LORD GUAN

LORD GUAN

WARRIOR, HERO, GOD

A Historical Novel

CHARLES N. LI

Regan Arts.

Regan Arts.
Copyright © Charles N. Li, 2025

All rights reserved, including the right to reproduce this book or portions thereof. Except as permitted under the U.S. Copyright Act of 1976, no part of this publication may be distributed, reproduced, recorded or transmitted in any form, in any medium, or by any means, or stored in any retrieval system or database, electronic or otherwise, without the prior written permission of the publisher.

For information, contact internationalrights@reganarts.com

This book is a work of fiction inspired by true events and by decades of historical research. Elements of the story are based on real-life occurrences, characters, and settings, and significant portions have been fictionalized for dramatic effect. This novel is a creative interpretation and not an exact factual account of historical events.

Regan Arts is committed to publishing works of quality and integrity. We are proud to publish this book; however, the story, the experiences, and the words are the author's alone.

First Regan Arts edition 2025

Library of Congress Control Number: 2024942389

978-1-68245-232-5 (Hardcover)
978-1-68245-233-2 (eBook)

Cover design by Richard Ljoenes Design LLC
Design by Neuwirth & Associates, Inc.
Page ii illustration: *The Chinese general Guan Yu on horseback* | Art Collection 2 | Alamy Stock Photo
Page xix illustration: Attributed to Katsushika Hokusai | *Guan Yu Seated (Chinese God of War)* | Japan | Edo period (1615–1868) | The Metropolitan Museum of Art

Printed in China

10   9   8   7   6   5   4   3   2   1

TABLE OF CONTENTS

List of Chinese Dynasties in Chronological Order		ix
Introduction		xiii
ONE	A Local Hoodlum	1
TWO	Guan Yu	10
THREE	The Martial Arts Camp	22
FOUR	Seeking a Mission	46
FIVE	Three Sworn Brothers	61
SIX	A New Militia	75
SEVEN	A Villainous Traitor	85
EIGHT	An Extraordinary Woman	129
NINE	A Fortuitous Opportunity	178
TEN	A Portentous Meeting	215
ELEVEN	The Battle of Vermilion Gorge	226
TWELVE	The Three Kingdoms	249
THIRTEEN	An Injury	295
FOURTEEN	The Loss of a Beloved Brother	298
FIFTEEN	The Last Battle	303
Epilogue		307
Acknowledgments		309
About the Author		311

To Kate, Rachel, Gabriel, Indy & Oliver
My family, my love, and my inspiration

LIST OF CHINESE DYNASTIES IN CHRONOLOGICAL ORDER

1. **LEGENDARY PERIOD:** early twenty-sixth century BC–late twenty-first century BC

2. **XIA DYNASTY:** late twenty-first century BC–early seventeenth century BC

3. **SHANG DYNASTY:** early seventeenth century BC–early eleventh century BC

4. **ZHOU DYNASTY:** early eleventh century–256 BC

5. **QIN DYNASTY:** 221 BC–206 BC

6. **HAN DYNASTY**
   Western Han dynasty (also known as Early Han, with its capital in Chang'an): 206 BC–AD 9

   Eastern Han dynasty (also known as Late Han, with its capital in Luoyang): AD 25–AD 220

   The last three emperors of the Eastern Han dynasty:
   Emperor Ling: date of ascension AD 168
   Emperor Shao: date of ascension AD 189
   Emperor Xian: date of ascension AD 189

7. **THREE KINGDOMS PERIOD:** AD 220–AD 280
   Wei kingdom, AD 220–AD 265

   Shu kingdom (also known as the Shu-Han kingdom): AD 221–AD 263

   Wu kingdom (also known as the Dong Wu kingdom): AD 222–AD 280

CHINESE DYNASTIES

8. **JIN DYNASTY:** AD 265–AD 420

9. **THE PERIOD OF DIVISION BETWEEN NORTH AND SOUTH:** AD 420–AD 589

10. **SUI DYNASTY:** AD 589–AD 618

11. **TANG DYNASTY:** AD 618–AD 907

12. **THE FIVE DYNASTIES PERIOD (ALSO KNOWN AS THE TEN KINGDOMS PERIOD):** AD 907–AD 960

13. **SONG DYNASTY:** AD 960–AD 1279
    Northern Song dynasty: AD 960–AD 1127

    Southern Song dynasty: AD 1127–AD 1279

14. **THE KHITAN DYNASTY** (also known as the Liao dynasty, founded by the Khitan ethnic group) lasted from AD 916 to AD 1125 in northern China and southern Siberia. The Khitan belonged to the Altaic ethnic family, which is probably related to the Xiongnu ethnic group.

15. **JIN DYNASTY (ALSO KNOWN AS THE JURCHEN DYNASTY, FOUNDED BY THE JURCHEN ETHNIC GROUP):** AD 1115–AD 1234. In pinyin spelling, the Jin of the Jurchen dynasty is identical with the Jin of the Jin dynasty that terminated the Three Kingdoms period. In Chinese logographs, the two Jins are completely different. They are also pronounced with different tones.

16. **YUAN (MONGOL) DYNASTY:** Kublai Khan, a grandson of Genghis Khan, ascended the imperial throne in AD 1271 and declared the beginning of the Yuan dynasty in China, even though Genghis conquered northern China decades earlier. The Yuan dynasty ended in AD 1368.

CHINESE DYNASTIES

17. **MING DYNASTY**: AD 1368–AD 1644

18. **THE QING DYNASTY** was founded by the Manchu branch of the Tungusic ethnic family. The Manchu are descendants of the Jurchens, who founded the Jin dynasty in the twelfth century AD. The Qing dynasty, the last imperial dynasty of China, endured from AD 1644 to AD 1911, when it was overturned by the revolution led by Sun Yat-sen.

INTRODUCTION

For centuries, Lord Guan (Guan Gong), named Guan Yu, also known as Guan Laoye "Grandpa Guan" and Guan Di "Emperor Guan," loomed large in the lives and psyches of Chinese people as a patron saint and a protector, until the establishment of the People's Republic of China in 1949. Every village and every neighborhood of a city in precommunist China had numerous Guan Gong shrines or temples where supplicants went to pray, burn incense, and petition for the fulfillment of their wishes. In 1977, when I visited Taipei, I counted seventy-two Guan Gong shrines and temples. Most overseas Chinese restaurants and stores keep a small Guan Gong shrine on the inside wall near the entrance. Patrons of those shops and restaurants typically mistook the shrine as paraphernalia for ancestor worship. Upon closer examination, one would discover that the image in all those shrines invariably showed a warrior with a ferocious yet righteous red face, sporting a big beard and holding a halberd. That image is Lord Guan, who became the god of wealth by popular acclaim in the sixteenth century, even though he never paid any attention to the acquisition of wealth in his lifetime. That is why Chinese business establishments keep a shrine for him.

The worship of Guan Gong began during the short-lived Sui dynasty (AD 589–AD 618), approximately three and half centuries after Guan Gong's death. The founding emperor of the Sui dynasty, a warrior of western pastoralist ancestry, promoted Buddhism, which was introduced into China by proselytizing monks from India and central Asia toward the end of the Late Han dynasty (AD 25–AD 220) in Guan Gong's lifetime. This new religion, malleable and adaptive, quickly took on Chinese characteristics, aligning itself with Confucian ethics and absorbing Chinese folk mythology. As the worship of Guan Gong proliferated among Chinese people, he was deified as Sangharama Bodhisattva in the Buddhist pantheon of gods in China. The deification enhanced Guan Gong's popularity.

Later in China's dynastic era, Guan Gong was deified repeatedly. Emperor Huizong of the Song dynasty (AD 960–AD 1279), a Taoist, made Guan Gong a Taoist god. The founder of the Ming dynasty (AD 1368–AD 1644), Zhu Yuanzhang, named Guan Gong Tian Huang, "the almighty (celestial) god." Toward the end of the Ming dynasty, when peasants rose in rebellion and the minority ethnic groups in China mounted military insurrections, the emperors and the imperial government tried to pacify the nation by invoking Guan Gong as the loyal celestial protector of the empire, hoping people would abide by one of Guan Gong's virtues, zhong, "loyalty to your sovereign." The penultimate emperor of the same dynasty, Xizong, who reigned from AD 1620 to AD 1627, established two statues of Guan Gong in the imperial palace and made the worship of Guan Gong a daily ritual.

During the final dynasty of China, the Qing dynasty (AD 1644–AD 1911), the ruling Manchu, in an attempt to legitimize their rule over the overwhelming Han majority, not only embraced Guan Gong as the almighty god but also created mythical legends of the ghost of Guan Gong guiding the founder of the dynasty, Nurhaci, and his son to victories in their conquest of northern China. By then, Guan Gong worship had evolved into a general practice with a religious fervor in China. Temples for Guan Gong worship sprang up everywhere in the country. People flocked to those temples as supplicants, pleading for the fulfillment of their goals, which could be directed at any desire or wishes, abstract or concrete, trivial or grandiose, frivolous or significant.

INTRODUCTION

At Guan Gong's birthplace, the city of Yuncheng in Shanxi province, an organization devoted to the study of Guan Gong, the Haizhou Guandi Temple Conservation Institute, is thriving with the blessing of the Chinese Communist Party. In front of the institute stands a giant bronze statue of Guan Gong, welcoming supplicating visitors and attracting tourists.

To sum up the history of Guan Gong in Chinese civilization, one could call him the martial saint, in opposition to the literary saint, who is Confucius. Confucius and Guan Gong are the two paramount figures in Chinese culture, the patron saints of the all-encompassing, complementary conceptual pair: wen, the world of humanistic pursuit, and wu, the world of martial endeavor, in Chinese metaphysics, education, government, administration, social order, and morality. Chinese people respect Confucius, the saint of wen, for his erudition, sagacity, and sapience, but worship Guan Gong, the saint of wu, for his indomitable courage, enduring loyalty, and unwavering rectitude. To the Chinese mind, Guan Gong is the avatar of righteousness, generosity, fairness, and courage. Without a doubt, he represents the paragon of virtue to the Chinese people.

A primary source of Guan Gong's military exploits can be found in *Sanguo Yanyi*, a Chinese historical novel attributed to the fourteenth-century writer Luo Guanzhong, although the contemporary Chinese text is the product of many recensions during the past seven centuries. In my youth, *Sanguo Yanyi* was one of a handful of novels that every Chinese teenager in secondary school read, often repeatedly. My schoolmates and I looked up to Guan Gong as the lodestar of our comportment, the golden standard of courage, loyalty, generosity, and integrity.

Sanguo Yanyi has been translated into numerous languages in Europe and Asia during the past two centuries. The earliest English translation was executed by British sinologist Charles Henry Brewitt-Taylor. It appeared in two volumes under the title *Romance of the Three Kingdoms* in 1925. Since then, many

INTRODUCTION

English versions, translated by scholars in England and America, have appeared in print. In all those versions, the title *Romance of the Three Kingdoms* endured.

Contemporary scholars in China have produced reams of articles and books on Guan Gong. Notwithstanding this impressive oeuvre, the details of Guan Gong's life remain mostly unknown. Even the dates of his birth and death are inferred from circumstantial evidence, and they are, at best, reasonable conjectures. The dearth of information on Guan Gong's natal family, his upbringing, his marriage, his education, his acquisition of martial skills, his own nuclear family including his wife, and to a lesser extent, his combat experience left a wide berth for my imagination as I wrote this novel. While a preponderant number of characters in this novel were people living in a tumultuous era toward the end of the Han dynasty, I took the liberty of inventing several personalities and describing many of the interactions between all characters as I saw fit.

Guan Gong devoted his life to the restoration of the Han dynasty, one of the greatest dynasties in Chinese history, ruled by the House of Liu. It endured more than four centuries (206 BC–AD 220) with a fourteen-year interlude when the House of Liu was deposed by Wang Mang, widely considered a villainous usurper in Chinese historiography. Historians marked this interlude by dividing the Han dynasty into Xi Han (Western Han) and Dong Han (Eastern Han) on account of the geographical locations of the two capitals of the two epochs, one (Luoyang) to the east of the other (Chang'an, which nowadays is known as Xi'an, a popular tourist attraction because of the partially excavated tomb of Qin Shi Huang, the First Emperor).

During the Han dynasty, China's territory expanded southward to present-day Vietnam and Southeast Asia, westward beyond the Uighur region of Inner Asia, and northward to Korea, Dongbei (northeast China), and Siberia, the original homeland of the nomadic Turkic, Mongolic, and Tungusic ethnic families.

INTRODUCTION

XVII

It was the Han dynasty that sealed the hallmark of Chinese civilization in East Asia when the Han emperors enshrined Confucian philosophy as the canon of ethics, polity, and national identity. During that dynasty, paper and a form of printing were invented, facilitating the distribution of portable books and the spread of education. Art, literature, historiography, as well as science and technology, flourished during the long periods of peace and prosperity under the sagacious reigns of several Han emperors. Expressions in Chinese language attest to the significance of the Han dynasty in the Chinese mindset. To date, the people of China refer to themselves as Han-ren "Han people," their spoken language as Han-yu "Han language," and their written texts as Han-wen "Han text."

It is not surprising that Guan Gong, a fiercely loyal subject born in the turbulent final years of that glorious dynasty, devoted his life to its restoration.

ONE

A LOCAL HOODLUM

In a little town on the alluvial plain of the Yellow River in northern China, the local hoodlum and rich landlord, S-Y Wang, stood at the edge of a large swath of farmland where the wheat and millet had already been harvested. He woke up early that morning and decided to survey the land of which he was the proud owner. Thirty years of age, he had inherited the property from his father, who had fallen victim in a recent cholera outbreak. Unlike his father, who had been a decent landlord sympathetic to his impoverished tenants, Wang was consumed by greed. The only thing that mattered to him was money. He was insatiable in his quest for wealth. To him, empathy or concern for other people was a sign of weakness. He treated tenant farmers as slaves even though they generated his income. In a year of good harvest, 40 percent of the wheat and millet produced by the tenant farmers went to S-Y Wang. In a year of poor harvest, typically caused by inclement weather, he raised his portion to 50 percent of the harvest. His tenants worked seven days per week. More than half of their children perished from malnutrition.

On this cold wintry morning, the land lay fallow. Wang surveyed his terrain with his head held high, as if he were announcing to the world, "This is my land, my territory!"

Medium height with a bulging midsection, Wang had a broad face, thin hair, long waist, and short legs. His shifty eyes and protruding ears made him look like a canine scavenger standing on its hind legs, trying to sniff out the remains of a prey killed by predators the night before. Standing at the edge of his domain, his facial muscles suddenly twitched. Jerking his head to his left, he saw an emaciated figure limping across his land. It was a tenant farmer he had condemned to destitution last month by canceling his contract to lease one acre of the land.

"Hey, cripple!" S-Y Wang growled, "What are you doing here? Get off my property this instant!"

Startled, Xiao Luo, the emaciated man with a cleft foot, quickly turned his skeletal body around and started to walk away from Wang's land. He happened to be crossing S-Y Wang's property because he was taking a shortcut on his way to the town market to see if he could collect some discarded leaves of napa cabbage to make a soup for his infant daughter. He would've preferred to collect some millet to make gruel for her. But that was out of the question. In those days of pervasive poverty, millet had become a staple food that occasionally filled the stomach of a poor tenant farmer, even though its habitual consumption was toxic and caused serious ailments of the digestive tract. The rich, like S-Y Wang, rarely ate millet. It was used occasionally for flavoring wheat or rice gruel. Their staple food consisted of steamed bread and noodles made from wheat flour.

For Xiao Luo, wheat flour was as precious as gold. He could hardly remember the sweet taste of noodles and the spongy consistency of steamed bread. The last time he enjoyed them, he was a young teenager, in the early years of Emperor Ling's reign. It was a year of bountiful harvest when the country was blessed with the right amount of precipitation at the right time

A LOCAL HOODLUM

of the growing season. Xiao Luo's father, who owned one acre of farmland at the time, brought home a sack of flour at the end of the harvest. For three days, the family feasted on fresh noodles and steamed bread, handmade by Xiao Luo's mother. They enjoyed the starch with stir-fried vegetables the family grew on a small plot of their land. The rest of the flour in the sack the family saved for the Autumn Moon Festival and the Lunar New Year holidays. For Xiao Luo and other peasants in the nation, those were the heady days of Emperor Ling's reign.

Since then, Xiao Luo's family farm had been repeatedly plagued by disasters: flood, drought, and locusts, not to mention the corrupt bureaucrats who preyed on them by levying unbearable taxes. But the imperial court paid scant attention to the affairs of the state. Sequestered in his opulent palace in Luoyang, Emperor Ling spent his days feasting, drinking, and frolicking with his concubines. A general malaise paralyzed the nation.

During a drought three years earlier, Xiao Luo's father was forced to sell his one acre of farmland to S-Y Wang for a pittance because, without a harvest, he needed the money to buy food for his family. Despondent and broken, Xiao Luo's father died shortly after the loss of his farm. He was not even forty years of age. In five months, Xiao Luo's mother, overcome by grief, followed her husband into the netherworld.

After the deaths of his parents, Xiao Luo worked twelve hours every day as one of S-Y Wang's tenant farmers. Hampered by his deformity, he couldn't produce enough grain to sustain his family after meeting the steep rent demanded by his landlord. Yet S-Y Wang complained bitterly against Xiao Luo for his subpar productivity. Last year, Wang lowered the boom on Xiao Luo by canceling his lease.

Without land to grow food, Xiao Luo faced hunger every day, scrounging anything edible to keep his family alive. He and his wife, with their infant daughter strapped on her back, spent a good part of each day trying to collect edible plants and berries in the hills, catching frogs and minnows in streams, and digging up tubers in forest meadows. But tubers were no longer bountiful, minnows and frogs were hard to catch without nets, and edible plants and berries became rare even in season. The only substances in ample supply were grass and kudzu, a fast-growing, bitter-tasting vine. Xiao Luo and his family teetered on starvation. Every day he and his wife suffered debilitating stress and anxiety from the fear of losing their infant daughter to malnutrition or disease. The little one's incessant cry tore at their hearts.

Even though life was abysmal, Xiao Luo maintained his dignity. He never begged as some despondent tenant farmers did. Every morning, he looked for temporary menial jobs in town, sometimes at the flour shop where he swept the floor, unloaded merchandise, and tidied up the interior, in exchange for a few taels of flour and millet so that his daughter could get a substantive meal. When he asked the store owner if he could be a regular employee, the answer was always negative. The store owner didn't mind hiring Xiao Luo for a few hours when he needed help but didn't want to commit himself to one more item of regular expense. Some days, the store owner would wave Xiao Luo away at the sight of him even though Xiao Luo had not intended to ask for work. It was so humiliating. But humiliation had become part and parcel of his life. If humiliation could bring some relief to starvation, he was willing to accept it. Survival, especially the survival of his infant daughter, always claimed the highest priority. He would suffer any amount of abuse for her sake. The only insult that he found difficult to tolerate was being called a cripple.

"It isn't my fault to be born with a cleft foot," he reckoned.

Now, early in the morning, the landlord, S-Y Wang, called him a cripple just for the fun of it. The more he thought about Wang's wanton insult, the angrier Xiao Luo became. His anger, aggravated by his empty stomach, quickly morphed into a bursting desire to take some action against Wang. Picking up a rock,

A LOCAL HOODLUM

Xiao Luo threw it in Wang's direction. But he was so feeble that the projectile traveled less than ten paces before it landed harmlessly between himself and Wang.

Wang, however, took great offense at Xiao Luo's action.

"What effrontery and brazenness from a person so low in rank!" Wang mumbled to himself.

He took a few steps toward Xiao Luo, picked up a bigger rock, cocked his arm, and heaved it at Xiao Luo with all his strength. The rock hit Xiao Luo square on his forehead, snapping his head back. He pitched backward and fell like a log.

Wang walked over, saw Xiao Luo's colorless face with eyes half-closed, showing only white. He poked Xiao Luo's ribs with his right foot. There was no response. Concerned, Wang bent over Xiao Luo to examine him more carefully. The wound on his forehead didn't look severe. There was some abrasion and minor bleeding. Shaking Xiao Luo's head did not elicit any response either. When Wang placed his right index finger under Xiao Luo's nose, he realized that the man was not breathing. Shocked, Wang stood up, surveyed his surroundings with shifty eyes. There was no one in sight. He took off for home like a rat with a cat in hot pursuit.

Xiao Luo's death caused a stir in town. It was the hot topic of gossip for days. On the evidence of his injury, the police concluded that he was murdered but couldn't find any clue about the identity of the murderer. Some townspeople pointed their fingers at S-Y Wang because of his propensity for violence. He had been known to slap his tenant farmers without any provocation. But their suspicion was speculative. No one witnessed the murder. When the police questioned Wang, he claimed that he was home the morning of the murder.

"I don't have the habit of loitering around town early in the morning," Wang declared to the police.

Xiao Luo's death soon became a case of unsolved murder. People began to lose interest in it. After his widow and infant daughter moved back to her parents' home in a nearby village, his death began to fade from people's minds.

Six months after Xiao Luo's murder, an upright member of the literati, having gained some recognition for his poems and brush-pen calligraphy, was appointed the new magistrate of the county with jurisdiction over five towns and villages, including S-Y Wang's property. Shortly after his appointment, the new magistrate decided to visit every town and village under his jurisdiction. When he arrived at the town where S-Y Wang lorded over everyone, Wang offered to throw a banquet in his honor. Even though the magistrate's staff had alerted him to Wang's unsavory character, he accepted Wang's invitation because it was customary for the richest man of a town to host a dinner in honor of a visiting magistrate. In addition, he thought the banquet would provide a convenient venue to lecture Wang on the virtue and benefit of compassion. Hoping to change Wang's wayward behavior, the magistrate wanted to exert some positive influence on the ruffian.

During the banquet at the yamen, which was the headquarters of the magistrate's representative in that town, the magistrate, quoting Confucius's words—"If you are generous, you have everything to gain; if you are kind, you will succeed in your enterprise"—admonished Wang to elevate his ethical standard and change his attitude toward the poor and the underprivileged. Wang listened obsequiously, praised the magistrate's erudition, and declared that he agreed wholeheartedly with the magistrate's eloquent rendition of the canon of a Junzi, "an honorable gentleman," which embodied the Confucian system of probity, erudition, and way of life.

"My goal in life is to follow the behavioral codes of a Junzi," Wang fawned over the magistrate, "even though I am not well educated. Having grown up in a merchant family and worked hard throughout my life, I never had a chance to study literature, history, and philosophy to attain the status of a Junzi. But I do my best to emulate his virtues."

It didn't require any acumen for the magistrate to see through Wang's servile mendacity. He had already been warned of Wang's notoriety, and he was aware of the townspeople's suspicion that Wang might have murdered Xiao Luo. But he wanted to see the reprobate himself and make an assessment. Their interaction at the banquet confirmed what he had heard about the ruffian, a self-serving and pathological liar. He would like to place Wang under arrest for suspicion of murder, but he needed a witness, and there wasn't one.

He had also heard that in addition to abusing his tenants and extracting usurious rent from them, Wang had a roving eye for teenage farm girls even though he had a wife and two concubines. With an arrogance inflamed by a sense of entitlement and a propensity for self-indulgence fanned by his idle life, he had evolved into a lecherous predator. Everyone in town knew that Wang had committed rape several times. Three victims in their early teens had killed themselves by drowning in the river because, having been violated by Wang, they had no hope of marriage. The town's matchmakers would not recommend a rape victim to a good family seeking a daughter-in-law, whether the family was local or from a nearby village. Yet none of the families of the three victims had filed charges against Wang because they feared retaliation. Losing a daughter was calamitous but not as life-threatening as losing the lease of the farmland that enabled them to eke out a living no matter how penurious and deprived.

The magistrate went so far as to openly solicit formal grievances and complaints from the tenant farmers against S-Y Wang. But nobody responded to his solicitation. They knew if they brought charges against the hoodlum, they and their families would be as dead as fish out of water. Wang held the ultimate weapon of canceling the leases of his land to them. The tenant farmers not only failed to respond to the magistrate's invitation to file charges against Wang, but a few of them also took the unexpected step of praising Wang to court favor with him. The magistrate listened to the praise with chagrin and exasperation.

He knew that an unscrupulous and greedy landlord like Wang was not a rarity, especially in those days of moral decay and pervasive poverty. In fact, he loathed scoundrels like Wang. Even more offensive than Wang's predatory behavior was his pretense. It was nauseating to hear him sing his own praise. The magistrate wished he had an excuse or the mandate to round up ruffians like Wang and lock them up. But he was a mere magistrate of a county in a large country, a small cog in the sprawling bureaucracy of a crumbling empire. No matter how much he desired to rid the society of predators like S-Y Wang, he would have a scant chance of gaining the support of his superiors. The higher bureaucrats might consider such an initiative an overreach of an ambitious local functionary, or worse, an act of insubordination. They might also succumb to Wang's bribery and rebuke the magistrate for taking rash actions against a landlord for unsolved crimes and accusatory gossip.

As the head of a county, the magistrate, with the assistance of his deputies in each town and village, collected taxes, facilitated and executed the imperial court's decrees, maintained law and order with the aid of a small police force, and served as both the judge and the jury of all criminal infractions and civil disputes within his jurisdiction. There was no incentive for him to do more than what was required of him. He had already gone beyond the call of duty, he thought, by lecturing Wang at the banquet and encouraging Wang's victims to step forward to file charges.

"What else can I do?!" he asked himself.

His top priority, beyond dispensing his normal administrative duties, was a promotion to a higher-level position in the civil service. If his record remained unblemished for a few more years and he was able to extend his social connections with high-level officials, sending them ample gifts on important occasions and festivals, he might be selected for the governorship of a province. For him, the governorship of a province, with authority over several million people, would secure a life of prestige, power, and wealth. He needed to focus on advancing his career, he reminded himself: "It would be foolish to spend my time and energy to engage in a struggle against hoodlums like S-Y Wang."

On his return trip to his yamen, the magistrate felt agitated and acted curtly to his staff. He did not like what he saw and felt frustrated that he lacked the means and power to improve the condition of people's lives in his dominion. His frustration was exacerbated by the knowledge that the people of the county looked up to him as an ethical and evenhanded leader. But respect from the people did not confer power. The only way forward for him, he reckoned, was to try to cast away from his mind unsavory characters like S-Y Wang. He hated escapism, but it made sense not to be overwhelmed by a persisting tragedy or fret over a national malaise beyond his control. Brooding over a bad situation beyond his authority and resources to make amends was not only futile but also self-destructive. He needed to hone the art of forgetfulness, he reminded himself.

Forget S-Y Wang! Forget abject poverty! Forget the suffering of the people. My salvation lies in seeing nothing, hearing nothing, and doing nothing, the magistrate repeated to himself in silence. To fortify himself with his rationalization when he retired to his private study, he consumed a jar of rose liquor, his favorite alcoholic beverage. The liquor soothed his nerves and made it easier for him to come to terms with the practice of seeing nothing, hearing nothing, doing nothing, and forgetting everything.

TWO

GUAN YU

In an adjacent county not far from S-Y Wang's town, an unusually robust and good-natured boy was born into an ordinary farming family during the early years of the reign of Emperor Ling. The parents named him Guan Yu, hoping the boy, keeper of the Guan lineage, would be nimble as a feather (yu). Neither rich nor poor, the family belonged to a dwindling pool of independent farmers. Guan Yu's father owned one and a half acres of arable land from which they eked out a living. Most of his neighbors had lost their farmland through the chicanery and machination of predatory officials and unscrupulous landlords. Guan Yu's family belonged to a lucky minority of small farmers who managed to hang on to their land.

In a year of good weather with a propitious amount of precipitation in the right season, Guan Yu's family could manage to plant and harvest two crops of wheat and millet, affording them the luxury of two meals of noodles, steamed bread, and fresh vegetables every day. Since the family members grew, harvested, threshed, winnowed, and ground the wheat they grew with great care, the flour they produced contained the maximal amount of nutrients, giving the noodles and bread made from their flour a resilient consistency because of its high content of protein. A portion of their flour went to the town merchants in exchange for salt, peanut oil, condiments, clothing, tools, and household necessities. The merchants favored Guan Yu's family and treated them with respect because of the upright character of the parents.

While growing wheat and millet, Guan Yu's family reserved a small plot of their land for growing vegetables, typically napa cabbage, cucumber, chili peppers, eggplants, long beans, daikon, ginger, and garlic. Most of the vegetables were eaten fresh, stir-fried with peanut oil, ginger, garlic, and salt. But a good portion of the napa cabbage, garlic, and ginger, all of which aged well, were stacked away in underground storage in their humble house built with mud and stones. The cool, dry air of the underground space preserved the vegetables throughout the year. During winter months when the field lay fallow under snow and ice, stir-fried napa cabbage was the most frequent dish to complement bread or noodles in Guan Yu's household. In the same underground storage, Guan Yu's parents also kept pickled daikon and pickled pepper in earthenware jars. Together with the stir-fried napa cabbage or other seasonal vegetables, the pickles added flavors and textures to the main staple of their diet.

Lunar New Year was the only occasion when Guan Yu's family had the luxury of eating meat, bartered from the local butcher with flour and napa cabbage. *Meat* always meant pork because pigs were raised for meat. Those families that owned a water buffalo, a cow, or a donkey used the animals for tilling the land and pulling carts. The animals worked hard but were treated as members of the families that owned them. The owners would never consider slaughtering a beast of labor for meat. As the Lunar New Year approached, everyone in Guan Yu's family looked forward to at least one dinner of pork dumplings. The dumpling feast made Lunar New Year a very exciting occasion, especially for the children, who also received haircuts, hot baths, and some new clothing.

Guan Yu's family, even though far from being affluent, observed a time-honored tradition of giving some of their food to their less-fortunate neighbors before the Lunar New Year, even though fewer and fewer people could afford to observe this charitable tradition in those days of hardship. The people of the county respected Guan Yu's parents for their generosity and kindness. They also adored Guan Yu because of his pleasant disposition and robust health. It was the consensus of the folks in the county that he would grow into a handsome young man with the sterling character of his parents. Many who had young daughters openly wished that Guan Yu would one day become their son-in-law.

At age five, Guan Yu joined his parents and two elder sisters working on the family farm. When he started in a summer harvest of wheat and millet, laboring in the field felt unbearably exhausting. In the evening his body, especially his lower back, ached. Sometimes, his arms and legs cramped up and hurt so much that he cried out in despair. Fortunately, his parents always allowed their three children to have playtime in the field, once in the morning and once in the afternoon. During the breaks from hard labor, the children played with bamboo, weaving small baskets with the pliant green bark they peeled from bamboo trunks, and searched for male crickets that they kept as pets in their handwoven baskets. The song of the male crickets, a territorial and courtship signal, was music to their ears.

The playtime lifted the children's spirits and enabled them to overlook their fatigue. By the time Guan Yu was six, the farmwork became routine, no longer distressing his body.

During winter, which was always harsh and frigid, as the north wind howled and the land froze, Guan Yu's family stayed indoors to avoid the inclement weather except on occasions of snowfall. The snowflakes excited the children. When heavy snow hit, the world was encased in fluttering white crystals, transforming the open space above the land into an amorphous world of magic. On those days, the children went out of their hovel home, braving the cold, running around to catch snowflakes in their hands. Most winter days, they were indoors, tending to their crickets, coaxing them to sing with long blades of grass by rubbing their bushy ends on the foreheads of the insects. When the girls embroidered, Guan Yu, on the order of his parents, did physical exercises.

His physical exercises consisted of calisthenics and lao niu gong di, which literally means "old bull tilling the land." Guan Yu's father supervised the boy's exercise sessions, instructing Guan Yu, "Lao niu gong di means supporting your stretched body horizontally on fingertips and toes for several seconds, and then dropping to an inch above the ground, before pushing up your body in a forward motion with your arms. The entire process looks like the surging motion of the earth as a water buffalo pulls the plow forward. Doing it repeatedly everyday will make you strong as a buffalo."

The physical exertion of the workout prescribed by his father kept Guan Yu warm in frigid weather. He loved it because it also dispelled ennui.

Reading and writing was another activity in Guan Yu's household during each winter day. Guan Yu's father taught his children to read and write, breaking the tradition of not educating female members of a family. The father thought educating the daughters would give them a leg up in life and help them to marry good husbands. Although not highly educated, Guan Yu's father had learned a few hundred logographs. That level of literacy enabled him to conduct transactions in town without being swindled. He wanted to make sure that his children achieved at least his level of literacy, reminding them at every opportunity that learning was the critical means to cultivate good character and improve quality of life. The father's dream was that Guan

Yu, his only son, would rise beyond the destiny of a peasant to become a professional with expertise in some arena. He didn't have a specific area of expertise in mind. His fervent wish was that Guan Yu would have a life less penurious and backbreaking than his own.

Guan Yu's father never verbalized his wish because there was a slim chance for his son to escape from peasantry. His wish was only a dream. Occasionally he indulged in dreams because they provided relief from the stark reality, no matter how ephemeral that relief might be. Even a fleeting thought of happiness was treasured in a dreary life.

Much to his father's chagrin, Guan Yu didn't take to learning literature with much enthusiasm. He applied himself to the point of acquiring as many logographs as his father knew, memorizing some passages of the classics, and developing an acceptable level of competence in brush-pen calligraphy. He studied just enough to placate his father.

Physical exercise, however, was another matter. Guan Yu loved practicing lao niu gong di, calisthenics, and rock lifting, a strengthening exercise Guan Yu took up himself. By ten years of age, he incorporated the exercise session into his daily routine regardless of the season. Even during harvest when everyone in the family worked feverishly, Guan Yu always tagged on an exercise session before dinner. After each session, he felt energized and gushing in optimism. When he was eleven, he learned to flip backward and forward on the dirt floor. His first flip startled his parents. They thought Guan Yu would inadvertently injure himself. But Guan Yu, gifted with exceptional proprioception and immense core body strength, executed the flips with ease and agility. He soon progressed to 360-degree tumbles in the air, living up to his given name, yu, nimble as a feather.

By the time he was twelve, he could execute ten repetitions of backward and forward tumbles plus fifty repetitions of lao niu gong di without pause. The speed with which he somersaulted in the air dazzled his parents and sisters. They watched him as if he were a traveling acrobat performing in a town square.

As for rock lifting, he steadily progressed toward lifting bigger and heavier rocks at ten repetitions per session and ten sessions per day. Once every three months, he went up the hills to search for a heavier and bigger rock to replace the one he had been lifting. Hauling a heavy rock from the hills to home in the early evening after a long day of farmwork was strenuous. But it gave pleasure to Guan Yu because each trip, in search of a bigger and heavier rock, meant that he had grown stronger. By the time he was sixteen, an expanding row of rocks, ranging from small ones weighing around ten catties to big ones more than 100 catties (130 pounds) lined the border of Guan Yu's family farmland. They marked the progress of Guan Yu's physical development over the years. Guan Yu was proud of his row of rocks, from small to large, lining his family's plot of land. They reminded him of his growing strength.

As Guan Yu developed physically, his appetite grew. It became a family concern. By age fifteen, he consumed twice as many noodles and bread as his father did at each meal. He seemed insatiable, gobbling up all leftovers at the dining table. But neither his parents nor his sisters begrudged him. His growing appetite spurred them to work harder than ever to increase their production of wheat, millet, and vegetables on their family land. Rising from bed before sunrise every morning, they tended and weeded the one and a half acres of their land, killed herbivore pests, loosened the dirt, fertilized the field with decaying leaves and night soil, watered the vegetables on sunny days, doing everything they could to maximize the yield of their crops and vegetables. Guan Yu's parents and siblings were proud of his bulging muscles, widening shoulders, chiseled torso, and nimble athleticism.

On a warm day toward the end of spring, Guan Yu, at seventeen years of age, was in the wheat field clearing weeds and loosening the earth with a hoe. He wore a loincloth without a shirt, his muscular body glistened with sweat in the sun. Suddenly a deep voice boomed, "What a physical specimen!"

Looking up, Guan Yu saw a barrel-chested, middle-aged man with a thin, flowing beard, thick eyebrows, piercing eyes, and a suntanned, leathery face on the main road not far from his family farm. Carrying a travel bag tied to a long spear over his broad shoulder, the traveler had stopped in his tracks, looking at Guan Yu admiringly. His posture and stance conveyed his supreme confidence and physical prowess. Standing at the edge of the road, he appeared to be a lone traveler.

In those days of political turbulence and social unrest, people were well aware that brigands and bandits infested the mountain roads connecting towns and villages. They preyed on a single traveler at every opportunity, robbing the traveler and killing him if he attempted to resist. Women never traveled without an entourage of bodyguards, and men, such as salesmen and craftsmen, usually traveled in armed groups. This spear-bearing man, who injected himself into Guan Yu's working family with an unsolicited compliment on the youngster's physique, was obviously a martial arts expert. His composure, his spear, and the fact that he was traveling alone suggested his martial expertise.

Having heard the stranger's pronouncement, Guan Yu's father, who was also weeding, stood up from his kneeling position in the field, bowed to the traveler in gratitude of his encomium, and responded, "That is my humble son, Guan Yu."

"Congratulations!" Smiling broadly and baring his white teeth, which displayed another sign of his robust health, the traveler said to Guan Yu's father, "Your son has the potential of becoming a great martial artist."

Such an unexpected compliment practically sent Guan Yu to heaven. *Elation* would not come close to capturing Guan Yu's feeling at that moment. He would love to become a martial artist. But his family could not afford to pay for lessons, and he never dared fancy a career divorced from his family plot of land. As the only son and heir in his family, he was expected to take over the small farm from his parents when they became old. Guan Yu was their pension and security in their old age. The traveler's compliment that Guan Yu could become a great martial artist was as stunning as it was unsettling to everyone in Guan Yu's family. The parents were too dumbfounded to come up with an appropriate response.

Oh! If only this stranger were a reliable soothsayer! Guan Yu reflected for a moment as he savored the stranger's words.

Guan Yu's soaring sentiment lasted only a fleeting second. He came back down to earth instantly, accepting that his place in this world had already been set in stone. The stranger was merely being kind and lavish. Jerked back to reality by a sense of duty to his family, Guan Yu felt a little dejected.

After a few seconds of silence, Guan Yu's father said to the stranger, "You are too kind. We are peasants, and my son is destined to continue the family tradition."

"Oh, what you said is usually true. But there are always exceptions. If you don't mind, let's talk! I have a proposition for you," the stranger said softly, his benevolent smile unfading.

Struck by the stranger's kindness and forthright persistence, Guan Yu's father offered, "Would you like to step into our home for a cup of tea?"

"I will be honored!" the stranger replied.

As the three sat down on two wooden benches, the only furniture other than a small wooden table next to the hearth in Guan Yu's home, the stranger revealed himself. He was, indeed, a martial artist. But Guan Yu and his parents did not expect him to be a grand master of the White Crane School, a celebrated branch of martial arts in boxing and armed combat. Living with two acolytes on a mountain approximately a half day's trek from Guan Yu's village, he shunned society while practicing martial arts, studying the classics, and farming the land. He and his acolytes rarely ventured out of their mountain retreat. They grew their own food, raised a host of domestic animals including two horses, and strived to be self-sufficient. The opportune encounter with Guan Yu and his father occurred during the grand master's return trip after attending a memorial for his own martial arts mentor who had died recently at his dojo on the famous mountain Huangshan (Yellow Mountain).

Over tea, Guan Yu's father wanted to know why the grand master chose the life of a recluse.

"Well, for very simple reasons," the grand master responded. "My acolytes and I can no longer endure the chaos and mayhem in our country. We are sickened by fractious conflicts between warlords, angry at an inept and dysfunctional government, and no longer wish to bear witness to the anguish and suffering of our people. Escaping into the mountains to seek a peaceful and simple life, my acolytes and I are fortunate to have found a hideout among towering pines, gurgling creeks, and enchanting wildlife."

After a sip of the hot tea Guan Yu served him, he continued while looking into the father's eyes intensely, "You are blessed with a son of amazing physique. I don't know him, but I am reasonably perceptive in evaluating people at first sight. We martial artists spend our careers honing our perceptual capability because, in mortal combat, the decisive factor of victory lies in accurately assessing the motivation, intention, and physical capability of an adversary. I believe that your son has an upright character in addition to being blessed with a superb physique. With proper training, he could become a great martial artist, and who knows, he might even become a great warrior to help restore the glory of the Han dynasty. I may be an escapist, hiding in the mountains from our calamitous world. But I am always on the lookout for an exceptional youth who may rise to the task of saving our country. I detect great promise in your son."

"Thank you so much for your compliment," Guan Yu's father responded. "You are too kind. Your generous opinion notwithstanding, I don't see any alternative to being a farmer in my son's future."

"Well, if you and your son are willing," the grand master responded, "I am happy to take him under my wing and train him in my mountain hideout. You can be assured that I will look after him as if he were my own son."

The grand master's response surprised Guan Yu's father. Guan Yu's father reckoned that, on the one hand, the grand master had made a tremendously generous offer to train and look after Guan Yu. On the other hand, regardless of what future such an offer might promise, accepting it would mean losing his beloved son, at least for several years in the immediate future. The grand master had presented a difficult dilemma for Guan Yu's father. As he was agonizing in his struggle to make a choice, tears welled up in his eyes. He didn't want to let go of Guan Yu. At the same time, he realized that the grand master's offer was a rare opportunity for Guan Yu to learn a new trade and perhaps embark on a better life with a bright future.

Guan Yu didn't want to leave his family either. His father, mother, and siblings had been the anchor of his life, the cornerstone of his existence. The Guan family might be poor, but their love and devotion for each other had helped them to overcome unspeakable hardship. Each day, their bonds grew stronger. They depended on each other and reveled in that dependency.

The grand master has made a tantalizing offer. But how can I abandon my parents and sisters? he asked himself silently. Doing so would be tantamount to abrogating my filial loyalty and deserting my loved ones.

Yet the prospect of becoming a martial artist beckoned with a powerful force. It promised a future that had appeared only in Guan Yu's fantasy. Torn apart by conflicting desires, each as strong as the other, Guan Yu left the decision of accepting or rejecting the grand master's offer to his father.

The grand master read the ambivalence of both father and son. He understood that he was asking the family to give up an enormous part of their lives if Guan Yu were to join his martial arts camp. Father and son were vacillating for natural and bona fide reasons. He made a gallant effort to lighten the negative impact of his proposition:

"My mountain retreat is less than four hours of walking distance from here." He said, "If Guan Yu trains with me, he can come home regularly. Bandits will not dare to lay hands on him when he travels between my retreat and here. He will remain your loyal and loving son. That will never change. I am merely offering a helping hand in developing his immense potential. Please allow me to repeat myself: there is a good chance that he will become a great martial artist and warrior."

This new information opened a window for Guan Yu and his father to consider accepting the grand master's proposition. To the father, the possibility of Guan Yu returning home easily and regularly mitigated the adverse impact of his absence. Even though the family would suffer a significant loss of labor if Guan Yu left for the grand master's martial arts camp, it remained possible for them to spend time with Guan Yu on a regular basis. Guan Yu felt the grand master's offer was reasonable. But being a loyal son, he stayed mum, giving his father a free hand to reach a decision.

"Let me consult with my wife," Guan Yu's father said, after a moment of thought, and left to find his wife in the field. By the time they came back to their hut, Guan Yu's mother was already sobbing. Apologizing incoherently between her sobs, she plunked down next to Guan Yu on the bench. The moment she buried her face on Guan Yu's shoulder, she could no longer hold back her sorrow. A flood of tears gushed down her cheeks. In a broken voice, she wailed, "My dearest son, my dearest son, is it true you are leaving?"

GUAN YU

"Mama, Ma—!" Guan Yu faltered in his attempt to console his mother. He had never been apart from his family, not even in his dreams. Now, his mother's sorrow made it appear that his departure was imminent. He couldn't help being overcome with sadness. Summoning all his strength, he regained his composure and said solemnly, "Mother, even if I follow the grand master to his mountain retreat, I am not leaving for good, and I promise to return every month. When the full moon hits the sky, you will find me at the door, and when there is a reason you should need me, I will return permanently."

Mother was barely mollified. Her tears continued to streak down her cheeks.

THREE

THE MARTIAL ARTS CAMP

Guan Yu was amazed by the atmosphere of the grand master's mountain refuge. It exuded energy and optimism. Everyone there projected a cheerful yet somber attitude. For Guan Yu, joining the camp was akin to stepping into a totally different world. Unlike the people in Guan Yu's village, whose demeanors and bearings betrayed the prevailing anxiety, gloom, and turmoil of the era, the grand master and his two acolytes were brimming with hope, compassion, and energy. They were untouched by the paralyzing malaise that afflicted Guan Yu's village. Neither cynical nor seeking self-advancement, the grand master and his acolytes lived with the belief that they would eventually participate in a restoration of the Han splendor created by Emperor Wu, the seventh emperor of Han dynasty who, during his fifty-four years of reign, enshrined Confucianism as the philosophical foundation the Chinese culture; enriched the country through trade and cultural exchanges with India, central Asia, the Parthian empire, and Rome via the Silk Road; established a meritocracy-based administrative apparatus to govern the country; promoted arts, crafts, music, and poetry; and lifted the spirit of the country.

THE MARTIAL ARTS CAMP   23

The secluded martial arts camp was self-sufficient and self-contained, an island in a sea of despair and turbulence. It had three people. Now with the arrival of Guan Yu, the community had grown to four. They formed a close-knit, supportive circle dedicated to the fine-tuning of their minds and bodies. The grand master behaved as an equal to his acolytes in all aspects of their daily life except the training of martial arts and the study of classics. During the daily sessions of martial arts practice and study of literature, the grand master assumed the role of a coach and taskmaster as the three pupils honed their physical and mental skills. In doing the numerous chores around the camp, he contributed his share of labor just like everyone else. The egalitarian atmosphere at the camp enhanced mutual affection and devotion among its members.

Every day, members of the camp community rose at dawn, when the sun climbed over the hills in the east. In the evening, darkness signaled bedtime. Exhausted from a full day of study, practice, and labor, everyone fell asleep the moment they lay down on the floor. There wasn't a lamp or candle at the camp. The grand master considered lamps and candles superfluous.

"A martial artist must have good night vision," he told the three young men. "In a night ambush, no one is going to light a lamp for you. Also, your night vision will improve with diligent training in darkness."

The camp's physical structures on a gently sloping meadow consisted of three simple wooden huts framed with large bamboo trunks. Between the bamboo trunks were thick planks of pine glued together with resins. There were no windows. Each structure had one door made of the same material as the rest of the wall. It had to be lifted out of the way for entry or exit. On the roof, layers of tightly bunched hay protected the interior from rain, hail, and snow. The thatched roof supported by interstices of willow boughs was steeply pitched to allow rainwater to run down to the bamboo gutters surrounding the house. The floor, made of thick poplar slats, was three feet above the ground. The elevation provided a luxury space to the inhabitants because it kept out the dampness of the earth and prevented vermin such as rats and giant centipedes from creeping into the house.

Every item of construction material, the bamboo, the wood panels, the slats and planks, the roof, the resin, came from the mountain.

One of the huts served as the dining and assembly place. It contained a hearth and a chimney built with stones and clay. Next to the hearth stood a simple wooden table with a bench on each side. Located in one corner of the hut was a row of books, newly created after the invention of paper and rubbing techniques. The grand master made sure that everyone understood that those books were the most important treasure in camp, not only because he spent most of his inheritance to acquire them but also because they contained a treasure trove of wisdom and knowledge. Another similarly structured hut, a few feet to the west, served as the sleeping quarters. All four of them slept on the floor in that hut. During the cold season, they covered the floor with a thick layer of hay that insulated the sleepers from the chill air. During the warm season, the hay was removed to avoid insect infestation. The third hut, the size of a sentry box, located between two towering pine trees a short distance downhill from the other two huts, housed a deep pit. That was the camp's outhouse. Every three months, camp members filled the pit with dirt and moved the box to a different spot among the pine groves.

A pristine creek on the other side of the compound supplied all the water camp members needed. On hot days, with the grand master's permission, the three youngsters doused each other with buckets of water along the creek in a joyful game of hide-and-seek among the riparian bushes.

After a breakfast of one egg per person collected from the nests of their chickens and ducks plus a large bowl of boiled millet and cornmeal flavored with salt and pepper, prepared by the grand master the evening before, camp members spent the morning on shadowboxing, sword combat with bamboo sticks, and various forms of strength-building exercises such as isometric stretching, repeated bouts of jumping in place, and kicking and punching bamboo poles planted deep in the ground.

Even though Guan Yu was the newcomer, it didn't take long for him to outperform his fellow acolytes in combat skills. He was stronger, faster, and more agile than everyone. To maintain equitable combat practice sessions, the grand master made it a rule, three months after the arrival of Guan Yu, that either he would act as Guan Yu's opponent, or Guan Yu would take on the other two acolytes simultaneously.

Guan Yu grew taller and stronger in camp, bulking up his arms, legs, and torso. The master was pleased with Guan Yu's physical development and his progress in martial arts skills. A model pupil, Guan Yu was a quick study and demonstrated exceptional intelligence. During six years under the grand master's tutelage, Guan Yu encountered only one comment from the grand master that could have a negative implication. One late morning at the end of a practice session, the grand master remarked, "My goodness, Guan Yu! You break so many bamboo sticks with your power strokes that the mountain will be denuded of its bamboo groves."

Lunch after the morning martial arts practice consisted of steamed bread and pickled vegetables. Afternoon was devoted to chores around the camp: tending to the crop and plants in the field; collecting firewood; grinding wheat and corn kernels; tidying up the houses and the grounds; feeding and caring for the chickens, ducks, and the two horses; and gathering material from the forest for repairing or replacing parts of the three huts. The grand master did most of the cooking while the youngsters pitched in to help if they were not preoccupied with other chores.

The dinner menu was identical to lunch. During the spring, when the chickens and ducks laid more eggs, camp members luxuriated in having hard-boiled eggs at dinner in addition to their steamed bread and vegetables.

After dinner, the four men discussed the canons of Confucian philosophy, focusing on loyalty, generosity, compassion, and integrity. While the grand master made it clear that moral principles of the Confucian philosophy constituted the foundation of life, he emphasized generosity because, in his opinion, human beings are predisposed toward greed and avarice.

The grand master preached, "Practicing generosity will fend off the development of narcissism and self-centeredness. Narcissism is one of the worst possible defects in a person. An honorable person always considers the welfare of other people, no matter how difficult and onerous the situation in which one lives. If a man is rich, his generosity will enhance his compassion and help the poor and needy. If a man is poor, his generosity will command respect and endearment from others.

"The accumulation of wealth should never be a goal in life!" The grand master liked to remind everyone from time to time, "Money is only a tool, not an end. It should never be the goal of life. Kindness, honor, loyalty, generosity, and the pursuit of knowledge constitute the essence and the gold standard of a happy and fulfilling life."

The young acolytes were sternly warned not to pick fights with anyone.

"You must be the master of your own feelings and temper," the master regularly reminded his pupils. Combat and violence are not a proper outlet for your emotions!"

Threatening or bullying another person was an absolute, inviolable taboo for a martial artist. According to the grand master,

THE MARTIAL ARTS CAMP

27

"One becomes a martial artist to help the weak, the meek, and the people in need. A martial artist fights only when there is a noble cause or when his life is being threatened."

The moral and philosophical discussions in the evenings had a profound impact on Guan Yu and his fellow acolytes. The teaching of the grand master forged their character and shaped their values.

Some days, the grand master led the young acolytes to analyze and parse the works of ancient Chinese scholars other than Confucius and his disciples. Taking out a book from his modest library, the master would read the philosophical discourse from an author, explain the text, and lecture on its significance. During those sessions, Guan Yu learned about Laozi, Zhuangzi, Xunzi, and Mozi and their philosophical musings, which were outside of the Confucian paradigm and did not constitute a part of the official canon. To Guan Yu, they posed interesting questions about the human condition and offered alternative worldviews from the Confucian perspective. Guan Yu had never heard about those philosophers before he came to the camp. He was startled to learn that Confucius was not the only scholar to be revered. He appreciated Xunzi's attempt to rectify the moral frailty of human beings and Laozi's and Zhuangzi's advocacy of humility and self-restraint, especially among men of power. He embraced wholeheartedly Mozi's preaching that the selection of leaders of a nation should be based on meritocracy, not genetic lineage. He learned that the practice of meritocracy was exemplified by the succession of the kings (Yao, Shun, and Yu) in the earliest period of Chinese history, more than two millennia before the Han dynasty.

To Guan Yu, much more interesting than philosophical discourse was the history book *Shiji* (Records of the Grand Historian) authored by Sima Qian, the pioneer historian who served as an official in the court of the magnificent emperor Wu. Before joining the martial arts camp, Guan Yu had never heard of Sima Qian or his monumental work, which not only chronicled the dynasties of China from Shang to Han but also contained the biographies of major scholars, warriors, officials, and individuals who had made important contributions to the Chinese civilization during the one and a half millennia ending with the Han dynasty. Guan Yu thought to himself, if literature were always as riveting as *Shiji*, he would not have objected to studying the classics as he had under his father's tutelage.

The grand master, being a martial artist, made sure that everyone delved into the entire range of military strategy and tactics presented in *The Art of War*, a book authored by Sunzi, a military general and scholar of the Eastern Zhou period. It was sobering for Guan Yu to learn from *The Art of War* that victory in war depended on intelligence, leadership, discipline, weather, and terrain much more so than it depended on weaponry, martial skills, and the numerical superiority of combatants. Later in his career, Guan Yu served under the command of one of the greatest military strategists, Zhuge Liang, who reminded him of the brilliance of Sunzi in the ways he planned and prepared for each battle.

Once a month, on the day of the full moon, Guan Yu returned to his family as he promised. To gain more time with his family, he took to jogging on those trips: from the martial arts camp to home one afternoon and from home back to the camp twenty-four hours later. The twice-monthly marathons, lasting almost three hours each way, were taxing but yielded some unexpected benefits: at the completion of each run, Guan Yu felt calm and relaxed, enjoying a sense of euphoria as if his perception had been sharpened and his mood boosted to a new height that made the familiar sceneries, instead of being ho-hum and lackluster, bright and scintillating. He became more sensitive to the color, the odor, the air, the sound of the streams, and the composition of the landscape around him. Even a cow plowing in the field looked beautiful. Unbeknownst to him, jogging brought exhilaration.

Another unexpected benefit of the runs was the improvement of his physical stamina. Guan Yu's endurance was already exceptional before his arrival at the martial arts camp. After eight monthly marathons, he noticed that the morning workout at camp became easy. This unexpected benefit buoyed him.

Guan Yu cherished his family visit. Happiness engulfed him as the full moon approached on the fifteenth day of every lunar month. His presence at home was always a celebratory occasion, a joyful reunion, perking up his parents and sisters. Upon his arrival, his family members launched into a flood of effusive compliments on his sculpted physique. Inevitably, the compliments were followed by a string of questions, some based on pure fantasy. But Guan Yu always had an answer to each question, even if it was absurd.

"Have you seen a tiger?"

("No, even though tigers live in the mountains, they are secretive and avoid human beings. I have heard their roars in the night.")

"Can you kill a tiger with your bare hands?"

("Nobody can. There is no truth in a man killing a tiger with bare hands. It belongs to the realm of folklore and fantasy.")

"What is your new secret stroke in combat?"

("A stroke may be lethal and lightning fast, but never secretive.")

"Are you becoming a warrior?"

("That is the future. I am not clairvoyant.")

"Does the grand master ever punish you?"

("No, never!")

When everyone sat down on the two benches in front of the hearth in their home, Guan Yu's father always gazed at him with adoration as if his son had just descended from heaven with a halo around him, while his mother typically plunked herself next to him on one of the two benches in order to pat and rub his head, reassuring herself that Guan Yu, no matter how much he had grown, remained her beloved child. Sometimes, she looked astonished at his bulging biceps and deltoid muscles. On one occasion, she told Guan Yu that his father was so proud of him that the elder Guan could hardly refrain from bragging to their neighbors that Guan Yu was well on his way to becoming a great warrior.

"I told him not to brag." She said, "But he went ahead anyway!"

Those were happy days, and happy days were always fleeting.

Halfway into the second year of Guan Yu's training at the martial arts camp, the grand master announced that Guan Yu should acquire equestrian skills.

"A warrior must be an expert horseman. It is a prerequisite!" the grand master declared.

By then, the foal born to the mare at the camp one year before Guan Yu's arrival had grown into a handsome brown steed, full of zest and bursting with energy. The master assigned the steed to Guan Yu, with the command, "From now on, he is your steed. You will ride him and care for him."

Honored by the grand master's generous assignment, Guan Yu worked hard to develop his riding skills. He and the steed soon became bonded. Every day, he saved a portion of his steamed bread at dinner as a treat for the horse, and whenever he found time, he took the horse to graze at meadows and glens where wild cabbage and other nutrient-rich plants grew. In return, the horse welcomed Guan Yu as its companion and master. When Guan Yu jumped on its back, it ears perked up, its head bobbed up and down, and its front hooves gently stamped the ground as if it were saying, "Where have you been? I have been waiting and waiting."

THE MARTIAL ARTS CAMP

After Guan Yu became a skilled horseman, capable of negotiating tortuous mountain trails at high speed, the grand master sprang another surprise.

He brought into camp an eight-foot-long halberd with a heavy blade, like a broad seax at one end and a sharp tip at the other end of the long bronze pole. The sharp ends of the weapon rendered it both a spear in the back of the pole and a formidable cutting, slashing weapon with a long reach in the front. A wavy motif was carved on the upper half of the shiny blade.

"This halberd is named Reclining Moon. It was forged by a renowned blacksmith who specialized in fabricating weapons. From now on, it will be your combat weapon." The master announced as if he had been planning for this occasion all along, "You will wield the Reclining Moon from horseback."

Guan Yu blinked in disbelief.

The grand master had thrown down a daunting challenge.

The halberd weighed about sixty catties (eighty pounds). Most of that weight derived from the heavy blade at the front end of the long pole. To wield that weapon deftly would require herculean strength from the hands, the arms, the shoulders, the pectorals, the core muscles, and most important of all, the thigh and leg muscles. Guan Yu knew he was strong enough to handle the Reclining Moon halberd with his feet firmly planted on the ground. Was he strong enough to swing and manipulate the same weapon on a horse's back? He wasn't sure.

By then, Guan Yu had learned that lower-body strength was the key to martial arts. He knew that a well-balanced, firm stance with legs apart at shoulder width and knees slightly bent constituted the most critical prerequisite for a martial artist in action. The stance set up a combatant with leverage and power to wield his weapon, whether the weapon was a fist, a foot, or an instrument. The power of the leverage stemmed primarily from the thighs, where the largest muscles of the body were located. The stance also facilitated rapid movements for dodging an attack, feigning a strike, or delivering a blow. Guan Yu understood that the moment a combatant lost his firm stance, he would become a sitting duck for his opponent to strike down.

The back of a horse, however, was not terra firma. A horse in battle was in perpetual motion. For a man sitting on horseback to strike with fluid and nimble manipulations of a heavy weapon like the sixty-catty halberd would require not only expert equestrian skills, exceptional strength, and gifted athleticism but also a talented and cooperating mount. Guan Yu wasn't sure he could do it.

The grand master saw Guan Yu blink and read Guan Yu's hesitation.

"Don't be concerned, Guan Yu!" The grand master tried to boost Guan Yu's confidence: "The horse and you are like twins, agile, powerful, and attached to each other. As for your own credentials, look at your thighs, they are as strong as the trunks of a mature willow tree; look at your arms, they are as thick as a grown man's thighs; and look at the abdominal muscles lining your midsection, they are as solid as a pile of bricks. No weapon could suit you better than this halberd. It is heavy, but you will learn to master it on your horse. When you do, you will be invincible!"

After a pause, the master ordered, "With this new assignment, you will be excused from farming every other afternoon, starting tomorrow."

The first thing Guan Yu had to learn in his new assignment was to ride and maneuver his horse without holding on to the reins.

"Your hands are for wielding the halberd," the master reminded him.

Using his body, legs, and feet, Guan Yu soon established a system of delicate, tactile communicative signals with his horse when he rode. The horse had already been in sync with Guan

Yu's movements, responding swiftly to Guan Yu's shift of body weight, soft kick, and gentle squeeze. As time passed, the back-and-forth messaging between horse and rider became much more nuanced and delicately calibrated. Without using the reins, Guan Yu practiced commanding the horse to charge forward, turn left, turn right, trot backward, make a U-turn, accelerate, halt, leap, and move sideways. It didn't take long for the horse to begin responding to the new communication codes. Much to Guan Yu's surprise, it delighted in the challenge of learning the system of interaction. After each training session, the horse raised its head and snorted as if it were telling Guan Yu, "You are good, and I can keep up with you!"

On a hot day, after a couple of hours of practice, Guan Yu took the horse to the creek and splashed it with buckets of cold water, and in response, the horse expressed its appreciation by pursing its lips and performing a cute little dance. The two of them, man and animal, now moved like a fused new creature, capable of all actions with precision and speed. They complemented each other in perfect harmony and reveled in each other's company. When Guan Yu walked in front of the horse on a trek through the woods, the horse rubbed his head against Guan Yu affectionately from time to time.

No sooner had Guan Yu become habituated to wielding the halberd on his horse in full gallop than the master set forth another challenge for him.

"It is time for you to develop a repertoire of fighting techniques," said the grand master to Guan Yu. "Most fighting techniques are improvised during combat in response to unanticipated situations, but a great martial artist always has a repertoire of moves practiced to perfection so that their execution becomes his second nature. In combat, a martial artist focuses his attention exclusively on instantaneous assessment and dissection of his adversary's capability and strategy; he strikes, swings, thrusts, chops in offense, and parries, blocks, dodges in defense, naturally and instinctively, at the most propitious moment without any hesitation."

The grand master designed three tactical moves as the foundation of Guan Yu's fighting technique.

One involved charging forward at full speed while holding the halberd in front of the horse and gyrating it at blinding speed with both arms.

"This move confuses and disorients your enemy, whether your enemy is a single combatant or an army," explained the grand master. "It is an attack. At the same time, it parries arrows and spears coming your way. It is called Breaking the Wave, as if you were wading into a raging surf. In battle, always remember to protect the front part of your horse, that is, his head, chest, and front legs. Some of your enemies will aim their spears and arrows at your horse to deprive you of your partner. Covering the horse with a thick hide will help. But too much armor slows it down and hinders its movement. That's why you should include a component to protect your mount in your tactical moves. Breaking the Wave will deflect weapons that may injure your horse.

"The second tactical move requires a sudden deceleration of your forward movement as you peek back at an adversary behind. Slide your grip inconspicuously toward the blade of the halberd pole as your pursuer closes in. When he is within reach, aim a mighty thrust of the sharp end of the pole backward at his torso. This is the Heart-Piercing Move."

The master continued, "The third is the Heart-Breaking Move." He said, "You feign defeat in a duel. Galloping away from your adversary, dragging the blade end of your halberd on the left side of your horse feigning defeat and pretending to escape. Then, twist your torso from left to right abruptly while swinging the halberd mightily in the same direction. The halberd will trace an arc covering more than one hundred and eighty degrees of air space, gathering speed until it finds its target."

These three moves became the bread and butter of Guan Yu's combat techniques. After one year of practice, at age twenty-one, he could, with one swing of the halberd, while galloping at full speed on his horse, chop into two pieces a straw man built around a solid wooden core. During practice, the master, standing at forty paces away, held up the target in the air and roared, "Ready, charge!"

Upon hearing the command, Guan Yu flew forward on his steed as he gyrated his halberd in front before raising the halberd to swing at the target.

Some days, the grand master rode the mare in tandem with Guan Yu on his steed into the mountain. In a hidden valley, the two galloped their horses together until Guan Yu surged ahead. The grand master took on the role of a pursuer, enabling Guan Yu to practice the Heart-Piercing Move and the Heart-Breaking Move.

One day, Guan Yu felt particularly energetic. He demolished thirty straw men without a pause in practice. The grand master jokingly complained that not only was he exhausted from playing the roles of coach and pursuer, but at the pace of Guan Yu's practice, the pine forest, like the bamboo grove in the mountain, would disappear.

Over the months, Guan Yu developed a template for new fighting tactics. They emerged almost naturally in combat practice with the grand master. As the horse trotted into combat, Guan Yu would hold his halberd low, nearly touching the ground, on the side of the horse so that the weapon was partly concealed from his opponent. At an appropriate distance, he swung up the halberd toward the opponent at blinding speed, like a swordsman whipping his sword from his waist to slash, chop, or pierce. Given the length, the weight, and the speed of

Guan Yu's halberd, an enemy with a sword, a spear, or a shorter weapon had little or no chance of parrying his powerful blows.

Later in his life, Guan Yu frequently alternated this template of moves with the Breaking the Wave technique when he charged into combat, baffling and intimidating his enemies.

Toward the end of Guan Yu's fifth year at the martial arts camp, as he prepared for the long run to visit his family on a day the full moon would rise in the evening, the grand master suggested, "Guan Yu, why don't you take the halberd and ride the steed to visit your parents."

The grand master's suggestion delighted Guan Yu. Riding a horse, even at a leisurely trot, would shorten his trip by half the time and afford more hours for Guan Yu to spend with his family. He couldn't wait to show his parents and sisters the Reclining Moon halberd and his newly acquired martial skill on the steed.

In the afternoon of that glorious spring day, holding his Reclining Moon halberd in his left hand, Guan Yu embarked on his homebound pilgrimage. Sitting high on his steed rendered the trip a completely new experience for him. The horse provided an elevated platform for Guan Yu to survey his surroundings, yielding a lofty, expansive view that was unavailable when he was on his feet. The high vantage point brought into Guan Yu's visual field new sceneries and objects that escaped his attention when he jogged along the same trail. The wooded landscape looked enchanting; the leaves and boughs of trees caressed him; a refreshing breeze soothed his spirit; songbirds, chirping and flitting about, entertained him. When the horse and Guan Yu reached an opening in the woods, they paused to view the beauty of the glade adorned with wildflowers, glistening in the sun, the vernal pools covered with velvety lotus leaves with radiant pink flowers among them, the honeybees and dragonflies happily buzzing around.

THE MARTIAL ARTS CAMP

The horse, trotting down the winding path in a buoyant mood, seemed to share Guan Yu's appreciation of nature's offering. Guan Yu felt blessed. An unexpected turn of fate had ushered him into an adulthood filled with verve, hope, and the promise of adventure. He was overcome with gratitude to the grand master and love for his parents. His parents didn't and couldn't train him in martial arts, but when the opportunity arose, they didn't hesitate to let go of him, giving up a pillar of their communal life so that he could pursue a new goal in life. He imagined building a comfortable home with an enclosed courtyard of fruit trees for them to retire in their old age. Even though the idea of providing generously for his parents appeared a far-fetched wish at the time, Guan Yu knew that it was not an empty dream. Nothing could hold him back in his pursuits. He felt he was on top of the world.

As the horse was happily trotting down the mountain with Guan Yu imagining a magnificent future, it suddenly stopped, raised its head high, flattened its ears, and neighed. Guan Yu thought the horse might have sensed the presence of a predator, perhaps a tiger or a timber wolf. Levelling his halberd, Guan Yu turned his head in every direction to scrutinize his surroundings. There was no sign of wildlife: no rustling among the bushes; no trampled grass; no footprints of a tiger, a bear, or a wolf; no alarm calls from birds. He did notice the presence of an unusual number of crows and magpies, common scavengers and carrion eaters. Perched on treetops, they cawed and cackled. Then, Guan Yu caught a whiff of a putrid stench and the smell of pungent smoke.

As the trail led Guan Yu out of the mountain, the cause of the sickening odors and the heightened alertness of the horse became clear. The plain before him looked like a killing field as if a marauding army or a powerful tornado had just swept through. Smoldering remnants of burned homes and structures, mangled human corpses, and trampled fields of wheat and vegetables covered the land. Even some of the poplar and willow trees along the river were damaged.

Alarmed, Guan Yu steered the horse toward his home and lunged into a full gallop for the remaining stretch of his journey.

As Guan Yu entered his hometown, a swath of charred ruins lay in front of him. Even the official compound of the county magistrate's principal subordinate was gone. The tall wall encircling it had crumpled into piles of stones, mortar, and shattered tiles. The intimidating black door on the south side, made of solid hardwood adorned with metallic hardware, through which horses, officials, and soldiers used to pass, had been reduced to a pile of charred remains. Before Guan Yu joined the grand master in his mountain retreat, that door had stood as an imposing structure symbolizing the magistrate's authority in the county.

Guan Yu could hardly believe what he saw. Is this a nightmare or a hallucination? he asked himself.

When he reached the southwestern side of the town, where his family's property stood, the grounds were littered with debris and corpses. Only the mud hearth of his parents' humble hovel was recognizable.

His heart pounding, his head exploding, his vision blurring, Guan Yu dismounted in front of his demolished home. He wanted to scream, but his voice left him. He thrusted his halberd back and forth, swung it left and right as if he were striking down invisible demons. The halberd swished in the air, making a menacing sound that was eerie in an environment of total silence. But it was all in vain, empty gestures of a delirious man who had lost his senses.

When Guan Yu regained his voice, he stopped attacking imagined enemies and began howling. Holding his halberd, he glared at his burnt home like a wounded beast ready to pounce on his enemy. But there was no enemy, no demon, not a single animate being, not even a stray cat. His grief, fury, and howl were met with silence, absolute silence.

Despondent, he let out a bloodcurdling scream and collapsed into a heap on the dirt. Tears pouring down his cheeks, his howl and bawl were reduced to a melancholy moan. When he stopped, he became catatonic, staring into the empty space in front of him that was once his home.

In the dead silence, a sudden squeak, like an aging door slowly swinging open, jolted Guan Yu from his catatonic state. Focusing his gaze in the direction of the squeaky sound, he saw an earthen-colored wood plank, like an aged cover of a coffin, had risen a few inches from the ground in front of the hearth of his vanished home, shedding ashes and dust into the air. He could feel that someone was looking at him from that opening, even though the person remained hidden. Grasping his halberd, Guan Yu walked menacingly forward. Suddenly, the old plank of wood flew into the air, and the head of Guan Yu's father popped up. In a desperate and hoarse voice, the senior Guan called out, "My son, Guan Yu! My son, Guan Yu!"

Guan Yu dropped his halberd, rushed forward, pulled the old man from the pit that was his family's underground storage space.

"Father! Father!" Guan Yu was beside himself as he held his father in a tight embrace, yelling at the top of his voice, "You are alive! Thank heavens. You are alive! Are you OK? Are you?"

Guan Yu's father tried to respond but couldn't summon his voice. He nodded with a painfully distorted face. A momentary relief enveloped Guan Yu, allowing him to be in command of himself. But tension and anxiety reclaimed him again immediately. With wide-open eyes, he asked, "Where is Mother? Where are my sisters?"

Farther shook his head in agony.

"They…are…gone!" He could barely speak as tears spilled sideways along the creases of his wrinkled face. "Oh! What calamity! What misery!" The old man started shaking and wailing.

Guan Yu struggled to steel himself from the devastating news. He had always been fearless and celebrated for his courage. As a young boy, he once stared down an angry water buffalo who lowered its head, snorted loudly, kicked the dirt with its front hooves, getting ready to charge a neighbor who froze in fear. Now he was fighting a battle against invisible devils in his own head. An avalanche of surging emotions threatened to send him over the edge. Guan Yu was in uncharted territory.

This is combat, he admonished himself in silence. In combat, a martial artist must remain calm. One of my master's cardinal rules!

Recalling the grand master's teaching helped Guan Yu regain some measure of composure, even though the emotional blow was devastating. In his rational mind, he knew that his priority was to console his father, and that priority required sensible actions.

Keeping a lid on his own feelings, he guided his father to the row of rocks lining his family's pot of farmland, the rocks that he used to strengthen himself daily before he followed the grand master to the martial arts camp. After they sat down on the biggest rock at the end of the row, Guan Yu wrapped his left arm around his father's shoulders and tried to keep his father's shaking body warm. It took the elder Guan a while before he regained some semblance of normalcy. Then he unloaded the burden of the tragic scourge that descended upon him the day before.

"Yesterday morning when your sisters went out to work in the field," Guan Yu's father began in a trembling whisper, "your mother and I, still in the house filling a water bucket, wrapping up a few wo wo tou (millet balls) for everyone in preparation of a long day of labor, heard rumbling in the direction of the big road, like a distant thunder. But it wasn't thunder, it was

THE MARTIAL ARTS CAMP

the sound of galloping horses leading a horde of running people pounding the road. When I opened the door, I saw that horde, wearing yellow turbans, but otherwise without uniform, running toward us. They were screaming, waving torches and assorted weapons, looking more like a mob than an army, charging toward our town in all directions like floodwater creeping through the terrain. Your sisters, their faces contorted in fear, were running desperately toward home, but the mob caught up with them and speared them in the wheat field. It was too late for your mother and me to run away. We decided to hide in our underground storage. There in the darkness of the storage pit, we sat for one full day and one full night, during which we, shivering in fear, heard footsteps of people walking through our house repeatedly and smelled burning fire. The bedlam raged on until the wee hours of the night. Then, quietness returned. But I did not dare to venture out of the underground storage space, not until I heard your voice when you were howling."

"Where is mother?" Guan Yu asked impatiently.

"She passed away early this morning. The loss of your sisters; the incessant, bone-chilling screams of people being killed, raped, and maimed; the inordinate fear; the uncertainty and its attendant tension were too much for her to bear. At dawn, she closed her eyes and departed. Until you showed up, I thought it was just as well that your mother had left this wretched earth. This is not a life worth struggling for."

At this point, Guan Yu's father stood up. Staring at his wife's corpse in the storage, he lapsed into a sob. Guan Yu held him in his arms. A host of emotions gnawed at him. There was anguish, sorrow, and bewilderment, the overwhelming loss of his mother and sisters, the destruction of his home, the termination of his family, the erasure of the first seventeen years of his life. There was also fury, fury that was so intense that Guan Yu was grinding his teeth and biting his lips.

"What sort of morons would kill innocent young girls?" Guan Yu wondered in disbelief, "What do they gain by burning down a whole town and committing such heinous atrocities?"

His fury began to overtake his sadness. The desire for vengeance burned in him. He wanted to kill the brigands, chop them down, lop their heads off, pierce their hearts, if he could only find those ignorant monsters.

"Where are you, imbeciles, savages, murderers?" Guan Yu screamed as he paced in front of his father like a caged tiger. "Come on! Attack me! Cowards, miscreants!"

The intensity of Guan Yu's anger jolted the elder Guan. He waved in front of Guan Yu with both arms, stopped him from pacing back and forth, and said softly, "We had better collect your sisters' bodies and take your mother out of the underground storage."

After burying his mother and sisters in a grave that he dug on the site of his destroyed home, Guan Yu surveyed the ruins of his childhood town and noticed that the Taoist temple, surprisingly, had been spared from destruction by the marauders. At the time, Guan Yu and his father did not know that the leaders of the bandits were Taoists. As followers of Taoism, the brigands never disturbed Taoist temples. Guan Yu went over to the temple and found several sticks of incense. Having lit the incense with a piece of amber from one of the ruins, father and son planted it on a makeshift grave for Guan Yu's mother and sisters. The elder Guan, standing at the grave, cupped his hands in front of his chest and bowed solemnly with trembling lips. Guan Yu was on his knees, his forehead in the dirt, as scenes of his mother patting his head and his sisters weaving cricket baskets in the field flashed through his mind.

The dirt of the grave was wet with the tears from father and son.

There was nothing left in their ancestral home other than memory. It was a humble home but rich and warm in spirit.

Guan Yu and his sisters were born there, as were his father and grandfather. Until Guan Yu broke the tradition, his ancestors, as far back as he knew, spent their lives there. Now, the home was gone, reduced to ashes.

Guan Yu stood up from the grave. He had to find a home for his father, but he couldn't think of any place. His grandparents died a long time ago, and he didn't have any surviving relatives. It became clear that the only option was to seek refuge in the martial arts camp.

Guan Yu lifted his father onto the back of the horse. Holding the reins, he walked in front as father and son made their way up the mountain.

Approaching the martial arts camp, Guan Yu became concerned about his decision to bring his father there. Other than the short encounter with the grand master five years ago, Guan Yu's father was a total stranger to the camp community.

Will the camp community accept my father? Guan Yu wondered anxiously, What do I do if the grand master takes offense at my father's sudden presence?

To Guan Yu's relief, the grand master welcomed Guan Yu's father warmly as if the elderly Guan had always belonged to the camp. The first thing the grand master told Guan Yu's father was that he would be a valuable addition to their small community. Guan Yu was so relieved that he had to restrain himself from hugging the grand master. But hugging your teacher was offensive in the Confucian codes of behavior. To express his gratitude, Guan Yu bowed deeply to the grand master.

It took Guan Yu's father a few months to overcome his grief. During those months, he rarely spoke. Seeking solace with long, solitary walks in the woods, he felt a radical amputation had been inflicted on him. An integral part of him had been removed, taken away, gone forever. Without his wife and daughters, he no longer felt like the same person he had been. A good part of him had died with them. There were moments when he wanted to end his life. But the presence of Guan Yu and the compassion of members of the martial arts camp sustained him and gave him strength to live on.

Gradually, Guan Yu's father became integrated into camp life, even though he did not participate in martial art training and study of the classics. With a lifetime of experience in farming and maintaining his humble home, he threw himself into the task of improving all aspects of life at the camp.

Shaping large bamboo into pipes with knives, he created a new irrigation system, ensuring adequate water supply to the crops.

Collecting cedarwood and resin from the mountain conifers, he built an insect-proof extension of their meeting/dining hut to store grains, informing everyone that the storage was necessary insurance against natural calamities.

"We must be prepared for lean years!" he announced to members of the community. "Leans years are inevitable. They are part of nature's cycle."

Mixing chopped grass and fallen leaves with dirt and night soil to make compost, he fertilized the crops and increased the yield of wheat, millet, and vegetables.

Building a fence around the cultivated field where camp members grew their food, he secured their crops against deer and other wildlife that might cause damage.

Gathering fallen branches from the grounds near and far from the camp, he refused to chop down trees for firewood. A tree was harvested only if he needed lumber for construction or repair. Before cutting down a tree, he always bowed to it and thanked the tree for providing him with the life-sustaining material he needed.

Digging a shallow gutter around each of the three huts in camp and piping the gutters downhill with hollowed bamboo

THE MARTIAL ARTS CAMP

trunks, he ensured that a heavy rainstorm would not flood the meadow on which the camp structures stood.

Clever and creative, Guan Yu's father knew exactly how to live off nature without damaging it. Watching him reorganize and reshape the farm at the camp, everyone was impressed with his skill, knowledge, and foresight. He improved camp life and became an indispensable part of that hermetic community.

Immediately after his father joined the martial arts camp, Guan Yu stopped shaving. It was, for him, a way of commemorating his mother and sisters, as if the added beard would preserve his memory of them. Unlike the thin and whiskery beard typical of many Han males, Guan Yu's beard grew thick and heavy. In six months, it sprouted from his chin and cheeks toward his chest. The pitch-black, long patch of curly beard earned him a nickname from members of his camp family, Mei xu gong, meaning "magnificent beard." That nickname not only followed Guan Yu throughout his life, but also became an enduring reference to him in legends and the annals of history long after his death.

FOUR

SEEKING A MISSION

At a festive dinner marking the Autumn Moon Festival of AD 185, more than one year after Guan Yu's father settled into the martial arts camp, the grand master opined, "Guan Yu, you have matured into a peerless martial artist, strong and skilled mentally and physically. It's time for you to embark on a new phase of your life in pursuit of your dream to become a great warrior."

Guan Yu's father chimed in with his full-hearted concurrence, and Guan Yu himself felt the urge to put to test all that he had learned at the knee of the grand master. It would suit him well to begin a new phase of life. For a start, he thought he would join the army in the capital, Luoyang.

At twenty-three years of age, Guan Yu had maximized his growth potential. Lean and chiseled, he stood at six feet two inches in height and 220 pounds in weight. With his martial art, equestrian skill, and the Reclining Moon halberd, he had matured into a formidable and intimidating warrior.

SEEKING A MISSION

On the day of his departure, Guan Yu's father cheerfully bade him farewell. For generations, the family had been peasants eking out a penurious life, which became increasingly precarious because of marauding bandits and predatory officials. Guan Yu was the first person to break out of that wretched family tradition. Proud and optimistic, his father felt that Guan Yu was stepping into a new world. He would miss his beloved son, but he had no regret seeing Guan Yu take off in search of a promising future.

The grand master chose to accompany Guan Yu out of the mountain. It was the master's way of saying a long goodbye to his prize pupil. This time, Guan Yu was heading northwest instead of his usual trek in the northeastern direction toward the home of his youth. During the trek, the grand master and Guan Yu walked in silence, each lost in his own thoughts. Guan Yu was riddled with anxiety, wondering what lay ahead. Questions bubbled up in his mind:

Will I fit into the military?

Is the military organization a meritocracy?

Will the senior officers recognize my martial skill and combat prowess?

He also tried to fathom the grand master's thoughts. He knew that both were saddened by their pending separation. For six years, they were inseparable. Yes, the grand master played the role of a teacher and Guan Yu the role of a pupil. But master and pupil now stood shoulder to shoulder in their martial prowess. More than respect, their affection for each other had deepened immeasurably.

Three hours after they began their trek, the grand master stopped to bid Guan Yu farewell. They had arrived at the foothills. A vast plain spread in front of them. The elderly man handed Guan Yu several silver coins for expenses along his journey, while Guan Yu marched on toward the capital city.

Even though few words were exchanged between master and pupil along the trek out of the mountain, the farewell was heart-wrenching for both. During the years Guan Yu spent at the grand master's mountain hideout, they shared their meals, slept on the same hay-strewn floor, grew their own food, and discoursed on philosophy, statecraft, and the human condition. Those years instilled in Guan Yu the conviction that the triad of a worthy and honorable life lay in loyalty to family, friends, and country; generosity to all; and compassion for sentient beings, humans as well as animals. The master was proud of Guan Yu for his physical, intellectual, and moral development, and Guan Yu revered his master for his art, modesty, and rectitude.

Without rendering their feelings in words over the years in the camp, they fed on each other's energy. The grand master had molded Guan Yu into a wholesome and superb warrior, while the pupil, blessed with talent and work ethic, made the reclusive elder feel that despite his hermetic existence, he had successfully passed on his art and spirit to a worthy heir and thereby might have contributed to the restoration of the Han glory.

By the time of his departure from the camp, Guan Yu had become, without any awareness of his transformation, far more attached to the grand master than he was to his father. Guan Yu's departure brought this attachment to the surface. It was not an issue of altering or abandoning filial loyalty. He remained unwavering in his devotion to his father, the only other surviving member of his family. But the grand master had molded him into a new human being, a full-fledged martial artist, confident in his capability and steadfast in his moral conviction. No longer a prisoner of his little family farm, he was now in search of a new pursuit to serve his country. But the awareness of his mission did not mitigate his feeling that leaving the grand master's camp meant severing the most important bond in his life. He couldn't help feeling overcome by an enormous void, a sense of infinite loneliness as if he had been cast adrift in a bitter sea.

SEEKING A MISSION

Why must my world, which has been nearly perfect, come to an end? Guan Yu asked himself while fantasizing, Why couldn't my master join me in the military?

Wiping tears off his cheeks and beard with his hands, Guan Yu soon caught himself in his indulgence of the childish wish.

"I am an adult now. It is time for me to strike out on my own!"

To divert himself from his grief, Guan Yu started hitting his rib cage with the knuckles of his right hand, which was gripping the Reclining Moon blade. The pain brought some sense back to him. He had to move on, but he could not refrain from capturing one more glance of his mentor.

When he turned his head back, he saw the broad shoulders of the grand master, wearing a coarse shirt and brown pants woven with thick fibers extracted from wild hemp in the mountain, walking steadily uphill. His thin gray hair danced in the breeze, his right hand gripped a long spear, his chosen weapon, swinging to and fro in sync with his strides as he receded into a sinuous path of the wooded mountain. Weeping, Guan Yu sighed and blamed the master's choice of a reclusive life on the decay of the Han dynasty. He knew that as the Han empire sank into anarchy, many honest, upright people, especially artists and the literati, chose hermetic lives. They had given up, said *no* to the world, and lived as recluses because they refused to serve a corrupt and inept court headed by a dunce of an emperor, Emperor Ling.

As he walked away from the mountain onto the main road toward Luoyang, Guan Yu's mood gradually changed. It began with overwhelming grief. But the grief gave way to a determination to dedicate himself to the restoration of the Han empire, a wish cherished by everyone in the grand master's martial arts camp. His sorrow from leaving the camp strengthened the wish. In honor of the grand master, his father, and his fellow acolytes, and in gratitude to their support and camaraderie during his formative years, Guan Yu promised himself that he would strive to lead an army, pacify the country, annihilate the brigands, sack the corrupt warlords, and eliminate the conniving palace eunuchs.

Guan Yu's aspirations were somber, ambitious, and grandiose, but they did not intimidate him. Feeling strong and purposeful, he pressed on in search of a new life grounded in the love and support of the grand master and his father.

Guan Yu's journey began uneventfully. Along the way, he passed by many burned and looted villages. Even in towns and villages that remained intact, beggars, young and old, were a common sight. Emaciated, vacant-eyed, and destitute, they wailed for food and alms from travelers. A pitiful sight of a wretched earth! Guan Yu wished that he were rich so that he could distribute money among them. The multitude of destitute rural people saddened him. He felt frustrated and angry.

The footpaths connecting cities and towns, especially in mountains, were infested with bandits and robbers. But the bandits stayed clear of Guan Yu. One glance at him and his long Reclining Moon halberd was sufficient to induce them to scamper. When he encountered small bands of conspiratorial men carrying weapons and loitering aimlessly on the roadside, his instinctive reaction was to subdue them. But the grand master's teaching held him back: "Never fight unless there is a justifiable and unmistakable reason. You will regret it if you ever harm an innocent man."

He held on firmly to the grand master's teaching.

"Conjecture is not evidential fact," he reminded himself. Those loiterers might look like brigands, he reckoned, he couldn't be sure that they were brigands. Besides, none of them ever glared at Guan Yu when he passed by. He reminded himself of the importance of controlling his emotions, especially his

SEEKING A MISSION

vengeful sentiments fanned by the murder of his mother and sisters at the hand of bandits.

When darkness fell on a mountain path, Guan Yu typically sought refuge in a rocky crevice or a hollow tree, dozing off as he sat cradling his halberd. If he were near a village, he often found a cozy sleeping spot in the middle of an old haystack in a field by pulling out a few bundles of hay. Occasionally he splurged by checking in to a roadside inn to enjoy a bath and a good night of sleep in a bed and replenish himself with a hot meal.

Every time he entered an inn, the keeper and staff inevitably stared at him with awe and fear, as if a celestial being from another world had descended upon them. Guan Yu's colossal beard, gargantuan size, nimble gait, and Reclining Moon halberd always stunned people. Fortunately, his politeness and soft-spoken queries tended to reassure people of his peaceful intent. After their initial shock, an innkeeper and staff members quickly regained their composure and understood that Guan Yu was not a threat but a gentleman.

Several days into his journey, Guan Yu came upon a remote valley tucked away in a rugged mountain chain. From the path along the side of a mountain, he had a commanding view of the valley in front of him. Its pastoral tranquility and simple elegance took his breath away. It was a hidden settlement without any sign of destruction, not a trace of the blight and malaise that plagued so many towns and villages along his journey.

It was late autumn, many days after his departure from the martial arts camp. The rice paddies in this hidden valley had turned golden. Some of the rice stalks fell flat in the field because of the weight of the grain. From a distance, the patches of fallen rice stalks looked like the footpath of some giant mythical creatures crossing the golden field.

At one end of the paddy field stood the hazy silhouette of three villages. Each appeared as a long row of white walls capped with a black pitched roof. The haze and the low clouds created an optical illusion that the roofs of those villages were undulating.

On the left of this halcyon landscape stood a row of hills, silent in a picturesque repose against sheaves of mountainous silhouette in the background. The nearest hills looked like a gigantic Buddha reclining on his side, a raised arm propping up his head as he kept a benevolent watch over the valley. The Luo River, a tributary of the great Yellow River, flowed between the Buddha's head and his raised arm. Becalmed on the plain, the river meandered past the villages like a gargantuan serpent, sustaining human settlements along its shore with flowing water. Branches of weeping willows, leaning over the river, swayed gently in a breeze. At each turn of the river, the bank where the current slowed almost to a standstill, patches of riparian green, smooth and verdant, looked like meticulously manicured gardens from a distance, where gaggles of snow-white geese and chocolate-brown ducks congregated, shaking their bodies, moving between the river and the bank, honking and quacking softly. Now and then, a black-and-silver carp leaped out of the river, twisting its shiny and sinewy body in the air, to snack on dragonflies.

In the valley's paddy fields, men and women wearing black costumes decorated with colorful patches were harvesting. Bending over their golden crop, they swung their sickles in rhythm and sang their harvest song in joy. In the courtyards fronting their villages, young men were threshing bundled rice stalks against slanted hardwood boards to separate the rice kernels from the hay. The kernels slid into a large bamboo bucket at the end of each hardwood board.

Here and there, haystacks piled high in the courtyards stood like sandstone kopje, sculpted and aromatic. The autumn breeze caressed; the balmy sun soothed. Overhead, flocks of migrating geese and cranes honked on their southbound migration, their formations resembling a simple Chinese logograph, ren 人, meaning "human/humanity," repeating itself in the sky.

Guan Yu could hardly believe what he saw. Hidden in the mountains, the valley had managed to escape the marauding bandits and the plundering bureaucrats. When he walked closer to the harvesting farmers in the field, he found the reasons for their good fortune.

Scattered over the field were weapons: swords, spears, lances, bows, and arrows within easy reach of everyone. Ready to take up their arms in a second, those farmers doubled as a self-defense force. Protected by steep mountains, this farming community maintained an undisturbed existence like members of his martial arts camp. They were also battle ready, fully prepared to defend themselves. Curious, Guan Yu approached the people working the field. Some of them paused in their harvest to look at him. Despite Guan Yu's halberd, they were not alarmed because, wearing a big grin, he was obviously benevolent.

"We are Hmong, but the Han people call us Miao, a derogatory name meaning barbarian," announced a middle-aged man, who spoke a regional Chinese dialect that Guan Yu could barely understand.

"Thank you for telling me who you are. I am Guan Yu and I apologize for the name Han people gave you. If you consider yourself Hmong, then you are Hmong. Please allow me to congratulate you on your bountiful harvest!" Guan said politely.

Surprised by Guan Yu's forthright apology and friendliness, the middle-aged man responded affably, "Yes, we work hard for our crops."

This was the first time Guan Yu had met a Hmong. He had heard of the disparaging Han names for some minority ethnic groups, such as Xiongnu, "the roaring slaves," and Xianbei, "lowly upstarts," referring to nomadic pastoralists from the north and the west of the Han empire. Guan Yu reckoned that because the northwestern nomads historically raided Han settlements along the border, the Han people, out of spite and fear, gave slanderous names to the raiders. But the Hmong appeared to be sedentary agriculturalists, just like the Han farmers. He couldn't understand why Han people called them barbarians.

With piqued interest, Guan Yu set forth to learn more about the Hmong.

Laying down his halberd, he volunteered to help the Hmong in their harvest to demonstrate his goodwill. Farming was what he'd done all his life until he moved to the grand master's camp. Even there, he'd lived as a part-time farmer to grow his own food. Here in the rice paddies of the Hmong, he showed off his mettle. His energy and proficiency astonished the Hmong and earned their admiration.

At the end of the day, the senior Hmong, who had initiated a conversation with Guan Yu earlier, invited him to stay in their village and treated him to tasty rice cakes and a special alcoholic brew made from sugarcane juice. Enjoying the company of his Hmong hosts and communicating with them through gestures and some Chinese words, Guan Yu stayed two nights.

During the mealtimes of those two days, he learned about the history and traditions of the Hmong people, and that there were many different Hmong tribes, speaking distinct Hmong languages, many of which were not mutually intelligible. Their ancestors used to inhabit the plains of the eastern seaboard of China, according to an elder in the village. But the Han people, sweeping from the north with an expanding population, forcibly took the arable land from them, expelling them into isolated pockets in mountain ranges. Some of them escaped into the tropical jungle of the deep south and never returned.

Guan Yu didn't like what he learned about his own people, the Han. Feeling guilty and shameful, he wondered what motivated Han to prey upon the Hmong. It wasn't fear or hostility, because the Hmong were not aliens and didn't belong to a different country. There were hardly any consistent physical differences between the Hmong and the Han. Members of both ethnic groups tended to have pale skin, almond eyes, straight black hair, a low ridge above the eye, and a nondescript nose that was never tall. Even the Hmong languages, though distinct, sounded like Chinese dialects. Taking account of the overwhelming similarity between the Hmong and the Han, Guan Yu suddenly became aware that his own reddish-brown skin, gargantuan size, and huge beard did not fit the stereotypical image of a Han person. Perhaps his ancestors belonged to an exotic ethnic group, he speculated. But he had never experienced any hostility on account of his uncommon physical features. After some cogitation, he couldn't come up with an answer to the question:

Why did the Han majority discriminate against the Hmong, take away their land, and chase them into high mountains and inhospitable jungles?

He then speculated that chauvinism might be related to narcissism, two opposite sides of the same coin of human frailty according to his grand master. The more narcissistic a person was, the more likely that person would harbor discriminatory attitudes toward others who were different in one way or another. But he wasn't sure. This was one occasion when Guan Yu wished he were a philosopher, even though in his teenage years, he disparaged philosophy as idle attempts to solve abstract, pointless riddles. In the past, he had heard people making derogatory statements about non-Han ethnic groups who spoke different languages and observed different cultural traditions. Chalking them up as momentary outbursts from ill-tempered people, he never paid much attention to that type of verbiage. Now he understood that the vilification of people different from oneself could lead to contempt, discrimination, and outright hostility. It was a human propensity of which he was ashamed. He would like to change or eliminate such a pusillanimous human trait. As for how to make such a change, Guan Yu didn't have a clue. He thought, someday, a new sage would teach humans to eradicate the feelings of contempt and discrimination against people with different language and culture.

Notwithstanding his awareness of another unflattering feature of human beings, Guan Yu was glad to have met the Hmong. He admired their way of life, combining farming with martial arts. They were not intimidated by brigands or invaders. Even though their martial skill conferred to them the power that other agricultural settlements might not have, they never lorded over their distant neighbors. Greed and power seemed to play no role in their pursuit of a simple life in harmony with nature.

Guan Yu also felt that the Hmong were the living example of a people practicing what his grand master never tired of reminding his pupils, that humans, being dependent on plants and animals, should not take any more than what was needed for survival. The grand master considered it disgraceful and pernicious that many humans trample plants, kill animals, and murder each other for power, wealth, and domination.

Another feature of the Hmong that attracted Guan Yu was the colorful patches on their black garments. The intricate patterns of the reverse appliqué, made of brightly colored textile pieces, rendered each patch into a blazing geometric montage. The Hmong didn't adorn themselves with gold, silver, or precious stones, the typical displays of wealth in the world. Only the reverse-appliqué patches decorated their costumes. Guan Yu was impressed by their folk art.

The attitude of the Hmong people and the bucolic tranquility of their villages left a deep impression on Guan Yu. An island in a sea of gloom and doom, the Hmong homeland presented a ray of hope, mitigating the dismal state of the country he had witnessed on his journey. It also lifted his spirits from the sadness

SEEKING A MISSION

of leaving the grand master's camp of martial arts. Even though the image of the grand master's back receding on the mountain path, the agony of the emaciated beggars along his trek, and the sight of his mother's and sisters' corpses still haunted him from time to time, a new optimism began to congeal in him. Perhaps there was still hope for peace and happiness in the country, Guan Yu thought.

At the end of his brief stay with the Hmong people, Guan Yu felt that he could live happily among them, had he not committed himself to a mission of reviving the Han dynasty.

Two days after leaving the Hmong region, Guan Yu came into the hilly neighborhood of S-Y Wang's town. Toward the end of his trek one late afternoon, still relishing the halcyon image of the Hmong homeland, Guan Yu heard, or he thought he heard, a very faint cry of a female as if she were being muffled. He stopped, turned his head from left to right like a barn owl trying to locate a mouse scurrying under the cover of darkness in the night. That muffled cry seemed to originate from a thicket of undergrowth about forty paces to the right of the footpath Guan Yu was following. He tiptoed over to the undergrowth.

To his astonishment, Guan Yu found a man pinning down a young girl on the ground. The man's left hand was covering the girl's mouth; his right hand was pulling apart her robe. In his frenzy, the rapist never saw or heard Guan Yu approaching.

A tsunami of rage engulfed Guan Yu.

Without laying down the Reclining Moon halberd in his right hand, Guan Yu, in one lightning swoop, grabbed the assailant's knot of hair on top of his head with the left hand, yanked him off the victim, and lifted him into the air. The assailant, hanging in midair, didn't even have the time to fathom what had happened when Guan Yu furiously shook him from one side to the other like a marionette dangling from Guan Yu's hand. By the time Guan Yu stopped and let go of the assailant, the rapist crumpled to the ground like a deflated accordion, his face white as chalk, his eyes motionless, his mouth agape, his head turned sideways.

When Guan Yu shook the rapist in the air, he inadvertently severed the man's spinal cord from his brain stem, resulting in instant death.

In the meantime, the young female victim had gotten up from the ground, mumbling something unintelligible, and ran away as if a demon were behind her. Guan Yu didn't give chase, even though he wanted to console her. But chasing her, Guan Yu figured, would've only aggravated the trauma that the assailant had inflicted on her.

It was not Guan Yu's intention to kill the rapist. In his fury, Guan Yu had wanted to teach him a lesson. The entire incident happened in a flash, affording no time for Guan Yu to think or plan a course of action. Now a man lay dead because of his actions. He could face a criminal investigation by the county magistrate. If found guilty, he could be imprisoned, even executed.

Guan Yu had neither the time nor the patience to undergo a judiciary hearing in front of a county magistrate even though he had a good chance of being exonerated on a factual basis, nor did he have faith in the competence and the integrity of the general officialdom. The deceased person's family, Guan Yu reckoned, if they were rich, might bribe the magistrate to have him convicted or beheaded no matter how well he defended himself in a judiciary hearing.

Without any further thought, Guan Yu left the scene of the incident and resumed his journey, albeit at a brisk pace, much faster than he was walking before the incident.

Guan Yu was lucky that no one, other than the rape victim, witnessed what had happened. The footpath was deserted at

SEEKING A MISSION

the time. Even the rape victim was not fully aware of what had transpired. She was so traumatized by the assault and so anxious to run away that she never looked at Guan Yu. By the time the poor girl reached home, she remained hysterical, incoherent, and completely out of breath. Between bouts of tears, she barely managed to tell her parents that by the grace of heaven, an emissary materialized to rescue her and enabled her to escape from the clutches of the villainous ruffian S-Y Wang. Even after she regained her composure, she couldn't offer much of a description of her savior.

"My savior was either a god or a demon," she told her parents. "He was a ferocious giant with a dark face, powerful enough to lift the ruffian S-Y Wang off my body as if Wang was a toy. I don't know what happened because once I got free, I ran away as fast as I could."

Lighting an incense stick, the parents prostrated themselves in front of a small ancestral shrine in their room and thanked the spirits of their ancestors for saving their daughter.

"Perhaps," the father told his daughter, "our ancestors had sent an agent from the dark region of the dead to save you from the jaws of S-Y Wang. You know, ghosts are powerful giants, usually have an unrecognizable face with bulging eyes and ferocious demeanor. You can see their statues guarding the entrance of some large Taoist temples."

They, of course, didn't know that S-Y Wang had died. In their minds, the ghost, while on a mission to rescue their daughter, merely lifted the evil man away from her and taught him a lesson.

Three days later, a collector of medicinal herbs, wandering in the mountains and foothills, accidentally discovered Wang's decaying body. The herb collector immediately reported his discovery to the yamen, the magistrate's office. A policeman, upon reaching the site, ascertained that the decaying body belonged to S-Y Wang, who, according to his family, had been missing for three days. The police didn't find any bruise or weapon-inflicted wound on the corpse other than the evidence, indicated by teeth marks, that part of S-Y Wang's legs had been consumed by some wild animals, most probably feral dogs. In the absence of any evidence and witnesses of foul play, the county magistrate ruled that S-Y Wang had died of an unknown accident and released the corpse to his family for burial.

FIVE

THREE
SWORN BROTHERS

Five days after Guan Yu inadvertently killed S-Y Wang, he arrived at the outskirts of a medium-sized city, approximately halfway toward Luoyang, the capital. At the city gate, affixed on a wooden board for government bulletins, was an official announcement, written in large logographs, seeking volunteers to enlist in the local garrison. From the bulletin and the chattering of the people standing in front of it, Guan Yu learned that the city faced the risk of being overrun by a ragtag army belonging to a cult that had evolved into a sizable military force consisting of tens of thousands of destitute farmers and desperados who had lost their livelihood. According to the bulletin, cult members wore yellow turbans and used yellow banners as their military insignia. Calling themselves the Yellow Turban Rebels, their leaders, three Taoist brothers with the surname Zhang, had proclaimed, "The Han dynasty is coming to an end and the Yellow Force is on the ascendency. We, the Yellow Turbans, are revolutionaries, the destiny of our country. Join us to usher in a new age of prosperity."

Despite the Yellow Turbans' leaders' slogans, prosperity was nowhere in sight. From the chattering of the crowd gathering in front of the bulletin board, Guan Yu learned that wherever the Yellow Turbans appeared, they left behind a trail of death and destruction as they looted, plundered, and killed at will. Official rural garrisons were no match to the horde of Yellow Turbans. The imperial government had adopted a policy of reserving its army for the defense of major urban centers in the country, leaving small cities and rural areas to be ravaged by the insurgents.

The information from the bulletin board and the conversations among the crowd gathered in front of it motivated Guan Yu to enlist in the local garrison. He now had evidence that the imperial officials were derelicts who could not even maintain law and order in the country, confirming what the grand master had said repeatedly in the martial arts camp. The imperial court had simply abrogated its duty to protect ordinary citizens. More exasperating than the government's inaction and ineptitude, Guan Yu came to understand from the chattering crowd that the Yellow Turbans, who were underprivileged and destitute before succumbing to banditry, chose to prey on people suffering from the same miserable fate that drove them to insurrection. They were cynical and unprincipled. Contrary to their leaders' claim of being revolutionaries, Guan Yu reasoned, the Yellow Turbans were a horde of cannibalistic predators.

The final realization that made up Guan Yu's mind to join the local garrison was that the Yellow Turbans were probably the same bandits who burned down his own hometown and murdered his mother and sisters. Two years ago, in the killing field of his native town, when his father told him that the mob that had killed his sisters and mother were wearing yellow turbans, he did not pay attention to that detail of his father's description of the mob. The government bulletin reawakened in him his

THREE SWORN BROTHERS

father's words. Standing among the crowd in front of the bulletin, Guan Yu felt a surge of anger.

"Savages! Vermin! Cowards!" He muttered to himself, "I will answer the call of this local government to join its garrison. It's time to hunt down the Yellow Turbans."

A man next to him heard Guan Yu's cussing. Taking note of Guan Yu's unusual physical presence, his Reclining Moon halberd, and the burning rage on his face, the stranger said with great courtesy, "Salute, sir! I heard what you've been muttering under your breath, and I totally agree with you. The Yellow Turbans are barbarous. Many friends of mine and I share your sentiment. We would be honored if you could join us to discuss and perhaps brainstorm over cups of wine a strategy to rout the Yellow Turbans."

Guan Yu turned to face this stranger. In a scholar's robe, he looked middle-aged, affable, and regal. But his long arms, large ears, benevolent eyes, and robust physical presence were atypical of a member of the literati. Speaking softly with confidence, the stranger came across as a thoughtful and sincere gentleman.

Guan Yu didn't see anything wrong with accepting the stranger's invitation. He had nothing to lose, and the stranger did not present a threat. As they walked away from the bulletin board at the city gate, Guan Yu learned that the stranger was named Liu Bei. Chatting amiably, they ambled into a wealthy neighborhood in the city.

Along the way, Guan Yu learned that Liu Bei was a member of the imperial clan, a distant descendant of Liu Bang, the founder of the Han dynasty, and he was living modestly in this town in Henan province as a plebeian, shying away from politics and public recognition. Lately, alarmed by the Yellow Turbans' insurrection and the decay of the Han dynasty, Liu Bei emerged from his seclusion. He felt, as a responsible citizen, it was time for direct action. Leading a group of friends and associates in frequent discussions on how to lift the Han dynasty from ruin, he had been on the lookout for like-minded people who might join his group of concerned citizens. When Liu Bei saw Guan Yu in front of the bulletin board, he felt he had found a superb candidate to recruit into his group.

After the serendipitous meeting, Guan Yu and Liu Bei took to each other spontaneously as if they were old friends. They agreed with each other on every subject they touched on: the urgency of combating the Yellow Turbans, the state of the empire, the importance of moral principles in life, the curse of greed and avarice, the connection between physical endeavor and intellectual pursuit. They spoke enthusiastically to each other as Liu Bei led Guan Yu toward a house belonging to Zhang Fei, an accomplished martial artist and a member of a wealthy merchant family, who was a close confidant of Liu Bei.

Immersed in their conversation, Liu Bei almost failed to notice that they had passed Zhang Fei's residence. When Liu Bei caught his error, he joked, "Guan Yu, you have a blinding impact on me!"

Zhang Fei's family residence was a spacious compound in the form of a walled quadrangle. The entrance was a large vermilion south-facing gate adorned with bronze handles. A black-tiled gable roof resting on four wooden columns sheltered the gate. A much narrower but similarly shaped roof covered the entire brick wall surrounding the compound. Inside the compound were several brick buildings decorated with lacquered cherry-wood windows and gabled roofs similarly styled as the one over the entrance door. Shaded balconies wrapped around each building inside the compound. The balconies with overhanging roofs kept out the hot sun and rain from the interior of each house during the summer and shielded the windows and doors from the sleet and snow during the winter. All the buildings faced a common courtyard occupying more than two acres of land. Stone paths from the buildings crisscrossed the courtyard. It was a classically traditional residence called siheyuan, meaning "harmony compound."

At one end of the spacious courtyard was a peach orchard, and in the center of the orchard stood a pavilion sheltering a round marble table with four lacquered rosewood chairs around it. The pavilion provided an ideal spot to practice calligraphy, study classics, train in martial arts, play board games, or enjoy tea and wine with close friends.

At the time of Guan Yu's visit, the peach blossoms had faded. However, the Osmanthus trees hugging the walls of the courtyard remained in bloom. Pale yellow and light orange, clumps of tiny Osmanthus flowers emanated a heavenly, sweet aroma.

No sooner had a servant seated Liu Bei and Guan Yu at the pavilion than a maid served up three ceramic cups with matching jars of Osmanthus-scented liquor. As the maid retreated, a bear of a man emerged from the house, bouncing energetically in huge strides toward the pavilion. Sporting a full face of protruding black whiskers that resembled more the spines of a hedgehog than a thick beard, he appeared powerfully built, as thick but not as tall as Guan Yu. Capped by bushy eyebrows, his piercing eyes sparkled with intensity. He had a flared nose, suggesting the potential for exceptional physical stamina. His lips parted in an impish smile. His hands were unusually large, and he wore loosely fitted black cotton pants tucked into a pair of black, ankle-length boots favored by traditional martial artists. Before Liu Bei could introduce Guan Yu and this exceptional specimen of a man to each other, Guan Yu had already surmised that his boisterous host was an accomplished martial artist.

"Welcome to my house. I am Zhang Fei, Liu Bei's bosom friend." Zhang Fei said, with a booming voice, as he filled the cups with Osmanthus liquor, "Let's drink to the renaissance of the Han dynasty!"

No sooner had the three men downed their first cups of liquor than Liu Bei proposed a second toast, "To the demise of the Yellow Turbans!"

Guan Yu roared with approval and said to his companions, "I cannot imagine two better toasts than what you have just proposed! You have warmed my heart."

It turned out that Zhang Fei had met Liu Bei several years earlier at the same government bulletin board outside the city wall where people were protesting the government's treatment of beggars. Liu Bei spoke at the gathering, pointing out that instead of beating the beggars and chasing them out of the city, the government should try to help them.

"No one enjoys being a despondent beggar," Liu Bei said in his short speech. "People become beggars because our country is disintegrating. They couldn't find employment and they couldn't enter a trade. We need a government to help the poor, not to punish them. The government could hire them to clean streets, repair roads, plant trees, reinforce river dikes, widen irrigation canals, and improve public services. There might be a minor initial cost to the imperial treasury, but public morale will improve, and productivity in the nation will increase. In the end, the imperial treasury will more than recoup its initial monetary outlay by helping beggars."

Standing in the crowd, Zhang Fei enthusiastically endorsed Liu Bei's suggestion and invited him to be a houseguest. The two of them found out that they shared similar worldviews. Both were compassionate patriots; both wanted a change in the way the country was governed, and both felt it was time to organize a movement to reinvigorate the country.

In the peach garden, Guan Yu told Zhang Fei and Liu Bei his humble origin and his training under the tutelage of the grand master in the martial arts camp. Zhang Fei revealed that since his childhood, he had wanted to be an expert martial artist. To support his ambition, his father employed the leading master of the Praying Mantis School of martial arts to coach the young son for years. Like Guan Yu, Zhang Fei was a skilled horseman. His favorite weapon was an extra-long metal spear, weighing well over sixty catties. Capable of tossing his spear from sixty paces away to pierce a two-inch-thick wooden board, he matched Guan Yu in strength and courage.

Unlike Guan Yu and Zhang Fei, Liu Bei grew up favoring books over martial arts. Even though he never aspired to be a warrior, he was not an armchair weakling. Throughout his teens and twenties, he trained assiduously in swordsmanship while studying the classics. By the time he met Guan Yu, he was in his late thirties, highly respected in his city for his erudition and his expertise in swordplay. In a world that sharply segregated intellectual pursuits (wen) from martial/athletic endeavors (wu), so much so that the literati, proud of being the people of wen, typically disdained all forms of physical exertion, Liu Bei stood out as a rarity who had attained excellence in both domains. In his view, training of the mind and training of the body were complementary and deeply connected. The swordplay sharpened his mind, enhanced his concentration, and improved his endurance in intellectual pursuits.

Conversely, the study of arts, philosophy, and literature helped him to appreciate the splendor of martial arts techniques that required tremendous mental dexterity to execute with precision and power. He admired Guan Yu and Zhang Fei for their incomparable attainments in martial arts just as much as he admired the poets and writers for their insights, ideas, and melodic juxtaposition of images and words. To him, intellectual pursuits were forms of mental exercise requiring agility and creativity just like the art of attaining martial or athletic excellence.

For two days, the three men got acquainted with each other. They reveled in each other's company. Unlike most of their contemporaries who hid their intents and held back their emotions, all three of them laid bare what was in their hearts to each other. They were forthright, honest, and passionate. They did not beat around the bush or speak in riddles, never hesitated to call a spade a spade, although among them, Liu Bei tended to be prudent and thoughtful, Zhang Fei bordered on impetuosity, and Guan Yu's temperament fell somewhere between the other two. All three loathed predatory characters who took advantage of the meek and the downtrodden. They considered generosity and loyalty the principal human virtues and cherished the vision of restoring peace and justice in the Han empire.

By the third day after meeting each other, they felt they had known each other for years. Full of trust, respect, and affection for each other, they exulted as if they had found their long-lost brothers.

In this atmosphere of exuberant camaraderie, Zhang Fei ordered his household staff to prepare a banquet on the third evening to celebrate the serendipitous meeting of the three friends that had quickly evolved into bonded brothers. All three felt they were embarking on a new and shared journey in life.

After the banquet, during which the three friends consumed many cups of Osmanthus liquor, Liu Bei proposed, to the delight of Zhang Fei and Guan Yu, that they should form a brotherhood.

The next morning, on their knees in the peach garden pavilion, the three men solemnly swore on the honor of their ancestors and their souls, in front of burning incense at an altar placed on the marble table in the pavilion, that they would dedicate themselves to the struggle of restoring the grandeur of the Han dynasty, and they would fight with all of their power to protect each other until the end of their lives.

In the brotherhood, Liu Bei took the honor and privileges of being the senior because he was the oldest among the three. Next came Guan Yu, while Zhang Fei, being the youngest, brought up the rear. Thereafter, friends and enemies referred to them as the Peach Garden Brothers.

THREE SWORN BROTHERS 69

Two days later, the three newly bonded Peach Garden Brothers received a miraculous blessing, an omen heralding a promising future of the enterprise that united them.

A dear family friend of Liu Bei's for several decades, who also happened to be one of the wealthiest men in the country, unexpectedly arrived in town. Accompanied by a contingent of armed bodyguards on horses and a train of burros bearing sacks of salt, he was on his way to inland provinces to deliver a sizable shipment of salt produced at his family-operated salt mines on the eastern seaboard. His wealth came from his family's business of producing and selling salt, an enterprise traditionally monopolized by the imperial court. During the reign of Emperor Ling's predecessor, several wise and farsighted court officials, in their effort to combat corruption and inefficiency, persuaded the emperor to abandon the government monopoly on the salt business in the country. People, for the first time, were free to harvest, transport, and sell salt. A large, corrupt, and inept bureaucracy controlling and managing the production, distribution, and sale of salt was dismantled. Instead of a dysfunctional bureaucracy, an excise tax was imposed on salt transactions. The new policy unexpectedly generated a vibrant new economic sector that benefited the country. Despite significant taxes, the salt business was profitable. It had a captivated market of fifty-eight million consumers, the population of Han China at the time, because everyone needed salt as a condiment and an essential preservative of vegetables, meat, and fish. The new market-oriented policy worked to the advantage of everyone: the consumers got easier access to salt at a competitive price, the imperial treasury received more income from taxation than it did under the policy of imperial monopoly on salt, the salt production increased, and its distribution was no longer hampered by corrupt officials.

The family of Liu Bei's friend had the vision to invest in salt production and distribution at the onset of free trade. They made a sizable fortune. After Liu Bei's friend took over the family business, he worked indefatigably. In addition to overseeing a salt mine in the estuary of the Yangtzi River, he regularly took charge of transporting a large quantity of salt from the eastern seaboard of the country to western inland provinces. On his current trip to Hunan province, he made a detour to stop at Liu Bei's hometown to visit his good friend and rest his contingents of bodyguards, animal drivers, and burros. He didn't expect to lodge his team at Liu Bei's humble home, but he knew that there was plenty of space in the harmony compound belonging to Liu Bei's bosom friend, Zhang Fei, whom he had met through Liu Bei several years ago.

Liu Bei and Zhang Fei were overjoyed at the unexpected visit of the salt merchant. They were also eager to introduce their sworn brother, Guan Yu, to him.

The merchant congratulated them on their newly founded brotherhood. He considered Guan Yu godlike. Much more than his physical presence, Guan Yu's modesty, serene confidence, and charisma deeply impressed the merchant. He had already known that Zhang Fei was a great martial artist and respected Liu Bei for his intellect, but Guan Yu commanded his admiration because the man with the magnificent beard seemed unique. Guided by his ideals, Guan Yu didn't care about money, didn't seek power, only exuded goodwill. He wanted to right the wrong and help the poor. The merchant saw Guan Yu as a paragon of virtue and was thankful for having met such a remarkable person, a rare embodiment of compassion, candor, and probity.

After Zhang Fei directed his house staff to accommodate the visiting merchant and his large team, he ordered up another elaborate banquet to celebrate the unexpected visitors even though the brothers had a banquet the previous day. That evening, the peach garden was transformed into a festive place

THREE SWORN BROTHERS

ablaze with lanterns, banquet tables, and merry diners. Sipping liquor and feasting on roasted boar, braised goose, stir-fried greens and mushrooms, and steamed golden carp covered with a dressing consisting of sesame oil, garlic, scallion, ginger, wine, vinegar, and salt, the salt merchant recounted to the three newly sworn brothers what he had witnessed during his journey.

"What I saw was sad and pitiful." The merchant sighed. "I passed by village after village suffering from unspeakable poverty; hungry farmers looked like emaciated zombies. They were listless and despondent. Most cities and towns, plundered by corrupt officials, were dilapidated, monuments in disrepair, pagodas crumpling, and steles vandalized. Some mountains and wilderness areas were denuded of trees and devoid of wildlife; roadways were infested with brigands and desperados, eager to pounce on vulnerable travelers.

"The Han empire is in ruin!" He lamented, "Even the sale of salt, which everyone needs, is depressed."

Even though the Peach Garden Brothers were cognizant of the dreadful state of the country, the merchant's vivid account of what he saw on his journey saddened them. In response, Zhang Fei told the merchant, "We hope to start a movement to restore law and order in our country."

"Yes," Liu Bei responded, "our first goal is to crush the Yellow Turbans and defeat the brigands."

"What brought the three of us together was our shared devotion to restore the Han empire," Guan Yu chimed in. "If the Han empire were a living organism, the Yellow Turbans represent a malignancy that needs to be excised before the organism itself can regain its health. We are preparing ourselves for military actions against the Yellow Turbans."

"How?" The merchant queried, "How do you propose to crush the Yellow Turbans? Their ranks are growing by the day. Even the imperial garrisons fear them. The high officials refuse to confront them."

"We will form our own militia," Liu Bei responded. "Our militia will not be an organization like the insurrectionists springing up everywhere. It will be a military column seeking collaboration with the official army. Even though many officers of the army have lost their way, we hope that our ardor and enthusiasm would inspire and arouse the rank-and-file soldiers. They might even join us if their commanders are unworthy of their loyalty. Here and there we might also have the good fortune of encountering some upright captains of the army who sympathize with our cause."

"It's not easy to organize a fighting militia," the merchant observed.

"No, it's not," Liu Bei agreed. "On that front, I have been assiduously networking over the last two years in this region covering three counties. Several hundred like-minded people, who are ethical, patriotic, and courageous, have promised to join a militia at a moment's notice. More significantly, a few days before your arrival, we had the good fortune of recruiting Guan Yu into our ranks. He and Zhang Fei, who are now my sworn brothers, will lead our militia to battle the Yellow Turbans. I think we have a good chance of success."

"That's music to my ears!" The merchant exclaimed. "I cannot think of a better group of leaders than you three to begin cleansing and rejuvenating our country: one sagacious member of the imperial clan, one towering expert of the Reclining Moon halberd, one incomparable master of the spear. Together, the three of you can defeat any brigands and insurgents!"

After a pause, he stood up, raised his wine cup and announced solemnly, "I am not a military man. Finance is my expertise and finance will be my contribution. I pledge, over this cup of outstanding Osmanthus wine, to hand over one thousand ounces of silver immediately as the first installment to support your grand enterprise. I salute you and wish you success."

THREE SWORN BROTHERS

That said, the four men emptied their cups and bowed together solemnly as if they had just launched a man-of-war against an invisible flotilla of pirates at sea. They were confident and optimistic.

Two days later, the merchant and his entourage resumed their journey to western Hunan. With the money he had contributed, Guan Yu and Zhang Fei purchased weapons, horses, armor, and other supplies for an army. Liu Bei, on horseback, called on important members of his network to meet at the square facing the yamen of his county magistrate on the day of the next full moon. It was a day of Guan Yu's choice because he used to visit his family from the martial arts camp every month on the day of the full moon. It was also the day he found his father in the underground storage of his ancestral home and learned the heartbreaking news of the murder of his siblings and the death of his mother at the hands of the Yellow Turbans.

When the militia gathered in front of the yamen, Guan Yu counted 294 people, including Zhang Fei, Liu Bei, and himself. Many volunteers brought bows and arrows in addition to their weapons of choice, which ranged from swords, broad knives, spears, chain whips, lances, and halberds to cudgels, battle-axes, hammers, dagger-axes, and battle spades. Liu Bei had purchased one hundred horses earlier from a horse ranch not far away.

As the militia assembled, those volunteers who were skilled in horsemanship formed the cavalry in front of the infantry. The three sworn brothers, also on horseback, led the column at the very front: Guan Yu with his Reclining Moon halberd on one side, Zhang Fei with his long spear on the other side, and Liu Bei in the middle carrying a special sword forged by the best blacksmith in the nation.

Behind the cavalry, the infantry, lined up five abreast, formed a column. The archers, each carrying a quiver filled with arrows on their back, brought up the rear.

The magistrate who came out of the yamen to greet this volunteer military battalion was so impressed by the militia that for a moment he fancied himself the commander of a victorious army. Smiling graciously, he praised the men for their loyalty and patriotism, thanked them for their proactive volunteer service, and announced that he had just received reports of several thousand Yellow Turbans sweeping down on a neighboring county in the south.

"The timing could not have been more propitious," Liu Bei exclaimed. "We will seize this opportunity to teach the brigands a lesson."

SIX

A NEW MILITIA

When the Peach Garden Brothers' militia approached the neighboring county in the south after three hours of march, they saw, from their high vantage point on a hill, a horde of Yellow Turbans steadily and successfully advancing against an army under the command of a court officer standing in a chariot pulled by two horses. The Peach Garden Brothers had not expected to see government forces in action. On this occasion, the imperial court had obviously made an exception to its laid-back minimalist policy of dealing with the Yellow Turbans, Liu Bei inferred. The banner fluttering on the chariot indicated the officer's rank as a high-level official of the court, the equivalent of a general. The Peach Garden Brothers didn't know that it was the initiative of this high-level official that led to the ongoing battle between the army and the Yellow Turbans. What caught the attention of the Peach Garden Brothers was the situation on the battlefield.

The government soldiers were fighting lackadaisically. Instead of staying in a tight formation to advance against their enemy, the soldiers spread out randomly. The battle was a chaotic, unorganized fight between individuals from the two sides. Even though the Yellow Turbans were equally undisciplined and disorganized, each of them fought with zeal and determination. It didn't take long for the Yellow Turbans to overcome the army, hacking and maiming the dispirited government soldiers. Shortly after the Peach Garden Brothers' militia arrived at the edge of the battlefield, they witnessed the imperial army retreating. Government soldiers scurried in all directions as they fled.

Taking stock of the lopsided battle unfolding in front of them, the Peach Garden Brothers realized that the Yellow Turbans were much more than a superstition-driven cult. The size of their deployment suggested that they had been successful in their recruitment.

The battle scene stirred up all kinds of thoughts in Guan Yu.

Growing up on a farm, Guan Yu understood the stereotypical mentality of the rural population. He knew that peasants tended to be hardy, yet docile, and they were, by and large, resilient, capable of quietly suffering unbearable hardships no matter how grim and impoverished their lives might be. But Guan Yu was also cognizant that if peasants were driven to starvation and faced destitution without the prospect of relief, they would resort to insurrection and become receptive to a demagogue's lies and propaganda. Taking up arms against the emperor represented the final straw of a despondent peasantry, their last attempt at survival. They might be unschooled in martial arts and untrained in military maneuvers, but their fury, like the torrent unleashed by a bursting dam, could be ferocious, powerful, and devastating.

From Liu Bei, Guan Yu had learned that the leaders of the Yellow Turbans were reprobate snake oil peddlers preaching insurrection, prescribing mantras, promoting superstition, and speaking with forked tongues to entice the desperate peasants to become their foot soldiers. From his own experience, he knew that the peasants were also ripe to succumb to demagoguery, and their plunder and wanton destruction were as much an expression of human deprivation as they were a symptom of the decline of the Han dynasty.

Deep in thought, Guan Yu nearly forgot that he was on the edge of a battlefield until Liu Bei jolted him back to reality with the question, "Well, Guan Yu, what do you think we should do?"

Guan Yu surveyed once again the battlefield in front of him. In his mind, even though the rebels deserved sympathy because they were duped by flimflam men, they did commit heinous crimes, including the murder of his own siblings.

"Let's go get them!" Guan Yu replied.

Liu Bei and Zhang Fei nodded their heads in agreement. Liu Bei then turned around to address the militia: "We will attack the Yellow Turbans," he announced. "But we will not charge. At one thousand paces from us, the enemies are too far away. We would be exhausted after running at full speed for that distance. Let us approach this battle with caution and discipline, preserve our strength, move forward cautiously in a tight formation, and wait for my order before initiating action."

When the commander of the Yellow Turbans saw the militia approaching, he was as surprised as he was infuriated: infuriated because the appearance of the militia interrupted his rout of the government force; surprised because an unknown column of fighters materialized suddenly out of nowhere on the battlefield, blocking his path to an imminent victory. He had no prior intelligence of the presence of a new military column in addition to the imperial garrison, which had only recently arrived in that county. He was puzzled that the militia did not wear any uniform, displayed no banners, and carried a mishmash of weapons.

"Who are these upstarts?" He muttered to his deputy, who held a chain whip made of braided, ductile metal with a sharp tip that could penetrate armor and inflict trauma at a range of six to eight feet. "A few hundred rabbles without uniforms, not even a banner or an insignia. Where did they come from?"

"I will take care of them," responded the deputy.

Twirling his chain whip, the deputy kicked his horse hard on its ribs. The horse reared and charged toward the Peach Garden Brothers. Looking like an apparition in a cloud of dust kicked up by his mount, the deputy commander of the Yellow Turbans let out a chilling shriek as he twirled his chain whip above his head.

With a smile, Zhang Fei moved toward the charging Yellow Turban slightly to his left. He partially concealed his long spear by holding it in his left hand close to his galloping mount. His adversary expected Zhang Fei to have a weapon, but he couldn't get a clear view of it.

A sword, a broad knife, a spear? the Yellow Turban commander was wondering.

What he didn't expect was the extraordinary reach of Zhang Fei's spear. Normally, a metal spear ranged from five to six feet in length. Anything longer would be unwieldy because of its weight. But Zhang Fei was no ordinary warrior. Endowed with extraordinary strength, he held a custom-made metal spear nearly eight feet in length. It could have been mistaken for a lance. But a lance was typically held by a soldier with two hands in combat. It was designed for thrusting against an advancing enemy or piercing a charging adversary on a horse. While most soldiers had difficulty swinging a lance swiftly and effectively because of its weight, Zhang Fei was able to maneuver his spear like a sword with one hand. He was strong enough to use his spear to slash, bludgeon, and thrust with amazing speed and dexterity.

Expecting Zhang Fei to have a weapon no longer than five or six feet in length, the deputy commander of the Yellow Turbans thought he had a short window to inflict a fatal blow to Zhang Fei with his ranging chain whip before Zhang Fei's weapon could reach him. That turned out to be a fateful miscalculation.

A NEW MILITIA

While the deputy's whip was still in midair, Zhang Fei thrust his spear diagonally toward his adversary's chest from the left side of his horse, and it found its target instantly. The deputy commander's whip fell to the ground and his horse galloped past Zhang Fei, dragging the blood-gushing corpse along its side.

Furious at the loss of his deputy, the captain of the Yellow Turbans, his cudgel raised high in the air, charged toward Zhang Fei. Guan Yu calmly trotted his horse forward to intercept the Yellow Turban captain. For a split second, Guan Yu's gargantuan size and flowing beard stunned his opponent. That momentary diversion gave Guan Yu enough time to swing his Reclining Moon halberd in an arc toward the midsection of his adversary with blinding speed. The halberd struck with so much power that the Yellow Turban captain's torso, gushing blood, flew into the air, as his horse ran past Guan Yu with the lower half of the captain's body still spouting blood in the saddle.

At that moment, members of the militia roared in cheers, raised their weapons, and charged the Yellow Turbans.

The stunning dispatch of the Yellow Turban commanders and the thunderous cheers of the militia demoralized the two-thousand-strong rebels so much that, for all they could fathom, Zhang Fei and Guan Yu were demons materializing from the nether world to punish them for their crimes. Panic-stricken, they turned tail at the sight of the militia's charging cavalry and fled in disarray. Zhang Fei, Guan Yu, and the rank and file of the militia instinctively went after their quarries. But Liu Bei, riding in front of the charging militia, in a booming voice, stopped all actions on the battlefield with the command, "Anyone who surrenders is free to leave. If you wish to join us, you will be welcomed as our brothers."

Then he turned around, addressing the militia at the top of his voice, audible to many Yellow Turbans, "Anyone who mistreats or abuses a surrendered soldier will be severely punished."

Many Yellow Turbans continued fleeing, but many surrendered. Liu Bei, with his wise and swift decision, averted a bloodbath. Following Liu Bei's command, the militia treated every surrendered Yellow Turban with courtesy. It didn't take long for the Yellow Turbans to see that members of the militia were merciful and disciplined. They also noted that Liu Bei, unlike their own commander, whose main concern was to enrich himself through looting, was in full command of his troops. As more and more Yellow Turbans surrendered, Liu Bei explained briefly to the captives the Peach Garden Brothers' mission. Many of them cast off their yellow turbans on the spot and joined the militia.

The commanding officer of the defeated imperial force was Dong Zhuo. At the beginning of his career as a low-level officer, he had gained recognition for his skill in archery and a flair for eloquence. Rising quickly through the ranks to become a general, he spent a fortune inherited from his silk-merchant father near Hangzhou, the silk capital of China, bribing and lavishly entertaining his superiors to grease his way upward in the mandarin officialdom, the wen branch of the government. As he advanced in his career, he also extorted money from his underlings and anyone who needed a favor from him. With success under his belt, he became obese, short-tempered, and irascible. In particular, he hated the eunuchs, calling them fake men. They irked him because he envied their proximity to the throne. His moral rectitude, if one could attribute any moral rectitude to such a man, did not rise beyond schadenfreude. People's misfortune gave him pleasure because it made him feel superior. His bodyguards and retainers were instructed to strike innocent citizens for being insufficiently subservient in his presence. When he appeared in public, pedestrians were obliged to bow low and avoid making eye contact with him. Often, he personally supervised the torture of people who complained about his

A NEW MILITIA

arrogance and cruelty. The residents of the capital considered him evil incarnate. In the imperial court, however, Dong Zhuo, with his guile and cunning, gradually accumulated influence and power. He even began to harbor imperial ambition, but prudence induced him to keep his treasonous aspiration to himself.

When the Yellow Turbans pillaged their way toward the county where the Peach Garden Brothers were organizing their militia, Dong Zhuo thought it was time for him to show his mettle. With the blessing of Emperor Ling, he led an expeditionary force from the capital to confront the rebels. In truth, he didn't give a damn about the Yellow Turbans. Embracing the military mission was a way for him to gain more power, combining the command of an army column with his high civil position in court. Lacking the courage and martial spirit of a warrior, he possessed neither the knowledge nor the charisma to lead an army. The rank and file, including most officers, considered him a coward and a schemer from the literati branch of the government, a renegade who had hoodwinked the emperor into appointing him to a commanding position in the military branch. No soldier wanted to risk his life for a commander who didn't care for the troops and whose only interest was his own career advancement. He might be the commander of a military column, but his soldiers considered him a joke.

In his cavalier way of leading a column of the imperial army to war, Dong Zhuo didn't bother to study his enemy or send scouts to gather information about the rampaging Yellow Turbans before reaching the battlefield. He thought of the Yellow Turbans as a horde of riffraff bandits, failing to understand that destitution and despondency could motivate and transform untrained peasants into ferocious fighters. The Taoist leaders of the Yellow Turbans might have fed the rank and file with lies and false promises. From the perspective of the desperate follower, a promised land no matter how distant was preferable to the agony of a lingering death by starvation.

On the battlefield, Dong Zhuo was quickly humiliated. When his disorganized and lackadaisical army retreated from the onslaught of the Yellow Turban desperados, Dong Zhuo fled the battlefield in a chariot with a few retainers. In his flight, he didn't even notice that Zhang Fei and Guan Yu had slain the Yellow Turban captains. By the time he learned that the Yellow Turbans were fleeing in fright, Dong Zhuo turned his chariot back and came face-to-face with the Peach Garden Brothers.

Instead of congratulating and thanking the Peach Garden Brothers, he barked with the condescending demand to know their official rank and source of authority. Liu Bei came forward in his customary humble manner, bowed in his saddle, and told Dong Zhuo that neither he nor the militia had any official title. Dong Zhuo grunted in contempt, turned his chariot around, and departed.

Zhang Fei was livid at Dong Zhuo's insolence. His eyes bulged, his cheeks puffed up, his nostrils flared, and his neck veins distended, he excoriated Dong Zhuo with a string of vituperative invectives.

"We have just saved your life," Zhang Fei bellowed, "you ungrateful, pusillanimous, dog-fart miscreant! How dare you treat my esteemed brother with such contempt. I will terminate your miserable, obesity-plagued life right here, this moment."

Without further ado, Zhang Fei cocked his arm and heaved his spear at Dong Zhuo. As the heavy spear flew toward Dong Zhuo's chest, Liu Bei, with a deft stroke of his sword, knocked it down, saving Dong Zhuo's life. Liu Bei then dismounted, picked up Zhang Fei's long spear, and handed it back to its owner.

"Let him go, my brother. We should not kill an imperial officer. Not at this juncture of our journey."

The incident left an indelible mark on Dong Zhuo. He heard Zhang Fei's cussing and was frightened out of his wits as Zhang Fei's spear hurtled toward him. Even though Liu Bei saved his life, he was too arrogant and shocked to acknowledge or show

A NEW MILITIA

83

any gratitude for Liu Bei's magnanimous act. His brief encounter with Zhang Fei was not only a devastating experience, but also a colossal insult. He could not believe that Zhang Fei, an unranked ordinary commoner, had called him a dog-fart miscreant. Seething with anger, Dong Zhuo swore that he would seek revenge.

In a single battle against the Yellow Turbans, the Peach Garden Brothers expanded their militia threefold in size to nearly one thousand members. After they returned to the county headquarters, the magistrate, overjoyed at the militia's victory, struck an agreement with the leaders of two adjacent counties to support and garrison the expanded militia. The allied counties reckoned that under the leadership of the Peach Garden Brothers, the militia could better protect them from the Yellow Turbans than the imperial army could. But the Peach Garden Brothers understood that the logistics and expenses of provisioning a garrison of one thousand troops were beyond the fiscal capacity of the three counties in the long run.

After long deliberations over several days, the Peach Garden Brothers decided to join the warlord Gongsun Zan, who headed a garrison in the north. Liu Bei had known Gongsun Zan ever since they studied classics under the same tutor in their youth. Pupils of the same mentor, according to Confucian ethics, were intellectual brothers. The two had kept in touch with each other ever since their youth. They might not be devoted to each other like the Peach Garden Brothers were, but they respected each other. During the turmoil of Emperor Ling's reign, while Liu Bei lay low in obscurity, Gongsun Zan, governing a large region on the northern border of China, became a powerful warlord. In the chaos of the Yellow Turban Rebellion and other rural uprisings during the late 180s, he remained nominally loyal to Emperor Ling. But he had ruled his territory like a sovereign. When Liu

Bei's emissary presented to him a proposal for alliance, Gongsun Zan accepted it enthusiastically. He reasoned that such an alliance would expand his military force and elevate his stature in the country.

In AD 186, the Peach Garden Brothers became officers in Gongsun Zan's army.

SEVEN

A VILLAINOUS TRAITOR

Meanwhile Dong Zhuo, the general of the imperial army rescued by the Peach Garden Brothers, returned to the capital, Luoyang, from his battlefield debacle. He reported to the court that he had vanquished a column of Yellow Turbans, several thousand strong. Without checking the veracity of Dong's report with the magistrate of the county where the battle took place, the mandarin officials of the court, following their characteristic indolence, accepted Dong Zhuo's claim. Upon their recommendation, Emperor Ling rewarded Dong Zhuo with five hundred ounces of silver and one hundred bolts of embossed silk and promoted him to the head of the imperial palace guards. One official, however, discovered Dong Zhuo's lie. He announced that the stunning military success against the Yellow Turbans belonged to a hitherto-unknown militia led by three unknown warriors. The next day, that official and his entire family were murdered. An investigation of the murder was launched without a conclusion. After two weeks, Dong Zhuo quashed the investigation.

As the commander of the palace guards, Dong Zhuo quickly went about the business of consolidating his power. He imprisoned and executed scores of officials who questioned the legitimacy of his activities. Corrupt, incompetent, yet shrewd and perfidious, he became the most powerful but also the most despised official of the court. The only person in court who could match him in political machination was the eunuch Jian Shuo, who had the ear of the emperor. Jian Shuo, was fed up with Dong Zhuo's imperious arrogance. He began to spread rumors that Dong Zhuo harbored seditious ambition and plotted secretly to overthrow the emperor, with the aim of persuading the emperor to have Dong Zhuo executed. An intense struggle between Jian Shuo's cabal of conniving eunuchs and Dong Zhuo's mendacious clique followed. The rivalry paralyzed the court and the government. Wallowing in his debauchery and annoyed by the incessant lobbying from the two opposing factions, the emperor stayed aloof and took no action to quell the fractious conflict or get to the bottom of the contradictory claims put forth by the opposing factions.

After several months of stalemate in the political struggle between Dong Zhuo's clique and the eunuchs, Dong Zhuo reached the limit of his patience. Having secured the support and collaboration of another group of high-level court officials headed by He Jin, who loathed the eunuchs because they blocked all access to Emperor Ling, Dong Zhuo led the imperial guards into the inner sanctum of the palace to kill Jian Shuo and his associates one night. But the imperial guards, stationed in barracks along the periphery of the forbidden city, had never been inside of the palace. Traditional policy prohibited them from entering the inner sanctum of the forbidden city until Dong Zhuo gave his rule-breaking order.

Unfamiliar with the palace grounds, the armed guards couldn't distinguish a eunuch from a host of other service personnel in the darkness of the night, let alone identify the senior eunuchs who constituted Jian Shuo's cabal targeted by Dong Zhuo. Dong Zhuo told the guards to pick out eunuchs by their foul odor because eunuchs, with both their penises and testicles sheared off at castration, were incontinent. The odor of urine had been the traditional telltale clue that enabled a mandarin official to detect the secret presence of a eunuch in court, usually hiding behind a screen at the rear of the throne to whisper advice to the emperor. But in the chaos and pandemonium created by the invasion of the armed guards, it was impossible for the soldiers to discern the smell of urine from other odors emanating from the frightened members of the palace staff and imperial household. Confronted with such a conundrum, Dong Zhuo ordered his charges to kill at will, sparing only females if they could.

It was a bloodbath. Many eunuchs were killed; so were a host of innocent members of the palace staff, although the emperor and members of the imperial family were unharmed.

After the massacre, Dong Zhuo emerged as the de facto ruler of the country, paying lip service to Emperor Ling's edicts while cowing all other officials at the court.

Three years later, Emperor Ling died at age thirty-three. His eldest son, the thirteen-year-old crown prince, ascended the throne as Emperor Shao.

As a boy, Shao was deeply offended by the murder of his widely admired tutor, Master Li, during Dong Zhuo's massacre of eunuchs. Master Li was a scholarly eunuch who stayed aloof from palace politics and intrigues. The young crown prince not only blamed Dong Zhuo for the murder of his revered teacher, but also found it inexcusable that Dong Zhuo violated the sanctity of the imperial palace by ordering the nighttime raid. In his private conversations with his mother, the empress dowager, the newly enthroned emperor expressed his desire to have Dong Zhuo executed. But the empress dowager, an intelligent autodidact who was savvy in palace intrigues, counseled prudence. She understood that in a power struggle, her son needed the backing of the military. The army in the garrisons of the nation was the only instrument capable of subduing Dong Zhuo's palace guards. The empress dowager knew that before her son could win the allegiance of the commanders in the nation, the young man was emperor in name only. She felt her son's frustration and believed that he should rightfully assume the Mandate of Heaven. But they needed to garner military support before they could take out Dong Zhuo.

"There will be a day of reckoning, but we must be patient and cautious," the empress dowager told the teenage emperor.

She didn't divulge to her son that she had secretly sent an emissary to the head of the garrison in her ancestral home region urging the commander to lead his army to the capital to take out Dong Zhuo. Aware that the palace was full of spies, she prudently adhered to her modus operandi that the fewer people knew of her plot, the safer she and her son would be.

The teenage emperor abided by his mother's advice and was careful not to betray his resentment of Dong Zhuo.

One day, however, the young emperor, offended and enraged by Dong Zhuo's insolence, protested loudly to his mother in her private chamber. He shouted at the top of his voice that he had had enough of the treacherous traitor and could no longer wait to eliminate him. An attending eunuch outside the chamber overheard the outburst. The eunuch, who had been assiduously seeking to worm his way into Dong Zhuo's inner circle, was delighted that a golden opportunity for advancing himself had fallen into his lap. Rushing over to Dong Zhuo's office, the eunuch reported the emperor's outburst.

The information alarmed Dong Zhuo. He reckoned that if the empress dowager and the emperor were plotting his elimination, he'd better act without delay.

In a private audience the next day, Dong Zhuo told the teenage emperor curtly that rebellions were breaking out

A VILLAINOUS TRAITOR

everywhere in the nation, the empire was in disarray, and the young emperor was derelict for not leading a military campaign against the most menacing rebels, the Yellow Turbans.

"Our country needs a new leader," Dong Zhuo bluntly declared in front of the emperor before he withdrew.

Shocked and frightened, Emperor Shao retreated to his private quarters. He didn't have a contingent of trusted bodyguards and he had no allies other than his mother. There was no recourse for him to counter Dong Zhuo's threat.

That afternoon, a eunuch who was one of Dong Zhuo's stooges brought a pot of hot wine to the emperor in his private quarters.

"This wine is a gift from Lord Dong Zhuo," the eunuch announced. "He wanted Your Majesty to drink it immediately."

Placing the pot on a table, the eunuch departed without uttering another word.

Shaken, the teenage emperor stared at the pot and turned white. His wife flung herself into his arms and let out a blood-curdling shriek as they wept in an embrace. They knew that the wine was poisonous. If the emperor refused to drink it, Dong Zhuo would kill him by some other gruesome means. Knowing that he had no chance to escape, he regained his composure. Sitting at his desk, the young emperor composed an elegy and tearfully chanted it for his wife:

> How fickle, my fate! How cruel, my destiny!
> Abandoning ten thousand chariots to avoid a war,
> I retreated, hoping to defend my dominion.
> Abused by a seditious minister, I have come to the
> end of my life,
> Leaving you forever to enter the silent underworld.

Overwhelmed with anguish, the young empress responded with her own poem:

As Your Majesty dies, your wife withers.
Even an emperor cannot alter the course of fate.
This is the moment that separates life from death.
Mourn me as I leave you with a grieving heart.

No sooner had she finished chanting her poem than she grabbed the pot of wine intended for her husband and gulped down a mouthful.

Seized by convulsion, she collapsed.

The emperor, shaking and sobbing uncontrollably, finished the rest of the poison in the pot.

The death of the young imperial couple did not satisfy Dong Zhuo's thirst for blood. According to his devious mind, when one kills a rival for power, one should exterminate all members of the victim's immediate family to forestall revenge in the future. The first target that came to his mind after murdering the emperor was the empress dowager. In the evening of that same day, Dong Zhuo had the empress dowager garroted. He then sent assassins to the hometown of the empress and had her entire clan murdered.

At the end of Dong Zhuo's murderous spree, the only surviving member of the emperor's immediate family was his half-brother, who had not yet come of age. Dong Zhuo spared him, not out of mercy, but in accord with his Machiavellian calculation. He needed a figurehead emperor to lend him the aura of authority to cow the warlords and the heads of garrisons of the nation before he could claim the imperial throne himself. The child emperor fit into his scheme seamlessly.

As soon as Dong Zhuo installed the child on the throne as Emperor Xian, he had himself appointed the grand preceptor of the emperor and the chancellor of state. In effect, he became the sole regent and the head of the government.

A VILLAINOUS TRAITOR

With the reins of power in hand, Dong Zhuo's first order of business was to recruit a great martial artist into his personal entourage. Paranoid, he needed a trustworthy bodyguard who was also a peerless warrior to protect him and lead his army. After many months of inquiry, Dong Zhuo settled on a man named Lü Bu. According to all sources of information, Lü Bu of Inner Mongolia seemed a perfect fit for Dong Zhuo's needs.

Widely known for his equestrian skill and marksmanship with bow and arrow, Lü Bu wielded a legendary weapon named fangtian huaji, "heavenly halberd." The weapon resembled Guan Yu's Reclining Moon halberd, but instead of a broad knife at the front end, it had a five-inch spearhead. Immediately behind the spearhead were two twenty-four-inch-long crescent blades affixed on three metal bridges extending from both sides of the shaft. It was a terrifying weapon, combining a long spear with two deadly blades that had sent scores of his opponents to Hades. On his left shoulder rested a priceless bow, constructed by a renowned craftsman from the horns of saiga antelopes that roamed the grassland of northern Mongolia. Perfectly balanced and immensely powerful, the bow required an archer with Superman's strength to cock the string. During a hunting trip on the steppe of Mongolia, Lü Bu once shot through two saigas with a single arrow.

On a battlefield, Lü Bu always appeared on a fiery steed from the Fergana Valley in central Asia named the Maroon Hare: maroon because of the red tint in its hair, hare because of its nimbleness and speed. The nomadic Bactrians of Fergana were renowned for breeding war horses that were swift, brave, and indefatigable. Lü Bu seized the Maroon Hare from a chieftain of a nomadic tribe in Inner Mongolia who fell victim to his fangtian huaji in a duel.

The spirited steed and its master projected an awesome and intimidating presence. Whenever Lü Bu rode onto a battlefield, the soldiers at his side roared in excitement because they expected Lü Bu to dispatch the head of their enemy, sack their morale, and initiate a rout. The soldiers believed that Lü Bu was invincible, and they were not wrong. Like Achilles, Lü Bu wielded a game-changing influence on the outcome of a battle in favor of his side.

As a warrior, Lü Bu was, indeed, second to none. In a skirmish between the Inner Mongolian garrison and the garrison under Gongsun Zan's command over a disputed area of grassland stretching more than two hundred miles in each direction, he had fought Zhang Fei to a standstill. At one point in the duel between the two, he trapped Zhang Fei's spear between the two blades of his halberd and came close to twisting it out of Zhang Fei's grip. The duel ended with Lü Bu retreating only because Guan Yu, concerned with Zhang Fei's safety, came to his brother's aid. Lü Bu did not see any possibility of victory in a battle against the combined assault of Guan Yu and Zhang Fei.

As a human being, Lü Bu belonged to the rank of scumbags. A narcissistic fop who sought to be flattered, he was greedy, fickle, and rapacious. With a malevolent gaze and evil eyes, he had a short temper, was incapable of self-restraint, and was predisposed toward violence. He killed at the slightest provocation and scoffed at the cardinal rule of Confucian ethics: loyalty. His loyalty, if one could even apply such a concept to him, was reserved for himself. Contemptuous of human relationships, he would interact with a person only if that interaction yielded some materialistic or utilitarian gain for him.

He never walked. If he was not riding the Maroon Hare, he would be strutting, bouncing on his toes like a stotting gazelle, as if he were broadcasting, "Look at *me*, the most virile specimen in the world!"

For two years, Dong Zhuo had heard of Lü Bu's incomparable martial prowess. He was particularly impressed with the legendary story of Lü Bu quelling a fractious confrontation between two battalions in the Inner Mongolia garrison to which Lü Bu

A VILLAINOUS TRAITOR

belonged. The captains of the two battalions, who originated from two different geographical regions and spoke two distinct dialects, never got along with each other. They had been feuding, treating each other as enemies even though it was their duty to collaborate as soldiers and officers under the same banner in the garrison of Inner Mongolia. One day, a scuffle broke out between soldiers of the two battalions over an argument about a frivolous topic. The scuffle soon escalated into an armed confrontation. As the two sides faced each other with mounting tension, Lü Bu showed up on his Maroon Hare. Planting his halberd firmly into the ground between the two groups, he announced, "I will aim an arrow at my halberd's left blade on my galloping horse one hundred paces from it. If I miss, I will leave you to settle scores as you wish; if I hit my target, you must disperse in peace because, if you don't, I will aim my next two arrows at your captains between their eyes."

The soldiers and captains couldn't believe what they heard. They assumed that Lü Bu was either bragging or bluffing. He might be an excellent archer, they reasoned, but one hundred paces covered a significant distance. Ordinary archers couldn't even shoot an arrow as far away as one hundred paces, let alone hit a narrow blade at that distance. Furthermore, Lü Bu had to make the shot on the back of a galloping horse, depriving him of stable ground on which to plant his feet. No one believed that an archer on a galloping horse could aim at such a small target accurately.

The captains of the two hostile factions, in agreement with their soldiers' assessments, cackled contemptuously at Lü Bu's offer and accepted it without hesitation.

With the Maroon Hare in full stride galloping away from the target, Lü Bu whipped out an arrow from his quiver, turned his torso around, drew the string of the bow to his chin, and released the arrow at about one hundred paces. The arrow hurtled through the air at lightning speed, whistling along its path.

Captivated, the soldiers on both sides of the confrontation followed the flight of the arrow in absolute silence. In a second, Lü Bu's arrow hit the narrow blade with a loud report. The halberd swayed from the impact of the arrow and the soldiers gasped in awe before they spontaneously broke out with thunderous applause.

When Dong Zhuo considered recruiting Lü Bu into his personal retinue, some of his trusted advisers warned him not to choose a person as fickle and unpredictable as Lü Bu. Being a master of duplicitous and Machiavellian tactics, Dong Zhuo dismissed his advisers' warnings. In his mind, he could handle and juggle any man, from a moral paragon to a deplorable knave, no matter how fickle that person might be. The advice and warnings of his aides elicited only contemptuous laughter from him. At this point in his life, the ascendancy to greater power was the only goal that mattered to him. If Lü Bu could enhance his military might, protect him from assassins, and help him to become a dictator, he wanted the man, fickleness and all.

Dong Zhuo had another reason to recruit Lü Bu. It was the memory of the insult he suffered at the hands of Zhang Fei more than one year earlier. That incident of being cursed and threatened had been gnawing at him constantly. He even suffered from nightmares seeing Zhang Fei's scowl and frightening glare, which always woke him up with a cold sweat. Revenge was never far from his mind. The only issue was *how*, until he found Lü Bu.

It appeared to Dong Zhuo that Lü Bu possessed the martial prowess to carry out his vengeance because, in Dong Zhuo's calculating mind, Lü Bu would overcome Zhang Fei in a duel.

Exercising the power of a regent, Dong Zhuo summoned Lü Bu to the capital in the name of the child emperor, Xian, ostensibly to attend a consultative conference on the threat of the Yellow Turban Rebellion.

A VILLAINOUS TRAITOR

As soon as Lü Bu arrived, Dong Zhuo, fully informed of Lü Bu's greed and vanity, wined and dined him. He flattered Lü Bu with encomium, honorific events, and precious gifts, including bolts of silk, sacks of silver, and a gold-plated chain mail. He also plied him with beautiful, seductive concubines.

After two weeks of being lauded and admired, Lü Bu was in heaven. In his heart, he felt that he was getting what had been due to him, a great warrior. Dong Zhuo seemed to be the kind of patron from whom he could derive great benefits. But he was shrewd enough to play hard to get so that he could maximize his gains. Far from matching Dong Zhuo in the realm of schemes and intrigues, he was nevertheless crafty enough to know that he needed to play his hand carefully and slowly. Keeping Dong Zhuo at a distance, he reckoned that if Dong Zhuo wanted his service, the price would have to be right.

On the day before Lü Bu was due to return to Inner Mongolia, Dong Zhuo unveiled the final move of a carefully orchestrated scheme to woo his quarry. He invited Lü Bu for a heart-to-heart chat in his private study lavishly decorated with polished marble floors covered with central Asian rugs. The study was well lit with silk lanterns hanging from high ceilings. Precious scrolls of calligraphy and landscape painting decorated the walls. All furniture in the study was studded with motifs of inlaid mother-of-pearl, gold, or jade.

"A magnificent warrior like you, my friend," Dong Zhuo mused wistfully as he and Lü Bu sipped wine in the opulent private study, "deserves an exalted rank in the imperial army commensurate with your ability. We may live in an era of chaos and conflicts. But you are destined to be a great general in the annals of warfare. "

"Thank you, sir, but I am far from being what you think," Lü Bu responded. His faked modesty didn't escape Dong Zhuo's shrewd mind.

"Allow me to be forthright and ask you a personal question." Dong Zhuo smiled as he seized the moment. "Are you content in the service of a garrison in Inner Mongolia? You know, I came from Gansu, a frontier region like Inner Mongolia bordering on the land of the nomadic marauders. Life is harsh and unpredictable on the frontier."

Far from feeling loyal to his current commander in Inner Mongolia, Lü Bu was aware that his words and behavior should conform to the principles of Confucian ethics. In his heart, Confucius's teaching meant nothing. To him, philosophical discourse and ethical principles were idle talks of bookworms and contemptible weaklings. But he understood the importance of paying lip service to the revered ethical norms of the society.

"I don't mind the harsh conditions of Inner Mongolia," he responded to Dong Zhuo. "Because I have pledged allegiance to my commander in chief, it is my obligation to be loyal to him."

"Well, Confucius has taught us that loyalty is a virtue," Dong Zhuo countered, "but he also instructed us to devote our primary loyalty to our sovereign and ancestors. Your commander in Inner Mongolia is not your sovereign. As the head of a garrison, he should be loyal, like all subjects in the empire, to our emperor. Yet, his actions suggest the opposite. He ignores imperial edicts, acts with impunity in Inner Mongolia, and refuses to transfer a portion of the tax income from his military region to the imperial treasury. In short, he is a warlord. Even worse than his lack of loyalty to our sovereign, he has never contributed toward the campaign against the Yellow Turbans militarily or financially. It is obvious that he intends to preserve his army and wealth to pursue his own ambition. I am not privy to his inner thoughts." Dong Zhuo paused to let the implication of his accusation sink in. "But I could say with certainty that far from being a loyal subject in Inner Mongolia, your commander has usurped the emperor's authority. I wouldn't be surprised if someone would consider him a traitor. But I choose to be charitable by calling him a warlord."

Taking a hard look at Dong Zhuo, Lü Bu decided not to respond. At that moment, he thought, the best strategy would be silence. Among other considerations, he wanted to keep Dong Zhuo guessing what his own course of action might be.

That evening, Dong Zhuo threw an extravagant farewell banquet in honor of Lü Bu. The two did not return to the topic of their earlier meeting. Only the exchange of pleasantries took place at the banquet. In the end, Dong Zhuo wasn't sure that he had reeled in his target, and Lü Bu showed no sign of revealing his true intention.

Two weeks later, Lü Bu came back to the capital accompanied by a small retinue of cavalry. Marching into Dong Zhuo's office, he laid a sack on Dong Zhuo's desk.

When Lü Bu opened the sack, Dong Zhuo saw the blood-stained head of the commander in chief of the Inner Mongolian garrison.

The acquisition of Lü Bu emboldened Dong Zhuo. Inflamed with his power, he promoted Lü Bu to the exalted position of general of the left of the Han empire and transferred a good amount of gold from the imperial treasury to him.

Notwithstanding the acquisition of Lü Bu, Dong Zhuo continued to be plagued by paranoia. He needed to ensure Lü Bu's loyalty. To that end, a new scheme came to his mind.

Concerned with Lü Bu's reputation of being fickle, he reasoned that if Lü Bu could become his son, then Lü Bu would be obliged to be loyal to him. Dong Zhuo calculated that even an extremely fickle person would not violate the cardinal rule of Confucian ethics, filial loyalty.

Two months after Lü Bu became the head of Dong Zhuo's bodyguards, Dong Zhuo staged a grand public ceremony, replete with pomp and oath taking over wine and incense, to adopt Lü Bu as his son. He wanted the entire world to know that he had become Lü Bu's adopted father, and therefore, Lü Bu would be bound to him by filial loyalty.

His paranoia mollified, Dong Zhuo became less anxious. His facial muscles stopped twitching; his eyes became less shifty; he enjoyed having Lü Bu by his side and began to indulge in his wanton way of life. He ordered the execution of officials as well as citizens who irritated him over the most trivial matters. Sometimes, Lü Bu carried out the executions on the spot in public. Whenever he saw a beautiful woman, regardless of her status and background, he either forcibly took her as a concubine or bestowed her to Lü Bu as a gift.

The two scoundrels created a reign of terror in the capital. Dong Zhuo, the Caligula, and Lü Bu, his enforcer. People loathed them. When Dong Zhuo and Lü Bu appeared in public, people scampered out of their way like baitfish darting away from marauding barracudas. Fearful, the residents of Luoyang were also furious. They yearned for revenge. The notoriety of the two sadistic scoundrels soon spread across the nation, deepening people's despair of the imperial government.

In the palace and the officialdom, Dong Zhuo's murder of the teenage emperor Shao and the empress dowager rankled everyone. As the information reached the general populace, people uniformly condemned Dong Zhuo as a degenerate regicide and a villainous traitor, deserving death by a thousand cuts. When the news of Dong Zhuo's infamous deeds and unbridled greed reached the Peach Garden Brothers, they were revolted. It caused Zhang Fei to holler at his senior brother Liu Bei, "You should've let me kill that cowardly obese swine on the battlefield years ago when he was running away from the Yellow Turbans. Look at what he has done, violating all norms of human decency, using Emperor Xian as a hostage, committing one atrocity after another."

A VILLAINOUS TRAITOR

Liu Bei told Zhang Fei and Guan Yu that the situation called for a national revolt. In order to organize a united front among the military commanders in the country, Liu Bei authored a proclamation summarizing Dong Zhuo's crimes and urging the heads of all garrisons in the nation to form a united front and take military action against Dong Zhuo. A retinue of personal emissaries from Liu Bei delivered the document to the head of each garrison in the nation.

"I hope Dong Zhuo will get his due," Liu Bei told Zhang Fei and Guan Yu.

When Liu Bei's emissaries returned, they reported that the heads of garrisons around the country, who had, by then, become warlords, were uniformly outraged by Dong Zhuo. But they did not commit themselves to military action against Dong Zhuo. Ironically, the most vociferous and vehement condemnations came from those who were suspected of harboring seditious ambitions themselves. They made proclamations, published essays, and rattled their swords in their castigation of Dong Zhuo for the purpose of covering up, if not expiating, their own treacherous designs. But they got cold feet when they were asked to commit resources to an alliance in a war against the villainous Dong Zhuo. They feared that a war would diminish their military strength in future power struggles. Without admitting their true intentions, they preferred to sit on the sidelines, watch the spiraling disintegration of the Han dynasty, preserve their own military strength, and pounce at the propitious moment to claim the Mandate of Heaven.

Fortunately, the best-known and most powerful warlord, Cao Cao, in Xuchang of Henan province, responded favorably to Liu Bei's proposal, on the condition that he, Cao Cao, would lead the combined expeditionary force against Dong Zhuo and his enablers in Luoyang. Liu Bei gladly accepted Cao Cao's demand, partly because Liu Bei was habitually modest, always willing to yield to a claimant for glory and credit of a movement initiated by him, and partly because Cao Cao, being the most powerful warlord, wielded considerable influence over the other warlords. Indeed, many warlords who originally hesitated at joining an alliance to punish Dong Zhuo took notice of Cao Cao's decision to join the alliance and followed suit.

Cao Cao was an intelligent and conniving general in addition to being a minor poet and scholar, earning respect from both the military and the literati. Shrewd and perceptive, he understood that behind the strongman facade, Dong Zhuo was nothing more than crafty and corrupt scum. Cao Cao estimated that an allied campaign would easily make short shrift of the traitor and his underlings. He also figured that heading the nation's military commandries to vanquish Dong Zhuo would establish him as the undisputed strongman in the empire, paving the way for him to pursue higher goals.

In accord with Cao Cao's plan, the allied force marched toward the capital, Luoyang, in four columns, from four directions: north, west, south, and east. Each warlord, departing from his home base, led his troops to join a column heading to the nearest gate of the capital.

Liu Bei, Guan Yu, and Zhang Fei and their militia were designated the vanguard of the northern column commanded by Gongsun Zan. Marching swiftly, the Peach Garden Brothers reached Luoyang ahead of Gongsun Zan's main force. They set up camp in the foothills at approximately one thousand paces from the north gate of the city.

The next morning, Lü Bu, with five hundred of his elite cavalry in tow, exited the north gate to probe and scout the Peach Garden Brothers' encampment. As soon as Liu Bei's sentries caught sight of Lü Bu and his men, they sounded the alarm.

Liu Bei, Guan Yu, and Zhang Fei picked up their weapons, mounted their horses, and came out of their camp with a platoon of soldiers. At fifty paces from their enemies, the Peach Garden Brothers halted as they heard Lü Bu yelling, "Traitors and renegades! I will kill you for invading the capital of the Han emperor. Come and meet your deaths!"

"We are loyal subjects of the Han emperor," Liu Bei responded calmly, "and we are here to mete out punishment to Dong Zhuo for murdering Emperor Shao and hijacking Emperor Xian's mandate."

"How dare you speak to me so crudely?" Lü Bu shrieked in anger. In a flash, he whipped out an arrow and shot at Liu Bei's head.

With a swing of his long spear, Zhang Fei deflected the arrow and charged Lü Bu on the left. No sooner had Zhang Fei's horse galloped toward Lü Bu than Guan Yu, concerned with his younger brother's safety, let out a thunderous roar and charged toward Lü Bu on the right. At five paces from his target, Guan Yu swung his Reclining Moon blade at Lü Bu's midsection while Zhang Fei, on the left, thrust his spear toward Lü Bu's neck. The two weapons approached Lü Bu like two shafts of thunderbolts converging from opposite directions. Unperturbed, Lü Bu, sitting in his saddle, didn't even raise his halberd. The soldiers behind him shrieked in alarm, believing in all certainty that Guan Yu's Reclining Moon blade would cut Lü Bu in half while Zhang Fei would flip away Lü Bu's upper body on the tip of his spear. At the very last moment as the weapons almost reached him, Lü Bu suddenly bent backward, flattening his torso on the back of his Maroon Hare, his lower legs anchored by his feet clamping around the horse's belly. Guan Yu's Reclining Moon blade whizzed over Lü Bu's flattened torso and Zhang Fei's spear missed its target.

As Guan Yu and Zhang Fei turned their mounts around, Lü Bu had already begun swinging his halberd in their direction.

Drawing an arc, it flew toward the necks of both brothers, threatening to behead them. Guan Yu, who was more proximal to Lü Bu than Zhang Fei was, barely had time to change his Reclining Moon blade into a vertical stance to block the oncoming halberd. The two weapons clashed in a deafening collision. Sparks flew. The immense power of Lü Bu's strike would have knocked the Reclining Moon blade out of the hands of most men. It was Guan Yu's exceptionally powerful grip that allowed him to hold on to his weapon. But Lü Bu's strike hammered the muscles and the tendons around Guan Yu's thumb on both hands. For a second, Guan Yu's hands felt numb. At that moment, Guan Yu feigned defeat. Dragging his Reclining Moon blade behind him as he galloped his horse away, he tried to entice Lü Bu to pursue so that he could execute his Heart-Piercing Move. But Lü Bu didn't bite. Instead of pursuing Guan Yu, he turned his halberd in the direction of Zhang Fei, bringing down his heavy weapon from high above Zhang Fei in a diagonal trajectory. Zhang Fei hadn't expected Lü Bu to switch his offense so swiftly from Guan Yu to him. There wasn't enough time to block the blow with his spear. Just as it looked that Lü Bu's halberd would split Zang Fei's torso, Zhang Fei's mount nimbly hopped sideways, saving him from certain death. Even though the lower blade of Lü Bu's halberd missed its target, its spear tip inflicted a gash on Zhang Fei's right shoulder.

Zhang Fei was livid. Ignoring his wound, he swung his horse around, leveled his long spear, and charged Lü Bu. Heartened that he had drawn blood from his opponent, Lü Bu positioned his halberd at an angle to Zhang Fei's spear, aiming to catch the approaching spear between the two blades of his halberd as he had in the last battle between the two. But before the two weapons became entangled, Guan Yu had returned to the mix-up. Thrusting and slashing, Guan Yu forced Lü Bu to parry the blows, freeing Zhang Fei to aim his spear at the side of the Maroon Hare. But the remarkable Maroon Hare leaped forward

A VILLAINOUS TRAITOR

and dodged Zhang Fei's spear. At this moment, the three combatants were disengaged. Each of them positioned at one corner of a triangle, and each had a moment to assess the situation. Guan Yu and Zhang Fei had earned Lü Bu's respect, while Lü Bu deeply impressed the two Peach Garden Brothers with his martial skill.

During this moment of disengagement, Lü Bu, recognizing the insurmountable difficulty of prevailing over the combined skill and power of Guan Yu and Zhang Fei, decided to retreat. Without uttering a word, while fixing his gaze on his adversaries, Lü Bu guided his Maroon Hare in a backpedal toward his platoon of cavalry. Zhang Fei wanted to give chase, but Guan Yu called him back. As Lü Bu and his troops took a slow tactical retreat into the city, the Peach Garden Brothers watched from a distance. They didn't wish to launch into a full battle before the arrival of all the allied forces.

That afternoon, all four allied columns arrived at the outskirts of the capital and set up camps at one thousand paces from each city gate. Liu Bei reported the morning skirmish to the warlord Gongsun Zan, his nominal commander, Gongsun Zan then requested the commander in chief, Cao Cao, to convene a strategic consultation of all commanders, including the Peach Garden Brothers. After some deliberation, they decided, as a first step of action, to initiate psychological warfare against Dong Zhuo's defense force in the city.

That night, the alliance soldiers took turns beating a hundred drums and banging a hundred gongs.

The ruckus created by the drums and gongs frightened the population in the capital. They anticipated a cataclysmic military confrontation, imagining the invaders scaling the city wall followed by hand-to-hand combat in the streets. People cowered behind closed doors in their homes. The streets were deserted, and the city looked like a ghost town. The only living beings in the streets were the troops under the command of Dong Zhuo and Lü Bu. They stayed awake all night on full alert. But the invasion never materialized.

The next morning, the drumbeating and gong banging stopped. Dong Zhuo and Lü Bu took an inspection tour of the city's four large wooden gates, each located at the center of one of the four sections of the square city wall. Every gate was bolted with a fifteen-foot-long and six-inch-thick hardwood plank. Behind each wooden gate, hundreds of soldiers armed with lances and broadswords were resting against the walls after a night of vigil.

Cognizant of Dong Zhuo's lack of popularity among the rank and file, Lü Bu worried about desertion. But he saw no sign of unrest. The soldiers looked tired. He figured that if the soldiers were properly fed and well paid, the alliance would have difficulty breaching the tall city wall.

Back in their headquarters, Lü Bu made clear to Dong Zhuo that the defense of the city depended on the morale of their army, and the morale of their army, in turn, rested on the compensation and rewards given to them. He demanded ten thousand ounces of silver to be distributed to members of the city garrison immediately. But Dong Zhuo never revealed that his wasteful extravagance had already depleted the imperial coffer. He didn't have ten thousand ounces of silver at that moment. Recognizing that the residents of the capital were his only possible source of money, he ordered his bodyguards to go to every home in Luoyang, rich or poor, to confiscate gold and silver jewelry, ornaments, or utensils.

While Dong Zhuo was busy pillaging the city of Luoyang for gold and silver, Lü Bu walked along the city wall to assess his enemy's intention. He could see the camps of the allied forces from the rampart on top of each city gate. Much to his relief, the invasion force did not appear in an attack mode. The allied soldiers looked alert but relaxed. Their horses, saddled, were feeding peacefully. Their archers, although within easy reach of

A VILLAINOUS TRAITOR

their bows and arrows, were not in formation. Their campsites did not appear as beehives of activity.

He surmised that the alliance did not intend to attack the city or breach the city wall, which meant that they would, most likely, lay siege to Luoyang.

Lü Bu correctly read the mindset of the allied leaders. Cao Cao and his commanders wanted to rest their troops after a long march from their respective bases. Being aware that even the most selfish warlords who did not join the alliance despised Dong Zhuo, the allied army did not worry about anyone attacking their supply lines or sneaking up on them from the rear. As for attacking the city, Cao Cao knew that scaling the city wall would be costly, favoring the defenders behind the ramparts on the wall. But time was on his side. A siege depriving the city of food supplies from the surrounding villages would, sooner or later, force Dong Zhuo to surrender or come out of the citadel to fight the allied army, fair and square, without the protection of the city wall.

Inside the city, Dong Zhuo, Lü Bu, and their captains met to consider their options. At the outset of their deliberation, Lü Bu pointed out that, under siege, the food in the city would not last more than one week. He advocated a strategy of concentrating their troops in a single formation to surge out of the west gate just before sunrise and mount an all-out onslaught before the rest of the allied forces at the other three city gates could join the battle.

Estimating that the allies had twice as many troops as the combined garrisons in the city, including the palace guards, Dong Zhuo and most of his underlings disagreed with Lü Bu. They chose to escape.

Lü Bu considered escape a cowardly option. He might be an incorrigible, puerile miscreant, but a coward he wasn't. In fact, holding all cowardly acts in absolute contempt, he believed that with his Maroon Hare and his fangtian huaji, he could hack through a wall of enemy soldiers. Arguing vehemently against Dong Zhuo and other commanders, he made it clear that a true warrior never ran away from a battle, no matter the risk and the difficulties. But Dong Zhuo considered Lü Bu's reaction to the siege the swaggering display of a hotheaded combatant unworthy of serious consideration.

For the first time, contempt for Dong Zhuo bubbled up in Lü Bu's mind. For several years, he had admired Dong Zhuo as a patron and a mentor, looking up to him as a genius, an indomitable operator. Now, he found out that Dong Zhuo was, at best, a cowardly genius. Concealing his contempt, but not his irritation, he demanded to know what made Dong Zhuo and his captains think that they could escape from the allied army surrounding the city.

Unexpectedly, Dong Zhuo, the crafty and cunning villain, had a trick up his sleeve. From an old eunuch in the palace, he had learned of a secret underground tunnel that linked the palace to a forest approximately two thousand paces west of the city wall. It was dug more than one and half centuries ago on the order of a high official in the court of Emperor Guangwu who restored the Han dynasty and founded what came to be known as the Eastern Han dynasty in AD 25, after the brief reign of the usurper Wang Mang. Emperor Guangwu was the one who chose Luoyang to replace Chang'an as the capital. Mindful of Wang Mang's palace intrigue that ended the first half of the Han dynasty, known as the Western Han, the high official who ordered the construction of the tunnel in Luoyang intended it to be a secret escape route for an emperor and his entourage if another seditious palace intrigue like the one that placed Wang Mang on the throne should materialize in the future.

Having confirmed the existence of the secret escape passage out of Luoyang, Lü Bu reluctantly concurred with Dong Zhuo's decision. However, his concurrence did not diminish his contempt for Dong Zhuo as a coward. It was a tactical move

A VILLAINOUS TRAITOR

107

to accommodate the decision of a superior who was fearful of combat.

That evening, Dong Zhuo announced to the palace staff that the boy emperor and his court would relocate westward to Chang'an, the gateway of the Silk Road and the capital of the first 212 years of the Eastern Han dynasty. Under the cover of darkness, the escape party began their exodus immediately after Dong Zhuo's announcement.

As Dong Zhuo, Lü Bu, Emperor Xian, members of his court, and several hundred palace guards emerged from the tunnel outside of Luoyang's city wall to begin their westward trek, Dong Zhuo, in his destructive craze, ordered a contingent of the palace guards to return to the palace and the city to set fire to the entire metropolis.

The fire lit up the night sky, and Luoyang turned into hell. Thousands of panicking residents died in the firestorm and the chaos. Many people were trampled to death. Many more injured. The destruction was horrendous, not to mention the loss of priceless national treasures housed in the palace, including scores of invaluable paintings, dozens of centuries-old bronze vessels, scrolls of brilliant brush-pen calligraphy, exquisite sculptures of jade and other precious stones, rare scientific instruments, a library of books including the first printed book in human history (using the technique of rubbing), archival records of the Han dynasty, and precious gifts from tributary kingdoms, vassal states, the Persian empire, and the Roman empire.

Frightened and confused, the residents of Luoyang wailed and howled. The fire was a catastrophic scourge that descended upon them with nary a warning.

The city was awash in tears and sorrow.

From their camps, the allied forces saw smoke and fire billowing from the city of Luoyang that night. They heard the heart-wrenching cries of despair of Luoyang's citizens. They didn't know what was happening, and they couldn't find out.

They were unprepared to attack the city. At any rate, scaling the city wall in darkness would be suicidal. The only thing Cao Cao and his commanders could do was put the allied forces on high alert as the fire raged in Luoyang.

Before sunrise, as daylight emerged along the eastern horizon, all four city gates suddenly swung open. Tens of thousands of victims of the firestorm poured out, surprising the allied commanders and soldiers. The Peach Garden Brothers were the first ones to approach the bereaved citizens. They quickly found out that Dong Zhuo had escaped. Pressed with the urgent tasks of extinguishing the fire and restoring law and order, the allied commanders did not give chase to the escaped party but threw themselves into the task of helping the residents of Luoyang. At first, they didn't know how Dong Zhuo managed to escape the besieged city. It was not until that afternoon that they discovered the secret tunnel among the ruins of the burnt palace.

Liu Bei was the only Peach Garden Brother who had visited Luoyang in the past. When he was a young boy, his father took him there on a pilgrimage, paying homage to the history of China. To Liu Bei's father and members of the educated elite, the capital city was not only the seat of imperial authority but also a sacred cultural monument and the repository of national treasures. Situated in the heart of eastern China and having served as the capital of the legendary Xia dynasty as well as the Eastern Zhou dynasty, Luoyang was full of legends, history, steles, temples, pagodas, and archaeological treasures. In the center of the city was the magnificent palace built for Emperor Guangwu, the founder of the Eastern Han dynasty.

During their visit, Liu Bei and his father walked around the perimeter of the palace. They saw that the two wings, known as the Southern Palace and the Northern Palace, were connected by a long boulevard. Each wing contained multiple ornate structures. Even though they couldn't see the palace grounds, they were awed by the enormous size and majestic beauty of the palace's layers of tiled roof.

"How could anyone set fire to such a legendary city and murder thousands of innocent citizens? What does Dong Zhuo gain from such a heinous and callous crime?" Liu Bei sighed, his face ashen, his eyes teary. "What a tragedy! What a travesty!"

When the Peach Garden Brothers arrived at the palace, the fire had leveled almost all its edifices. The cavernous hall where the officials conducted business in the presence of the emperor had collapsed, enormous wood columns still smoldering in the ruins. The storage buildings and their invaluable contents were reduced to ashes. The palace grounds were strewn with charred debris. The air filled with smoke and soot. Charred corpses were everywhere. Horrified by the devastation, Liu Bei, Guan Yu, and Zhang Fei were speechless.

While the allied soldiers were struggling to put out the fire in Luoyang, calm its citizens, and restore order, Dong Zhuo's escape party had gone some distance west of the forest after emerging from the secret tunnel. Along the way, Lü Bu ordered everyone to pick up the pace of the march. Within a few hours, the elderly and infirm members of the party collapsed from exhaustion. They were cast by the wayside and left to die.

It took nearly two weeks of trekking for Dong Zhuo's party to reach their destination. During the trek, Dong Zhuo's soldiers plundered and looted, inflicting unspeakable atrocity on the citizenry along the way.

For Dong Zhuo, the trek from Luoyang to Chang'an was long, arduous, and unbearable. The hardship of the journey inflamed his paranoia. He was agitated and excessively demanding. Even after his lieutenants requisitioned a horse for him outside of Luoyang, he found the travel exhausting. His fatigue was made worse by his awareness that he now faced the onslaught of the nation's military commanders. He became suspicious of everything and everyone, including members of his inner circle. Several of his military guards were executed on the slimmest evidence of making disparaging comments about him. Lashing out at his close subordinates repeatedly, he even began to question Lü Bu's loyalty. Gone were the days of unchecked power and luxury in Luoyang, where he lavished rewards on Lü Bu incessantly as the two of them terrorized the capital with their atrocity.

Lü Bu, being a mercenary, understood the travail of long-distance trekking. Greedy as he was, he did not expect a life of comfort on the road and tolerated the hardships of long-distance travel with aplomb. For Dong Zhuo, being confined to the saddle every day was pure torture. Plagued by constant pain in his buttocks and lower back, he became exasperated by midday. In the afternoon, he yawned, cussed, grumbled incessantly, and strained to sit upright on his horse. In the evening, he sorely missed the fine dining to which he was accustomed. To console himself, he resorted to excessive alcohol consumption.

One evening in his tent, dazed by the liquor he had already consumed and in a moment of confusion exacerbated by his paranoia, he, believing that Lü Bu was an assassin, grabbed a spear and flung it toward Lü Bu. But Dong Zhuo was so disoriented that the spear barely reached the vicinity where Lü Bu stood. Lü Bu snatched the spear on its downward flight and proceeded to walk out of Dong Zhuo's tent. The incident surprised and irritated Lü Bu even though it didn't frighten him. Shortly after tossing the spear at Lü Bu, Dong Zhuo came to his senses, realizing that he had committed a serious faux pas, antagonizing his premier bodyguard and his best asset. He yelled after Lü Bu that he, Dong Zhuo, did not intend to harm Lü Bu. But Lü Bu walked away in silence with the spear in his hand.

Before the spear-throwing incident, Lü Bu had thought that he and Dong Zhuo had risen beyond the usual transactional relationships that dominated his life. After all, Dong Zhuo, on his own initiative, took the trouble to become Lü Bu's foster father in a public ceremony. Even if there was no love between them, because neither of them was capable of love, their mutual dependency appeared to be solid and mutually beneficial. Neither of them had friends, but the two of them had reached a level of trust and collaboration that was close to a friendship. The spear-tossing incident, however, drove a wedge in that budding relationship. In Lü Bu's mind, it revealed that Dong Zhuo was not beyond killing him. That revelation cast a shadow on his view of Dong Zhuo and drove him to question the nature of their relationship.

Being self-centered, narcissistic, and violent, Lü Bu had never entertained a rosy view of any human being. His life, the life of a ruthless mercenary, consisted of an unending series of polar extremes: victory or defeat, conquest or surrender, kill or be killed. Survival, instant gratification, and the acquisition of wealth dictated all his actions. After joining Dong Zhuo, he came close to reaching an exception of his cynical and sinister view of life. The father-son relationship with Dong Zhuo had brought him some contentment, mitigated his hostility, and mollified his fury against the world. He had begun to chart a new life. Now out of nowhere came the spear incident. It rekindled his sinister view of the world. He realized that the chummy relationship between Dong Zhuo and him was skewed heavily in favor of Dong Zhuo. Dong Zhuo held all the power while indulging him to wallow in a bubble. This new revelation began gnawing at Lü Bu. Convinced that the Dong Zhuo era of his life was just a brief interlude, he felt compelled to explore new possibilities. He muttered to himself, "I need to regain my independence!"

When Dong Zhuo and his party drew near Chang'an, the capital of the Western Han dynasty, he sent an advance party to announce the arrival of the boy emperor. Settling the young emperor and his attendants into the old palace of the Western Han, Dong Zhuo decreed that henceforth Chang'an would be the capital once again. The decree had little practical consequence outside of Chang'an because by then Dong Zhuo's treachery had been recognized nationally. Even the most loyal subjects of the Han dynasty conceded that the great dynasty, after nearly four hundred years, had ended with Dong Zhuo's murder of Emperor Shao and the empress dowager.

While Dong Zhuo was settling down in Chang'an, leaders of the alliance failed to reach a consensus on further actions against him. Their disagreement meant that they would not pursue the escaped traitor, which, in effect, spelled the end of the alliance. Subsequently, the leaders returned to their respective home bases and resumed their independent existences. There was, however, a change in their attitude. Most of the warlords, such as Yuan Shao and Gongsun Zan, who used to acknowledge nominally their subordination to the Han emperor, no longer paid any attention to the boy emperor, Xian, in Dong Zhuo's custody. They conducted affairs in their territories as fully independent states, and they vied with each other for dominance.

During the campaign against Dong Zhuo, the benevolent reputation of the Peach Garden Brothers attracted thousands of new followers from the general population. By the time of the alliance's dissolution, the Peach Garden Brothers' militia had expanded into a formidable army. With the blessing of Cao Cao, who was eager to return Liu Bei's favor for helping him to become the commander in chief of the erstwhile alliance, the Peach Garden Brothers took over the southwestern portion of Xu province, near the expansive Jing province, the territory of Sun Ce, an up-and-coming warlord gaining power and prestige south of the Yangtzi River. The warlord of Xu province had passed away without an heir, and his subordinates chose to invite the Peach Garden Brothers to be their commanders.

While Cao Cao gave his consent to the popular acclaim to have the Peach Garden Brothers as commanders of Xu province, he annexed the eastern portion of Xu province, incorporating it into his own territory. The Peach Garden Brothers, grateful for having acquired their own foothold, reaffirmed their commitment to serve the people and presented themselves as the heirs of the Han dynasty. They governed their dominion with the loyal support of the people. Their popularity soon propelled them into contention for national supremacy, even though they were far from being dominant in military strength.

In the meantime, the former commander in chief of the alliance army, Cao Cao, claimed Luoyang and its surrounding territory, consolidating his position as the most powerful warlord in the nation.

In Chang'an, Dong Zhuo never recovered from the trials and tribulations of the long journey of exodus from Luoyang. He began to deteriorate mentally and physically. Paranoid and irascible, he ordered executions of people with the slightest excuse in and out of the imperial court. In his presence, no official dared to offer any advice, express any opinion, or speak his mind. Behind his back, everyone wished his reign of terror would end soon. Even Lü Bu, who used to stay by Dong Zhuo's side in Luoyang at all times, began to keep a distance from him.

Isolated, Dong Zhuo took great offense at Lü Bu's newfound independence. He felt that all the money and effort he had poured into securing Lü Bu's service had not paid off, and the entire enterprise of recruiting Lü Bu turned out to be a bad investment. He even entertained the thought of eliminating Lü Bu should an opportunity arise. But he was cautious, not revealing his secret desire for fear of provoking Lü Bu into open rebellion. Caught between the annoying present situation and a potentially dangerous future, Dong Zhuo sought solace in alcohol more than ever. One day, plagued by a sudden swell of paranoia, he, once again, heaved a spear at Lü Bu in his office.

This time, Lü Bu took serious offense. Dodging the spear, he stormed out of Dong Zhuo's office, no longer doubting that Dong Zhuo would kill him at an opportune moment.

One day, while confiding his grievance against Dong Zhuo to a senior minister of the court, he mentioned the second spear incident, grumbling that he no longer felt safe in Dong Zhuo's presence. The minister, who had been eager to recruit Lü Bu into his cabal, divulged a secret assassination plot against Dong Zhuo he and a group of court mandarins had been planning. Startled by the information, Lü Bu fixed his gaze on the minister, trying to ascertain the veracity of what the minister had said. Detecting a trace of fear in the minister's expression, Lü Bu inferred that the minister was probably not an agent-provocateur in Dong Zhuo's service, and therefore, the secret assassination plot was most likely not a test of Lü Bu's putative loyalty to Dong Zhuo. But Lü Bu wanted confirmation. He demanded to meet with the entire group of conspirators. After two days, the official gave his consent and made the necessary arrangements.

During a meeting at an inn outside of Chang'an at the gateway of the Silk Road, Lü Bu was convinced of the sincerity of the conspirators and agreed to join them. But he wanted an answer to a question that had been weighing on his mind.

"Dong Zhuo and I are father and son. If a son entertains the thought of killing his father, wouldn't that son be condemned as a pariah forever?"

"You need to wake up, my friend," the minister responded. "Are you certain that Dong Zhuo is your father? Would a real father try to spear his son repeatedly? Did it occur to you that making you an adopted son was Dong Zhuo's tactic to keep you on a leash? You have to understand Dong Zhuo's devious mind. Adopting you as a son is merely his tactic of controlling you!"

The minister's rejoinder hit Lü Bu hard. Its reverberation, intensified by Lü Bu's anxiety, which had already eroded his trust and respect for Dong Zhuo since the escape from Luoyang, led him to the conclusion that, in self-preservation, he needed to strike against Dong Zhuo before Dong Zhuo could kill him.

Never a man of hesitation, Lü Bu wasted no time taking action once he joined the cabal of conspirators against Dong Zhuo. The afternoon after meeting the conspirators at the gateway of the Silk Road, he went to Dong Zhuo's office near the palace. There were two armed soldiers standing guard at the bottom of a flight of granite stairs. On top of the stairs was a large square demarcated by polished granite balustrades, and at each of the four corners of the square stood two fully armed guards. In the middle of the elevated granite square was an imposing hall in the style of a palatial structure where an emperor held court. Following established custom, Lü Bu placed his halberd on a weapon rack next to two guards in the vestibule before entering Dong Zhuo's workspace located deep in the recesses of the cavernous hall.

When Dong Zhuo saw Lü Bu walking toward him in huge strides, oozing tension that distorted his face, he growled from his chair behind his desk, "What do you want?"

Without uttering a word, Lü Bu pulled out a stiletto hidden inside his robe and thrust it toward Dong Zhuo's heart. Panicking, Dong Zhuo rose from his seat to defend himself with outstretched arms. As Dong Zhuo was halfway up from his seat, Lü Bu's weapon missed Dong Zhuo's heart. It penetrated Dong Zhuo's fat belly instead. In agony, Dong Zhuo squealed like a pig being slaughtered. A surprised Lü Bu immediately pulled out the stiletto and plunged it into Dong Zhuo's chest. He could feel the weapon hitting the soft tissue of the heart after penetrating the bony chest wall. Blood gurgled from Dong Zhuo's mouth as he collapsed back into his chair, moaning. Using the same weapon, Lü Bu then severed Dong Zhuo's head.

The two guards in the vestibule heard Dong Zhuo's squeal and rushed in with drawn swords. Halfway into the hall, they met Lü Bu, who was holding Don Zhuo's head in his left hand.

The soldiers charged. Lü Bu, with a powerful stroke of the stiletto in his right hand, tracing an arc from left to right, parried both swords of the soldiers and slashed the right arm of one. While swinging his stiletto, he also inflicted a vicious kick at the groin of the other soldier. As the two soldiers reeled in pain, Lü Bu dropped the stiletto, reached for his halberd on the weapon rack, and proceeded to exit the hall.

Alarmed by the screams and ruckus, other members of Dong Zhuo's bodyguards rushed toward his office. By the time Lü Bu was out of the building, a full platoon of armed soldiers was running up the stairs of the elevated granite square. Lü Bu, on top of the stairs, leveled his halberd at the charging soldiers and barked in a booming voice, "Halt, if you wish to live!"

Lü Bu's ferocity and reputation stopped the platoon of body-guards in their tracks. Raising Dong Zhuo's head, still dripping blood, Lü Bu roared menacingly with a fierce stare, "Your master is dead. Now vanish before my fangtian huaji dispatches you to hell!"

In an instant, the guards turned tail, ran down the granite stairs, and disappeared. It was spring, AD 192.

After the cabal of conspirators in the imperial court learned of Dong Zhuo's death, they cast his fat-laden corpse at a square in the center of Chang'an. Residents of the capital so detested Dong Zhuo that they inserted a wick into his belly button. Fueled by Dong Zhuo's copious belly fat, the wick burned for days.

After Dong Zhuo's death, his lieutenants, cognizant that the mandarin officials of the court would publicize Dong Zhuo's crimes and possibly punish members of his inner circle for their complicity, pleaded for amnesty. Their plea was rejected.

A VILLAINOUS TRAITOR

Desperate and fearing for their lives, they mounted an armed rebellion even though they had not secured Lü Bu's participation. In a brief armed confrontation, ministers of the court and their troops slew most of Dong Zhuo's loyal subordinates. At this point, Lü Bu knew that Chang'an was not a place where he could tarry any longer.

Where to? he wondered.

Detesting administrative chores, lacking interpersonal skills, and incapable of navigating political quagmire, his only option was to sell his military service and his martial prowess to a patron. Thus, Lü Bu resumed his former life as a wandering mercenary, serving one warlord after another. The warlords who were vying for power in this tumultuous era coveted Lü Bu's martial skill and combat experience, but they also found his arrogance, narcissism, and fickleness menacing. He bounced from the warlord Yuan Shu to Yuan Shu's archrival and cousin, Yuan Shao. Then he sought shelter under Zhang Yang, someone he had fought against when he was in the service of Yuan Shao. By AD 194, having been shunned by warlords across the nation, he begged Liu Bei of the Peach Garden Brothers to accept him into their army.

Both Guan Yu and Zhang Fei, who loathed Lü Bu, objected to accommodating Lü Bu, but Liu Bei, always forgiving and merciful, prevailed over the objection of his sworn brothers by arguing that they should give the mercenary the benefit of the doubt.

"For years, Lü Bu had been serving the villainous traitor Dong Zhuo," Liu Bei said. "It is not surprising that he had adopted some of his master's unsavory traits. In some ways, people are like apples. When apples are in the company of a rotten one, they tend to rot faster than normal. Perhaps Lü Bu may change for the better in a morally upright environment."

In the army of the Peach Garden Brothers, Lü Bu behaved reasonably well under the watchful eyes of Guan Yu and Zhang Fei. Then, he grew tired of being a law-abiding citizen and found life under Liu Bei's leadership unbearably tedious and ho-hum. The Peach Garden Brothers lived frugally, never ogled beautiful women, and imposed strict codes of conduct among their troops in their territory. Looting, raping, and plundering, for example, were punishable by death. Gone were the days when Lü Bu swaggered around Luoyang like a demigod, appropriating any valuable objects he saw and taking any woman he desired. He even began to regret that he had killed Dong Zhuo.

Driven mad by ennui in Peach Garden Brothers' martinet camp, Lü Bu decided to strike out on his own as a wandering martial artist.

A few months later, he joined a band of brigands in Inner Mongolia, his old haunt at the beginning of his career. They established a base camp at Crescent Lake, a natural wonder with a bubbling spring among the great sand dunes in Shazhou (present-day Dunhuang) on the southeastern edge of the Gobi Desert. From there, the bandits raided the frontier towns and villages to the east, posing a threat and becoming a nuisance to both the Peach Garden Brothers and Cao Cao.

Alarmed by the mayhem and chaos created by Lü Bu's bandits, Cao Cao amassed an army of ten thousand and personally led it to attack Lü Bu's base camp at Crescent Lake. The ensuing battle lasted several days. Lü Bu tried his best to inspire his followers with unprecedented bravery as he and his Maroon Hare repeatedly charged into Cao Cao's army, killing scores of soldiers each time. In the end, waves and waves of sword-slashing and lance-thrusting soldiers, supported by hundreds of archers of Cao Cao's army, overpowered Lü Bu's force wherever the bandits appeared. Most of Lü Bu's followers were killed. Some managed to escape into the heart of the Gobi Desert on their Bactrian camels. When Cao Cao's soldiers finally surrounded Lü Bu near a sand dune, he had no choice but to surrender.

A VILLAINOUS TRAITOR

Tied up with ropes and kneeling in front of Cao Cao, Lü Bu played his best hand for self-preservation, attempting to sell his service as the greatest warrior of all time. Fully aware of Cao Cao's intelligence and ruthlessness, he did not plead for mercy. Instead of begging for acceptance, he couched the offer of his service in an analysis of the state of the nation.

"The murder of Emperor Shao marked the end of the Han dynasty. Civil war is engulfing our nation." Lü Bu summoned his eloquence to the best of his ability. "At present, there are three contenders for domination under heaven. They are your lordship, Liu Bei of the Peach Garden Brothers, and Sun Ce, the fast-rising warlord of the south. The Peach Garden Brothers are popular. Guan Yu and Zhang Fei are superb warriors. They may expand their influence and territory up to a point. However, their resources are limited because they are unwilling to impose heavy taxes on the people in their territory. Sun Ce's base includes the rice-rich domain south of the Yangtzi River. With the wealth to pursue his ambitious goals, Sun Ce, a wily leader assisted by several brilliant military strategists, is a serious rival of your lordship. But you, my lord, have two advantages over Liu Bei and Sun Ce. Firstly, you are the most gifted general of all time, and secondly, you control the Central Plain, the richest and the most populous region of the nation. With the addition of a peerless warrior like me in your service, you will be able to defeat the Peach Garden Brothers and Sun Ce. I believe that your lordship is well poised to become the founding emperor of a new dynasty."

Shrewd Cao Cao listened to Lü Bu's analysis with amusement. Pursing his lips with his customary Machiavellian smile, he refused to favor Lü Bu with a response and ordered Lü Bu to be summarily executed on the grounds that he was a moral degenerate, having repeatedly made a farce of the Confucian canon of loyalty. Banditry was the secondary charge Cao Cao leveled against him.

After Lü Bu's execution, a fleeting pang of regret flickered in Cao Cao's mind. He had lost one of the greatest warriors who could be useful to him in his contest with other warlords for supremacy. He wished he didn't have to kill the man, but what choice did he have?

"All political decisions involve some degree of gambling." His mental calculator was ticking feverishly. "This unprincipled man has already murdered two of his patrons. I could be the next victim if I retained him. For him, the concept of loyalty doesn't exist."

In the same train of thought, Cao Cao was impressed with Lü Bu's assessment of the political situation of the country. Indeed, he was surprised by Lü Bu's ability to proffer such an accurate analysis, a cerebral feat unexpected from a mercenary. Like what Lü Bu said, there was no doubt that Sun Ce, with a well-financed army, would be a major contender for national power. Cao Cao knew he had to prepare for an eventual military confrontation against this rising star from the Yangtzi River basin. The Peach Garden Brothers, Cao Cao thought, constituted a threat in a different way.

"As Lü Bu correctly observed, the Peach Garden Brothers' strength lies in their popularity, but they are not ruthless enough to win it all," Cao Cao mused.

With a sly smile, he muttered to himself, "It's hard not to like the Peach Garden Brothers. They are ethical and compassionate. Even I am fond of them. I should mount a campaign to charm them into my camp."

But Cao Cao's counselors disagreed. They argued against a charm campaign, noting that being an ambitious member of the Liu clan that founded the Han dynasty, Liu Bei had the advantage of enjoying some legitimate claim to the imperial throne. A succession claim on the ground of ancestral lineage by Liu Bei might be tenuous. However, being a member of the imperial clan remained an important asset. That asset, in addition to his popularity and the unwavering devotion of Guan Yu and Zhang Fei, made Liu Bei a formidable contender for national power.

"A person who has the potential of becoming an emperor will not be charmed into serving your lordship as a subordinate," the counselors pointed out to Cao Cao. Unanimously, they recommended immediate military action against the Peach Garden Brothers: "We should nip their rise in the bud before they become too powerful."

After several days of contemplation, Cao Cao found his counselors' recommendation compelling. Together, they devised a plot. Instead of taking military actions against the Peach Garden Brothers, Cao Cao and his strategists designed a scheme to approach Xu province, the territory under the control of the Peach Garden Brothers, with stealth and deceit. They drafted a fake letter from Liu Bei inviting Cao Cao and a small contingent of cavalry to Liu Bei's headquarters to refresh their alliance. The letter was carefully crafted by a group of experts. A calligrapher imitated Liu Bei's handwriting perfectly. A seal maker produced a copy of Liu Bei's personal seal based on an image the seal had made in an earlier document on file. Cao Cao made sure that the paper and the wrapping of the letter were the same as those customarily used by Liu Bei. The letter looked authentic in every detail.

With that letter in hand, Cao Cao led three hundred of his best cavalry toward Xu province. They had to stop at two defense strongholds along the way. When Cao Cao showed the fake letter to the captains in charge of those checkpoints, the defenders did not suspect foul play and allowed Cao Cao's contingent to pass through without sounding any alarm.

Upon reaching the vicinity of Liu Bei's headquarters, Cao Cao rested his troops. At midnight on the second day, Cao Cao and his troops sneaked into Liu Bei's headquarters while everyone in Liu Bei's party was sound asleep. The surprise attack wreaked havoc in Liu Bei's camp. When the soldiers and officers were rudely awakened, they didn't know what was happening or who was attacking them. Amid chaos and confusion, Cao Cao captured Guan Yu. But Liu Bei and Zhang Fei escaped. They sought refuge in the territory of Yuan Shao, the warlord under whom the Peach Garden Brothers' initial militia served.

Cao Cao was overjoyed with his swift and resounding success in expelling the Peach Garden Brothers from Xu province. His army didn't suffer a single casualty. In addition, they captured Guan Yu asleep in his bed, which was an unexpected prize. In a jubilant mood, Cao Cao proclaimed a general amnesty for all prisoners of war captured from the Peach Garden Brothers, permitting them to either join Cao Cao's army or return home as civilians. That amnesty turned out to be a mistake because most of the captive soldiers ended up rejoining Liu Bei in Yuan Shao's territory, enabling Liu Bei to rebuild his army. They, like the general population, believed that Liu Bei was the most caring leader and the most compassionate commander. They didn't want to serve a less deserving person than him.

As for Guan Yu, Cao Cao made it clear to his underlings that he would deal with the prize captive himself.

When Guan Yu, tied up with ropes, was brought to him, Cao Cao rose from his dais, walked toward Guan Yu, personally untied him, and apologized for his subordinates' disrespectful action of placing him in bondage. He then invited Guan Yu to sit at the dais with him to share a jar of liquor. As the two men sipped liquor, Cao Cao, complimenting Guan Yu for his martial prowess, bravery, and impeccable character, announced to his camp, "I am appointing Guan Yu as my deputy commanding general for our army."

Guan Yu was embarrassed. Here he was, a prisoner of war, being made a deputy commander by his captor!

A VILLAINOUS TRAITOR

123

The appointment of Guan Yu was a brilliant stroke by Cao Cao. Desperately desiring Guan Yu's service, Cao Cao was well aware of Guan Yu's reputation as an unfaltering champion of ethical principles. He knew Guan Yu would never submit to anyone or switch his allegiance from his sworn brothers. By making Guan Yu the deputy commanding general of his army, Cao Cao simply sidestepped those issues.

In Guan Yu's mind, his loyalty to Liu Bei and Zhang Fei remained absolute. They were sworn brothers. Now, Cao Cao not only treated him honorably but also made him a commander of Cao Cao's army. In fairness, Guan Yu felt obliged to repay Cao Cao for his magnanimity and generosity.

Two months after his capture by Cao Cao, Guan Yu seized an opportunity that arose unexpectedly.

Yuan Shao, the warlord who hosted Liu Bei and Zhang Fei at the time, was alarmed that Cao Cao had annexed Xu province, which belonged to the Peach Garden Brothers. Since Xu province bordered his own territory, he considered Cao Cao was now posing an ominous threat to him. Anticipating Cao Cao's invasion, Yuan Shao decided to strike first, but Cao Cao had not yet moved his main army into Xu province. Yuan Shao sent his best general, a formidable warrior, the axe-wielding Yan Liang, at the head of an army group to invade Xu province. Guan Yu, having learned of Yuan Shao's action, realized that if he defeated Yuan Shao's invasion force, he would have conveniently atoned for the compromising and embarrassing position in which he found himself. Thus, he volunteered to confront Yan Liang and his army with three hundred cavalry, telling Cao Cao, "I will slay Yan Liang and defeat his army."

Initially, Cao Cao rejected Guan Yu's offer. But Guan Yu's insistence and candor changed Cao Cao's mind. Cao Cao figured that Guan Yu couldn't possibly be conniving to double-cross him. He was confident that duplicity, chicanery, and schemes were beyond Guan Yu.

If Guan Yu commits himself to a task, he will give his life to accomplish it, Cao Cao calculated.

With Cao Cao's approval, Guan Yu led the detachment of cavalry to Xu province.

It was a bright day on the battlefield where the sun shone on the soldiers led by Guan Yu and Yan Liang. By any standard, Guan Yu's position looked precarious. His force numbered three hundred; his enemy had a combined force of three thousand. It was highly unlikely that three hundred cavalry could overcome an adversary ten times its size.

As the two opposing sides took stock of each other, Guan Yu, on his mount, suddenly charged into Yan Liang's army with his Breaking the Wave move. As he gyrated his halberd in a circular motion at high speed, shafts of blinding sunlight reflecting from the broad metallic blade of his halberd disoriented Yan Liang's soldiers and dispersed them. Instead of fighting, they had to shade their eyes with their hands. Guan Yu, in a matter of seconds, slashed his way into the center of his enemy, where he surprised the commanding general, Yan Liang, at a moment when he was preoccupied with battle preparation. Surprised and stunned, Yan Liang, sitting in his tent, did not expect actions, least of all actions against a warrior like Guan Yu, who suddenly materialized in front of him. With one mighty swing of his halberd, Guan Yu beheaded Yan Liang.

The sudden death of their commander thoroughly demoralized Yan Liang's officers. Their troops, disoriented, started fleeing, enabling Guan Yu's calvaries to score a decisive victory against an overwhelming army.

Back at Cao Cao's headquarters, Guan Yu told his fellow officers that the killing of Yan Liang and the defeat of Yuan Shao's army was his payback to Cao Cao for treating him with honor and generosity; he was now ready to rejoin his sworn brothers.

A VILLAINOUS TRAITOR

One of the officers immediately reported Guan Yu's words to Cao Cao. Much to the informer's astonishment and contrary to his expectation, Cao Cao responded, with a deep sigh, "Guan Yu is an avatar of bravery and loyalty. I wish I had the privilege of securing his service. Let him go! I don't wish to be remembered in history as the executioner of such a magnificent and noble warrior as Guan Yu."

Thus, Guan Yu was reunited with Liu Bei and Zhang Fei in Yuan Shao's territory. But Yuan Shao, angry that Guan Yu had caused him to lose an important warrior, made it clear that the Peach Garden Brothers were no longer welcome in his territory. One of Yuan Shao's overzealous subordinates, eager to curry favor with his lord, went so far as to mount an assassination attempt on Liu Bei without Yuan Shao's approval. But the assassin, before he could act, was caught and killed by Zhang Fei.

Expelled by Yuan Shao, the Peach Garden Brothers sought refuge in the territory of Liu Bei's cousin, Liu Biao, a mediocre man and a weak warlord in the southwestern region covering the middle Yangtzi River basin. Reluctant to turn away a kinsman but at the same time wary of Liu Bei's intelligence and popularity, Liu Biao stationed the Peach Garden Brothers in a region further south where the migratory expansion of the Han people had already begun penetrating. The region was hilly, swampy, heavily wooded, and sparsely populated by non-Han ethnic groups. Its climate was semitropical, and its people, other than the non-Han ethnic minorities, which constituted the majority in that region, were primarily hardy frontier settlers.

There, in the swampy frontier, the Peach Garden Brothers languished for several years while other warlords vied for domination in the north and the east. During those years, Cao Cao continued to engage Yuan Shao in military confrontations. But neither side could score a decisive victory to vanquish the other.

Meanwhile, Sun Ce, a major rival of Cao Cao's, was injured by an assassin sent by Cao Cao.

During a hunting trip, the assassin, embedded in Sun Ce's army, shot Sun Ce in the back with an arrow. His bodyguards promptly hacked the assassin to pieces. But Sun Ce's injury was severe. After two weeks, he died of sepsis caused by the deep wound. His brother, Sun Quan, a brilliant strategist as capable as, if not more gifted than, his elder brother, took over the control of the Sun family territory covering several provinces southeast of the Central Plain, including the fertile lower Yangtzi River basin and the southern coastal region of China. Funded with ample tax revenue from his rich and expansive region, Sun Quan created a new kingdom named Wu, referred to by some historians as Dong (Eastern) Wu, and declared himself king.

Having been exiled from the heartland of Han China, namely the Yellow River basin extending southward to the Yangtzi River region, the Peach Garden Brothers were rendered irrelevant in the contention for national power. In an underdeveloped region of southern China, they patiently began a process of recruiting soldiers and officers to rebuild their army. Guan Yu's prior experience with the Hmong people helped them recruit minority people in that region. Under his guidance, the Peach Garden Brothers and their subordinates treated the minority people with respect and courtesy and successfully recruited many youngsters into their army. Since the region, full of rivers and lakes, tended to be waterlogged during the monsoon, most of the new recruits were skilled sailors and boatmen. Taking hints from the local geography and his new recruits' expertise, Guan Yu organized a lightly armed naval force consisting of fast-moving sampans that could dart across the surfaces of rivers and lakes like arrows, regardless of the depth of the water. With horns and flags, he devised a communication system for his flotilla of sampans. Each sampan was operated by two rowers, two soldiers armed with bows and arrows, and a fully armored signaler who directed the movement of the sampan in coordination with other sampans. Liu Bei and Zhang Fei, delighted with Guan Yu's innovative idea of establishing a naval force, congratulated him enthusiastically.

More significant than their success in recruiting new soldiers and establishing a navy, the Peach Garden Brothers enticed a military engineer and brilliant strategist, Zhuge Liang, to be their chief of staff. At the time, Zhuge Liang led the life of a recluse, like Guan Yu's mentor, the grand master of the White Crane School of martial arts. Even in seclusion, Zhuge Liang enjoyed a reputation for his brilliance across the country. He was celebrated for his erudition, analytical capability, and political acumen, earning him the nickname Sleeping Dragon, *sleeping* because he refused to serve any warlord and chose to live humbly. His hermetic cottage home happened to be in the mountains not far from where the Peach Garden Brothers were stationed.

When one of Liu Bei's counselors recommended that Liu Bei should recruit Zhuge Liang to be his chief of staff, Liu Bei asked the counselor to invite Zhuge Liang to a meeting. However, the counselor said that Zhuge Liang would not leave his mountain cottage to meet anyone, not even the emperor. In response, Liu Bei, with Guan Yu and Zhang Fei in tow, trekked up the mountain to call on Zhuge Liang. The four men met in Zhuge Liang's humble shack, exchanged pleasantries, discussed affairs of the Han empire, and sipped tea. When Liu Bei proposed that Zhuge Liang should join him and take charge of the Peach Garden Brothers' enterprise, Zhuge Liang politely declined. He made it clear to Liu Bei that he did not wish to play a role in the pursuit of power. One month later, Liu Bei, Guan Yu, and Zhang Fei trekked to Zhuge Liang's remote abode to repeat their earlier proposal, but Zhuge Liang remained steadfast in his refusal to abandon his hermetic life, regardless of how lofty his position might be in the Peach Garden Brothers' organization.

Another month elapsed. The Peach Garden Brothers climbed the mountain path to Zhuge Liang's home a third time to woo him. Moved by the Peach Garden Brothers' perseverance and determination and impressed with their modesty, rectitude, and steadfast loyalty to the Han empire, Zhuge Liang agreed to emerge from his seclusion to be the chief of staff of the Peach Garden Brothers' military force in their endeavor to restore the Han dynasty.

The recruitment of Zhuge Liang was a great scoop on the part of the Peach Garden Brothers. It sent tremors among all the warlords in the country. The addition of Zhuge Liang significantly boosted the potential of the Peach Garden Brothers in the national struggle for supremacy.

As Zhuge Liang and the Peach Garden Brothers pondered their future, Liu Bei's cousin, their reluctant host, Liu Biao, died of illness. The deceased warlord had two sons who didn't get along. Feuding, the brothers jostled for inheritance. One of them declared himself a vassal to Cao Cao to gain an upper hand over his brother. Zhuge Liang suggested that the Peach Garden Brothers should lay claim to the region as their base for an eventual war against Cao Cao. But Liu Bei rejected the suggestion. In Liu Bei's mind, his cousin's sons belonged to the Liu clan. Loath to use force against his relatives, Liu Bei also felt morally obliged not to take advantage of his younger kinsmen and rob them of their territory.

While the Peach Garden Brothers and Zhuge Liang were deliberating their next strategic move, Cao Cao led his army southward and annexed the territory belonging to Liu Bei's demised cousin, further strengthening his position as the dominant warlord in the nation.

EIGHT

AN EXTRAORDINARY WOMAN

Xian-Hui (Sage), the petite, sixteen-year-old imperial concubine, exquisite and beautiful, had spent two days since her arrival in her chamber in the imperial palace sobbing intermittently. The chamber was a large rectangle, the ceiling vaulted and high, the hardwood-latticed windows covered with a delicate, translucent white silk, like a membrane that let in the light but kept out the pests. On the floor, wool carpets from the steppes of central Asia and the Uighur land blazed with rich, radiant colors displaying stylized, geometric representations of flowers, pomegranates, and fawns. Everything in her room was either silk in imperial yellow, rosewood in amber red, or lacquer in dark maroon. Blazing peonies, made of inlaid mother-of-pearl, adorned both the rosewood and lacquer furnishing, suggesting that the occupant of this chamber would rival the splendid flower in its delicate and alluring beauty. Hanging over a vanity placed against the wall on one side of the room was an enormous round mirror with a pair of carved phoenixes lining its border. Made of polished bronze, the mirror emanated a golden sheen. Two white jade qilins, the auspicious, dragon-like hoofed creatures of pan-Asian mythology, sat crouching on marble pedestals flanking the vanity. On the wall facing the vanity hung a large wood panel on which a beautifully executed logograph, zhong, "loyalty and devotion to the sovereign," one of the central tenets of Confucianism, was carved and painted in black.

But the exquisite and tastefully furnished chamber did not please Xian-Hui. The palace, with all its aura of beauty and glory, did not catch her attention. The lure of wealth, prestige, and potential power did not tempt her. The large panel of calligraphy with that lone character, zhong, appeared intimidating. But her fury shielded her from its imposing glare. She hated, with a passion, being an imperial concubine, even if it implied the possibility of becoming an imperial consort, a position second only to that of the empress, the highest role a concubine could aspire to. She was furious at being plucked from her parents' home in Suzhou near the eastern seaboard, deprived of the prospect of pursuing a life of her own choice and denied a role in choosing her own matrimonial partner. She came from an exceptionally unconventional family where females as well as males were educated and encouraged to be independent, assertive, and cerebral. She did not subscribe to the convention that males were superior to females. She saw herself as a free human being, as intellectual as any gifted literati of the opposite sex.

The eunuchs and other palace residents found her anguish bewildering. They recognized neither the iron will nor the overwhelming intelligence beneath her youthful beauty. To them, women, like any other possessions, were owned and traded by men for service, profit, and pleasure. Accustomed to women embracing this tradition as their fate, all people, including the palace denizens, considered imperial concubines the luckiest of the weaker sex. It was beyond everyone's comprehension that Xian-Hui did not rejoice in her good fortune for being chosen a member of the imperial household, in which she could, if she were lucky, one day rise to a great height and seize enormous power. The people of her hometown, Suzhou, shook their heads in disbelief upon hearing that Xian-Hui was distraught at becoming an imperial concubine. The men and women of the palace thought she cried because of fear and ignorance, the antithesis of what she felt. In her own mind, the day the eunuchs came to claim her under the imperial mandate of seeking beautiful young women to be concubines of the Son of Heaven was a day of infamy. It marked the end of her dreams and ambitions. She felt her life, on the cusp of embarking on a path of discovery and exploration, had been brought to an abrupt halt. The tears she shed in her palace chamber were not the tears of weakness or self-pity. They came from her frustration and fury, intensified by the humiliation of being subjected to an examination, upon arrival in the palace, to verify her virginity.

Xian-Hui's father, a convention-bucking member of the land-owning gentry, loved his talented daughter. Ever since she was a young girl, her intellectual gift and prodigious memory stood out like a bright star. She could recite *The Book of Odes* and held her own in spirited debate with her father's literati friends on deep philosophical issues:

Are humans innately evil or benevolent?

What is the cosmological significance of the hexagrams of *The Book of Changes*?

Why is Confucianism superior to Taoism?

Awed by his daughter's intellectual prowess, Xian-Hui's father brought her up as a free spirit. He educated her, nurtured her, and encouraged her to think freely and originally. By the age of twelve, she was already adept at articulating her own thoughts and intent on taking charge of her own life. A celebrated beauty in Suzhou, she attracted an unending string of marriage proposals from rich and socially elevated families ever since she was thirteen. Yet, neither her father nor she gave a moment of thought to those propositions regardless of the status of the suitor and the amount of gold and silver promised to her family. All proposals of marriage were met with immediate rejection reinforced by an unambiguous message that there was no possibility of reconsideration.

Rumor swirled, from those who projected their own mundane ambition upon the person they envied and misunderstood, that Xian-Hui was saving herself for the Son of Heaven. People dismissed her father's claim that his daughter aspired to be a poet, wanted to seek her own matrimonial partner, and planned a life of intellectual pursuit. They didn't believe that she disdained conventional success in wealth and prestige. Everyone could see the young girl's intelligence. But the lofty goals of feminine independence and aspiring to be a poet seemed outlandish and disturbing. To most people in Suzhou, those claims were nothing but a ruse for covering up father and daughter's grandiose, ambitious design for becoming members of the imperial court. After all, how could a woman, destined to be a wife and a mother, become a successful poet and intellectual?

How preposterous!

All the great poets and sages, from Qu Yuan to Song Yu, from Confucius to Mencius, from Laozi to Zhuangzi, were men. Furthermore, why should a young girl choose her own husband? Choosing a son-in-law was the duty and the inalienable right of a young woman's parents.

Thus, the rumor of a rare, untouchable beauty in Suzhou saving herself for the emperor traveled far and wide, until it reached the scouting eunuchs who traveled the country to seek unparalleled beautiful girls for the emperor's harem. To the anguish of both Xian-Hui and her father, that rumor turned into reality. Without any warning, as if a thunderclap suddenly roared from a clear, blue sky, the scouting eunuchs descended upon Xian-Hui's home one day and proclaimed that they would escort her to the imperial palace in Luoyang to become a member of the imperial harem.

The year the eunuchs snatched Xian-Hui away from her life was AD 187. A mild summer had just begun in Luoyang, the capital city of the Eastern Han dynasty. The nation was in turmoil; the economy in tatters; insurrections sprang up across the country; many people, especially the peasantry, suffered from unspeakable privation.

Xian-Hui, after secluding herself for two nights and one day in her room, stopped shedding tears. Her anger had not subsided. She felt just as violated as before. But the futility of venting her emotions took hold of her. Like it or not, she was a captive in the palace. Remembering her father's teaching, "Adversity always lurks around the corner. When it shows its cruel face, do not fold and crumple. Confront it and take charge of yourself!" she resolved to apply her resources to find a way to extract herself from this damnation. It didn't take long for her to conclude that she had only two logical possibilities of action: submit or escape.

Submission was out of the question. It meant death in every sense except the physical one. Being young and healthy, she had never thought about death before, other than abstractly equating it with the termination of physical existence. Now she came to see that death could also mean the end of free will, the closure of intellectual exploration, the demise of the mind. Submission was tantamount to becoming a living dead. To her, a life confined to the material realm, no matter how opulent, was pointless, not worth living. It was clear that she had only one sensible option: *escape*.

She understood that escaping the palace would be extremely difficult, if not impossible, no matter how patiently and carefully she crafted a plot. To begin with, the palace was walled off from the outside world as a forbidden city, heavily guarded twenty-four hours a day. Without an official permit and a proper escort, no one could enter or exit the palace grounds. Beyond the guards and the physical barriers, she knew that the punishment of a captured runaway concubine was death by garroting, a gruesome way to end life. To escape from the imperial palace was never a normal course of action entertained by a concubine no matter how desperate and miserable she might be. Xian-Hui also understood that, even if she managed to escape from the palace, she would need to find a suitable destination, a place to hide from the authorities, a shelter that offered some measure of protection.

She had none!

Home in Suzhou, the only place she knew, was out of the question. That would be the first place where the authorities would go looking for her if she managed the unattainable feat of escaping from the palace. If the authorities found her in Suzhou, they would not only take her back to the palace to be put to death but also behead every member of her extended family as a coconspirator.

Yet the overwhelming odds against escaping and its risky consequence did not faze Xian-Hui.

I must pursue my goal with patience and supreme caution, she told herself.

She didn't have a plan yet. It needed to evolve and develop. At the same time, she knew the importance of being prepared for improvisation and decisive actions, in case an unexpected opportunity presented itself. Even as a teenager, she was wise and prudent.

Now that she had reached the decision to escape in her mind, it defined her life and gave her strength to survive in bondage as she bided her time to arrive at a plan. The first step, she reasoned, was to acquaint herself with her surroundings.

The first person she saw, when she eventually ventured out of her room, was a young eunuch, standing close to her door, suggesting that he had been assigned to her as an attendant. Perhaps he was the one who brought her meals in lacquer bowls and dishes during the past few days while, in her anger and sorrow, she hardly ate any food and did not even cast a glance at the deliverer. As the eunuch bent down in a deep bow, Xian-Hui took measure of him.

He was no bigger than Xian-Hui herself. His face still retaining the innocence of a young boy, the eunuch seemed kind and somewhat unsure of himself. She figured that he was in his early teens, probably a new initiate into the life of castration, a prerequisite for serving in the quarters of the imperial concubines. That meant, Xian-Hui inferred, he had recovered from the knife not too long ago, and the psychological scar of mutilation probably remained raw and sensitive.

She pitied him.

"What's your name?" Xian-Hui asked gently.

"My surname is Ma. You can call me Little Ma," the eunuch answered in a thin voice without raising himself from the deep bow.

"Can you show me around? That is, to places where we are allowed to go. I'm new here."

"Of course, it will be my pleasure. My job is to please you. Do you think you'll enjoy visiting the pavilion where some of the imperial treasures are on display? It's only about one hundred paces from the quarter of the noble concubines."

Xian-Hui nodded with a smile.

As Little Ma straightened himself and looked at Xian-Hui's face for the first time, her radiant smile and elegant features struck him like a thunderbolt. His natural reaction was to stare at her and adore her. Being aware that such behavior by a eunuch would be grossly offensive, he quickly lowered his head and averted his eyes as they proceeded to walk out of her chamber.

LORD GUAN

Out in the open, Xian-Hui took a deep breath. After days of confinement, first in a hansom, then in a palanquin, and finally in a private concubine chamber, she savored the liberating feeling of breathing the fresh air in open space, as if she were a bird newly released from a dark dungeon. Wide-eyed and somewhat apprehensive, she took in a panoramic visual sweep. The magnitude and magnificence of the palace staggered her.

She was brought into the palace in an enclosed palanquin at night from the south gate of the capital city, Luoyang, after five days of an unrelenting, rocky ride in a hansom pulled by two horses. At every stop, of which she saw nothing and spoke to nobody, she was escorted into the quarters of high government officials to rest, while everyone, in deep bow, refrained from looking at her. On the outskirts of Luoyang, a welcoming party consisting of four eunuchs smiling obsequiously in front of a palanquin met her without any fanfare. As soon as she transferred into the palanquin, it rolled and rocked in tune with the synchronized grunts of a team of laboring men who bore it on their shoulders. Toward the end of the ride, she heard the barking of soldiers as her entourage passed through a heavily guarded gate at the end of a tunnel that, she found out weeks later, was an opening through the thick and tall wall surrounding the forbidden city. Other than the exchange of brief questions and answers between the guards and the escorting eunuchs, which indicated that they were on palace grounds, she had not heard nor engaged in a conversation throughout the five-day trip.

Upon arrival in the west wing of the palace, she was ushered into her chamber. Freshly brewed green tea with the scent of sweet chestnut and a bowl of delicate fruit, including lychee and dragon's-eye fruit, awaited her on a small dining table. In that opulent room, she had been sequestered, lamenting her fate. Now, as she stood outside the concubine quarters and took in the sight, she found the beauty and grandeur of the palace

AN EXTRAORDINARY WOMAN

even more impressive than the exaggerated description of the emperor's residence she had heard in her hometown.

The walkway where she stood was twenty paces wide, covered with gray bricks set in a hexagonal pattern of mosaic design. Running north–south, it was so long that Xian-Hui could barely make out the silhouette of the architectural structures at the north end. On the south end, which was much closer, the walkway ended in a majestic rampart that appeared to be a part of the wall surrounding the palace. She figured that it would require at least a few minutes of brisk march to reach that rampart. Lining the walkway, at five paces apart, were enormous, glazed, green ceramic pots with embossed golden dragons. Each pot contained blooming chrysanthemum, blazing yellow, luscious maroon, and deep purple. The single-level buildings on both sides of the walkway were distinguished by their steep, golden ceramic-tile roofs with upturned ends displaying a miniature dragon at each corner. The rows of glazed tiles glittered in the morning sun, adding to their beauty and magnificence. Behind, more similarly structured roofs of buildings situated on higher grounds rose in sheaves, creating a picture of layered golden hills. Extending over the veranda that wrapped around each building, the roof, like a sculpted canopy, sheltered the windows, the doors, and the bright-red lanterns from the sun and rain. Thick vermilion colonnades, supporting the heavy roof, stood at ten-pace intervals. They provided the final touch of grandeur, befitting the imperial status of the structure. Even the richest Taoist temple in Xian-Hui's hometown, Suzhou, did not come close to matching these structures in beauty and grandeur. Yet, Suzhou was one of the wealthiest cities in the empire because of its thriving silk industry and the fertile soil enriched by the nutrient-laden water from the tributaries of the Yangtzi River. Xian-Hui's curiosity was aroused:

What could the rest of this forbidden city hold in store for her?

With Little Ma leading the way, Xian-Hui turned into an east–west-oriented thoroughfare. Here the surface of the road was paved in rectangular slabs of polished granite. While the chrysanthemum-lined walkway from which she and Little Ma came was twenty paces wide, this thoroughfare reached an astonishing sixty paces in width. It was an impressive boulevard adorned on both sides with large statues of dragons, phoenixes, lions, qilins (unicorns), cranes, and tigers, each one carved from a massive block of white granite. At a distance, Xian-Hui could see a rumble of mandarins, some in official garments with elaborate hats indicating their ranks and some in military outfits without their weapons, crisscrossing the wide thoroughfare, going from one majestic hall to another. A series of similarly designed halls rising into the sky at different heights lined both sides of the thoroughfare. Xian-Hui inferred that they were the buildings in which the emperor and the mandarin officials conducted affairs of the nation.

No sooner had Xian-Hui and Little Ma turned into the thoroughfare than Little Ma gestured that they should climb a wide flight of marble steps on their right. At the top rose a stately pavilion of the same architectural design as all other buildings in the palace, except this one was round, a rotund jewel that stood out among all the rectangular or square buildings on palace grounds. Two elderly eunuchs sitting at the entrance recognized Little Ma and greeted Xian-Hui politely. They retrieved a lantern from a nearby shed. After lighting the lantern and handing it to Little Ma, one of the eunuchs offered a warning in a soft murmur.

"Beware! It's dark inside. The hall is filled with treasures strewn everywhere. The windows do not let in enough light for you to see your way. Make sure that you hold the lanterns in front of you so that you won't trip over precious objects!"

As Little Ma raised his lantern above his head to light the way for Xian-Hui inside the cavernous, dark pavilion, she saw

AN EXTRAORDINARY WOMAN

a hodgepodge of objects, large and small, some on pedestals, some on tables and benches, some just sitting on the floor. There were bronze sculptures, ceramic vessels, textile products, jade and ruby ornaments, taxidermic renditions of strange animals that she had never seen before. Some objects looked like technological instruments. Others looked like contraptions from a fantasy world. On the wall hung numerous wooden plaques of calligraphy and painting. Their color had faded in different gradations. In sum, the inside of this rotund building looked like an abandoned museum with precious objects randomly strewn everywhere.

"This pavilion houses the items of the imperial treasure that no longer catch the emperor's fancy," Little Ma said apologetically. "But His Holy Majesty's lack of interest does not diminish their value. You will find some extremely precious art, rare objects, and bizarre instruments here."

As they began to wander around, two long, curved white objects resting in a silk-lined box on a wooden table caught Xian-Hui's attention. Tapering from a bigger hollow end toward a sharp solid point, the cylindrical objects seemed to be made of coagulated cream.

"What is this?" Xian-Hui asked, as she put her hand on one and felt its cool, sensual surface.

"I don't know," answered Little Ma as they bent over, examining the object.

"Ah, you like ivory," a boy's voice came from behind.

Startled, Xian-Hui and Little Ma turned around. The voice belonged to a large man, pudgy in the cheeks, bulging in the midsection, with eyes like two slits taking flight into his temples. Draped in a scholar's gray robe, he looked middle-aged, kind but authoritative.

"Master Li, greetings!" Little Ma bowed deeply while gesturing at Xian-Hui. "This is concubine Xian-Hui who arrived in the palace two days ago."

LORD GUAN

"I know, I know. I'm delighted that you enjoy His Holy Majesty's toys." The large man smiled and spoke to Xian-Hui in his boyish voice. "Let me tell you what ivory is," he said gently. "It's the tooth of the largest terrestrial animal living in a remote part of the world. This pair is a gift from Pius Antoninus, to our late Emperor Huan, who preceded our Son of Heaven on the dragon throne. Far down south in the jungle where barbarians live, we have a similar animal, only much smaller. These animals are called elephants."

"Thank you, sir, for enlightening us," Xian-Hui responded. "But who is Pius Antoninus?"

"Oh, he was the emperor of a country headquartered in a city called Daqin (Rome), thousands of li to the west, way beyond the Western Regions that were conquered by our great general of the cavalry Ban Chao more than one hundred years ago. Commanding an army of seventy thousand, Ban Chao headed further west after pacifying the oasis kingdoms of the largest desert in our part of the world. They scaled a formidable mountain reaching to the sky, marched continuously for two years while conquering city states and fighting skirmishes with barbarians along the way, until they reached an inland sea. There, on the shore, Ban Chao established a military base, and made peace with a nation called the Parthia. From the Parthians, he learned of their long-standing and more powerful nemesis, the Daqin empire. Eager for direct contact with the government of that legendary empire, Ban Chao dispatched a lieutenant with a detachment of cavalry westward until they came upon a garrison guarding the eastern border of the Daqin empire. Assuring the garrison commander of his peaceful intent, Ban Chao's lieutenant and his soldiers stayed in that Daqin fortress as guests for many days before embarking on their long trek back home. That's how our Han dynasty and the Daqin empire came into contact. Anyway, the Daqin emperor, Pius Antoninus, died twenty-six years ago, in AD 161. He was

AN EXTRAORDINARY WOMAN 141

a wise and accomplished emperor who cultivated a special interest in our part of the world, probably because he was a governor of western Asia before ascending the throne of the Daqin empire. He was succeeded by his adopted son, Marcus Aurelius, seven years before His Holy Majesty, our Emperor Ling, became the Son of Heaven in AD 168. While Emperor Ling still reigns, Marcus Aurelius passed away in AD 180. His son, Lucius Commodus, is Daqin's current reigning emperor. Sadly, Commodus is weak and humdrum, without any ambition and grand design, even though his father, Marcus Aurelius, was magnificent and visionary. A quintessential example of hu fu quan zi, 'tiger father, doggerel son.'

"Commodus showed no interest in our realm," Master Li carried on, "even though we traded with the Daqin empire through the intermediaries of Sogdians and Parthians along the Silk Road. If General Ban Chao were alive and the Han dynasty still prospering, this could have been a golden opportunity for us to take down the Daqin empire."

He, then, mused, as if he were alone, "Then our Son of Heaven would rule all corners under heaven. Wouldn't that be earthshaking!"

But he quickly recovered from his reverie as Xian-Hui spoke.

"I always thought that China was the whole world, and the world was China. I know on the fringes of our empire are the uncivilized Xiongnu (Huns) in the north, hordes of savages in the southern jungle, and many uncultured tribes in the west. But I've never heard of another nation such as Parthia or another empire such as the Daqin. You are so knowledgeable, Master Li. I'm fortunate to make your acquaintance."

"You speak well and learn quickly. How exceptional! I'm just as honored to make your acquaintance," Master Li responded politely.

"Could I ask you more questions, Master Li?"

"Of course! Please!"

"How did Antoninus's embassy travel thousands of li to reach our capital, Luoyang?"

"I don't know the details. But they came by camel caravans traversing enormous deserts and scaling great mountains. Their journey took two years to complete. During that journey, the embassy faced great perils and endured tremendous hardship. Their route nowadays is called the southern Silk Road because via that road, our silk, unknown to people outside of China, reached Daqin through a chain of intermediary traders, and the Daqin people, who admired and coveted silk, bought it with their gold and silver. You should know that both the northern route and the southern route of the Silk Road were mapped out more than two hundred years ago by the intrepid soldier diplomat Zhang Qian at the behest of our illustrious and sagacious Emperor Wu, who reigned for fifty-four years from 141 BC until 87 BC. About one hundred years later, General Ban Chao, guided by the map and instructions provided by Zhang Qian, conquered all the kingdoms along the routes. Both Ban Chao and Zhang Qian played pivotal roles in extending the domain of influence of our Han dynasty westward and southward."

"Oh, yes, Zhang Qian!" Xian-Hui reacted excitedly. "His missions and expeditions are in the celebrated historical treatise *Shiji*, Records of the Grand Historian. I have not yet read the sections that describe his explorations and conquests. But my father told me many stories about Zhang Qian's trailblazing exploits in the Western Regions and central Asia that lasted an astonishing thirteen years."

"You read?" Master Li, lifting his eyebrows, was shocked.

"Yes, I've learned the classics under the tutelage of my father since I was four and I would love to be a poet."

"Truly impressive! You are unique among all the noble concubines. Since you know about Zhang Qian, let me show you something connected to another warrior of our Han dynasty

AN EXTRAORDINARY WOMAN

143

by way of this beautiful bronze horse statue right in front of us, resting on the same table as the ivory tusks."

Xian-Hui noticed that the bronze statue, with its head raised high, lips pursed, mouth slightly agape, and tail raised in an arc not only captured the spirit of a magnificent, spirited horse, but also depicted, in impressive detail, its powerful, muscular physique.

"This is a statue commemorating the beloved heavenly horse belonging to the same illustrious Emperor Wu who commanded Zhang Qian to explore the west. Every morning before attending the affairs of state, the illustrious Emperor Wu practiced his equestrian skill on his heavenly horse. The real horse, also known as a blood-sweating horse because of the reddish tint of its perspiration, was brought back by General Li Guangli from Fergana on the western steppes of the Pamir Mountains. In 103 BC, Emperor Wu ordered General Li Guangli, at the head of an expeditionary army of sixty thousand soldiers, to attack Fergana for a second time. The emperor wanted to punish Fergana for refusing to meet the court's demand for a tribute of one hundred blood-sweating horses. After a yearlong journey, marching nearly eight thousand li, General Li sacked the important city called Samarqand in the heart of Fergana and brought back hundreds of the legendary horses to the great delight of Emperor Wu."

Xian-Hui and Little Ma were spellbound by Master Li's historical anecdotes. Even though Xian-Hui and Little Ma could count themselves as members of the educated elite among more than fifty million people in the Han empire, they had no idea of the extent of the Han dynasty's glorious past. They had heard of the legendary Emperor Wu. They knew that the Han empire at various times was powerful and prosperous and extended far beyond the great plains of the Yellow River basin and the Yangtzi River basin. But in their lifetime, the Han empire was besieged by internal rebellions and barbarian invasions. It was teetering toward collapse. Xian-Hui and Little Ma were heartened to learn from Master Li some of the old glories of the Han dynasty.

Lifted by his own account of earlier Han military conquests, Master Li wanted to show Xian-Hui and Little Ma other glorious achievements of the Han dynasty. He guided the two to a corner table on which a beautiful lacquer box held a book consisting of a stack of yellowish paper artfully sewn together.

"This is the first paper book in our country, presented to the late Emperor An about seventy years ago, commemorating the invention of paper." Master Li cleared his throat. "Yes, paper, a mundane material that you and I take for granted nowadays. I cannot overstate its importance! The inventor was one of my illustrious predecessors in the palace, Master Cai Lun. Before Cai Lun, all books were made of bamboo slats on which each word must be carved. As a pile of bamboo slats, a book was cumbersome and heavy. A person could not carry even one book with him. Cai Lun's invention of paper enabled the application of rubbing in bookmaking."

"Pardon me for interrupting, Master Li." Xian-Hui couldn't contain her curiosity. "What is rubbing?"

"First, a scribe writes the left-right inverse of every word of a book onto bamboo slats." Master Li smiled patiently. "A skilled carver then carves away a quarter of an inch of the surface of each bamboo slat, leaving the strokes of the words standing like ridges. With ink spread on the ridges, you can press a sheet of paper on the bamboo slat to produce one page of a book instantly. When all the pages of a book have been produced by rubbing, they are sewn together as a book."

Like a natural spring, Master Li's train of thought, once spouting, couldn't stop. He carried on his narrative: "The technology of rubbing makes it possible to produce multiple copies of a book. To make a long story short, Cai Lun's invention laid the foundation for improving literacy and facilitating teaching. It also spawned a booming new trade across our country,

AN EXTRAORDINARY WOMAN 145

involving traveling salesmen, each of whom is accompanied by a train of donkeys carrying sacks of paper, ink, and books carved in inverted logographs on bamboo slats. They are the traveling bookstores on donkey backs. When a client wishes to purchase a book, the traveling salesman produces a copy for the customer on the spot in a matter of a few hours. Thanks to Master Cai Lun, we can now carry a book in one hand wherever we go. I assume that your father's books are made of paper, noble concubine."

"Yes, all our books at home are made of paper. But they are not as beautifully bound as this one made by the inventor of paper."

As Xian-Hui turned the book cover, a thin wooden plate wrapped in silk embroidered with a dragon, she instantly recognized what the book was. The pleasure of recognition led her to exclaim, "This is *The Book of Odes*, the collection of lyrical poems dating as far back as one thousand years ago."

She remembered chanting those poems as her father struck a chime to produce the musical note that matched the tone of each syllable. Each line of every poem consisted of four single-syllable characters, for all 305 poems in the book. She had learned most of them at the knee of her father, who explained each word, described each symbol, clarified each metaphor, and illuminated the theme of each poem in his effort to provide her with a context for understanding *The Book of Odes*. The memory transported her back to those happy times, in the courtyard of her home, willows swinging in the wind, finches darting among the branches, where she studied and recited the poems, in sync with her father's chime: four chimes, a pause; four chimes, a pause; she whirled around blissfully, recalling her father's face brimming with pride at her impeccable mnemonic prowess. Lost in her reminiscence, she started reciting the first stanza of *The Book of Odes*, almost like singing a lullaby:

Guan guan ji qiu, (The ospreys screech,)
zai he zhi zhou. (over the islet in the river.)
Miao tiao shu nü, (The shapely, demure maiden)
jun zi hao qiu. (makes a gentleman shiver.)

"Brava, brava!" Master Li applauded. "You ought to be a poet! You are a poet!"

Jolted out of her reverie, Xian-Hui felt a surge of tears in her eyes. Partly to conceal them and partly in contrition of her sudden, uninvited display, she bowed as if she had committed an offense for showing off her knowledge. The bow helped her to recover her composure, leaving only a slight trace of sadness and some embarrassment on her face.

"Now that you have seen the first paper book of the world," Master Li intoned, "you should also see the original copy of the first dictionary of our written language compiled around eighty years ago. This dictionary contains more than nine thousand entries listed under five hundred and forty radicals."

"Here it is, the first copy of *Shuowen Jiezi*." Master Li found the dictionary in a nearby corner, an enormous pile of dark bamboo slats. "Look at this pile and you will immediately appreciate the importance of the invention of paper! This dictionary was compiled before Cai Lun invented paper. I am not demeaning the significance of the dictionary, which is, of course, a monumental achievement. Indeed, it represents the splendor of our Han dynasty. But as you can see from this heap of bamboo slats, without paper, few people could use it, and even fewer could own it. Now it is a dictionary available across our country in a stack of paper sewn together, weighing less than two catties." Master Li unknowingly raised his voice, betraying the pride he took in recounting Cai Lun's singular invention.

As the group navigated their way among treasures randomly stored in the hall, Master Li announced enthusiastically as he led them to a shiny, bronze object that looked like an urn.

AN EXTRAORDINARY WOMAN

"Let me show you a different kind of treasure." Master Li pointed at the bronze contraption. It looked like a large sphere sitting on a tapered stand. On the surface of the upper sphere protruded eight evenly spaced longitudinal handles, each of which was an upside-down dragon. Each dragon faced a free-standing bronze toad with its mouth agape. The very top of the sphere was a circular plate with a nodule. The plate looked conspicuously like a pot cover.

"This is not a large pot for cooking soup, or a jug for holding wine, or an urn for burning incense," Master Li said with a smile. "It is a scientific instrument of great significance, called a seismograph, invented by Zhang Heng less than sixty years ago. I don't know if you have heard of Zhang Heng. He was a polymath, an incomparable genius. In addition to his numerous inventions, he also discovered, through intricate mathematical study of the movements of celestial bodies, that the light emanating from the moon reflected the light from the sun. Everyone thought the moon was a shining star, until Zhang Heng proved that it merely reflected the light of the sun."

Spellbound, Xian-Hui and Little Ma felt like two wide-eyed pupils in a hallowed pantheon of learning as they listened attentively to Master Li. Neither had expected their casual, ad hoc excursion to turn into a lesson of appreciation of the inventions and intellectual achievements during the Han dynasty. They were grateful to the master.

"Let me tell you how the seismograph works." Master Li's voice was brimming with excitement. "If an earthquake strikes our country at a distant location, even several hundred li away from Luoyang, this seismograph is capable of not only detecting the quake but also indicating its direction from our capital by having the longitudinal dragon closest to that direction disgorge a small metallic ball into the mouth of the gaping toad.

"What you see here is the original version of the seismograph invented by Zhang Heng. He built it with his own hands. In the Hall of Virtue, where high officials conduct affairs of the state, there is a new version forged from silver. It's there because the government needs to know when and where an earthquake strikes a part of our country, so that aid can be sent to that location without delay."

"Is this inventor the same Zhang Heng who laid down the canons of the metric system for writing poetry?" Xian-Hui queried.

"Yes, that's him. Poetry happens to be another dimension of his talent. That's why he has the reputation of being a polymath, a universal genius, pushing forward the frontiers of mathematics, astronomy, and technology, as well as literature," Master Li replied.

Little Ma had expected Master Li, being his teacher and having served more than forty years in the palace, to be knowledgeable. But he could not anticipate Xian-Hui's erudition and intellectual acuity. At age thirteen, he had just begun to learn the classics under the tutelage of Master Li. Aspiring to become a scholar, he thought only males could become learned. Never had he met an inquisitive and knowledgeable young female like Xian-Hui. But he was beyond awed by Xian-Hui's intellectual precociousness. The way she spoke and the way she conducted herself, which conveyed both confidence and modesty, was more impressive than anyone he had met, except for Master Li, whom he revered. Even though he barely knew her, he began to idolize her to the point of endowing her with magical qualities. He looked at her adoringly. In his eyes, she was beautiful and magnificent, like the incomparable peony in full bloom. It was not her fragrance and femininity that attracted him. Such things escaped his perception. Having been castrated at age twelve, he had not experienced and would never experience romantic love. But the castration did not prevent him from yearning for the joy and warmth of bonding with a person he adored, especially when the person happened to belong to his generation. It was a primal yearning unaffected by the physical devastation inflicted on him, a yearning for human connection beyond carnal desire and across the gender divide. He was drawn to her by her intellect, her composure, and her vivacious spirit. Her attractiveness was further enhanced by a reassuring kindness. He felt an avalanche of feelings for her. It would be heavenly to have her in his family, he thought, a family that he would like to establish someday even though siring children was beyond his reach. He had no idea how he could attain that goal. But he was sure of one thing: his family would be different from the family headed by his father and mother who forced him to become a eunuch less than two years ago. The memory of being pinned down by four men who held his limbs apart, and experiencing the searing pain, as if someone repeatedly applied a red-hot iron at his crotch, continued to haunt him in his nightmares. He remained incontinent most of the time, leaking urine at the most inopportune moments. The embarrassment and humiliation of wetting his pants were as excruciating as being forced to undergo the mutilation by knife. To date, he couldn't bear to look down at his crotch. Of course, there was nothing to look at other than scars and a tiny orifice that still tormented him periodically with a burning sensation when urine dribbled through. All the appendages in that part of his body, the scrotum, the penis, had been lopped off.

He understood that he owed his life to his parents, and filial piety required him to be obedient to them. But he felt that they had already extracted from him most, if not all, of what he owed them. After the ordeal of castration, he came within a thread of death from fever and infection. Recovery marked the beginning of a new life, even though he had no inkling of what the new life had in store for him. He felt that the life given to him by his parents had slipped into the past, and he wanted it to stay that way so that he could pursue a new life peacefully and freely. Yes, if he came to great wealth someday, he would give his parents a share of that wealth in the spirit of filial piety. But he no longer felt the warmth of kinship or the affection of attachment to his parents as he now began to feel toward Xian-Hui. The sentiments stemming from and nourished by affectionate familial ties normally brimmed with trust, adoration, and a sense of belonging. They conferred strength to an individual, defined one's identity, and helped to shape one's mission in life. Those sentiments had left Little Ma. Like a ship lost at sea, he had been adrift emotionally for nearly two years, feeling infinitely lonely. Now, suddenly, he wished to hitch his fate to a young imperial concubine whom he barely knew. He was aware that such a wish, which emerged so unexpectedly, quickly, and almost inexplicably, was inappropriate and even preposterous. But he didn't choose the wish. It was not something he planned for, not a goal that he established through either logical reasoning or premeditation. The wish rose from the depths of his heart. A mysterious and powerful force drove him to adore Xian-Hui. He was painfully aware that he needed to keep his wish a secret, yet he couldn't refrain from looking at Xian-Hui longingly, until Master Li interrupted his dreamlike adoration with the announcement that he had to leave with Little Ma for an important assignment.

"I wish I had more time to show you around, honorable concubine. But duty calls and Little Ma must come with me," Master Li said to Xian-Hui apologetically.

"I wish the same. There is so much I can learn from you, Master Li. Thank you very much for your kindness and generosity."

"Now, we will escort you back." Master Li gestured in the direction of her chamber.

"Oh, there is no need. It's only a short distance. I know how to go back."

"No," Master Li said firmly. "This is not a safe place. We would be remiss if we didn't escort you to your chamber."

AN EXTRAORDINARY WOMAN

"We're in the palace. It must be the safest place in the empire!" Xian-Hui countered innocently.

Master Li laughed, his head tossed back, and his torso bent in the same direction, as if he were searching for stars in the sky. When he straightened up, his laughter stopped abruptly and his face turned somber, with a tinge of sadness.

"More murders and atrocities are committed here, in the imperial palace, the forbidden city, than anywhere else in the empire. Everyone here, members of the imperial family included, is in danger of being murdered. People in the palace are always vigilant and fearful. When access to ultimate power, the power of the imperial throne, is at stake, nothing matters, not decency, not morality, not even familial relationships. A father may kill his son and a son may murder his parents. Such mayhem only happens in the palace. Well, I *hope* it only happens in the palace."

Mater Li paused as he reflected on his own words.

"I hope the Confucian code of ethics upholding familial relationships is not violated elsewhere under heaven, and the palace represents an anomaly. Let me tell you about the gory death of a Han imperial consort, who lost a struggle to place her son on the throne some years in the past. Normally, a condemned consort is put to death by strangulation, and members of her clan, if the crime involved treason, would die by beheading. But this consort's rival, who happened to be the empress dowager, showed a theatrical fair in her cruelty and vindictiveness. After successfully installing her own son on the throne, she ordered a gruesome menu of punishment for the consort, her vanquished opponent. First, the guards gouged out the victim's eyes. Then, they cut off her nose, ears, lips, hands, and feet. Finally, while the victim was writhing in agony but still alive, they tossed her into a pigsty as fodder for the voracious animals.

"Now, anywhere in the nation, the perpetrator of such atrocities would be put to death by a thousand cuts. In the palace, this gruesome incident is just mundane, collateral damage of power struggles, and power struggles never cease to occupy the center stage in the imperial palace.

"I don't mean to frighten you, noble concubine," Master Li continued. "But you should know that death always hovers nearby in the palace. You will learn. In the meantime, Little Ma and I are late for our assignment. Please let us walk you back."

Xian-Hui returned to her chamber, shocked and chastened by Master Li's conflicting messages. Their encounter began with a narrative of the marvels of the Han dynasty, delivered with unbridled enthusiasm and genuine sincerity, but ended with a warning, amplified by the bloodcurdling atrocities committed in the palace, the home of the Son of Heaven. She resolved to learn more about the history of Han to understand its glory and folly. At the same time, she was relieved that Master Li, by condemning the horror of the palace intrigues, had cast aspersions on a fundamental tenet of the Confucian ethic: blind obedience to your sovereign. She needed that psychological lift, inadvertently proffered by Master Li, because she had already, in her heart, rejected the role of an imperial concubine. She stared at the solemn calligraphy, zhong, "loyalty and devotion to your sovereign," on the wall in her chamber. It still carried a ton of weight, but it began to look less intimidating.

"Well, I have a lot to learn," she reflected. "But I'll start with the practical issues. First, I must find out how the palace works and who its denizens are."

That evening, she began firing questions at Little Ma when he brought her dinner. He answered her questions eagerly to the best of his knowledge. She found out that the palace held 458 concubines, more than six hundred eunuchs, and close to twelve hundred maidservants. She wanted to know about the man on the throne, Emperor Ling, who was the reason for her being brought into the palace. But Little Ma demurred, "You should ask Master Li about His Holy Majesty. Master Li knows everything.

"One thing I do know about the Son of Heaven," Little Ma added with a smile, "is that if and when he favors you with his presence one night, all the red lanterns outside of your chamber will be ablaze."

Xian-Hui bit her lip, fighting back the anger and indignation that surged and churned inside her.

Men only think of women as their daughters, wives, concubines, mothers. In short, we, females, are nothing but appendages of men. Even castration does not spare a man from viewing women as appendages, she thought to herself. But I shouldn't blame Little Ma. He could not possibly understand that I consider such a "favor" from the emperor the ultimate violation and travesty.

I will escape! Thoughts began to race through her mind. After all, there are four hundred and fifty-seven other concubines, all of whom are young and beautiful, and most, if not all, would connive and do anything to become the recipient of the emperor's favor. They understand that a concubine could ascend to power and prestige only if she gave birth to a son. They are content to be man's appendage. I do not share their mentality. I must leave, get out of this prison! In the meantime, I'd better make myself inconspicuous and unworthy of any favor to the eunuchs who choose concubines for the emperor every day.

As Xian-Hui's mind churned, she tactfully changed the topic of her conversation with Little Ma.

"Is Master Li an honest and upright person?" Xian-Hui looked at Little Ma intently.

"Oh, yes! On that point, I can vouch with absolute confidence. Only a righteous man like him could have survived in the palace for forty-some years without being poisoned or executed.

Power and money do not interest him. Staying clear of intrigues in the palace and shying away from cliques that vie for power, he seeks solace in the pursuit of knowledge, although he is generous enough to devote a good part of his time and energy to disseminating his knowledge and wisdom to young eunuchs like me. His erudition is universally acknowledged. Even the emperor appreciates his encyclopedic mind. He tutored the two sons of the emperor before they were sent away for the sake of their safety. The court regularly seeks his advice on issues and policies concerning the Western Regions. It's rumored that he reads several exotic languages and speaks Sogdian, the most common language used by the traders of the caravans along the Silk Road."

"Yes, I can see he is very learned in my brief encounter with him." Xian-Hui nodded her head. "I am glad that he is a good man. Do you think it is possible for me to learn from him regularly?"

"Let's find out. Tomorrow morning, he will teach me the centerpiece of Confucius's thought, *Daxue, The Great Learning*. Let's go together. I am sure that your presence will please him."

"Wonderful!" Xian-Hui began to feel a little cheerful. But she wanted to steer the conversation back to palace politics: "A while ago, you mentioned palace intrigues and cliques vying for power. Who are the people involved in those intrigues?"

"I don't really know." Little Ma hesitated. "All I can tell you is that the most powerful man here is the eunuch Jian Shuo. I have hardly laid eyes on him. According to rumors…"

Little Ma looked behind himself uncomfortably to make sure that no one was lurking about.

He then lowered his voice. "According to rumors, Jian Shuo acts like a surrogate emperor. Emperor Ling, I understand, does not like his official duties. Delegating his authority to Jian Shuo most of the time, the emperor prefers not to deal with affairs of the state. Even personnel decisions, such as the appointment of high-level government officials, often fall into Jian's hand. Over the years, Jian managed to place many members of his clan as senior eunuchs and powerful officials of the court. They form the core of a clique that dominates both the government and the palace. Beyond his clansmen, Jian commands the loyalty of many other officials and eunuchs who choose to serve him because of their own greed and cowardice. He owns tens of thousands of acres of prime agricultural land not far from the capital. With his money, he buys adherents and allies."

"How many eunuchs belong to Jian's core group?" Xian-Hui pressed on.

"Somewhere between thirty and forty. Almost all of them are related to each other as brothers, nephews, and cousins. Many of them joined the service as adults. Some are married and have children. Imagine a grown man with a wife and a family willing to suffer the knife and all the consequences to become a eunuch for the sake of gaining wealth and power!"

Little Ma had a pained look on his face as he continued: "You know, if you run into a eunuch with a deep voice, shifty eyes, and oozing sycophancy, you will have, most likely, met a relative of Jian's. They have a man's low voice because they were castrated in their adulthood. Jian's kinsmen are always exceptionally charming. You must beware of their facades and slippery tongues! They cultivate anyone and everyone who has the potential to access power. You never know, one day you might become the emperor's favorite concubine. They know that they should cultivate you early in your career."

For a moment, Little Ma's words, *become the emperor's favorite concubine*, stung Xian-Hui like yellow jackets. But she kept her composure, because she understood that Little Ma did not mean to hurt her. He was probably complimenting her when he said that. Instead of showing her annoyance, she smiled, as Little Ma continued his narrative on palace politics.

"Jian and his kinsmen are so skilled at being obsequious that they have elevated flattery into an art form. They wield it as a powerful and effective instrument to advance themselves and gain what they want. I suspect that Jian personally trains his people to perfect their art of flattery. It's probably the reason behind his refusal to let Master Li, the official in charge of educating eunuchs, teach his clansmen. They are, if you can imagine, so good at flattery that they could likely coax a crouching tiger to emerge meekly from its lair or a flying crane to descend gleefully from the sky. Even a sitting emperor willingly yields his authority to the honeyed tongues of those obsequious jackals!"

Little Ma's sudden rhetorical flair surprised Xian-Hui. She thought it was entertaining. At the same time, she knew that he was venting his feelings. But Little Ma was not done.

"Of course, when a person becomes a sycophant, he also acquires the persona of a bully. Sycophants and bullies are inseparable twins, mirror images of each other. In my interactions with members of Jian's gang, I have learned that the more polished the sycophant, the more viciously he bullies people below him in ranks. Just the other day, one of them slapped me for not bowing to him deeply enough. As a novice eunuch, I am, you know, nobody, and I have nothing of value to them. So, they treat me like a doormat."

Suddenly, Little Ma's voice took on a solemn and beseeching tone: "You must never repeat to anyone what I just told you, because if you do, my head will roll in no time! One never knows who or where Jian's spies are. I am putting my life on the line by telling you these things. I want to protect you, but you must not betray me."

Xian-Hui was touched by Little Ma's display of trust in her. Although she did not expect it, she was not surprised. She sensed a spontaneous loyalty and a kindred spirit in this young boy since she'd first laid eyes on him shortly after her arrival at the palace, and she was grateful to him for trusting her.

"I promise I will never repeat to anyone what you told me. Thank you for favoring me with your trust and thank you for your friendship. I want to be your friend too."

Tears began to well up in his eyes when Little Ma heard what Xian-Hui said, especially the words *I want to be your friend too.* She was so candid and spoke so unpretentiously. Her words made him feel that his secret wish of establishing a familial bond with Xian-Hui might not be too far-fetched and preposterous after all.

As he lowered his head to hide his teary eyes, Little Ma figured that he had made significant progress toward realizing his goal of becoming connected, in some manner, with Xian-Hui. It strengthened his resolve to serve Xian-Hui and enabled him to swallow his tears quickly.

The next morning, Xian-Hui, fresh from a good night of sleep, was primed to meet Master Li for the second time. She wanted to learn more from him about palace politics, but she also looked forward to a discourse on Confucius's *Daxue, The Great Learning.* She had studied it under her father's tutelage and knew its importance in Confucian philosophy.

When Little Ma and Xian-Hui arrived at Master Li's study, the door was wide open, suggesting that he was anticipating his pupil. A square, midsize room, the study was as functional as it was austere. There was no silk, no lacquered furnishings, no paintings or sculptures, no elaborate decoration, and no precious stone. Other than the book cabinets that lined three walls of the room, the only furniture consisted of a small table and several wooden chairs. The fourth side of the room had two large windows through which the sun was pouring in. As Xian-Hui and

Little Ma tiptoed into the room, Master Li was standing by the windows, gazing at the palace grounds.

Their footsteps jarred him from his thoughts, and he wheeled around.

"Ah, good morning to you, noble concubine. What brought you here?"

"Little Ma told me that you are offering a lesson to him today on the most important work of Confucius. Without seeking your permission beforehand, I'm tagging along. Am I intruding, Master Li?"

"No, no, no. On the contrary, your presence honors me. But a noble concubine does not need to learn from an old bibliophile. There are senior noble concubines who can enlighten you on matters that are completely beyond my grasp. Such matters may be more important than pedantry."

Having been reassured of Master Li's moral integrity by Little Ma, Xian-Hui decided to take a chance and spoke boldly to him.

"Master Li, what you call *matters that are beyond your grasp* do not interest me. I am, if I may be forthright, *not* born to be a concubine. Let me be honest. I prefer to be a poet."

Xian-Hui's sudden confession of her aspiration, which flirted with treason, startled Master Li, while her courage and ambition commanded his admiration.

"Did you not consent to be an imperial concubine?" Master Li queried.

"No, certainly *not*! No one asked for my consent. I was plucked from my home in Suzhou, stuffed into a hansom, and brought to Luoyang, where I was transferred to a palanquin and carried into the palace. All against my wishes."

"I am so sorry." Master Li shook his head. "It's unfortunate that my colleagues did not seek your consent. Eager to please the Son of Heaven, some of them take matters into their own hands and ignore the proper procedure. They think they know best. Unfortunately, I have no influence on them and cannot reverse their actions. But I will be delighted to guide you in your intellectual pursuit."

"Thank you so much, Master Li. I am deeply grateful to you for your kindness and generosity." Xian-Hui bowed deeply.

For the first time since her capture by the eunuchs, she felt that her life had turned a corner. There was a glimmer of hope. She had found two potential allies in two dramatically different people: Little Ma and Master Li. What they had in common was decency and kindness. In addition, both seemed to be genuinely fond of her.

In the meantime, Master Li turned his attention to his pupil.

"Now, Little Ma, let's begin our lesson. Have you been studying *The Great Learning*? What can you tell me about it?"

"I've devoted a good amount of time perusing the book." Little Ma responded respectfully, "There are many vocabulary items that I need you to explain. So far, my impression is that the book focuses on how a prince or a sovereign can rule wisely and how a monarch can create harmony under heaven. I fail to see its relevance to ordinary folks like me."

"It is true that the sovereign holds the key to a harmonious state, because he sets the example for the empire," Master Li responded. "But if the sovereign is the only virtuous one, harmony will not prevail under heaven. The root of a harmonious state derives from the cultivation of moral character at the mass level, because cultivation of moral character promotes a healthy family life, a healthy family life serves as the foundation to a civil society, a civil society leads to a robust government, and a robust government guides a nation into a state of harmony. The teaching of *The Great Learning* applies not just to a prince or a king, it implies that every human being bears the responsibility of acquiring virtue, and virtue entails the caring for humanity, the nurturing of family, the understanding of the world, the acquisition of knowledge, the sincerity of thoughts, and the rectification of the heart. That's why this book is entitled *Daxue*,

The Great Learning. It urges us to follow a path of perfecting ourselves in life by becoming virtuous. Bear in mind, the opening sentence, set in four phrases, yields the incipit, daxue, as well as its theme:

> *Da xue zhi dao (The way to the great learning*
> *begins with)*
> *Zai ming ming de (understanding and illuminating*
> *the illustrious virtue,)*
> *Zai qin min (loving and renovating humanity.)*
> *Zai zhi yu zhi shan (It ends with ultimate kindness*
> *and benevolence.)*

The rest of the book elaborates on this theme."

Master Li paused for a moment and continued: "Virtue, in Confucius's thought, has nothing to do with the supernatural. One does not have to rely on some fictitious, omnipotent being to become virtuous. In other words, virtue belongs to this world: this concrete, practical world inhabited by humans and other sentient beings; it does not need or presuppose supernatural beings. This is a fundamental philosophical canon articulated by Confucius. It stands apart from Taoism and other schools of thought, which invoke the concept of God to justify their leaders' actions. Often, the invocation of God is a cover-up of immoral behavior, an excuse for insincere thoughts, or a justification, a ruse for corruption, duplicity, inhumanity, and transgressions. A glaring example is the Yellow Turban Rebellion that is currently plaguing our country with insurrection, murdering, and looting. They claim that God is on their side, that they have been chosen by God to replace the Han dynasty. Let's make no mistake about it. What's called a god's will is always some person's will, whether that will and its invocation happen to have crystallized in the person's conscious or unconscious mind. Like everything belonging to humans, a so-called god's will can be good or bad. The god's will invoked by the leader of the Yellow Turban Rebels, for instance, is horrendously evil. The beauty of the Confucian thought is that it dispenses with the notion of god. It offers guidance to our daily behavior based on common sense and universal human needs."

Xian-Hui took to heart every word of what Master Li said. She felt that the master's brief exposition had encapsulated and clarified the essence of *Daxue, The Great Learning*. Her father, whom she loved and admired, couldn't have done better.

"Now, let's go through your vocabulary. Next time, you will have to tell me about Confucius's elaboration of the theme of *The Great Learning*."

Then Master Li beckoned to Little Ma, "When we finish with the vocabulary of the book, the floor will belong to Xian-Hui."

She was overjoyed, not only at the prospect of being granted an opportunity to articulate her own thoughts but also at being addressed by her name. For the first time, the master didn't use the term *noble concubine* to refer to her. It signaled that he no longer maintained an officious facade in her company and perhaps he empathized with her in her objection to being a concubine.

After some time, during which Xian-Hui sat patiently as Master Li taught Little Ma the new vocabulary in *The Great Learning*, Master Li looked in Xian-Hui's direction.

"Now, let Xian-Hui speak."

"Thank you for your enlightening dissection of *The Great Learning*. I will always remember that an ideal state rests on moral principles and morality is every person's concern. That is the essence of Confucius's thought. Everyone must strive to live ethically without succumbing to the allure of wealth and power. Greed and avarice are at the root of human evil." Xian-Hui leaned forward in her chair and looked straight at Master Li. "Your explanation is both edifying and illuminating. I would love to be your pupil. Could I come again with Little Ma?"

"You'll be most welcome. But you should not spend too much time with me, so as not to arouse any suspicion or incite malicious rumor. Of course, you can always join Little Ma when he has his weekly lesson. Today Little Ma will introduce you to a few of your sister concubines, those who have earned our respect for their probity. Even though I understand your disdain for mundane matters in the palace, I think you have much to learn from some of your fellow concubines."

"Thank you, Master Li. It was arrogant of me to dismiss all concubines so callously and so casually when we first met. You have my apology. I was merely venting my indignation at my captors when I said I didn't care to learn from other concubines."

Xian-Hui was glad to have the opportunity to make amends for her intemperate pronouncements when she first met Master Li. On reflection of her own behavior, she became aware that she had been recklessly indiscreet in her interaction with the master. She understood that her indiscretion was a consequence of her fury at being made an imperial concubine. If Master Li were not a compassionate and empathetic man, her outburst could have resulted in her death. Master Li's graceful reaction to her sentiment confirmed what Little Ma had told her. The master differed from other eunuchs who would betray anyone and commit any atrocity to seek career advancement. Considering that Master Li was a cautious and reserved senior eunuch, she began to think that it would be proper to wait for a propitious time before asking him questions about the palace politics. At the end of the lesson, she bowed to the master, bade him farewell, and left with Little Ma.

Upon Xian-Hui's departure, Master Li examined their interaction. He felt sorry for her predicament, but her intelligence, courage, and sincerity left an indelible impression on him. Fully aware that she risked her life by revealing her feelings to him, he felt somewhat protective of her. In his view, a courageous, independent, and inquisitive mind like hers should be nurtured.

He took solace in the fact that Little Ma was assigned to be her attendant, an arrangement in which he played no role. He knew Little Ma was his loyal acolyte, well-informed but uninvolved in palace intrigue for power, and felt comfortable with the arrangement, because being Xian-Hui's attendant, Little Ma would be a valuable and trustworthy ally for Xian-Hui to navigate all the dangers and treacheries in the palace.

Much to Master Li's surprise in the weeks that followed, Xian-Hui displayed an emotional and intellectual maturity beyond expectation of a person of her age. Astute and savvy, she had an uncanny instinct to avoid the unscrupulous without being offensive. Never expressing an opinion on any person or issue, she listened attentively and spoke sparingly in her interactions with others. Unlike every other concubine who sought attention at all times, she preferred to keep a low profile and seemed content to be an inconspicuous member of the emperor's harem. Once a week, she faithfully attended Little Ma's lesson with the master. Her participation enriched the intellectual discourse and benefited all three of them. Sometimes, Master Li took such pleasure in her inquisitiveness and cognitive dexterity that he neglected his primary duty of tutoring Little Ma.

Xian-Hui enjoyed the weekly lesson even more than Master Li did. It reminded her of her happy days with her father. More importantly, it provided her a venue for winning the master's trust. She wanted him to be an avuncular ally and a source of information, without expecting him to offer her a helping hand in her mission to escape. He was a venerable, if powerless, fixture in the palace. Xian-Hui understood that for him to help a concubine escape would be a betrayal of the institution with which he identified. She would never burden him with such a treasonous plot. The mission to escape was hers and hers only. She intended to plumb his knowledge of the emperor and the palace, and she wanted to make sure that he would not hold anything back if she asked him the questions that had been on her mind ever since her arrival in the palace. When the opportunity arrived, she couched her question in Confucian ethics.

"Master Li, I have some burning questions, practical questions about the palace. In the spirit of *The Great Learning* by Confucius, I would claim that my questions are critical to my pursuit of moral certitude."

"Well, I'll do my best to give you answers. But you must bear in mind that I am just an old bookworm, hardly a savant of the affairs in the palace."

"Can you briefly tell me about His Holy Majesty and the way he functions as a ruler? As an ordinary citizen, I've never seen the Son of Heaven and never heard him talk. When he and his entourage leave the palace, citizens are required to avoid looking at him. It is strange that I don't have the faintest idea of the man to whom I belong as a concubine. I don't know what he looks like, I don't know his personality, I don't know his worldview, and I don't know what he likes or dislikes."

"If I answer your questions," Master Li began, "do I have your word of honor that my answer will never be revealed to anyone else? Of course, Little Ma here is like a son. He knows my heart."

"You have my word of honor. That's the least I can do. You have already given me so much. I am forever indebted to you."

Without any further ado, Master Li began to summarize the history of Emperor Ling's reign.

"Emperor Ling is a descendant of Emperor Zhang, who reigned more than a century ago, between AD 76 and 89. Before ascending the dragon throne at age twelve, Emperor Ling held the title of marquess of Jieting. When the preceding emperor, Emperor Huan, died in AD 168 without an heir, his wife, the empress dowager, became the regent. Shrewd and unscrupulous, she chose as emperor the marquess of Jieting, a pampered minor without vision, grand design, or a good education, so that she could corral power in her own hands and place members of her clan in critical positions in government. As the empress dowager and members of her natal family took steps to monopolize imperial authority, she advised the young emperor to indulge his senses and pay no attention to affairs of the state. He gladly accepted her advice and was content to be a titular Son of Heaven."

Master Li paused. He wanted to scrutinize Xian-Hui's reaction and make sure, once more, that his trust in her was not misplaced, because his words were treasonous. She sat impassively without a word, her facial expression neutral, and her eyes fixed on the master, just like an attentive and studious pupil. After the cautious old eunuch was satisfied that Xian-Hui could not harbor any intention to harm him, he carried on.

"But the empress dowager's attempt to concentrate power in her natal family alarmed and irked those politically ambitious eunuchs who had been accustomed to exercising their influence through their proximity to the Son of Heaven. An intense and ferocious rivalry between the political eunuchs and the empress dowager's faction ensued. It ended in a palace coup during which my fellow eunuchs slaughtered their enemies, including the empress dowager and her entire clan, young and old, male and female. I must confess that I supported the coup as a reaction to an earlier plot hatched by the dowager's father to kill the leading eunuchs. The coup took place almost twenty years ago. At the time, as an immature eunuch, I had not risen beyond the simple-minded view that the world was divided in black versus white, good versus evil, us versus them. I was unable to appreciate the shades of gray in human affairs, the merit of moderation, the importance of diversity, and the futility of revenge. The bloodshed and atrocity brought on by the coup opened my eyes to the folly of vendetta and extreme reaction. I've regretted supporting it ever since. Nothing justifies murder. Yet, twenty years ago, I was an accessory to murder. From that point on, I've eschewed politics and devoted myself to scholarship.

"Let me return to our Son of Heaven, Emperor Ling, a benevolent person who, as I said, never showed any interest in government as a minor. Well, he came of age many years ago, but remains unchanged even though he has already been on the dragon throne for nineteen years. Faithfully and willingly abiding by the late empress dowager's advice to stay aloof from the affairs of the state, His Holy Majesty's interest lies in the indulgence of the senses... Well, you will find out from the concubines you know. With an indolent emperor, my power-hungry and greedy colleagues have, once again, hijacked the throne. Today, they dominate the court and rule the nation in the name of the emperor. Cunning and treacherous, they have instituted heavy taxation that drives the peasantry into destitution. Their insatiable greed and corrupt practices have depleted the national treasury. Their harsh and brutal policies have pushed the people, out of desperation, into rebellion. For sure, the leaders of the Yellow Turban Rebellion are treasonous snakes. But their call for rebellion would have fallen on deaf ears if the ordinary folks in the country had not been reduced to unspeakable misery and abject hunger by the rapacious policies of my colleagues. Those eunuchs use flattery and their physical proximity to the emperor to discredit the enlightened policies recommended by the loyal officials in the government. They are a curse to the Han dynasty. Sadly, and unfortunately, we are witnessing a precipitous decline of the greatest empire on earth. The recent earthquakes and drought are ominous harbingers of the end of a dynasty."

Master Li sighed. He would have gone on recounting a litany of shame and disasters in the country, had he not checked himself because of his concern for being overheard. At his age, he cared little about his own life, but did not wish to endanger the safety of his two young friends.

From his seat, he looked out at the golden roofs of palace buildings, glittering under the sun, displaying the glory of the

AN EXTRAORDINARY WOMAN

great Han dynasty that had survived for nearly four hundred years other than a brief interlude when Wang Mang, a relative of an imperial consort, usurped the throne.

So magnificent, yet so precarious!

He felt exhausted by his own pessimism and dire prediction, like a veteran sailor with tied hands watching his cavalier and inept captain steer their ship into a gathering storm. The pending doom exasperated and depressed him. Yet he couldn't refrain from calling for retribution for the evildoers.

"My nefarious colleagues in the palace, wallowing in their intrigues and luxuriating in their wealth, will pay for their crimes and venal schemes sooner or later. There will be a rude awakening."

Following his prediction of retribution for the crimes of the eunuchs, Master Li admonished his two pupils, "You two are pure and uncontaminated. I hope you will always follow the way of *The Great Learning*."

Xian-Hui had not expected such a gloomy assessment of the empire. She was shielded from poverty by her landowning father who, unlike many other landowners, treated his tenant farmers with decency. She had heard of rebellions, especially the Yellow Turbans'. Three years ago, they laid waste to most of the northeastern region of the nation and came close to threatening her home in the Yangtzi River basin until their senior leader was killed in a battle with the imperial army. Her father, a member of the Confucian intelligentsia, considered the Yellow Turbans a horde of ignorant and superstitious renegades beguiled by a few flimflam men, who professed to be Taoist prophets and miracle workers designated by God to implement an apocalyptic change. Xian-Hui remembered that her father threw a banquet for his friends and tenant farmers to celebrate the death of the senior Yellow Turban leader. But the death of a self-appointed prophet had not ended the rebellion. Pockets of marauding Yellow Turbans, who no longer possessed the military strength to sack a city defended by imperial garrisons, continued to pillage rural areas. At Xian-Hui's home, her father had to hire a contingent of mercenaries to protect his land, his family, his tenants, and their families.

Both father and daughter had heard many rumors about the court's feeble and inept policies of dealing with the Yellow Turbans. The most disturbing one claimed that some of the conspiratorial eunuchs had secretly entered a pact with the Yellow Turbans, hoping to use the rebels as their own independent military force in a contingency that might develop from their raging political battle against those generals and government officials who opposed them. This rumor explained why the eunuchs counseled the emperor to stay clear of a policy of eradicating the Yellow Turbans. Their strategy was to hold the rebels in check and use them as a counterbalance against court officials.

Of course, one could not count on rumors as facts. Xian-Hui's father tended to dismiss rumors, especially rumors about the Son of Heaven. To Xian-Hui's father, rumors were mostly malicious alley talk to which an honest man should never pay much attention. A Confucian scholar never challenged an emperor's authority or questioned his integrity, unless irrefutable proof existed, beyond reasonable doubt. A scholar's first obligation was to uphold the canon zhong, "loyalty and devotion to the sovereign."

Xian-Hui recognized that Master Li, like her father, was also a Confucian scholar marked by a strong belief in moral rectitude. More importantly, she understood that the master was an unimpeachable source of information about the emperor and the government. He might not be involved in palace politics, but the perfidious manipulators and the backstage machinations did not escape his attention. His account of palace politics lent credence to the rumors about a dysfunctional imperial court Xian-Hui had heard at home. She now realized that her father, who insisted on not blaming the Son of Heaven for the

AN EXTRAORDINARY WOMAN

abysmal conditions in the nation, was misled by his blind loyalty. The country was under siege, the economy in ruins, rebellions everywhere. Even more disturbing to Xian-Hui than Master Li's forceful indictment of the imperial court, life in the palace showed no sign of any awareness of a national emergency or a ruinous economy. Little Ma gave all the indications that the profligate way of life in the palace remained standard practice at all levels in the forbidden city. In short, the palace was a sybaritic haven of a ravenous horde of parasites. Living in the palace, one would never know that the Yellow Turbans and bands of brigands were burning down the country, killing tens of thousands of people. Neither would a palace denizen have any inkling about the poverty, suffering, and privation of the peasantry.

Little Ma, too naive to share his companions' keen interest in national politics, was nonetheless taken aback by Master Li's alarming forecast. It frightened him. But Master Li was his teacher. In the absence of a father, a young man owed his loyalty and filial piety to his teacher, according to Confucian ethics. Naturally, his trust in Master Li did not waver, even though some of the master's predictions and analyses bordered on treason. He didn't fully grasp how an indolent emperor and a group of conniving eunuchs could destroy a nation. The only words of Master Li that resonated deeply with his own experience were *the destitute peasantry*. Peasantry was his origin, his ancestral background. The second son of four children of a tenant farmer in a village located at some distance east of the capital, he knew hunger and deprivation as far back as he could remember, until his parents sold him to become a eunuch at age twelve.

As he mulled over Master Li's assessment of the state of the empire, it dawned upon him that perhaps his parents were not as cruel and coldhearted as he'd thought when they sold him. Perhaps his parents could no longer feed him or themselves, and selling him was the only alternative to death by starvation. Perhaps, by this point in time, death had already claimed some if not most members of his family. His parents never explained to him their reason for selling him, and it was not a son's prerogative to question or find out his parents' motivation. Master Li's description of the state of the empire inadvertently revealed a possible explanation of his parents' action, which, cruel as it might seem, was more humane than death. As a young boy, he had witnessed the grisly way of dying by starvation, skeletal bones pushing out of the body, abdomen bloated like a balloon, eyes sunk deep into their sockets, skin cracked like a sunbaked mudflat, flies crawling in and out of every orifice. The thought of death by starvation gave him the chills. Yes, perhaps his parents, by selling him, saved him and possibly other members of his family from that gruesome fate.

The revelation jolted Little Ma.

He cringed from a sudden sense of guilt for having harbored an unforgiving fury against his parents. If he could achieve some level of conventional success and if, by that time, his parents were still alive, he swore in silence, he would lift them out of destitution.

Gloom enveloped all three, teacher and pupils, as Xian-Hui and Little Ma quietly took leave of Master Li. They were overwhelmed by the prospect of the collapse of the Han dynasty, a dynasty founded by the magnificent Liu Bang and set in glory fifty years later by one of his descendants, the incomparable and indefatigable Emperor Wu. The end of a dynasty always began with chaos and anarchy: a nation relegated to the primitive rule of the survival of the physically strongest, as in the animal kingdom, where the strong and fierce preyed on the weak and meek. It meant an end to civil order and the collapse of social structures. In the ensuing chaos, an untold number of people would perish from mayhem, starvation, and disease. Unthinkable as it might seem, the end of the great Han dynasty was what Master Li predicted. It weighed heavily on Xian-Hui and Little Ma as they took leave of Master Li.

AN EXTRAORDINARY WOMAN

As the months went by, Xian-Hui settled into a routine that kept her occupied. The routine did not bring happiness, but neither did it inflict pain. Inspired by Master Li, she began working through Sima Qian's Records of the Grand Historian, chapter by chapter, all one hundred and thirty of them. The vivid description of events and historical figures in the book lightened her task of wading through an enormous web of information. Sima Qian's biographical sketches of emperors, noblemen, warriors, philosophers, and other notable persons over the past millennium were captivating. Of all the biographies, one stood out and caused her to read it over several times. It portrayed the only woman whom Sima Qian deemed important enough to be included in the pantheon of important people in his monumental historical treatise.

This exceptional woman was the wife of the founding emperor of the Han dynasty, Empress Dowager Lü. Much more than a wife, she ruled by the side of her husband, who not only relied on her advice, but also delegated to her most of his imperial authority whenever he went away on military expeditions. Effective, farsighted, and resolute, she consolidated the Han empire while her husband, the emperor, devoted himself to military conquests to expand his empire. After the death of her husband, she gathered the reins of power in her hands, established absolute authority, and emasculated her son, the young emperor and the legitimate heir to the imperial throne. In the biography of Empress Dowager Lü, Sima Qian focused on her ruthless pursuit of power, portraying her as a merciless, vindictive woman obsessed with schemes to vanquish her enemies and competitors. In fact, the empress turned out to be none other than the woman who ordered the gruesome dismemberment of a rival concubine, the protagonist of that bloodcurdling palace killing described by Master Li during Xian-Hui's memorable first encounter with him. Only between accounts of her atrocious deeds, Sima Qian acknowledged that during the fifteen years of her reign, she enacted wise and sensible administrative and fiscal policies, appointed gifted civil servants, and led the empire to peace and prosperity.

As Xian-Hui mulled over this biography of Empress Dowager Lü, she began to develop a highly unconventional view that a woman might be just as capable as a man to be a sovereign ruler. She felt that Sima Qian's negative portrayal of the empress was unfair. After all, Xian-Hui observed, plenty of male sovereigns, during their rise to power, committed regicide, patricide, fratricide, and other unspeakable atrocities, and in the process, broke every moral principle that ever existed.

"It's normal for men to vie for power," Xian-Hui muttered to herself. "As they fight and scheme, they employ whatever means necessary for victory. People expect murder and mayhem from them. But if a woman, like Empress Dowager Lü, seizes power and vanquishes her enemies aggressively as men do, her deeds are portrayed as more heinous, flagrant, despicable, and unforgivable than a man carrying out the same deeds!"

"History needs to be rewritten," she contemplated, "and instead of aspiring to be a poet, I ought to become a historian."

When Xian-Hui critiqued Sima Qian's writing of Empress Dowager Lü to Master Li, he disagreed.

"Women, by nature, are not as cruel and ruthless as men. They are mothers, daughters, and wives; they nurture the young. Nursing a baby and raising an infant requires kindness and forbearance. So, you can understand that whenever a woman, such as Empress Dowager Lü, abandons her conventional role to become aggressive and bellicose, even though no worse than most male sovereign rulers, she raises eyebrows and invites condemnation. As a rule, a man kills and plunders on his way to power. It is no less evil or condemnable than a power-seeking woman who leaves no prisoners behind. But humans have

AN EXTRAORDINARY WOMAN

173

become inured to men's barbarism. We even expect it. When a ruthless male warrior wages one bloody battle after another to create an empire, we admire and revere him. That's the cultural norm that has been inculcated into our mentality. For better or worse, we don't think of women wielding weapons, lopping off people's heads, and laying waste to a city. Empress Lü is a rare exception, and exceptions tend to titillate the intellect as well as the senses. There is an old saying: shu da zhao feng, 'the bigger the tree, the more wind it catches.'

"There is hardly any tree bigger than the one symbolizing Empress Dowager Lü. Sima Qian is the greatest historian our nation has ever had. History commemorates the landmark events of the past, the connections between those events, and above all, the significant players who helped shape those historical events. I don't think Sima Qian intended to vilify the empress when he highlighted her atrocities. He merely followed his instinctive reaction, namely, astonishment, to the exceptional qualities of the empress and her bold actions as he wrote about her."

Xian-Hui saw a point in Master Li's argument. It mitigated her resentment against the historian Sima Qian, but did not change her opinion that women were dealt a rotten hand in life. She chose not to carry on further the debate with Master Li on that topic. Continuing such a debate seemed futile. To her, he remained a man, even without the full anatomical complement of that gender, and a man always saw a woman as nothing more than a daughter, a wife, and a mother. She venerated Master Li as a scholarly man of virtue. More significantly, the philosophical and intellectual discussions with him provided her with the only relief from her confinement in the palace.

While her relationship with Master Li developed along the intellectual dimension, Xian-Hui nurtured her friendship with Little Ma, earning his complete devotion. She began to see him as a little brother, someone who considered her welfare even more important than his own. He always brought her what she needed, which, of course, was his professional obligation as her attendant. He brought her the news, be it gossip or official decrees. He saw her every day, as his duty required of him. Xian-Hui noticed that he showed up at her quarters even when duty didn't call for his presence. But she did not place much importance on his frequent appearances.

During the same period, Xian-Hui, following Master Li's advice, befriended many fellow concubines. She preferred and sought out those who had not yet given birth to children. Without children, they belonged to the more vulnerable enclave of the emperor's harem. Most of them retained some pleasant qualities because they were less obsessed with the pursuit of power. A concubine without offspring from the emperor lacked the platform from which to launch her ascent up the totem pole of dominance in palace politics. Those barren concubines welcomed Xian-Hui as one of their own. They also respected her for her erudition and independence.

On the occasions when a special courier was made available to deliver the concubines' letters to their families, they flocked to Xian-Hui's chamber. Even though the palace provided scribes at their service, they preferred Xian-Hui to write their letters because they felt safe and comfortable confiding their feelings and yearnings to her. She had established a reputation as someone who never gossiped. A secret divulged to her stayed with her and never reached anyone else. If they wished to send sensitive information to their family, Xian-Hui would be their trusted scribe. They respected her, not only because she was literate, but also because she stood for honesty, discretion, fairness, and courage as her name implied. But they were also bewildered by her way of life in the palace. Her refusal to attend to her physical beauty confounded them. She never powdered her face or applied rouge to her lips. Her hair was always somewhat disheveled, and she wore oversize robes, hiding her curves. On the

AN EXTRAORDINARY WOMAN

quirkiness of her physical appearance, they probed, but found no explanation. Xian-Hui typically met their concerned inquiries with the cheerful response, "This is just the way I am. I've never paid attention to my appearance. When I was a little girl, everyone thought I was a boy."

Some of the friendly concubines offered advice to Xian-Hui, trying to help her realize that she would have no future in the palace if she continued to neglect displaying her beauty and physical attraction. To those friends, she always responded to their well-intentioned advice with the explanation, "I don't care. I'll be happy to return home as a spinster when I reach twenty-six years of age."

Of course, they couldn't know that she purposely made herself unattractive. Indeed, Xian-Hui did everything in her power to avoid being the recipient of the emperor's favor. She made sure that everyone in the palace knew that she liked books, loved reading, and cared about nothing else. The eunuchs who brought her into the palace thought they had made a mistake by selecting a concubine who inexplicably took after the reclusive and austere Master Li. They considered the master an overly contemplative monk, and counseled Xian-Hui to change her ways. She listened to them attentively but took no action to alter her appearance. Exasperated, the eunuchs gave up on her and figured that she was destined to be a nonentity and eventually would be returned to her home as a spinster.

Every morning when the emperor conferred with his trusted eunuch to decide which concubine he should favor that day, Xian-Hui was left off the list drawn up by the eunuch. The eunuch who compiled the list each day faithfully followed two guiding principles. First, he wanted to please his master. Since all concubines were beauties, he sought the lascivious and the voluptuous with well-defined curves. Secondly, he used his position to extort money from the concubines. The more a concubine paid him out of the gold and silver she brought with her to the palace, the more likely she would be included in his list. But he played no role in determining which concubines received the greatest favor of all, which was a visit to the Garden of Delight. That decision rested exclusively with the emperor.

If a concubine pleased the emperor the night before or sometime in the past, she might be invited to join him and several other favorite concubines in his secluded Garden of Delight during the summer months. The garden, surrounded by tall walls, was in a hidden corner of the palace. If the emperor and his concubines entered the garden, all eunuchs had to withdraw. According to palace rumors, that secluded enclave was the place for lurid and salacious activities between the emperor and his favorite concubines. In the confined world of imperial concubines, there was nothing more tantalizing and titillating than the gossip about who was invited to the Garden of Delight. Many who were gleefully bragged about their experiences: how they frolicked around, nude, in the midst of gardenia, jasmine, Osmanthus, and *Magnolia champaca*; how they bathed in marble tubs filled with aromatic running water at an ideal, soothing temperature suited to the weather; how they consumed the most delicious and exotic fruits of the season: the golden peaches of Samarqand, the scarlet lychees from Annam, the emerald grapes of Turfan, the luscious melons of Hami, the flaming pomegranate of Sogdiana; how they fortified themselves for marathon sex with aromatic liquor and delicious dumplings made with meat, exotic herbs, Korean ginseng roots, fresh and newly erupted horns of antelopes, and other aphrodisiac ingredients; how they disrobed the emperor and titillated him; how the emperor spent most days in that garden during the warm season engaged in quixotic lovemaking.

Above all, they talked about an alfresco pavilion where a reclining swing with a pair of stirrups spread wide apart hung from the rafters at just the right height to face the midsection of the standing emperor. That was the emperor's favorite

AN EXTRAORDINARY WOMAN

contraption in which to place his concubine. There, His Holy Majesty preferred to be on his feet during fornication. He liked visual stimulation. The sight of the female anatomy excited him, and the sight of himself repeatedly penetrating a swinging female enraptured him.

Rumors circulated about the stamina and legendary sexual appetite of the emperor. Some concubines even attributed magical power to him for his insatiable carnal desire. On one occasion, a concubine, inebriated on the evening before her obligatory retirement to her natal home for having reached the age of twenty-six and failing to produce any offspring, commented with sarcasm, "Well, our Son of Heaven may not be much of an emperor. But he is definitely the best man at sex!"

Such ribald gossip and lewd accounts of imperial sexual practice always made Xian-Hui blush. She didn't care to hear them, but they validated what Master Li told her during her first weeks in the palace: the emperor had no interest in affairs of the state. She now fully understood what the master meant when he said that the Han dynasty no longer had an emperor to discharge his imperial duties, and a headless empire was destined to collapse.

During all these months of learning about palace life while carving out a niche for survival in that environment of intrigue and debauchery, Xian-Hui never dropped her vigilance in search of an opportunity to escape. But none, nothing that even remotely resembled an opportunity, arose. Each morning, she reminded herself of the number of days she had been in bondage.

It was the five hundred and forty-ninth day, January 18, 189.

NINE

A FORTUITOUS OPPORTUNITY

A blustering winter day. The sky was gray. The north wind, howling. Trees bent and shaking in the bone-chilling wind. Bleary-eyed and depressed, Xian-Hui got up early, wrapped in a woolen coat. From the slits between the wooden window shutters in her chamber, she could see the unlit lanterns hanging in the porch swinging erratically. The explosive blows of gale-force wind punctuated the high-pitched whistles created by air currents swirling around the icicles hanging from the roof. The noise sounded like an excruciating practice session of an amateur music ensemble, cacophonous, dreary, and irritating. The cold and the darkness exacerbated Xian-Hui's melancholia.

Marking the five hundred and forty-ninth day she had successfully averted the emperor's favor, Xian-Hui wondered how much longer her luck would endure or when she would get a chance to escape, to be free from this bondage, to reclaim her life and explore the world beyond her confinement. The frigid interior of her chamber, dimly lit by an oil lamp and the sunless sky outside, weighted down by heavy and dark clouds, gushed gloom and sadness. She felt pessimistic, infinitely lonely, and grief-stricken. Just as tears began to trickle down her cheeks, an urgent, loud knock on her door jolted her.

When she opened the door of her chamber, Little Ma was standing there, pale as the frost around him. His face and robe were stained with spots of fresh blood. Shaking uncontrollably, he attempted in vain to speak as his chattering teeth hampered his articulation. Plagued by his tremor, he, in desperation, resorted to gesticulation by crossing his throat with the index finger of his right hand repeatedly.

Alarmed, Xian-Hui closed the door, pulled up a chair for Little Ma, wiped the blood off his face, and examined him carefully. His neck was intact; he had suffered no wounds on his face or head. The blood splattered on him belonged to someone else, Xian-Hui inferred. Before she could announce that he had not suffered any injury, Little Ma broke into tears. In halting words between sobs, he told Xian-Hui, "They... killed... him. Killed... him. They... slit... Master... Li's throat."

"Who? Who killed Master Li?"

"Soldiers. A horde of soldiers." Little Ma bit his lower lip as he tried desperately to regain his composure. Xian-Hui could see the horror on his contorted face.

"Little Ma. You're safe now. You are in my chamber," Xian-Hui said softly in a firm voice. "Soldiers will not enter the quarters of the imperial concubines. You must collect yourself and tell me what happened."

"I have to go," Little Ma said as soon as he took hold of himself. "I must leave the palace before the soldiers kill me. But I want to see you first."

"No, don't go. Stay here!" Xian-Hui's voice took on an imperative tone. "My place is safe from the soldiers. It's against the rules for them to enter the quarters of the concubines. The soldiers belong to the imperial army, do they?"

"Yes, they are from the imperial army, not the Yellow Turbans," Little Ma confirmed. "Their uniform showed their regiment, a unit under the command of General Dong Zhuo, the general who allegedly made his reputation fighting against the Yellow Turbans."

As Little Ma's panic subsided, he began to see the merit of Xian-Hui's assessment that he would be safe in her chamber. Once again, he recognized Xian-Hui's wisdom and presence of mind as he had experienced on many other occasions during the past one and a half years. She always kept a cool head, applied her intelligence, and held her emotions at bay. He should always listen to her, he reminded himself, follow her lead, and be obedient. Drawing a deep breath, he started recounting what had happened.

"The whole thing, an avalanche of events, started yesterday evening when Master Li asked me to sit with him in his study, the room where he usually tutored me. Plagued by insomnia and reluctant to stay in his bedroom, which is in a separate building, he looked depressed and spoke pensively. He wanted me there to keep him company and listen to him late into the evening, something he had never done before."

Little Ma paused. His mind now cleared, and a vivid memory of the last eight hours crystallized in his head.

"At first, Master Li talked about his long life. He was fifty-nine years of age, a senior by all accounts. One more year, he would've made the class of sagacious elders according to Confucius. But the soldiers denied him that opportunity. It's so unfair, so cruel! The man had never harmed anyone."

Tears streamed down his cheeks. He had to pause again before drying his face with his sleeve. With a sigh, he resumed his recollection of Master Li's final hours.

"Intermingled with reminiscence of his own life, Master Li recounted the splendor of the Han dynasty, his favorite topic. You know how much he loved history, especially Han history. Evaluating one emperor after another, he declared solemnly that an emperor must be a visionary military leader capable of

A FORTUITOUS OPPORTUNITY

rousing his people to fight for the expansion of the empire. His heroes were Emperor Wu (the Martial Emperor) of Western Han and Emperor Guangwu (the Shining Martial Emperor) of Eastern Han. I could sense his excitement when he talked about the exploits of those two exceptional leaders, how Emperor Wu stabilized the Han dynasty in its early years, and how Emperor Guangwu rejuvenated it two centuries later. By the time his historical narrative reached the recent years, he became very emotional. Speaking somberly, he lambasted Emperor Ling for his cavalier attitude and nonchalant indolence. According to the master, Emperor Ling had failed his people and betrayed his ancestors. But his most damning indictment was aimed at his fellow senior eunuchs. Enumerating their crimes, from deceiving the emperor, conspiring with the Yellow Turbans, and murdering loyal officials to stealing from the national treasury and confiscating the legitimate property of loyal citizens, he accused them of committing treasons repeatedly. They should have died a thousand deaths, he said. I think he wanted to pass on his personal observation of what has been transpiring during the past few years in the palace. I was chosen to bear witness to his testimony of the last chapter of a collapsing dynasty. Like any accomplished Confucian scholar, he considered historiography one of the pillars of literature, and wanted to make sure that his knowledge was passed on to future generations. Perhaps he had a premonition of his imminent death, because when he talked about current events, he was grief-stricken."

"What events?" Impatience overtook Xian-Hui for the first time in her interaction with Little Ma.

"He began by telling me the shocking news that Emperor Ling has been gravely ill for many days. It happened suddenly and unexpectedly. Only a few senior eunuchs know, and they have stonewalled the news. It's winter. No one in the palace expects to see His Holy Majesty making his way toward the Garden of Delight. People assume that the Son of Heaven is spending these frigid days in his private, heated quarters with his favorite concubines. As a rule, he rarely shows up in the Hall of Virtue where the mandarin officials conduct government business every day, normally under the leadership of the emperor. That is why his absence has not caused any alarm. At the beginning of the emperor's ailment, the senior eunuchs expected a quick recovery. But his health continued to deteriorate, even though he is barely thirty-two years of age. As the emperor lapsed into a coma and the prospect of recovery began to fade, words of his impending death leaked out two days ago. Instantly, the news ignited an all-out war for succession among two opposing factions, one led by the empress and her brother, the other headed by the fawning eunuch I have told you about, Jian. The empress has a young son whom she wishes to place on the dragon throne, while Jian is scheming to make the son of his closest ally among the concubines the next emperor. Being the most powerful eunuch, Jian was privy to the emperor's condition. By the time the empress found out belatedly that the emperor was near death, she went into a rage because it meant that her rival, eunuch Jian, had gained a head start in the machination for succession. Then, another twist to this life-and-death struggle for the ultimate power unfolded.

"Mindful of the long-standing and venomous rivalry between eunuch Jian and the empress, the Son of Heaven had secretly sent both sons, his only two male heirs, out of harm's way by the time they were teenagers. They were taken to two distant locations to be raised as marquesses. No one in the palace knows their whereabouts. That's why you have never seen the two young princes on the palace grounds, and you don't hear about them either. Master Li told me that the emperor expected to live to a ripe old age, and he had adamantly refused to address the issue of succession by anointing one of the sons as the crown prince. The emperor's refusal to name a crown prince, however, had intensified the intrigues and murderous battle between the

A FORTUITOUS OPPORTUNITY

two factions in the palace. Sending his sons away from the court was his way of ensuring that his sons would not die mysteriously, either by poison or an alleged accident in the palace. He might not love his children, but he would go to great lengths to avoid the notoriety of violating the cardinal rule of filial piety: never allow your family lineage to end with your own death. Now the sudden, unexpected collapse of the emperor's health has created an emergency, as if a fuse connected to a keg of gunpowder has been lit. An all-out power struggle among potential contenders for the throne has begun to take on great urgency. The chaos created by the succession crisis is even more intense and convoluted than usual because the two eligible candidates are not only minors but also unknown to the court and the senior officials of the government."

"But why did the soldiers come into the palace? Why did they kill Master Li?" Xian-Hui couldn't connect the murder of Master Li with what Little Ma had said so far.

"Master Li did not anticipate that the soldiers would enter the palace early this morning. He did say that many government officials were fed up with the venomous battle between eunuch Jian and the empress. One notable person in particular, General Dong Zhuo, who himself harbors grand ambitions, has been waiting in the wings to seize power. He commands the imperial guards as well as the military garrison charged with protecting the capital. Master Li said that he wouldn't be surprised if General Dong would stage a coup by siding with the faction in the succession battle that would yield him the greatest political benefit. Such a coup, according to Master Li, is always accompanied by a great deal of bloodshed. I don't know for sure, but I guess General Dong decided to support the empress and massacre the eunuchs, especially those of the senior rank.

"At around five o'clock this morning, Master Li was quietly resting in his chair after his lengthy reminiscence and discourse, and I was dozing off next to him. Suddenly, the rhythmic sound of synchronized footsteps pounding the palace grounds woke me up. Before I could rub the sleep out of my eyes, soldiers kicked down the door and burst into our room. Without uttering a word, they slit Master Li's throat. It was so quick that I don't think Master Li even knew what happened to him. I squeezed my eyes shut, expecting to be killed the next instant. But the soldiers paused, and one of them barked, 'Leave him! Just a kid!' Then they left the room as suddenly as they came in.

"That was when I got up and started running in the direction of your chamber. Along the way, many soldiers with unsheathed weapons were marching to different areas of the palace. The palace looked like a military staging ground for a major battle. Halfway over here, I ran into a young boy attendant of eunuch Jian. Panicky and out of breath, he looked as pale as if he had just been visited by a ghost. He said that soldiers had broken into the room where he and Master Jian were sleeping, arrested them, and dragged them into a courtyard where General Dong stood waiting. On the order of the general, the soldiers disemboweled eunuch Jian before cutting his head off. The general then turned to the boy attendant and told him to get out of the palace, yelling after him as he was running away, 'Run, little eunuch. Leave the palace! We are ridding the nation of wicked parasites like you.' That was only a few minutes ago."

At this point in Little Ma's narrative, Xian-Hui suddenly stood up. With a stern and determined voice that startled Little Ma, she barked, "The general is right. We should leave the palace."

"But you are not a eunuch!" exclaimed Little Ma.

Instead of responding to Little Ma's protest, Xian-Hui took out a pair of long scissors from her dresser and commanded Little Ma to cut off her hair.

"Why? What are you doing?"

A FORTUITOUS OPPORTUNITY
185

"Listen, Little Ma." Xian-Hui's imperative voice betrayed a hint of tension and impatience. "I am leaving the palace, and I would like you to come with me. But if you prefer to stay, that's fine. I will leave by myself."

"No, no, no! I'm coming with you; I'll go anywhere you want to go!" Little Ma, shocked by Xian-Hui's stern voice and frightened by her fierce ultimatum, protested, "I had wanted to leave. But you told me to stay."

"Hurry, help me cut my hair so that I can look like a young boy." Xian-Hui handed him the pair of scissors.

For a moment Little Ma still hesitated as he thought about the repercussions of harming the appearance of an imperial concubine, but Xian-Hui's air of authority and sense of urgency overcame his fear. He sheared her lustrous, long black hair with uneven cuts, leaving her head like a small molehill with tufts of grass sprouting at different heights. From a trunk that accompanied her to the palace, Xian-Hui took out a man's hat, her father's hat, which she had brought as a souvenir by which to remember him. The hat covered her unkempt hair and made her look like a handsome young boy.

"I have two old sheepskin coats," Xian-Hui said. "Let's put them on and leave immediately."

"But where are we heading to, ma'am?"

"Don't call me ma'am! From now on, I am Little Wong, your fellow eunuch. You hear? Now, call me by my new name."

"Yes,... Lit... tle... Wong."

"No, no, not with hesitation! Say it with conviction."

"*Yes, sir!* Little Wong," Little Ma responded like a soldier at drill.

"Put on your sheepskin coat. We are walking out of the palace at this moment. Remember, if a soldier asks who we are and where we are heading, tell him that we are new initiates among the eunuchs and that we are following General Dong's instructions to leave the palace at once."

As they walked toward the nearest palace gate in the bitter cold and gusty wind, Little Ma repeated his earlier question in a whisper: "Where are we heading?"

Without looking at him, Xian-Hui answered, "We will figure that out after we get out of the palace."

As they approached the nearest gate on the south end of the palace, Xian-Hui and Little Ma caught sight of many lance-bearing guards patrolling on top of the city wall, each carrying a longbow and a quiver of arrows on their shoulder. Hearts pounding and choking with fear, Xian-Hui and Little Ma lowered their heads and bravely marched forward. Four soldiers with an officer standing on the side stopped them at the gate.

"Hold there! Who are you?"

"We are recently initiated eunuchs," Little Ma answered in his trembling boyish voice. "Our master has been killed and General Dong ordered us to leave the palace."

In the dim light of the early winter morning, Little Ma and Xian-Hui appeared even smaller than they were, and Xian-Hui's beauty was not noticeable.

"When and where did you see General Dong?" the officer demanded.

"In the main courtyard, not too far from the Hall of Virtue. We are assistants to Master Li, who had been killed in his study."

"Master Li?" The officer expressed surprise, "I have heard of him. An elderly scholar, known as a rare man of integrity among the perfidious eunuchs. It's a pity that he got killed."

Turning to the soldiers, the officer barked, "Let these young eunuchs go, before they become entrenched parasites like their elders."

As they walked past the gate, one of the soldiers yelled, "Go, you seedless freaks, and don't return! If you do, we will cut off your other end."

A FORTUITOUS OPPORTUNITY

187

Xian-Hui and Little Ma walked briskly in silence until they melted into a crowd of pedestrians beyond the perimeter of the palace. As they slowed down their pace, Xian-Hui had to summon all her willpower to resist the urge to look back and make sure that no palace guards came after them. Her fear and anxiety demanded her to check what was behind her. But her logical mind recognized the futility of such a gesture, not to mention its potential for arousing other people's suspicion that the two of them were fugitives on the run. Like a prey animal seeking a herd of its own kind for protection from predators, she kept a few steps ahead of Little Ma, hoping that the pedestrian traffic would become heavier. It was not until they reached the commercial district where the shops had just opened their doors that tension began to drain from her. Safe among the early morning shoppers, she felt at once exhausted and relieved. After more than one and a half years of living in bondage, she had finally regained her freedom against all odds. She knew she was incredibly lucky to get out of the palace. No one noticed the absence of Xian-Hui in the chaos that followed General Dong's massacre of eunuchs. By the time they did, two days later, no one made an issue of it. The palace officials assumed that Xian-Hui, an inconspicuous and unimportant concubine, had fallen victim to some overzealous soldiers during the chaos and confusion of General Dong's murderous intrusion.

Almost an hour after leaving the palace, Xian-Hui allowed herself to look back. No soldiers, no eunuchs. The palace was no longer in sight. The suffocating tension she held within her chest began to melt away. Her confidence was restored.

She patted Little Ma on his back. "You were good, very good in your exchange with the guards at the palace gate. I am proud of you."

Little Ma smiled broadly. He too was proud of himself for not panicking in front of the soldiers, but his proud feeling didn't compare to the happiness brought on by Xian-Hui's compliment. It was the first time he felt some reciprocal affection from Xian-Hui. In the palace, she seemed to be aloof and distant even though she was always kind and considerate. Now she showed some feelings. Little Ma began to harbor the thought that Xian-Hui was moving closer to him. This new phase of their relationship was heartwarming and gratifying to him. A surge of optimism and happiness coursed through his veins. He felt that his rotten fate had taken a sharp turn in a promising new direction. At this moment, he was glad that Xian-Hui and he were walking away from their past, an abominable life in the forbidden city. He looked forward to his future by the side of the person he adored.

Perhaps we can become a family, like a brother and sister dependent on each other as we forge a new life, he thought to himself. I will attend to her needs as I did in the palace, with care and devotion. Her happiness is always my mission.

"Now, noble concubine, can you tell me where we are going?"

"I'm Little Wong, *not* concubine, remember?" Xian-Hui corrected him brusquely.

"Sorry! So where are we going, Little Wong?"

"Out of the city. Out of Luoyang."

"Really? Then what?" Little Ma was mystified.

"We will find out when we get there."

Finding the city gate was easy for Xian-Hui and Little Ma. Travelers converged toward it in the early-morning hours, carrying luggage on foot or riding in carts pulled by donkeys. Intermingled with the travelers were residents going about their daily chores. It was easy for Xian-Hui and Little Ma to differentiate the travelers from the locals. The locals meandered a bit, looking at the shops. The travelers walked more purposely away from the center of the city. Xian-Hui and Little Ma followed the travelers. Along the way, restaurants with long wooden counters displayed bowls of hand-pulled noodles mixed with scallions, braised pork, and a variety of spices. Behind the counter, a rich

A FORTUITOUS OPPORTUNITY

broth made from pork bones, chopped napa cabbage, garlic, and ginger boiled in two steaming pots. The calls of the proprietors hawking their culinary products and urging passersby to enter their shops had a singsong aspect. Each huckster had his own way of hawking, highlighting the specific culinary ingredients in his singing. Some of the singing was colorful, like short operatic arias, others were somber, resembling religious chants. A few hawkers looked as if they were enjoying their own vocal performances. The singing, in addition to the sweet aroma of the boiling broth, made the steaming soup and noodles on such a cold winter day nearly irresistible to anyone nursing an empty stomach.

"Do you have money?" Little Ma looked at the food wistfully. "I'm famished."

"Yes! Let's eat." The prospect of sitting down at a counter of a noodle shop appealed to Xian-Hui. Both of them needed a rest from the nerve-racking escape out of the palace.

Little Ma practically jumped with glee. "How come you have money? I was certain that we would have to endure hunger."

"I brought along fifty silver pieces in the inside pockets of my sheepskin coat, the money my father gave me when I left home. I have been saving it just for this journey."

The food stop not only satisfied their hunger but also lifted their spirits. Rejuvenated, they resumed their trek at a faster pace, stopping only at a clothing store because of Xian-Hui. She ducked into it and bought a woman's robe and three young men's casual outfits made of tough coarse material, two for herself, one for Little Ma. In half an hour, they reached the south city gate.

The gate turned out to be a brick-lined tunnel, about one hundred paces long and ten paces wide. The tall city wall extending from both sides of the tunnel maintained the same one-hundred-pace depth for a considerable distance before tapering off to a wall five paces in thickness. Directly on top of the tunnel rose a magnificent building of the same architectural design as that of the palace buildings, except its roof tiles were black instead of the imperial yellow. Parapets lined the entire space on top of the wall. It was an awesome rampart swarming with soldiers, some patrolling, some standing on guard, and some standing in formation.

Much to the relief of Xian-Hui and Little Ma, there were no soldiers guarding either end of the tunnel. There were no signs of military action either. People on the streets were conducting their affairs normally. Through the tunnel, a steady stream of farmers was entering the city, hauling grain and their winter produce: flour, millet, onion, cabbage, yams, garlic, eggs, apples, and persimmons. Some herded farm animals in front of them: sheep, goats, and pigs. Some transported cackling chickens packed in large bamboo cages. Some pushed carts covered with fishing nets under which foul-smelling, quacking ducks tried desperately to escape. Some carried pairs of water-filled buckets in which carps and catfish were struggling to breathe. Each of those sturdy, bow-legged carriers balanced two buckets on a pole across his shoulder. All those people were the food venders and suppliers for the population inside the city. Compared to them, the travelers leaving the city were few, forming a trickle of light traffic in the opposite direction. It was obvious to Xian-Hui and Little Ma that residents of the capital had not yet learned of the mayhem and killing that had occurred in the palace. Even the soldiers patrolling on top of the city wall, wearing the uniform of General Dong's regiment, showed no sign of high alert.

Exiting the city of Luoyang did not evoke any nostalgia or joy from Xian-Hui and Little Ma. Confined to the palace, neither knew the city of Luoyang. They had no attachment to it. For Xian-Hui, exiting the city meant nothing more than the completion of the first phase of her journey to freedom. Once out of the city, her fear of pursuers evaporated, but she remained fully cognizant that the new phases of her escape would be challenging, and she needed to maintain a high vigilance.

A FORTUITOUS OPPORTUNITY

At a short distance beyond the city gate, Xian-Hui announced, "We must find the caravansary."

Little Ma, taken by surprise, asked, "Why the caravansary?"

"Well, for me, the safest choice is to go far away. Do you remember how Master Li told us about caravans that travel the Silk Road? I would like to hitch onto a caravan and head west."

Little Ma was alarmed.

"A caravan goes to the Western Regions, which is far, far away. Do you want to settle in a place where Huns, Sogdians, Bactrians, Tocharians, and other barbarians live? They will eat us alive!"

"No," Xian-Hui assured him. "It's a long way before the caravan reaches the eastern border of the Western Regions in the Gobi Desert. From Luoyang, the caravan goes to Chang'an, the old capital, which is many hundred li to the west from where we are. From Chang'an, the frontier remains another three hundred li to the west. We will choose a place to separate from the caravan before it enters the Gobi Desert."

Little Ma sighed with relief. "That sounds reasonable. If you want to find the caravansary, I suggest that we head south toward the Luo River. The river runs east and west. We came out of the southern gate of the city. So, if we keep heading south, we should hit the river. The caravansary should be along the riverbank where camels can be watered, the traders can replenish their food supply from the surrounding farms, and the non-Han traders do not have to contend with urban hostility and Han condescension."

"Good reasoning, Little Ma!" Xian-Hui nodded.

As they trekked toward the Luo River, deep groans and occasional roars drifted toward them from afar. Those vocalizations did not come from the domestic animals with which they were familiar, so they surmised that they came from two-humped Bactrian camels, the beasts of burden of a caravan. The camel vocalizations became the beacon that guided them to their destination.

It was midday when they arrived at the riverbank and found what they were looking for. The caravansary appeared to be a large campground. Along the riparian meadow, a row of yurts stood, each a dome of thick felt woven from camel hair. Smoke drifted out from openings on top of some yurts. Different yurts exhibited different shades of gray and brown, betraying different ages of the camel hair. From a distance, the yurts looked like a row of enormous mushrooms sprouting from the earth.

At a distance further upstream, a flock of camels, some standing, some sitting, were tethered to a long rope secured at both ends on the trunks of two large willow trees that stood twenty paces apart. Not far from the camels were a pack of horses tethered to several poplar trees. A large black yak-skin tent tied down on stakes looked conspicuously like the headquarters of the caravansary. The entry to the tent was covered by a thick, rectangular flap of sheepskin.

Standing in front of the entrance, Little Ma sought guidance from Xian-Hui.

"Should we go in?"

"Of course, what's the alternative? We need to find the people who run the caravan." Xian-Hui became a bit impatient.

The inside of the tent, despite an open hearth with a roaring fire, did not feel significantly warmer. Permeated with the rancid odor of liquor and pungent roasted mutton, the air smelled sickening to Xian-Hui and Little Ma. There were perhaps a dozen or so people sitting around the fire in the middle of the tent below the circular vent. None of them looked like Han people. Sipping their drinks, they appeared to have just finished their lunch and looked ready for a nap. The unexpected intrusion of Xian-Hui and Little Ma momentarily disrupted the indolent ambience. For a few seconds, the caravanners stared at the two in silence. They were trying to figure out the reason for the sudden appearance of two underaged Han. The youngsters didn't look like thieves; they were not hostile;

A FORTUITOUS OPPORTUNITY

193

they seemed just a tad timid and bewildered. Then, a bearded elderly man sitting behind the hearth broke the silence with a mild accent marked by an intonation that was obviously not Chinese.

"What can I do for you?"

Xian-Hui and Little Ma noticed the man's salt-and-pepper hair, aquiline nose, blue eyes, and leathery skin. Wearing a brimless flat-crowned cylindrical hat made of yellowish sheep fur and a heavy, yak-skin overcoat with matted, long yak hair on the inside, he followed up his question with a friendly smile to reassure Xian-Hui and Little Ma.

"We would like to travel west with the caravan," Xian-Hui answered. "Am I speaking to the leader?'

"That would be my friend Habib, sitting here next to me." The man pointed to a tall, wiry fellow in his prime. "What do you say, Habib? Do you want to take on two young travelers?"

Habib wore a heavy beard that was pitch-black and kinky. It covered most of his face below his owlish eyes. His nose stood out like a long, thin kopje on an African savanna. His oily hair was black and curly, spreading downward from his hat like cresting waves. Xian-Hui and Little Ma could hardly see his lips behind the beard until he opened his mouth, baring two rows of yellowish teeth. He projected strength and confidence.

"It will cost you money." Habib spoke matter-of-factly in a guttural voice.

"How much?" Xian-Hui asked.

"For the two of you, half an ounce of silver per day, the cost of food and water will be included."

"We accept," Xian-Hui responded instantly.

"There are rules that you must follow. As the head of the caravan, I take responsibility for its safety, and I decide the route we take, the stops we make, the time we rest, the places we camp, and the food we eat. Is that agreeable with you?"

"Yes, sir," Xian-Hui responded. "We agree."

"Now, I have to ask you a few questions." Habib stood up and walked toward Xian-Hui and Little Ma. Carrying a long, curved sword by his waist, he was tall and intimidating. "First of all, what are your names?"

"I'm Little Wong. This is my cousin, Little Ma," Xian-Hui answered calmly.

"Where are you going?"

"We haven't decided yet. But we want to head west. We will let you know when we wish to separate from the caravan."

"You won't have many opportunities to drop out once we leave the Han territory, though it will take us many days of travel before we reach that point. May I ask why you are heading west?"

"We are former eunuchs. The palace no longer needs our service. We also lost our family because of the Yellow Turban Rebels." Xian-Hui responded calmly, "The capital, Luoyang, is too crowded and too chaotic for our taste. We have relatives in Chang'an, but if we find a town to our liking before Chang'an, we may try to settle there."

"Ah, eunuchs, no wonder you sound like a girl." Habib held back his smile. "Chang'an is about ten days of trekking from here. We hug the southern bank of the Yellow River until it turns up north into the Ordos region. From there, we go directly westward, skirting the Wei River. Along the way, the farming communities are predominantly Han. But the more westward we go, the more ethnic variety and the fewer Han people we will encounter. The most common settlements belong to Huns, Sogdians, and Tanguts. Many of them have assimilated into the Han people's way of life and became sedentary farmers. Of course, there are also a few towns on the way to Chang'an that you may find attractive. In the old days, the caravan never came this far east. Our route, the Silk Road, ends in Chang'an. Nowadays, we come all the way to Luoyang whenever we have special cargo for the Han imperial court. I wish the Han capital had remained in Chang'an. We and

A FORTUITOUS OPPORTUNITY

195

our camels do not appreciate the humid climate here, not to mention the noise, trash, beggars, thieves, foul air, and dense population. The humidity of Luoyang mats our hair, the noisy crowd gets on our nerves, the hustle and bustle disturbs our spirit. The beggars and thieves annoy us. We are people who favor open air, big sky, soaring mountains, enormous space, and above all, borderless grassland where the grass undulates in the wind like the waves of a sea. When we are confined to a small, crowded area, we and our animals become irascible. That's why the camels, reacting to the slightest provocation, spit and roar. So, we make our stay in Luoyang as brief as possible. Normally at the end of a long journey, we like to set up camp at a caravansary for one week or longer to relax and recover from the ordeal of long-distance travel. But in Luoyang, we stay for only two days. Tomorrow, we will load up our cargo and provisions to begin our westward journey. It's a quick turnaround for the sake of our health and our animals. Coming to Luoyang is a hardship for all of us."

"Thank you for the information." Xian-Hui bowed. "You are very kind. May we stay at the caravansary tonight?"

"That's a decision to be made by my Sogdian friend Demetrios here," Habib gestured toward the elderly man sitting behind the hearth who had greeted Xian-Hui and Little Ma at first. "I am sure it can be arranged."

"Not a problem, not a problem," Demetrios said in fluent Chinese. "One of the yurts is available. It costs you one ounce of silver. I'll throw in a free dinner. Let me show you to the yurt."

"Thank you, Mr. Di-mi…" Embarrassment marked Xian-Hui's face as she struggled to pronounce Demetrios. "Pardon me. Your name is difficult to pronounce."

"It's Greek." Demetrios chuckled. "I was born in Bactria far from Greece. Some of us, Sogdians of Greek origin, have long names like Eucratides, Theofanos, Athanasakos. They will strain your memory and twist your tongue if you are accustomed to monosyllabic or bisyllabic Han names."

As Xian-Hui and Little Ma followed Demetrios out of the tent, beyond the leather door flap, they were awestruck by the dramatic change of the scenery from just a few minutes earlier. Like magic, the winter landscape in shades of gray had transformed into a glittering world of white during the time they were inside the tent of the caravansary owner. A thin layer of snow covered everything: the tent, the yurts, the ground, the barren trees, the brown grass, even the camels, which, with their heads held high, seemed to welcome the relief of the aridness brought on by the dry snow. The air smelled clean and fresh. The meandering river, absorbing the gentle snowflakes, seemed to be moving imperceptibly. White crystalline snowflakes fluttered in the air, falling reluctantly.

"How beautiful!" Demetrios exclaimed. "Fresh snow reminds me of my youth when I guided caravans through the great deserts and magnificent mountains. If you ever cross the Taklamakan Desert or scale the Pamir Mountains and encounter a gentle snowfall, you will feel, at times, that you are in harmony with heaven and earth. In those majestic and enormous spaces, heaven and earth are linked by the falling snow to become an integrated whole, quiet, peaceful, and all-embracing. Of course, nature dwarfs us, makes us humble. But as you merge into it, even as a tiny insignificant human, you forget your greed, your ambition, your possession, your worldly pursuit and become content with life. You feel at peace with yourself. It's that serenity, that contentment that I miss, now that I am the proprietor of a caravansary. Well, my young friends. Old age has imprisoned me. I can no longer bear the burden of a long-distance trek through the harsh desert." Demetrios sighed. "That's what old age does to a man. It ties him down and deprives him of his freedom. But it's not your concern. Youth remains with you. You have a future to look forward to. Well, here is your yurt. Let me start a fire in the hearth."

A FORTUITOUS OPPORTUNITY

When Demetrios lifted the heavy, oversize sheepskin flap hanging over the entrance, a raised wooden threshold was revealed. Stepping beyond the threshold, Xian-Hui and Little Ma, having taken off their shoes at Demetrios's instruction, walked onto a soft floor composed of several layers of felt that yielded gently to their feet. The cozy interior accentuated by the softness of the felt-covered floor was a welcoming relief to Xian-Hui and Little Ma after the tense march out of the palace and the city. They were surprised. Unlike the large black yak-skin tent whose bottom edge stayed a few inches above the ground, allowing a cold draft to enter the interior, the yurt provided an airtight dome with a small vent on top. The circular felt wall enclosed a snug space. A frame of hardwood sticks supporting the felt cover converged from the floor onto a wooden ring at the center of the dome. Three wolf pelts on the floor marked the spots for sleeping and sitting. At the center of the yurt stood a hearth made of large pebbles rising two or three inches from the felt floor. A ring of sand wall, several inches high, held the fire inside the hearth. The vent at the top of the yurt let out the smoke from the fire. It was the same opening framed by a hardwood ring on which wooden sticks supporting the yurt were fastened.

Demetrios made a small fire in the hearth, which warmed up the interior instantly.

"Take a rest," Demetrios advised as he took his leave. "I'll expect you for dinner in the large, black yak-skin tent at sunset."

In the protective and cozy warm yurt, Little Ma's nervous energy that had possessed him since dawn began to give way to exhaustion. He felt an overwhelming fatigue creeping all over his body, from his feet to his back and neck. As he lay down on one of the wolf pelts, he struggled to keep his eyes open as he fought to stay awake. Before yielding to his exhaustion, he wanted to express his astonishment at the way Xian-Hui interacted with Habib and Demetrios.

"Cousin Wong, the way you spoke, the answers you gave were impeccable. You thought of everything and were prepared for every encounter. You are a genius!"

"I am not a genius, and I don't get what you mean."

"I mean you were so smooth, so casual, in your interactions with Habib and Demetrios, answering their questions convincingly without hesitation. Before we left the palace, you must have worked out in your mind the kind of questions people might ask and the answers you would give."

"No," she responded, "I improvised. I had no idea of who we would run into and where we would end up. It was not possible for me to anticipate what sort of questions people might ask me."

"You improvised?" Little Ma lifted his head from the wolf pelt and opened his drooping eyes in bewilderment. "That's incredible!"

He had always admired Xian-Hui. Now he felt she was almost a goddess capable of navigating through any situation, coping with any hardship, standing up to any challenge. She bordered on omnipotence. There was no need for him to worry about his safety with her. Heaving a sigh of relief, he dropped his head on the wolf pelt and fell asleep.

When he woke up, it was almost dark. He could see Xian-Hui sitting on the other side of the hearth. She had changed into the rough outfit she bought on the way to the caravansary, the sheepskin coat folded next to her.

"Noble con... I mean, Cousin Wong," Little Ma caught himself and shook his addled brain. "Shall we go eat?

"Yes. Remember, Cousin Ma, the less you talk, the less likely you are to make a mistake. Let other people talk. And if you have to say something, the safest way to is to ask questions, OK?"

"Yes, Cousin Wong."

In the big black tent, half of a sheep carcass was being roasted on a spit over the hearth. Demetrios stood behind it with one knife in each hand, slicing hunks of meat dripping with fat to

A FORTUITOUS OPPORTUNITY

serve his customers. In front of the hearth sat a pile of ceramic dishes and a row of jars holding salt, cumin, garlic, mint, caraway seed, ground white pepper, crushed red pepper, pulverized green pepper, and spicy sauces Xian-Hui and Little Ma had never seen before. Around the tent, people were eating mutton and drinking black tea boiled in a huge pot while talking boisterously in exotic languages. A few people were drinking a pungent alcoholic beverage as they ate their mutton. Xian-Hui and Little Ma didn't know what alcoholic beverage it was. But they could tell from the odor that it wasn't a Chinese liquor, which was typically brewed from fermented sorghum and then distilled.

Wearing fur, leather boots, and a variety of hats, most of the diners sported heavy beards and carried stilettos on their belts. Much to the surprise of Xian-Hui, no one used chopsticks. They ate with their right hands, picking up the roasted mutton dripping with fat and stuffing it into their mouths.

Behind the roasting mutton, Demetrios beckoned to Little Ma and Xian-Hui, waving a knife in the air.

"Come over and get some mutton."

Fatty mutton didn't suit the palate of Xian-Hui. She stared at the hunk of meat on her plate, picked it up with her hand, and dropped it back instantly, shaking her hand like a cat shaking its wet paw at the edge of a stream. Both the food and the manner of eating turned her stomach.

Unlike Xian-Hui, Little Ma chomped on the meat with gusto. Observing Xian-Hui's reaction, he said, "Try the spices. They neutralize the fat."

"No. I can't eat mutton fat."

"Let me help you." An imposing man in his prime with a mug of tea in his hand approached, speaking perfect Chinese. He had green eyes, pale skin, and a shock of wavy brown hair. He plunked down his drink and drew his stiletto. With great dexterity and lightning speed, he trimmed off the fat and sliced the lean meat into small chunks on Xian-Hui's plate.

"Thank you, thank you." Xian-Hui took the young man's measure as she picked at the meat. He seemed sincere in his friendliness. "I'm Little Wong. This is my cousin, Little Ma."

"I'm Gu, Habib's deputy. He told me about you two this afternoon. Han people are rare in a caravan. I'll look after you."

"Are you Han?" Xian-Hui asked, suspecting that he wasn't.

"Well, you can say that I am, but you can also say that I am not," Gu replied. "My ancestors came from Liqian, a rural town on the northwestern edge of the Gobi Desert, more than one thousand li from here. Liqian was settled by a detachment of Roman legionnaires a long, long time ago. Roman legionnaires are soldiers of the Daqin empire. Some of my ancestors are Romans, some are Han, some are mixtures of the two, and some might be descendants of other ethnic groups. I grew up in a small town not far from Chang'an where my father settled down as a blacksmith after years of being a sharpshooting archer guarding caravans."

Xian-Hui remembered learning about the Daqin empire from Master Li. "But what were Roman soldiers doing in the Han empire?"

"That's a long story." Mr. Gu looked beyond Xian-Hui. "I'll tell you a brief version.

"The Roman legionnaires of Liqian originally served under General Crassus, the governor of Syria in the Daqin empire more than two hundred years ago. In a battle against the Parthians from Persia, a long-standing enemy of Daqin, Crassus was killed, and his army decimated, except for a small contingent. This contingent of soldiers didn't want to return to the Daqin empire to face humiliation and possible persecution for their defeat by the Parthians. So, they headed east, going further away from Daqin. Along the way, they hired themselves out as mercenaries to different city-states, until they reached the Western Regions of the Han empire. There, they settled in a place that came to be known as Liqian."

Xian-Hui had never met a person who openly admitted his mixed racial origin. She felt a little embarrassed because Gu's affability and decency totally contradicted the disparaging image of non-Han races that was deeply ingrained in her through her upbringing. Instinctively she considered a non-Han person uncouth if not barbarous. Yet Gu was anything but inferior. He spoke Chinese natively, he was the deputy to the leader of the caravan, he had an imposing physical presence, he kindly offered to look after them, and he gave no indication of being ill at ease with his mixed ancestry. Besides embarrassment, Xian-Hui felt confused. Discriminatory sentiments and traditions in the face of contrary evidence caught her in a web in which she hadn't the faintest idea how to navigate herself. She would have been overwhelmed by her confusion if she were not, first and foremost, a quick-witted, levelheaded person. Deftly carrying on the conversation, she asked, "Do you still have relatives in Liqian?"

"Only distant cousins."

"It must be an interesting community. How do people there make a living?"

"Most of them are farmers. But some men take after their legionnaire forefathers. They prefer not to be tied down to the land. Like my father, those intrepid young men leave Liqian in search of adventurous professions."

"Coming from a warrior lineage, you carry the martial spirit in your blood. My cousin and I are fortunate to be under your care."

"There are several Liqian people who serve as professional guards in this caravan. We are not mercenaries because we don't fight for a king or lord. But we are all trained in martial arts and military skills."

The mention of martial arts perked up Little Ma.

"Mr. Gu, can you tell us about the caravan and the trip that will start tomorrow?"

"The caravan will move at maximum speed toward Chang'an. Neither our camels nor we, the caravanners, like the Han country. We will rush through the eastern portion of our journey. From Chang'an, we will cross the neck of the Gobi Desert where Shazhou (Dunhuang) is located. From Shazhou we head toward the oasis, Yiwu (Hami), where we will rest for a few days. Then, we'll embark on a long trek westward, tracing the northern fringes of the Desert of No Return (Taklamakan), an enormous and unforgiving desert that would swallow up travelers if they didn't have experienced guides. That's why it is called the Desert of No Return. Along the northern rim of the Desert of No Return, the first oasis where we can replenish our animals and ourselves is Turfan; the second oasis is Kuqa. After Kuqa, we head to Kashi (Kashgar), the most important trading post on the eastern foothills of the Pamirs. We'll end our journey there and transfer our merchandise to a different team of caravanners. That new caravan will climb the Pamirs and transport the merchandise westward to Tashkent, Samarqand, and Syria. The entire journey, our journey to Kashi, covers almost ten thousand li. It will take three to four months depending on the weather and other conditions."

Gu took a sip of his drink. It emanated a strong odor of alcohol and rancid milk like the alcoholic beverage several people were drinking as they chomped on their mutton. Distracted by the odor of the drink, Little Ma interrupted Gu: "Mr. Gu, can you tell us what you are drinking?"

"The best stuff on earth! Fermented mare's milk, a strong alcoholic drink favored by all people in the Western Regions. It is called koumiss. You want to try some?" He thrust his mug toward Little Ma.

"No, no. Thank you for the offer. I apologize for interrupting your talk about the caravan. You were bringing up several exotic places. They are fascinating."

A FORTUITOUS OPPORTUNITY

"Yes, living in the Han empire, you have probably never heard of the places in Western Regions. But let me first tell you something about our caravan. We have thirty-eight camels, eight horses, and fifteen caravanners, plus the two of you as guests. Most of our camels carry supplies and merchandise; a few will have people on their backs. The blood-sweating horses are for our best martial artists. This is an unusual configuration of men and animals for a caravan. In the good old days, the beasts of burden would outnumber humans three to one, and we didn't bring horses along. Nowadays, the Silk Road is plagued by brigands. The army of the Han no longer patrols the desert. On the Silk Road, each caravan needs to protect itself with a military escort. All fifteen of us caravanners, including Habib, are battle-hardened soldiers and martial artists. In addition, each of us is proficient in at least one other skill, such as animal care, constellation reading, cooking, hunting, the identification and use of medicinal plants, familiarity with the Gobi and the Desert of No Return. Like my Roman ancestors, I started my career as a mercenary. After a long apprenticeship, I learned the trade of guiding caravans on the Silk Road."

Fascinated, Little Ma couldn't wait to start trekking west. He wanted to start the journey immediately. Even tomorrow seemed to be too late. Deserts, mountains, oases, brigands: stuff that stirred a boy's imagination and spurred his wandering spirit. Little Ma was beginning to feel that he was regaining the boyhood that he had lost when he entered the palace in servitude.

"Please tell us about Shazhou, Yiwu, Turfan, and the other places you mentioned along the Silk Road. Who lives there? What kinds of strange people and animals will we encounter?"

A waning smile marked Mr. Gu's face. Being aware that most Han people considered other ethnic groups uncultured, he hesitated for a moment.

Xian-Hui, aware of the awkward situation, interceded.

"Please don't take offense at my cousin's choice of words. He does not mean any disrespect when he uses the expression *strange people*. To him, it means people who are different from the Han. He and I grew up in Han country. We don't know any non-Han people and we are fascinated by what you've told us."

"I understand." Somewhat assuaged, Gu took a swig from his mug before continuing his narrative of the Western Regions.

"In the Western Regions, you will find people of many ethnicities with different physical features, wearing different garments, speaking different languages, gesturing in different ways. People may have dark skin, light skin, golden hair, black hair, brown eyes, blue eyes, tall noses, flat noses, angular faces, round faces, showing every gradation of these physical categories. People may be tall or medium height, wearing a beard and a hat of different shape. Among the ethnic groups, Sogdians, Persians, Greeks, Yuezhi (Tocharians), Semites, Huns, Zang, Tanguts, and Bharati represent the better-known ones. There are Han people, but they are never the dominant ethnic group in the Western Regions. In some areas, you will run into Parthians or people of the Persian empire. Further west, the Daqin empire is enormous in geographic spread and ethnic complexity. Along the Silk Road, you will encounter many different languages. Even among our caravanners, six different languages are represented. But we mostly rely on Sogdian during our journey. Beyond Kashi, the traders prefer Aramaic. At every place, the local people have their own native language. I can speak only a few words in those languages."

"Please forgive me for interrupting." Xian-Hui stopped Gu's narrative. "You have brought up so many names of people that I have never heard of. Could I just ask you to elaborate a little bit of one or two? For example, who are the Bharati?"

"Oh, the people of Bharat!" Gu smiled. "I am glad you asked because Bharat is a large country with many ethnic groups. It is cordoned off from the rest of the world by enormous mountain

A FORTUITOUS OPPORTUNITY

ranges that are so high that their summits are usually hidden in high clouds. It is far from here in the southwest direction. Bharat has several great rivers along which different civilizations arose."

"Ah, Bharat, my teacher, Master Li, told me about it once," Little Ma chimed in. "The people of Bharat extol a set of behavioral codes called sanatana dharma that emphasizes benevolence, patience, compassion, and self-restraint. Master Li thought highly of the codes. But sanatana dharma is also a system of beliefs revolving around the cycle of death and rebirth, which never made sense to me."

"Well, you are not the only one puzzled by the idea of rebirth. I don't think there is such a thing," Gu responded. "Death and birth, I understand! Rebirth? It is pure fantasy. In the desert, all dead creatures, if not eaten by living animals, eventually disappear in sand. Their bones are reduced to grains of sand. Sand is eternal. It doesn't become something else."

As thought-provoking as Gu's response might be, Xian-Hui wanted to steer the conversation back to Gu's narrative about the people and nations along the Silk Road.

"My companion, Little Ma, accidentally led you into a discussion of some obtuse issues. Could you please tell us more about the Silk Road?"

"Alright." Gu laughed. "Let me tell you about the two closest non-Han cities along the Silk Road. They are Yiwu in the Gobi and Turfan in the Desert of No Return, two important oases in two great deserts. Even though the Han dynasty has been ruling Hami for many years, the people of Hami never assimilated into the Han civilization. Situated on the eastern foothills of the Celestial Mountains, Hami is home to many Huns and Sogdians. During summer, a sweet, intoxicating aroma of melon infuses the air of Hami. Everyone in the Western Regions considers the Hami melon a great delicacy. It is juicy, sweet, and heavenly!

"The other important city-state is Turfan. The home of Tocharians, a people whose language bears a lot of similarities to Greek, Turfan has its own unique characteristics. A huge depression on the northern rim of the Desert of No Return, it is freezing cold in the winter and scorching hot in the summer. The one constant feature of Turfan is its relentless aridity. A bowl of water in Turfan in open air will disappear quickly through evaporation if you don't drink it or cover it up. You cannot see a single body of water anywhere in Turfan. No river, no lake, not even a pond. Yet, it is one of the greenest oases in the world. Vegetation thrives in Turfan because of an ingenious underground water supply system constructed by generations of inventive engineers many hundreds of years ago. The local people call this water system karez. It consists of wells, dams, and canals, all underground. The wells store the water flowing down from the Celestial Mountains through subterranean canals. Within Turfan, underground waterways connect the wells and supply water to every household. The underground system prevents any loss of water by evaporation in the arid air. It also protects the water supply from disruption or pollution by sandstorms, which occur frequently in the Desert of No Return. Most impressively, the system allows the water to flow everywhere by its own natural pressure, which derives from its source high up on the snowcapped Celestial Mountains. When you walk in Turfan, you feel the scorching dry desert air. It cracks your lips and sears your lungs. But you also hear the gurgling sound of flowing water underground. It is the most comforting and reassuring sound because you know you can have water whenever you need it, and you need it constantly. Turfan grapes and raisins are delicacies famous throughout the region. Every neighborhood has a tall, cone-like brick structure full of small openings. Like an upside-down gigantic beehive, the structure allows the people of Turfan to make raisins by placing fresh grapes in each opening. The aridity and the heat turn the grapes into sweet and soft raisins. When we stop in Turfan, we buy at least fifty catties

A FORTUITOUS OPPORTUNITY

of raisins for the rest of our journey, and they are more delicious than the best candy in the world."

Gu's description of the raisins made Little Ma's mouth water. In the palace, he had heard about the grapes from Turfan. They were a delicacy reserved for the emperor and his favorite concubines.

"Cousin Wong, are we going all the way to Turfan?" Little Ma turned to Xian-Hui.

"Perhaps," Xian-Hui responded. "Let's finish our dinner and retire early so that we can be ready for our journey tomorrow."

Turning to Gu, she said, "Thank you so much for preparing us for our journey, Mr. Gu. As you can see, my cousin is very excited. So am I. You can count on us faithfully following your instructions during the trip."

As Xian-Hui and Little Ma took leave of the dining tent, Gu said, "Remember, we will move out at the crack of dawn."

When the caravan reached Chang'an, Habib set camp on the western outskirts of the metropolis, along the shore of the Wei River, the largest tributary of the Yellow River. To Habib's surprise, a small party was already in camp there, and it wasn't a caravan. The party consisted of several horses, some adults, a few youngsters, a small band of armed bodyguards, and an oxcart carrying furniture and household sundries. They looked like an emigrating Han family. Following the tradition of greeting other caravans already at a campground, Habib walked over to introduce himself. As he approached the main tent, a middle-aged man came out to meet him. Average height, slightly bent over, and dressed in long garments, the man appeared a quintessential mandarin official. Bowing, he and Habib greeted each other. With a pained facial expression, the man said, "My name is Cheng, a refugee from Han China's civil war and banditry."

208 LORD GUAN

After informing Cheng that he was leading a caravan carrying bronze vessels and a variety of ceramic pieces into the Western Regions, Habib said, "I hope you are not heading onto the Silk Road. Without camels, you cannot survive the Gobi Desert, not to mention the Desert of No Return."

"No, no. We are not going that far. We hope to settle in Shazhou at the beginning of the Silk Road," Cheng responded. "I have heard of Shazhou's Crescent Lake, with a natural spring bubbling a copious amount of crystal-clear water, and the Singing Sand Dunes next to the lake. My children do not believe that a mountain could sing. They couldn't wait to see it and hear its song."

"Well," Habib said, "the mountain, which consists of several enormous sand dunes, does not literally sing. But when strong wind whips up, it blows the sand into the air along the ridges of the high dunes. As the grains of sand grind against each other along the ridges, an eerie sound is produced as if the dunes were singing."

"Ah! You have explained the mystery of the singing mountain. Thank you," Cheng responded.

"As for the Crescent Lake, yes, it is miraculous!" Habib continued. "Especially in view of its location between the dunes in the driest part of the Gobi. At the foot of the tallest sand dune, a fresh spring bubbles up and feeds a crystal-clear lake in the sand. The lake is shaped as a crescent moon. It is a welcoming sight and a lifesaving gift to people like us who traverse the Gobi and the Desert of No Return for a living. I think you and your family will like Shazhou. The air there is pristine. The people are nice and the climate balmy."

"Thank you." Cheng bowed. "We look forward to making our home in Shazhou."

That evening, Habib invited the Cheng family for a dinner of roasted lamb. During dinner, Cheng, having discovered that Xian-Hui and Little Ma were former eunuchs in Emperor Ling's

A FORTUITOUS OPPORTUNITY

209

palace, revealed that he had recently left his post as the governor of Bingzhou province because the warlords had made it impossible for him to govern. The chaos and armed strife in China drove him to emigrate to the Western Regions. He confessed that the decision to emigrate was difficult and heart-wrenching, tantamount to self-imposed exile. But Cheng did not see any hope for the Han dynasty, and he did not wish to subject his family to the risk of perishing in a war-torn country. He had been assiduously studying the Western Regions ever since he assumed the governorship of Bingzhou province, which included several frontier regions. As the Han nation sank into anarchy, he chose to start a new life by taking his family to Shazhou, an area partly colonized by Han agriculturalists after Emperor Wu defeated the Huns in 121 BC and stationed a garrison there. Three centuries after Emperor Wu's conquest, Shazhou now flourished as a multiethnic prefecture with a thriving economy, too remote to be of interest to the power-craving warlords. The warlords focused their efforts on controlling the Yellow River basin and the Yangtzi River basin, the two grain-rich regions with large populations that constituted the heart of China. Cheng knew he and his family would be safe in Shazhou, out of the region of contention among warlords. Feeling a connection with Xian-Hui and Little Ma on account of their previous lives, he was glad to meet them at the beginning of his emigration. He told them the current news about the imperial court. According to Cheng, the imperial court had become totally dysfunctional. Cao Cao had corralled the reins of power and harbored imperial ambition.

"I can visualize the end of the Han dynasty," Cheng told Xian-Hui and Little Ma.

"You mean to tell me that there isn't a single warlord who is loyal and moral?" Xian-Hui wondered out loud.

"I don't know," Cheng said. "I heard that there is a militia headed by three good people called the Peach Garden Brothers who wish to resuscitate the Han dynasty. They defeated a column of the Yellow Turbans not so long ago. Unfortunately, without a rich economic base and a big army, they stand little chance contending for national dominance. They are loyal subjects with good intentions. But I am not sure that the Han dynasty is salvageable."

"Where are they? I mean the Peach Garden Brothers," Xian-Hui asked.

"I don't know for sure. They might be in the southern part of Jing province. They did have a base in Xu province but lost their territory to wily Cao Cao. Now they are settling in the southern part of Jing province as guests of the warlord Sun Ce. They have a sterling reputation among people who live in areas under their governance."

"Well." Xian-Hui contemplated as she responded to Cheng's words. "Good people are rare in this world. Good leaders are even rarer. If what you said about the Peach Garden Brothers is accurate, I would like to join them if I could."

Xian-Hui's response astonished Cheng. He didn't expect such a resolute and definitive pronouncement on a weighty issue from so young a person. Furthermore, her preference stood out in contrast to his choice of emigration. To begin with, he was not proud of his choice, being painfully aware that emigration amounted to the last resort of a desperado. It meant abandoning one's ancestral heritage, bringing up one's children in a different culture, severing all social connections, and facing unknown challenges in a new environment that might or might not be better than the society one was abandoning.

Xian-Hui, unintentionally, had induced Cheng to question the wisdom of the direction in which he was taking his family.

Perhaps my pessimism has overwhelmed me and drove me to a rash decision, Cheng thought to himself. He became pensive, stopped eating, and excused himself from the dinner party.

Back in his tent, Cheng felt agitated. He reexamined his situation. Yes, the Han dynasty was coming to an end. Yes, the nation was war-torn. Yes, he could no longer execute his duties as an honest provincial governor and the safety of his family was uncertain.

Does my situation call for so drastic a move as to leave the world to which my ancestors and I belong? he asked himself. Will my family and I thrive in an alien region? What will happen to my children? Will they grow up to be Han people?

Question after question welled up in his mind. He thought he had examined them when he considered emigrating to Shazhou. As conditions in his home province degenerated to a point that the life of his family became threatened, he stopped mulling over those questions seriously. Now, the same questions resurfaced. He still had no answers for them. He felt sad, confused, and bereaved. Logical reasoning seemed to have escaped him.

That night, plagued by anxiety, he tossed and turned for hours before falling asleep. When he woke up in the morning, a revelatory decision, unexpectedly, crystallized in his mind: "I will give my family and myself one last chance in my country: join the benevolent Peach Garden Brothers. If life under the Peach Garden Brothers is also unbearable, I will emigrate and leave my country."

The decision lightened his burden. Cheerfully, he sought out Xian-Hui and told her that he and his family, instead of heading toward exile in Shazhou, had decided to join the Peach Garden Brothers in southern Jing province. He wanted to thank Xian-Hui for suggesting that living in a region governed by benevolent leaders might be wise.

"Yesterday you told me that you would like to join the Peach Garden Brothers." Cheng told Xian-Hui, "If you wish to do so, you are welcome to travel with us to Jing province."

Xian-Hui was pleasantly surprised.

"Thank you very much for your kind and generous offer. Let me talk with my cousin Little Ma."

Upon learning that Xian-Hui wanted to go to southern Jing province, Little Ma was shocked. Xian-Hui's choice made no sense to him. In his mind, they had barely escaped the chaos and pandemonium of the palace in Luoyang and reached the edge of a promising new life, it was incomprehensible that Xian-Hui wanted to return to that quagmire of conflicts, intrigues, and politics in the Han empire. He knew nothing about the Peach Garden Brothers, nor did he care to learn about them. He wanted to roam the great steppes of the Western Regions, gallop over the waves of the grassland, camp under the big sky and glittering stars, experience the immensity of the Desert of No Return, admire the snowcapped mountains that cordoned off countries like Bharat, explore exotic places like Turfan and Kashi, participate in adventures with people like Habib and Mr. Gu. He wanted freedom, freedom from a life of servitude, freedom from bondage, freedom from cruel traditions, freedom from conniving officials, freedom from oppressing conventions. To him, the Western Regions stood as a promised land where he could forge a new life, adopt a new identity, and pursue his dreams. But he couldn't bear the thought of parting with Xian-Hui. They had been inseparable for nearly two years. When Xian-Hui said that she was going to join the Peach Garden Brothers in Jing province, his heart skipped a beat. Swallowing hard, he said to Xian-Hui, "Why do you want to join some people you don't even know? They are probably the same as all those people in the palace vying for power, people like eunuch Jian and his cabal, General Dong Zhuo and his coconspirators. We escaped from the palace to leave behind that rotten world. I don't want to go back, but I also don't want you to go back. You have been my lodestar, and I am your devoted servant. I want to stay with you. Please, I beg you…"

Little Ma was so grief-stricken that he lost his voice and started sobbing. Suddenly, it dawned on Xian-Hui that Little Ma might be in love with her. She never envisioned that a eunuch

A FORTUITOUS OPPORTUNITY

could fall in love, not understanding that Little Ma's love for her stemmed from his adulation for her and his hunger for familial attachment, like an abandoned prepubescent boy, seeking to hitch his life onto a mature woman in his romantic imagination. He felt totally devoted to Xian-Hui. On Xian-Hui's side, she treasured Little Ma's devotion, cared for him, and wanted to help him find a new life. But she had no doubt that they were not meant to be together forever.

"Listen, Little Ma," Xian-Hui said softly but firmly. "You have been a wonderful friend. Practically a brother. But I need to live among my kind of people, and you are eager to seek a new life and adventure in foreign land. I cannot go with you, and you will be miserable if you follow me. It is best for us to part ways. Tomorrow, I will leave with Cheng's party heading to Jing province while you go west with Habib and Mr. Gu. I am sure that they will take good care of you. Here is the money for you to pay Habib and some more."

As Xian-Hui turned to walk away from Little Ma, a surge of sadness nearly overpowered her, but she did not stop walking, confident that her words and action were best for both. She heard Little Ma, inconsolable and heartbroken at that moment, sobbing behind her. But she never looked back.

The next morning, when Xian-Hui showed up at Cheng's camp carrying a small sack, Cheng was stunned and speechless. Upon recovery, he blurted out, "Little Wong, I don't understand. You are a eunuch, aren't you?"

Xian-Hui, radiant in a beige silk robe, an indigo sash around her waist, and a matching scarf over her short pitch-black hair, which had already begun to grow back, smiled confidently.

"No, I disguised myself as a eunuch to travel safely. Since you have a platoon of bodyguards, I no longer feel the need for the disguise. My name is Xian-Hui."

Recovering from his shock, Cheng stuttered, "Of course, of course. You will be well protected. You are very beautiful if you don't mind my saying so."

"Well," Xian-Hui responded, "my beauty is more a curse than a blessing. It has caused me great distress and hindered my pursuit of a worthy life."

"Oh, I am sorry to hear that. I am happy to be your avuncular friend. It is rare for me to meet a woman like you. I hope that, from now on, you will be free and you will meet people who support and appreciate you in your pursuits. Shall we begin our journey? It will be a long one."

TEN

A PORTENTOUS MEETING

Not long after Cheng, Xian-Hui, and their party entered the southern region of Jing province, skirting lakes, fording streams, bypassing swamps, and traversing forests, they came upon hundreds of busy soldiers on a lakeshore, herding mules to haul trees they had felled, hewing planks of wood from tree trunks, bending wood studs and planks over fire, assembling boat frames with hardwood studs and resin, honing wooden pegs with their axes, and drilling holes on boat frames for the pegs to fasten wooden planks onto the boat frames. They were building small sampans and large junks at multiple stations where the completed wooden frames sat on elevated platforms. It was an inspiring sight of enthusiastic and hardworking military men as if they were a regiment of skilled carpenters and craftsmen.

Among them was a colossal man with a magnificent beard, his forehead glistening with sweat, moving among laborers, cutting trees, hauling wood, sawing trunks, bending wood planks and studs over amber charcoal, hammering pegs that bound the siding onto boat frames. This man with a big beard was everywhere even though he appeared to be the boss because the soldiers listened to him when he talked. But he acted like a member of the working crew without pretension and worked as hard as, if not harder than, everyone else. In a buoyant mood, he also seemed to have a knack of shoring up the spirits of the entire crew, patting people on the back, brushing off sawdust and wood chips from their shoulders, removing debris and small tree branches from the workplace.

Cheng and Xian-Hui stopped in their tracks and marveled at the sight. They had never seen so many people working so hard in such good spirit. When Guan Yu noticed that the traveling party was gawking at him and his crew, he waved.

"Hello there!" Guan Yu's voice boomed.

"On our way to join the Peach Garden Brothers," Cheng responded, "we have stopped to admire the way you and your crew are working, so cheerful and harmonious."

"Yes, my soldiers are precious jewels. They come from many different ethnic groups in this region, Hmong, Mien, Jingpo, Thai, Yi, Bunong, Dai, Han, and so on. We constitute a multiethnic task force building a naval fleet. Except me, everyone here is skilled. I am their pupil and assistant," Guan Yu said. "Oh, did you say that you were looking for the Peach Garden Brothers? I am one of them. Obviously, you are on a mission. Go talk to my senior brother, Liu Bei, and our chief of staff, Zhuge Liang. Just follow the road. Our headquarters is not far off."

"A multiethnic task force. I have never heard of such an organization. What a glorious concept and a splendid achievement! Congratulations!" Xian-Hui commented.

Guan Yu looked in Xian-Hui's direction. When he did, he was transfixed, mesmerized by her poise, confidence, and eloquence. In his experience, most Han women didn't speak so freely in public or offer their opinion so spontaneously, least of all expressing a favorable view of non-Han ethnic groups.

"Thank you, thank you. My name is Guan Yu. Honored to make your acquaintance," Guan Yu responded.

A PORTENTOUS MEETING   217

"I am Xian-Hui. We will meet again."

As much as Guan Yu was impressed with Xian-Hui, she was fascinated by Guan Yu. What struck her was his bursting energy, forthright personality, and absolute unpretentiousness. He seemed to exude kindness, a kindness that obviously touched and inspired the people who were working with him. Instead of treating soldiers with condescension as many commanders did, Guan Yu worked among them as an equal. He also made them laugh with his incessant, lighthearted banter, lifting everyone's spirits, often at the expense of belittling himself.

What an interesting man! Xian-Hui thought to herself.

At the Peach Garden Brothers' headquarters, Cheng explained the reason for his presence and briefly summarized his credentials to the guards. He asked for an audience with Liu Bei. Within minutes, Liu Bei appeared at the gate.

"Welcome to my humble headquarters, Governor Cheng." Liu Bei bowed. "I am honored by your presence. Our enterprise will be invigorated with the addition of your talent."

"You are too generous, Lord Liu Bei," Cheng responded. "My family and I admire your mission and seek refuge in your domain. I would be honored if you could assign me a role in your enterprise, so that I could contribute toward your effort to restore the Han dynasty."

"That will be wonderful. I am sure that we can put your administrative experience to good use. In the meantime, my people will help you and your party to settle in our expanding compound. Ah, here is our chief counselor, Zhuge Liang." Liu Bei gestured in Zhuge Liang's direction as he entered the headquarters.

"I am delighted to meet you, Honorable Zhuge. Your reputation is far-flung."

"Ah, I am just a plodding bookworm, trying to help Lord Liu Bei. You arrive at a propitious time when we need people with administrative experience. We are building a navy and preparing for a major battle with Cao Cao who, by now, occupies the largest territory and commands the most powerful armed forces in the nation. Let us talk tomorrow. After a long journey, you and your family should settle in and rest up."

"Thank you, Honorable Zhuge. We are one family plus a young lady, Xian-Hui. I hope it is possible for us to be housed separately."

"Not a problem. Not a problem." Zhuge Liang directed the household staff to guide the travelers to their respective rooms.

That evening, Liu Bei hosted a dinner in honor of Cheng's party. During the dinner, the conversation tended to gravitate toward the political situation of the nation. When politics was not discussed, people focused their attention on Xian-Hui. Everyone wanted to know where her family home was, why she was so erudite at such a young age, what she was doing in a caravan heading to the Western Regions, etc. Cheng told what he knew of her, how they met at a caravansary where she was disguised as a eunuch, how she inadvertently gave him the idea of joining the Peach Garden Brothers and then abruptly announced she would join the Cheng family to come to Jing province. In answering people's questions, Xian-Hui did not demur as young women often did. She responded with candor but did not divulge the information that she was an imperial concubine who escaped from Emperor Ling's Luoyang palace. Even her traveling companions, Cheng and his family, were not privy to that information.

The Peach Garden Brothers were fascinated by Xian-Hui's story. But they all sensed that she withheld some crucial information about her past. In addition, they were all mystified by her dismissal, if not outright rejection, of her beauty. She clearly did not like to be complimented for it. Guan Yu found her so intriguing that he approached her with an uncommon request after dinner: "Since you are such an intelligent and

A PORTENTOUS MEETING

learned lady, I would be honored if you would play a game of weiqi (Go) with me. Being a warrior, I am, as you can guess, far from being erudite as you are. Weiqi is a game of strategy, deploying beads to gain territory on the board, like deploying troops in a war to rout your enemy. When I was young, I learned to play this board game at the knees of my grand master in a martial arts camp, but never became very good at it. That's why I never played the game with my elder brother, Liu Bei, or our chief of staff, Zhuge Liang. Both are experts who can beat me handily. Perhaps you wouldn't mind giving me a lesson, Lady Xian-Hui."

Xian-Hui was happy to accept Guan Yu's challenge, which struck her as another out-of-the-norm behavior. Men typically praised a woman for her beauty, never competing with her in a game of strategy and mental agility. Her father was the only exception. In addition, Guan Yu launched his request with such casualness and humility that Xian-Hui couldn't possibly turn him down. It would have been impolite and inconsiderate if she did. Xian-Hui also thought it would be fun to play a game of weiqi with a renowned warrior. Without further discussion, the two of them retreated to an adjacent conference room to start the board game with black and white beads.

"Perfect!" Guan Yu said as he and Xian-Hui took their seats facing each other. "I am dark as a raven, and you are white as ivory. Naturally you take the white beads and I'll take the black beads."

Xian-Hui laughed. "You are not as dark as a raven, just suntanned and in robust health."

"Well, I am no good at simile or, for that matter, any figure of speech. Literary devices are too sophisticated for a simple person like me. Let's begin our game. It is customary for white to make the first move."

Twenty minutes later, Guan Yu conceded. Xian-Hui had his beads cornered and surrounded.

"So much for a warrior!" Guan Yu said after losing the game. "I need you as my strategist."

"No, you don't," Xian-Hui retorted, "you already have a genius strategist in Zhuge Liang."

"Yes, Zhuge Liang is a genius. I am glad he is on our side. But he is not *my* strategist."

Xian-Hui blushed but didn't respond. She stood up and bade Guan Yu good night. Guan Yu was astonished by his own bold declaration. He had not planned on saying what he said. The words just tumbled out of his mouth spontaneously. He hoped he had not offended Xian-Hui, whom he, unaware of a host of his own feelings, admired.

Back in her room, Xian-Hui felt agitated. She had never taken an interest in any man. Realizing that there was something about Guan Yu that appealed to her, she tried to get to the bottom of it.

Was it his cheerful personality?

Was it his exceptional level of energy?

Was it the way he interacted with people: warm, gentle, and candid?

Was it his disregard for convention and lack of inhibition?

Was it his commanding presence?

She couldn't decide.

Everything about Guan Yu was unusual. Unusualness was the only feature about him that she was sure of. It seemed to capture all his qualities.

The next morning, Guan Yu asked for a private conversation with his senior sworn brother, Liu Bei.

"Dear brother," Guan Yu didn't beat around the bush, "I don't know how to describe my feelings. But I think I am in love with Xian-Hui."

A PORTENTOUS MEETING

Liu Bei could hardly believe what he heard. Totally focused on his work and his martial arts, Guan Yu had never shown any interest in women. Flicking his bushy eyebrows, Liu Bei asked Guan Yu in all seriousness, "Are you sure? Do you know what you are saying?"

"Of course! You know me well." Guan Yu explained, "It is not easy for me to say such things. Sleepless for hours last night, I recognized the cause of my insomnia was my love for Xian-Hui. At the beginning of meeting her, I admired her for her poise and intelligence. I wasn't looking for love. But love came looking for me, suddenly and unexpectedly. When I woke up with the understanding that I had fallen in love with her, I didn't know what to do and still don't know what to do. That's why I am here seeking your counsel."

"Good!" Liu Bei responded, "It is time for you to be married, and I think there isn't a woman better suited to you than Xian-Hui in the whole world."

"What should I do?" Guan Yu wondered.

"Don't do anything." Liu Bei said with a broad smile, "Leave the matter to me."

That afternoon, Liu Bei asked Xian-Hui to accompany him on a promenade along the bank of a nearby lake surrounded by weeping willows. It was a temperate day in late summer with a soft breeze. The willow branches swayed gently over the water. From the bushes around the lake, fledglings of songbirds were testing their wings in preparation for their autumn migration southward.

"Today I am taking on a task that I have never done in my life," Liu Bei told Xian-Hui with a smile.

"What is that?" Xian-Hui's curiosity was piqued.

"I am playing the role of a matchmaker."

"Matchmaker!" Xian-Hui was further surprised. "For whom?"

"For you and my dear brother, Guan Yu." Liu Bei's face glowed with pride. "I think marriage between you two is preordained, made in heaven."

"But I have no interest in being a wife," Xian-Hui declared emphatically.

"Perfect!" Liu Bei giggled. "And my brother, Guan Yu, has no interest in seeking a wife. That's why you two are a perfect match. Guan Yu needs a counselor, a strategist, a cerebral partner in life. He knows you are more intelligent and erudite than he is. That's why he adores and loves you."

Xian-Hui looked surprised. But then she wasn't, recalling that Guan Yu told her yesterday at the end of their board game that he wanted her to be his personal strategist. She had not known him for long. But he was easy to know, hiding nothing, speaking his mind, calling things as he saw them. Fearless and forthright, he was unique in the world with which she was familiar, where people customarily concealed their desires, disguised their feelings, never meant what they said, and never said what they meant, where a yes could mean no and a no could mean yes, where interpersonal communication was conducted through inferences, implications, innuendos, and second-guessing, where everyone struggled to debunk and interpret another person's words and actions with the help of the context and history of their relations. It was as if people didn't share a common language and needed an interpreter whenever they conversed with each other. No wonder reticence was considered virtuous, and speaking in riddles regarded as brilliant in Han culture, Xian-Hui suddenly realized.

"People are afraid of divulging what is in their hearts and fearful of being misinterpreted," muttered Xian-Hui to herself. "That's why Guan Yu is such a breath of fresh air! Therein lies his charm!"

A PORTENTOUS MEETING 223

With that understanding of Guan Yu and the equally unforeseen revelation of her own emotions, Xian-Hui looked at Liu Bei and said, "Yes, I will marry him."

"Congratulations!" Liu Bei cried out in joy. "You have made my day. I will arrange the matrimonial ceremony!"

At their insistence, Xian-Hui and Guan Yu had a simple and brief matrimonial ceremony in the garden of the Peach Garden Brothers' military headquarters the following morning. Zhang Fei set up a small shrine with burning incense in a bowl surrounded by lotus flowers and many cups of rose liquor on a table next to a lotus pond. Zhuge Liang served as the master of ceremonies, facing the wedding couple, who were flanked by Liu Bei and Zhang Fei. Xian-Hui, radiant in her crimson silk gown, was all smiles. Guan Yu, wearing a long indigo robe and a matching hat, his beard neatly trimmed, was jubilant. When Zhuge Liang declared their marriage a union of true minds, pure and glorious as the lotus flower, the small group of people including Cheng and his family broke into applause.

The wedding ended with many rounds of toasts proposed by Liu Bei, Zhang Fei, Zhuge Liang, and Cheng, wishing the newlywed couple happiness. Afterward, Guan Yu rejoined his crew of shipbuilders to work. Xian-Hui went to her room to compose a letter to her parents, whom she had not contacted in consideration of their safety since she escaped from the imperial palace. Being married to Guan Yu, she felt that it wouldn't be rude for her to request a special messenger from the camp of the Peach Garden Brothers to deliver a letter to her parents all the way in Suzhou on the bank of the Yangtzi River along the eastern seaboard.

When the messenger reached Xian-Hui's parents at their home in Suzhou and handed them Xian-Hui's handwritten letter, which they recognized immediately from her calligraphy, they could not believe that they had regained their daughter. They thought that she had perished when Dong Zhuo set fire to the palace and Luoyang. In shock, they asked the messenger twice if Xian-Hui was really living in Jing province. The messenger's repeated assurances induced a flood of tears from the elderly couple even though they tried desperately to hold back their surge of emotions.

After regaining their composure, Xian-Hui's parents thanked the messenger profusely, invited him into their home for tea and rice cakes, and treated him as if he were an angel bringing a miraculous tiding from heaven. When they learned from Xian-Hui's letter that she was married to one of the Peach Garden Brothers, they would've jumped in ecstasy, had they not been inhibited by the self-restraint instilled in them since childhood. They were aware of the Peach Garden Brothers' sterling reputation and felt proud that one of the brothers had become their son-in-law.

One year later, Xian-Hui gave birth to a son. Her parents, ecstatic at becoming grandparents, sold their home in Suzhou and relocated to Jing province to live with Xian-Hui and Guan Yu, shocking their neighbors and friends in Suzhou because the nation's timeless tradition called for a newlywed couple to move into their parental home, preferably the groom's parental home, to be near their ancestral roots. It was unconventional, if not sacrilegious, for parents to move to the home of a newlywed offspring. The removal of Xian-Hui's parents to Jing province generated a lot of gossip among their neighbors and friends in Suzhou. People disparaged the parents' motivation for such a tradition-breaking, nonconforming behavior. In the eyes of the people of Suzhou, the departure of Xian-Hui's parents represented the culmination of the couple's eccentric manner of bringing up Xian-Hui, from educating her to become an intellectual to aiding and abetting her to rebel against the traditional role of a female as an appendage to a male.

A PORTENTOUS MEETING

For Xian-Hui and Guan Yu, having Xian-Hui's parents in their household was a blessing. Under the doting care and tutelage of his grandparents, Guan Ping grew up to become a cheerful, well-rounded young man, talented in both martial arts and intellectual pursuits.

ELEVEN

THE BATTLE
OF VERMILION GORGE

The day after Xian-Hui's wedding, Guan Yu, Zhang Fei, Liu Bei, and Zhuge Liang reached a decision to ask Cheng to oversee logistics for their military operation, charging him with the responsibility of ensuring the free flow of food, supplies, weapons, equipment, and personnel. Cheng couldn't be happier with the assignment and plunged into his job with total devotion. After spending one month to establish a logistics system within the Peach Garden Brothers' army, he felt that he had regained his governorship of a state without the shackle and pressure of corrupt and incompetent colleagues. To Cheng, the camaraderie in the camp of the Peach Garden Brothers was uplifting, the spirit of the rank and file exhilarating.

As Cheng tackled his job with enthusiasm and confidence, Guan Yu and his crew were training diligently for naval warfare on the Yangtzi River. The mainstay of their newly created navy consisted of scores of sampans, each of which was manned by four soldiers: two rowers in the middle, one archer at the stern with quivers of arrows at his knee, and one lancer at the bow. When Guan Yu's navy maneuvered in tactical exercises, the sampans darted like a horde of gigantic water striders on a predatory hunt across the surface of a body of water.

Xian-Hui helped Guan Yu to create the organizational structure of the navy. It was her idea that every ten sampans formed a platoon, and every five platoons formed a fleet headed by a junk from which the fleet commander directed the action of the platoons. The river people from the Dai and Yi ethnic groups taught Xian-Hui, Guan Yu, and his officers a signaling system, using colored flags in various configurations. Each platoon leader, who replaced the lancer at the bow of his sampan, and two signalers on each junk bore the responsibility of communication with other boats of the flotilla.

Xian-Hui was always present at battle drills. With her infant son strapped on her back, she observed every move of the boats and advised Guan Yu on tactics to surround imagined large enemy ships. When Guan Yu's navy charged upstream, a flotilla of sampans moved synchronously in a tight formation, flanking their commanding ship, which was a large junk loaded with rowers, soldiers, archers, and equipment. At the sight of enemy ships, the flotilla split into several columns, speeding across the water to attack each enemy ship from two sides. The sampans moved upstream and downstream with equal agility. They navigated around eddies and submerged rocks like kayaks maneuvered by expert kayakers.

Curious, Cheng asked Zhuge Liang the reason for creating a naval force.

"We anticipate a major battle with Cao Cao, who has assembled a powerful flotilla of several dozen junks in a cove upstream from the Vermilion Canyon on the Yangtzi River," Zhuge Liang explained. "You know the Yangtzi River is the major artery for transportation in this region. Whoever controls the Yangtzi River will lord over Jing province and Shu (Szechuan) province. Shu province is a large, fertile basin surrounded by high mountains drained by the Yangtzi and its tributaries. We intend to take over the Shu basin as our base for launching our national campaign."

"Yes, Shu province is upstream along the Yangtzi River." Cheng nodded. "The mountains surrounding Shu province protect the basin from land invasion. That leaves the Yangtzi River the only gateway to enter the basin. If one wishes to safeguard Shu, one will have to control the Yangtzi, ergo the navy!"

"Bravo! Bravo! You grasp the situation totally." Zhuge Liang applauded. "Cao Cao is an intelligent general who understands the strategic importance of the Vermilion Gorge as a choke hold along the Yangtzi River. That's why he is amassing a naval task force in a cove nearby. Our job is to destroy his navy before he seizes control of the waterway."

"I have two questions, Honorable Zhuge," Cheng said. "First, please tell me about the Vermilion Gorge. I am not familiar with local geography."

"The Vermilion Gorge is on the eastern border of Shu province where the Yangtzi River exits onto the plains." Zhuge Liang explained, "It is an awesome canyon with two walls of solid, dark-vermilion rock rising almost one li from the river without any vegetation as if some mythical titan, wielding a gargantuan sharp knife when our world was being created, had cut smoothly through a mountain of solid rock to let the Yangtzi River exit the Shu basin. When you sail through the gorge, you feel like an insignificant creature at the bottom of an enormous slot, boxed in by sky-high vermilion cliffs on both sides, deafened by the sound of the raging water tumbling eastward, and if you crane your neck to look up the vertical walls surrounding you, their height is of such a scale that it will make you dizzy. Aside from being an awesome spectacle of nature, the Vermilion Gorge guards the Shu basin like a gate guarding a citadel. The major flow of commerce and people in and out of Shu province passes through the Vermilion Gorge. We must control it, if we wish to take the province of Shu."

THE BATTLE OF VERMILION GORGE

"Thank you, Master Zhuge." Cheng cupped his hands together and raised them high to express his appreciation. "My second question concerns our upcoming battle against Cao Cao. You have stated that Cao Cao has already amassed a large navy with dozens of gigantic junks in a cove upstream beyond the Vermilion Gorge. Our naval force consists of a few dozen sampans with three midsize junks stationed downstream from the Vermilion Gorge. A battle between us and them would appear lopsided in their favor. How are we to proceed?"

"A good question." Zhuge Liang smiled. "We need a clever plan and a miracle, both of which I cannot divulge at this time. Our immediate task is to form an alliance with the warlord Sun Ce. It won't be easy because he also wants to acquire the Shu basin."

"Just before I left Chang'an to come here," Cheng said, "Sun Ce was rumored to be critically ill. By now, his younger brother, Sun Quan, has probably succeeded him. I am friendly with Sun Quan's chief of staff, Zhou Yu, a cerebral and portly man. It will be my pleasure to serve as your emissary to seek their alliance against Cao Cao."

"Excellent, excellent!" Zhuge Liang responded, "Could you get on the road as soon as possible to visit Zhou Yu and persuade him to be our ally?"

"Of course," Cheng exclaimed. "It is my duty to contribute to our mission. I am delighted to take on the assignment."

Two weeks later, Cheng returned to report to Zhuge Liang triumphantly that Zhou Yu had agreed to attack Cao Cao's military base at the foothill northeast of the Vermilion Gorge in coordination with the Peach Garden Brothers' naval action along the Yangtzi River. Zhou Yu reasoned that Cao Cao, given his control of the imperial court, the rich Yellow River basin, and the province of Xu, was already too powerful and menacing. If Cao Cao were left unchecked, he would swallow up other warlords. At this moment, it seemed strategically advantageous to check Cao Cao from pushing his large army south to gobble up the Shu valley and the territory belonging to the Sun clan. Zhuge Liang's proposal for a coordinated attack on Cao Cao came at a propitious moment in his strategic analysis of the current state of affairs.

For Zhuge Liang and the Peach Garden Brothers, the alliance with Zhou Yu against Cao Cao relieved them from the burden of defending against Cao Cao's infantry in the north, so that Zhuge Liang could focus his troops on the upcoming battle at the Vermilion Gorge. Seizing the opportunity provided by the new alliance with the Sun family, Zhuge Liang immediately transferred Zhang Fei and his cavalry from the northern frontier of Jing province to reinforce Guan Yu in the forthcoming naval battle.

Upon Zhang Fei's arrival in the headquarters, Zhuge Liang sent Cheng to secretly procure a large quantity of oil, sulfur, batches of dry hay, and twenty small sails to be fitted on sampans.

"Choose twenty sampans and the most trustworthy soldiers who are also the best swimmers to install a mast at the stern and load the incendiary material at the bow of each boat. Tie the sampans into a row, stretching from one bank of the river to the opposite bank." Zhuge Liang ordered Cheng, "Swear the soldiers to secrecy! They are forbidden to talk about what they are doing for the next few days."

As the preparation for the naval battle neared completion under the watchful eyes of Xian-Hui, Zhuge Liang revealed his strategic plan.

"We will not fight against Cao Cao's superior fleet. That will be costly, not to mention that Cao Cao's junks are likely to overwhelm our smaller vessels. We will burn them before they can unleash their superior power on us."

"How do we burn Cao Cao's fleet?" Guan Yu, full of doubt, inquired.

THE BATTLE OF VERMILION GORGE

231

"We will send twenty sampans loaded with incendiary materials into Cao Cao's fleet to burn them when they sail down the river to fight us," Zhuge Liang answered.

"How do you send sampans upstream against the current?" Zhang Fei challenged.

"We will need a miracle with which we may be blessed any day." Zhuge Liang laughed.

"A miracle!" Guan Yu was alarmed. "The Taoist priests are the only people I know who talk about miracles. It is their standard ruse to dupe gullible people. If you don't mind my rudeness, I would like to know when you have become a priest of Taoism."

"No, no," Zhuge Liang retorted, "I have no use for religion. The miracle I am talking about is wind. Easterly wind, to be more precise. Our flotilla of sampans will ride the wind upstream on sails to reach Cao Cao's junks."

"But it is autumn now," Guan Yu was practically yelling. "Easterly wind ends in late spring!"

"Yes, you are right!" Zhuge Liang tried to calm down Guan Yu. "Except the sea along the coast breeds hurricanes in summer and early autumn. Hurricanes bring powerful southeasterly winds that could reach several hundred li inland. I am counting on one coming our way. That's why I have been asking my attendants to carry me to a high mountain peak east of the Vermilion Gorge every morning so that I can observe the weather front along the coastal region. But you must not say anything about my plan. The attendants who carry me up and down the mountain peak every morning believe I go there to meditate and summon supernatural power. I told them that on the mountaintop, I would be closer to heaven, and it would be easier for gods and immortals to hear my supplication. There, cupping incense in my hands, I chant coded mantras with my eyes shut, my body shaking, as if I were possessed by some invisible spirit. My attendants were scared out of their minds when they first saw me in that bewitched state. They couldn't stop from gossiping about my rituals, speculating and debating the nature of the immortals I was invoking, whether those immortals would be evil or benevolent, powerful or ho-hum, dangerous or harmless. They are my unintended, uninstructed, self-motivated propagandists. I want them to spread their gossip, honestly and earnestly, that I am invoking magic in the upcoming battle. You must understand that, as a rule, the most effective propagandists are the ones who are unaware of their role. If they gossip 'facts,' people will believe them."

"Why are you taking all this trouble to spread false information?" Zhang Fei asked innocently.

"I want to intimidate Zhou Yu, Sun Ce, and Cao Cao, instill fear in them, and gain an upper hand in our struggle against them." Zhuge Liang smiled.

"Master Zhuge, you are, indeed, a miracle worker," Guan Yu cried out. "Now I understand why you have ordered Cheng to procure incendiary material and sails. I hope the weather cooperates with us."

"If your mission is righteous, nature will be most likely on your side." Zhuge Liang asserted, "Unlike Cao Cao who wishes to terminate the Han dynasty and Sun Ce who wants to ascend the imperial throne, we are on a righteous path to seek a Han renaissance. Tomorrow morning at dawn, please join me on my trip to the mountaintop. I mean both of you. We can observe the clouds and the weather pattern together."

Guan Yu and Zhang Fei were delighted by the invitation.

Early next morning, Guan Yu and Zhang Fei accompanied Zhuge Liang to the mountaintop. Ten attendants carrying Zhuge Liang in a palanquin rocked their way up the mountain path while singing in unison to relieve the strain of bearing the palanquin. With weapons in their hands, Zhang Fei and Guan Yu walked behind in giant strides.

THE BATTLE OF VERMILION GORGE   233

Upon arriving at the mountaintop, Zhuge Liang began his usual ritual, burning incense, chanting incomprehensible mantras, invoking the immortal spirits, and occasionally shaking.

Shortly after Zhuge Liang began, several men showed up on the other side of the meadow where Zhuge Liang had set up his altar and paraphernalia. Dressed shabbily and collecting herbs, they loitered around. One asked a palanquin carrier what Zhuge Liang was doing. An attendant immediately interrupted Zhuge Liang to report the interlopers.

"You can tell them the truth. The chief of staff of the Peach Garden Brothers' army is here to summon gods and immortals to vanquish Cao Cao," Zhuge Liang said calmly.

Then he turned to Guan Yu and Zhang Fei and whispered, "Enemy spies! From which camp, Zhou Yu's or Cao Cao's, I cannot tell."

When he heard *enemy spies*, Zhang Fei's eyes bulged as if they were ready to pop out of their sockets.

"Should I kill them?" he asked Zhuge Liang.

Zhuge Liang beckoned to Guan Yu and Zhang Fei, "Let's walk away from everyone so that we can speak privately."

Waving their subordinates away, the three men walked some distance into a bush before Zhuge Liang admonished Zhang Fei, "No, no, no! Don't do anything against the spies. Ignore them. I want them to report to their master that I am engaging in magic. In fact, I think they might very well be Zhou Yu's spies," Zhuge Liang continued in his whisper.

"What?" Taken aback, Guan Yu was barely able to hold his voice down. "Zhou Yu is our ally!"

"Yes, all the more urgent for him to spy on us." Zhuge replied, "Zhou Yu and his lord, Sun Ce, want to gobble up the Shu basin just as eagerly as we and Cao Cao do. For all we know, Sun Ce might have already departed from this world. But that doesn't change the chess game. His younger brother, Sun Quan, a capable general, would follow Sun Ce's policies and listen to Zhou Yu's advice. Zhou Yu is trying to figure out how we prepare for the naval battle in the Vermilion Gorge so that he can deal with us more effectively in the future. There is no reason for Cao Cao to spy on me at the mountaintop. His spies are probably disguised as local fishermen traversing the stretch of the Yangtzi River around the Vermilion Gorge to count the number of our vessels and figure out the formations of our fleet."

Guan Yu and Zhang Fei were dumbfounded. They were awed by Zhuge Liang's ability to read the minds of his rivals and stay a couple of steps ahead of them. It was his custom to position himself at a vantage point where he had a clear view of his rivals while concealing himself in darkness.

"Oh, well!" Guan Yu sighed. "This is all beyond me. I am just a warrior, and I am glad that you are our chief of staff!"

Zhuge Liang leaned back and laughed.

"Well, an effective team should be composed of people with different talents," Zhuge Liang observed. "We make an excellent team because you and Zhang Fei are intrepid warriors who command and inspire our soldiers, Liu Bei is a charismatic leader who can call on people to move mountains, Xian-Hui is a perceptive tactician who can solve difficult problems, and I am the strategist who plots our way forward. Now, let's read the distant clouds and see if we can detect the miracle we need."

To Zhuge Liang's delight, as the sun began to rise at the eastern edge of the sky, he saw dense cumulostratus clouds at a distance. Moving in a northwesterly direction, the clouds seemed to be gathering strength.

"Heaven is on our side!" Zhuge Liang exclaimed. "A squall is brewing. A southeasterly wind will rise from the horizon. Let's hurry back to put our plan in motion before rain dampens the explosive power of our incendiary sampans."

Back at their base, Xian-Hui learned of Zhuge Liang's plot. She thought it was brilliant and advised Guan Yu to have twenty

THE BATTLE OF VERMILION GORGE

sampans tied together in a phalanx. According to Xian-Hui and Zhuge Liang's plan, the bow of each sampan was loaded with bales of hay mixed with sulfur and oil. A square sail was affixed to a mast at the stern. No sooner had the wind begun to whip up white caps on the river, with sprays blowing upstream, than a soldier, selected because of his expertise in swimming, set sail on each of the twenty sampans. Riding the wind behind their sails, the phalanx of sampans, stretching from one bank of the Yangtzi River to the other, was cutting through the current toward the Vermilion Gorge at an astonishing speed.

As soon as Cao Cao's scouts saw the approaching sampans, they rushed to report to their master. Delighted, Cao Cao thought Zhuge Liang was handing him an easy victory on a silver platter. He ordered his junks, already chained together, to ride the current downstream at top speed, with scores of rowers in each junk propelling the boats to move even faster than the roaring current to ram Zhuge Liang's sampans. He figured the sampans would disintegrate in multiple collisions with his powerful and heavy junks.

As the two sides were still forty paces apart in the Vermilion Gorge, Zhuge Liang's soldiers on the sampans set fire to their incendiary cargo, abandoned ship, dived into the river, and swam downstream. The bow of each sampan mushroomed into a gargantuan fireball as the sail at the stern, untouched by the fire, remained fully driven by the southeasterly wind. The burning sampans shot upstream toward Cao Cao's fleet of junks. The collision of the two phalanxes of ships set off explosion after explosion, reverberating between the vertical walls of the Vermilion Gorge. The gorge was transformed into a burning furnace hemmed in by thousand-foot-high cliffs. Zhuge Liang's soldiers in camp, even at a considerable distance downstream, could feel the heat radiating from the inferno in the gorge. Most of Cao Cao's officers, archers, rowers, and foot soldiers, scorched and injured, died. The battle was a massacre.

While Cao Cao's navy was burning, Zhou Yu mounted a surprise attack on Cao Cao's garrison northwest of the Vermilion Gorge. Unprepared and not expecting any hostile action, the garrison surrendered without a fight. As Zhou Yu's troops were busy processing their prisoners of war, a scout reported that the flagship of Cao Cao's junks had beached itself on the northern shore of the Yangtzi River approximately one li upstream from the Vermilion Gorge. A platoon of light cavalry surrounding a portly figure disembarked from the junk and galloped up a mountain path. Zhou Yu surmised that the portly figure was Cao Cao. It would have been futile for Zhou Yu's troops to give chase because, from their location, they would have to scale a ridge to reach the escaping party. By the time the chasing party arrived at the spot where Cao Cao was sighted, Zhou Yu estimated, they would not be able to determine which escape route up the mountains Cao Cao's party had taken.

Considering the sighting of Cao Cao's small party on the north shore upstream from the Vermilion Gorge, Zhou Yu inferred that the Peach Garden Brothers had triumphed over Cao Cao. Just as he was wondering how the Peach Garden Brothers pulled out a victory over Cao Cao's overwhelming force, Zhou Yu's scouts reported that Zhuge Liang had burned Cao Cao's navy in the Vermilion Gorge.

It was impossible for Zhuge Liang to burn Cao Cao's fleet, Zhou Yu thought to himself. After all, Cao Cao was upstream, the Peach Garden Brothers were downstream, not to mention Cao Cao's fleet had an overwhelming advantage in size, equipment, and firepower. I had hoped that the battle would endure for days, inflicting heavy losses on both sides, leaving us, the Sun branch of the triumvirate, invincible.

"How did Zhuge Liang manage to burn Cao Cao's fleet of junks?" Zhou Yu asked the scouts impatiently.

"We had reported to you, before the battle, that Zhuge Liang was summoning magical spirits on the summit of a

THE BATTLE OF VERMILION GORGE

high mountain near the Vermilion Gorge," the leading scout explained. "Today, the day of the naval battle, the weather pattern took a miraculous change. It was miraculous because we are at the beginning of the autumn season and autumn wind always hails from the north or northwest. But this afternoon, an out-of-season squall from the southeast materialized suddenly and dramatically. Obviously, Zhuge Liang summoned the squall with his magic. With the wind blowing from the east to the west, whipping up white caps on the Yangtzi River, Zhuge Liang's phalanx of sampans loaded with incendiary material sailed toward Cao Cao's superior fleet of large junks. The two sides collided in the Vermilion Gorge. The entire gorge became a fireball. Cao Cao's fleet was incinerated. His troops either drowned or burned to death. It was a brutal and pitiful sight."

The news of Cao Cao's defeat shook Zhou Yu.

"If Zhuge Liang possesses magical power in addition to his brilliant mind," he reckoned, "we will not be able to compete with him. It is imperative for us to eliminate him by any means as soon as possible."

It didn't take him long to come up with a clever scheme.

Without delay, he sat down at his desk and composed a congratulatory letter inviting Zhuge Liang to participate in a celebration of the resounding victory of their alliance against Cao Cao at Zhou Yu's headquarters. A trusted emissary was dispatched to deliver the invitation to Zhuge Liang immediately.

Upon arriving at Zhuge Liang's camp, the emissary found Zhang Fei, his long spear in hand, blocking his way at the entrance.

The emissary bowed politely and told Zhang Fei that he came to deliver a personal invitation from Zhou Yu to Zhuge Liang.

"Ha ha! Zhuge Liang has been expecting your master's invitation," Zhang Fei barked. "He knows that it is a dirty little trick to lure him to a death trap. That's why he sent me to stop you."

238   LORD GUAN

At this point, thinking about the treacherous plot conceived by Zhou Yu, Zhang Fei began to get angry, his neck veins protruded, his face turned ferocious, his voice became dark and menacing. Growling, he warned the emissary, "Because you bring evil tidings, I would have preferred to pierce your chest with my spear and dump you in the Yangtzi River as fish fodder, if Master Zhuge had not explicitly forbidden me to do so. Go back to your master and tell him that Master Zhuge has anticipated his treacherous scheme. Go, this moment, before I kick you into the dirt!"

The emissary, trembling with fear, mounted his horse without uttering another word and disappeared in a cloud of dust.

When the emissary reported to Zhou Yu what had transpired in front of Zhuge Liang's tent, Zhou Yu sighed and muttered to himself, "I am no match to Zhuge Liang. A genius, he reads my mind and stays one step ahead of me. It's unfortunate for my lord, Sun Ce. No, Sun Quan."

Distraught over Zhuge Liang's brilliance, Zhou Yu, the master strategist of the Sun regime, suffered a momentary lapse of memory, forgetting that his new master was Sun Quan, the younger brother of Sun Ce who had died of an illness one week before the Battle of the Vermilion Gorge.

Recognizing Zhuge Liang's superior intellect, Zhou Yu was depressed. Faced with his own inadequacy and inferiority in competition with his rival, Zhuge Liang, he became forlorn and downcast in his chair. Suddenly, he felt a sharp pain in his chest and suffered from shortness of breath. A dark mood of gloom and doom overcame him.

After the humiliating debacle at the Vermilion Gorge, Cao Cao retreated to Luoyang, seeking refuge in the heartland of his territory. Sun Quan took over the eastern portion of Jing province and Yangzhou province, covering most of the south-central seaboard. Liu Bei and Zhuge Liang, while leaving Guan Yu and his regiments in charge of western Jing province, decided to enter the Shu basin along the Yangtzi River.

The Shu basin was part of Han dynasty's large Yi province, situated between the Tibetan cultural domain in the west and northwest, the Jing province to the east, and bordering the impenetrable tropical jungles in the south. The Yangtzi River flowed from the high Tibetan plateau eastward, exiting the Shu basin at the Vermilion Gorge. The river, fed by water from more than a dozen tributaries draining the surrounding mountains, was a deep and navigable artery of commerce and transportation throughout the basin. As Liu Bei, Zhuge Liang, and their navy slowly moved upstream along the river into the basin, they hardly met any resistance. Their armada of sampans and junks, replete with colorful flags for communication, created an impressive pageant for the people living along the banks. Led by an awesome junk where soldiers beat their drums to coordinate the movement of the rowers sitting in the bowel of the junk, the oars of Peach Garden Brothers' fleet of sampans followed the same beat, hitting the water simultaneously in rhythm. The rowers chanted as they pulled their oars through the water to propel the boats upstream.

The bulk of Peach Garden Brothers' infantry, led by Zhang Fei, entered the Shu valley on land, marching westward along the banks of the Yangtzi River in coordination with the upstream journey of their navy. But the infantry column on land soon fell behind the naval vessels.

At a major frontier pass along the riverbank, west of the Vermilion Gorge, Zhang Fei and his column were confronted by the local garrison headed by an aging general, Pang Tong, who refused to grant passage to Zhang Fei's troops on the grounds that Zhang Fei could not produce a permit from the Han imperial court. When Zhang Fei's army took up position for a battle with the defensive force, Pang Tong refused to come out of his citadel to fight. As Zhang Fei's troops beat their drums and Zhang Fei himself galloped back and forth in front of the citadel's gate, waving his spear and screaming calumnies at Pang Tong, the defenders paid no attention. Pang Tong ordered his soldiers to stay behind the tall stone wall that blocked the pass. They had reinforced the locked gate with a bronze sheath on the outside and large tree trunks harvested from the nearby mountains on the inside. Zhang Fei wanted to set fire to the thick wooden gate of the pass. But their arrows with burning tips could not penetrate the bronze sheath. When his troops attempted to approach the gate to burn it, they were forced to retreat because the defenders on top of the wall rained arrows and spears on them.

After several days of stalemate, Zhang Fei ordered his infantry to scale the steep rocky mountain on the side of the pass to circumvent the citadel. Most of the soldiers, who grew up on the coastal plains without mountaineering skill, balked at Zhang Fei's order. Livid and sulking, Zhang Fei was at the end of his wits until a group of Qiang minority members in his troops came to his rescue, claiming that they were at home on vertical rocky walls because rock climbing was a favorite recreation in their homeland.

"When we were teenagers, we scaled rocky precipices for fun." They told Zhang Fei, "We think you and your cavalry should stay in front of the pass to distract the defenders, while we climb up the rocky mountainside, bringing ropes made of hemp from the local villages. Once on top of the rocky walls, we will drop the ropes down for the rest of our troops to scramble up."

The climb was a nerve-racking, though exciting, experience for Zhang Fei's soldiers. Most of them made it without accident. On top of the mountain, their legs and hands still shaking from the strain of climbing the rocky wall, the soldiers were so proud of themselves that they danced with joy.

THE BATTLE OF VERMILION GORGE 241

When those rock climbers descended from the mountain and raided the citadel from behind, Pang Tong, facing assault from both front and back, realized that he had no choice but to fight. Leaving his infantry to resist those who scaled the rock, Pang Tong led his cavalry out of the gate to face Zhang Fei.

The duel between Pang Tong and Zhang Fei was intense and protracted, pitching an aging but wily veteran against a young and impetuous adversary. Pang Tong wielded a big broadsword; Zhang Fei prodded with his long spear. They fought back and forth on their horses, thrusting and slashing at each other while blocking, deflecting, and dodging blows. Pang Tong, drawing from a wealth of experience, gave Zhang Fei all he could handle. During the early rounds, Zhang Fei, irked by Pang Tong's resilience and hampered by his own impatience, almost got hit on several occasions. As the duel went on, however, Pang Tong began to tire. His fatigue emboldened Zhang Fei. When Pang Tong thrust his broadsword at Zhang Fei's head, the thrust was neither powerful nor intimidating. Instead of parrying the thrust, Zhang Fei galloped his horse toward the sword as if he were welcoming Pang Tong's weapon. At the last instant, he abruptly tilted his head and torso to the side. As Pang Tong's sword missed its target, Zhang Fei, still advancing, came face-to-face with Pang Tong. With one sweep of his left arm, he grabbed Pang Tong by his belt, lifted him off his horse, and tossed him in the air toward one of Zhang Fei's cavalry officers. The officer, seeing Pang Tong being flung toward him in midair like a log, dropped his weapon and caught the fallen warrior with two arms. By the time Zhang Fei turned his horse around, Pang Tong was forced by his captors onto his knees.

Zhang Fei, on his horse, facing Pang Tong, commanded, "Order your troops to surrender!"

"Hell no! A warrior never surrenders to a mutineer!" Pang Tong shouted back.

"In that case, I will have you beheaded."

"Go on!"

As the executioner raised his axe, another thought flashed through Zhang Fei's mind. He raised his hand and roared, "Stop!"

In one rapid-fire sequence of actions, Zhang Fei rolled off his horse, helped Pang Tong to his feet, and untied him. While Pang Tong was still in shock, Zhang Fei bowed to his captive and said, "Pardon me for being so rude, General Pang Tong. I would never execute someone as loyal and brave as you are. You are free to leave. If you do, I only regret that you are depriving me of the privilege of having by my side a warrior more noble and more capable than I am."

Moved by Zhang Fei's humility and merciful gesture, Pang Tong said, "I will be pleased to serve under your command."

Zhang Fei held Pang Tong's arm and replied, "I am honored to have a new comrade in arms. Welcome, Pang Tong, into the army of the Peach Garden Brothers. You and I are now the cocommanders of this military column."

The thought that flashed through Zhang Fei's mind that stopped him from having Pang Tong executed was Liu Bei's standard approach to captured enemy officers. He often managed to induce their surrender with courtesy, magnanimity, and humility. Zhang Fei had witnessed Liu Bei deploying that tactic repeatedly. He also remembered his brother's favorite dictum, which Liu Bei took pains to reiterate to his followers at every opportunity: "Killing a person should be the last resort after all other possible alternatives have been exhausted, even if that person happens to be your enemy."

Zhang Fei was so proud of his success converting Pang Tong from an enemy to an ally that he declared in a missive to Zhuge Liang that with Pang Tong's collaboration, he was looking forward to an unimpeded march all the way to the capital of the Shu province, Chengdu.

Indeed, the westward march of Zhang Fei's military column toward Chengdu was smoother than he had expected. During two decades of service in the Han dynasty army in Shu basin, Pang Tong had trained and mentored most of the active officer corps in the region. When he and Zhang Fei approached a town or a strategic pass, the commanding officer of the local garrison did not see any reason to wage a battle against their mentor and former commander, especially after Pang Tong explained to them that the Peach Garden Brothers wished to include them in the enterprise to resuscitate the Han dynasty. At Pang Tong's urging, one garrison after another along the way to Chengdu pledged their allegiance to the Peach Garden Brothers.

On their way into the heartland of Shu valley along the Yangtzi River, Zhuge Liang and Liu Bei's armada sent teams of sailors and soldiers ahead to spread the news that they were not invaders but loyal subjects of the Han dynasty on a mission to restore it. They also made it clear that they did not intend to replace any local officials if the officials were not engaged in corruption, larceny, or oppression of the general populace.

As the naval fleet of Liu Bei and Zhuge Liang moved upstream, some local people came out of their homes along the shore to see the spectacle of the armada as if it were a military parade. Some of the villagers were Han; many belonged to Yi, Dai, Qiang, Zhuang, Bai, Naxi, and other ethnic groups. They cheered when they heard that the Peach Garden Brothers planned to remove corrupt and oppressive officials in their region.

Along their voyage, Liu Bei and Zhuge Liang were impressed with the way the people of the Shu valley tamed their mountainous land and turned it into an agricultural basket producing copious amounts of rice, vegetables, and fruits. The farmers employed an innovative way of farming the steep slopes of the mountains flanking the Yangtzi River and its tributaries. As a result, terraces graced the mountain slopes with intricate curvy geometric patterns, transforming each mountainside into a beautiful stack of curvatures with undulating plants. Each curvy terrace was fed by thin, glimmering waterways providing lifelines to the plants.

Rising straight up each steep mountain slope, teams of farmers in their ethnic costumes propelled river water up the slopes by pedaling ingenious water pumps constructed from wood. Attached at the end of each of the two vertical sticks of a pump was a bucket that dipped into a water trough. The pumps began from the edge of the Yangtzi River. When a person, holding on to a horizontal bar above each pump, stepped down on a pedal with one foot, this caused the bucket to scoop up water from the river. When that person stepped down on the other pedal with the other foot, the bucket was lifted out of the river and its water dumped into a trough a few feet uphill. Then another person laboring on another pump propelled the water a few more feet uphill to the next trough up the mountain. Each chain of pedaling pumps transported water from the river to a holding pond on the highest terrace near the mountaintop. Gravity then allowed the water in the pond to flow through a network of narrow channels that irrigated the entire mountainside.

Liu Bei and Zhuge Liang marveled at the local farmers' clever way of converting the steep mountain slopes into productive agricultural fields. They were also pleased to see locals emerging from their homes along the shoreline to chat with some of the vanguard soldiers and sailors because they happened to share a minority language as their native tongue.

Impressed with the terrace farms and the friendly disposition of the people, Liu Bei and Zhuge Liang were delighted with their collective decision to choose the Shu valley as their home base.

"The Shu basin is an amazing place," Zhuge Liang observed, "full of hardworking people, covered with fertile farmland, blessed with abundant waterways! Without seeing this place in person, one would have thought that the Shu basin was a remote, impoverished region of mountains and wilderness in western China. I am glad that our rivals, in their ignorance, covet the Central Plains around the Yellow River and the coastal region. Being the heartland of all dynasties since antiquity, the Yellow River basin and the coastal plains are historically significant. The Shu basin may not be the center stage in the history of our nation. But it is blessed with productive farms, a large population, and the protection of high mountains. It is a perfect base from which to conquer the entire country. I have learned an important lesson by coming into the Shu basin. It is important to study history. It is equally important not to be held back by history. We worship our ancestors, venerate our past, honor our traditions. Even our language codifies the future as behind us and the past in front of us, suggesting that the past deserves more of our attention than the future does. I have no quarrel with our ancestors, our culture, and our traditions. They offer us valuable lessons and edifying precedents. But we must strive to further innovate on the foundation of what we learn from the precedents they set. Otherwise, we will never improve upon the work of our ancestors or surpass their excellence."

"Yes, the Shu basin is a paradise, locked away in the great mountains of the southwest of our country. I love the ethnic groups here," Liu Bei responded with a big grin. "They are the same people who constitute the backbone of our navy. We would not have been here without their support. Guan Yu deserves all the credit for galvanizing the minority ethnic groups into our ranks. I am glad that we have come to their heartland. This voyage is my first visit to a place where the Han people do not constitute the majority."

"Well, with Guan Yu's thick beard, brown complexion, and gargantuan size, he might be a member of an ethnic minority himself, perhaps one of his ancestors is a nomad in the northwest!" Zhang Fei laughed. "Some time ago, I told him that he might carry the blood of Xiongnu from the Ordos region, which is not far from where he grew up. But he claimed that his parents never said anything about non-Han ancestry. He did admit that his father had a dark complexion. If the father was of minority ancestry, he probably would not wish to admit it as he lived among Han peasants."

As Zhang Fei was on a thought train about the ethnicities of the people in the Han empire, he articulated his new revelations: "Come to think of it," Zhang Fei wondered out loud, "the physical features and complexions of Han people cover a wide spectrum, from ivory skin to dark skin, from straight hair to kinky hair, from narrow, almond-shaped eyes to wide, oval eyes, from flat noses to aquiline noses, from small stature and short legs to considerable height. I've heard that missionaries from Tianzhu (India) these days are spreading a religion called Buddhism in our country. It has found a sympathetic ear among many Han people. Those missionaries have settled in our country, married Han women, and sired offspring, injecting another non-Han lineage into the Han people. In the north, the nomadic raiders, Xiongnu, sometimes settled as farmers and married Han women. In the west, intermarriage between Han, Zang, Qiang, Xianbei, and other minority people is common. In the south, mixtures of Han and many ethnic groups such as the Hmong, Thai, and Vietnamese probably have existed throughout history as the Han people swept southward. I wouldn't be surprised if every Han person has some non-Han ancestry. In my opinion, this whole rigmarole of Han vis-à-vis other ethnic groups seems to be a mythology, an artificial demarcation. It serves no purpose other than promoting schism."

"I agree. The only thing that matters is that we are all human beings," Liu Bei interjected. "Ideally, human beings should accept and respect each other independent of physical features and cultural traditions. But the world is not ideal. I have a much

THE BATTLE OF VERMILION GORGE

simpler view of people in this world. There are good people and bad people. Bad people polarize a society, create schism, promote animosity, and feed on hatred. They are the scum of the earth, causing animosity, war, and all our woes. Sadly, there is no escape from bad people, wherever you live or go. Like critters, they are everywhere. I admit that my simplistic view becomes not very simple when we consider gradations of good and bad. What I call the scum of the earth are extremists on the undesirable end of the spectrum. Perhaps recognizing that we are all limited in our perception, and our evaluations of people are nothing more than subjective opinions and sometimes resentful feelings, will help us not to be judgmental."

"Bravo, Lord Liu!" Zhuge Liang chimed in, "You are the philosopher king, sagacious and insightful. As the chief strategist, I wish to raise a pragmatic issue. Where should we settle our headquarters in the Shu valley?"

"Well, I favor the traditional capital of the Shu valley, Chengdu, famous for its dense network of irrigation channels, an engineering feat initiated by the First Emperor, Qin Shi Huang, more than four hundred years ago," Liu Bei opined. "At any rate, we will have to go there because it is the seat of the major Shu garrison. I hope the commander there will not oppose us. Zhang Fei is already marching toward the garrison along the northern bank of the Yangtzi river. We will meet up with his column of troops there!"

In Chengdu, the head of the garrison turned out to be someone who had met and admired the Peach Garden Brothers when the nation's commanderies formed an alliance to campaign against the villainous traitor Dong Zhuo. During the campaign, the Chengdu commander witnessed how the Peach Garden Brothers operated, how their disciplined troops never looted or harmed the populace, how they treated their captives with kindness and compassion, how they respected the captains as well as the soldiers of other commanderies. In his memory, the Peach Garden Brothers stood out as caring and judicious leaders, a world apart from most other commanders whose only interest was to pursue wealth and power with abandon.

Liu Bei, however, didn't remember the Chengdu commander because the allied expedition against Dong Zhuo included scores of commanders from across the nation. But he figured that they must have met during the expedition against Dong Zhuo. He knew that Cao Cao, who took over the imperial government shortly after Dong Zhuo's death, had not replaced the chiefs of the commanderies as remote as Chengdu was. It took time and effort for a newly established central government thousands of li in the east to project its power to distant locations like Chengdu in the Shu basin.

When the commander of the Chengdu garrison heard that the Peach Garden Brothers' navy was approaching, he came out of his headquarters to welcome Liu Bei at the waterfront with open arms. In a meeting the next day, he agreed to integrate his command into the army of the Peach Garden Brothers. In appreciation of his magnanimity and cooperation, Liu Bei promoted him to a higher rank in command of the Chengdu garrison.

TWELVE

THE THREE KINGDOMS

After the Peach Garden Brothers settled in Shu valley, there was a brief lull in hostility between members of the triumvirate warlords: Cao Cao, Sun Quan, and Liu Bei. But Sun Quan remained miserable and discontent. He felt that he ended up with an unfair deal after all the confrontations and maneuvers. The entire Jing province, in his view, should belong to him. It had always been an integral part of his family's domain. More than one year ago, he had given permission to the Peach Garden Brothers and their troops to stay in the western portion of the province for the sake of an alliance against Cao Cao during the Battle of the Vermilion Gorge. By now, since the Peach Garden Brothers had successfully taken over the Shu valley, he reckoned that they should've yielded western Jing back to him. He sent letters repeatedly to Liu Bei and Zhuge Liang, demanding the return of western Jing. Zhuge Liang advised Liu Bei to ignore Sun Quan's demand.

After six months of no response from Liu Bei and Zhuge Liang, Zhou Yu, Sun Quan's chief adviser, tried a new approach. He arrested the entire family of Zhuge Liang's brother, Zhuge

Jin, who happened to be residing in eastern Jing. Sun Quan then sent Zhuge Jin to Chengdu to inform Liu Bei and Zhuge Liang that if the Peach Garden Brothers refused to yield western Jing province, the entire family of Zhuge Jin, young and old, male and female, would be executed.

When Zhuge Jin arrived in Chengdu and asked to meet with Liu Bei, Liu Bei queried Zhuge Liang, "Why is your brother coming all the way to Chengdu to see me?"

Zhuge Liang replied with a smile, "The reason lies with our territory in Jing province. I suspect that Sun Quan and Zhou Yu are using my brother and his family as hostages to coerce us to give up western Jing."

"How do you know?" Liu Bei was surprised.

"Well, it is my conjecture. But I think my conjecture is on the mark."

"That will put us in a tough situation. How do we deal with it?" Liu Bei asked.

"I have a plan. This is what we do." Zhuge Liang whispered to Liu Bei for a few minutes. "Just follow my plan when my brother arrives."

When Zhuge Jin entered the meeting hall of Liu Bei's headquarters, he immediately fell on his knees in front of Liu Bei and started weeping. In a broken voice, he pleaded, "Sun Quan has imprisoned my entire family. He told me that he will execute them if you don't return western Jing to him."

Liu Bei raised his voice with a frown. "Extortion! Extortion! How despicable! As much as I feel for you, Zhuge Jin, I cannot give in to extortion, because if I do, more extortions will follow."

At that moment, Zhuge Liang made his appearance, helped his brother onto his feet, and wept.

"I am so sorry that you and your family are being held as pawns in a territorial dispute between Sun Quan and the Peach

Garden Brothers," Zhuge Liang said. "I hope my lord, Liu Bei, will take pity on members of the Zhuge clan."

Liu Bei thought for a while and responded, "Since the family of my chief of staff is at stake, I will accede to a compromise. I will yield half of western Jing to Sun Quan. That is the best I can do."

Back in eastern Jing, Zhuge Jin delivered Liu Bei's written concession to Sun Quan and Zhou Yu, who, then, released Zhuge Jin's family members. When Sun Quan's officials came to claim the three counties yielded by Liu Bei, Guan Yu, who had been governing western Jing with the assistance of Xian-Hui, rejected them outright. In response, the officials produced Liu Bei's handwritten concession as proof of the validity of their claim. Guan Yu looked at the concession document and dismissed it with a wave of hand, saying, "Liu Bei might have consented to yield half of western Jing. But I am in command here, and I disagree with Liu Bei."

As Sun Quan's officials protested, Guan Yu picked up his halberd and roared in anger, "Haven't I made clear that I disagree with Liu Bei? Are you deaf? Scram before my temper overtakes me!"

Scared out of their wits, Sun Quan's officials scrambled out of Guan Yu's headquarters and returned empty-handed to Sun Quan and Zhou Yu. They reported in detail their short but frightening encounter with Guan Yu. Infuriated by Guan Yu's insolence, Sun Quan wanted to wage war against Guan Yu immediately.

"Not so fast, my lord!" Zhou Yu counseled. "First, let's invite Guan Yu to a luncheon by the bank of the river that separates our territory from western Jing. If he crosses the river with a naval flotilla, we will rain arrows on them from the bank and kill them during their crossing. If he comes with a few bodyguards on a single boat, we will overpower them after lunch. If Guan Yu rejects our invitation, then we will wage war against him. My assessment of Guan Yu's character tells me that he will accept your invitation. His bravery and pride will blind him to the risk of crossing into our territory."

Sun Quan thought the plan recommended by Zhou Yu made good sense. Accepting Zhou Yu's advice, he commented, "War is costly, and the outcome of a war is unpredictable. It should be our last resort after the failure of all other approaches."

They wrote a letter of invitation. To signal their seriousness, they both signed the letter and assigned Zhou Yu's senior deputy, Lu Su, to hand deliver it.

Upon receiving the invitation, Guan Yu consulted with Xian-Hui. Xian-Hui recommended acceptance of the invitation, even though she suspected that the invitation was merely a guise to capture or kill Guan Yu. She discreetly whispered into Guan Yu's ear long instructions that she had developed with the guidance of Zhuge Liang. Armed with Xian-Hui's detailed instructions, Guan Yu accepted the invitation. He told Lu Su that he would cross the river at noon the next day.

Zhou Yu was overjoyed at the news of Guan Yu's decision. He said gleefully to his entourage, "Guan Yu, a great martial artist, all brawn, no brain. He is walking into my trap! Tomorrow he will die."

That night, under the cover of darkness, Zhou Yu had his troops dig up two rows of deep trenches at forty paces from the bank of the river. Scores of archers and lancers concealed themselves in the trenches before workers covered the trenches with wooden planks and dirt, leaving many small openings for air. The soldiers were instructed to maintain absolute silence until they heard a gong signal, at which point in time they should push aside the wood planks and emerge from the trenches to kill Guan Yu and his entourage.

THE THREE KINGDOMS   253

Early in the morning, a spotless white tent was set up halfway between the camouflaged trenches and the riverbank. In the center of the tent, a rosewood table and three armchairs were placed. Near midday, attendants brought to the table three wine jars, three wine cups, and utensils for three diners. Sun Quan and Zhou Yu then took their seats at the table facing the river. Everything was in plain view of Guan Yu's troops on the opposite bank.

Before Guan Yu started to cross the river, his deputies, who had been vigilantly watching the activities on the side of Sun Quan and Zhou Yu, cautioned him against going. They didn't feel comfortable because the entire setup smelled of treachery, and Zhou Yu was well-known for designing deceitful plots.

"Don't worry," Guan Yu told them calmly, "I am fully prepared. Zhuge Liang and my wife have anticipated all the possible scenarios that might happen. We know Zhou Yu is a master of treachery. Your job is to prepare the ten fastest sampans equipped with sails and long shields, each one to be manned by three of our strongest sailors. I will attend the meeting on Zhou Yu's side of the river alone. You people on this side of the river watch me carefully. When I give a signal by waving my halberd, the sampans should dash across to fetch me back."

With that instruction to his subordinates, Guan Yu boarded a sampan to cross the river without any bodyguard, accompanied only by a single attendant holding his halberd and a strong sailor who rowed the boat across the river.

When Zhou Yu saw Guan Yu standing alone on a sampan, he was beside himself with glee.

Guan Yu will belong to me shortly! he muttered to himself.

Upon Guan Yu's arrival, Zhou Yu met him at the riverbank and guided him into the tent where Sun Quan sat. The soldier holding Guan Yu's halberd stood at attention outside the tent by the entrance. The three men exchanged pleasantries, commenting on the humid climate, the abundance of wildlife, the rich variety of semitropical vegetation, and the multitude of ethnic groups of the south. After consuming a few rounds of drinks while eating dishes of venison and exotic birds, Sun Quan said to Guan Yu, "I have generously allowed you and your brothers to stay in Jing province for several years. Historically, the province has always belonged to my family. By now, your brothers and Zhuge Liang have taken over the Shu basin. I think it is time for you to leave my territory."

"I am enjoying this exquisite lunch," Guan Yu responded with a smile. "Why are you spoiling such a pleasant occasion by bringing up thorny issues like a territorial dispute? You know very well that I am just a martial artist, not a politician."

"Your elder brother, Liu Bei, has already agreed to return half of western Jing to us." Sun Quan began to raise his voice. "I have his written consent. Why do you refuse to honor his commitment?"

"Well," Guan Yu retorted, "you've invited me to lunch. I am grateful to you for your friendly gesture and generosity. But I did not come prepared for a debate on a territorial dispute, and I am certainly not in a confrontational mood. Since you refuse to act as a gracious host, I am leaving."

Abruptly, Guan Yu stood up, took one giant step to snatch his halberd from the hands of his attendant, and with his left hand, grabbed Zhou Yu by his neck. Flinging Zhou Yu on his back as if Zhou Yu were a piece of armor, Guan Yu stepped out of the tent and waved his halberd. In the meantime, Sun Quan's archers dared not unleash their arrows at Guan Yu for fear of striking Zhou Yu who was draped over Guan Yu's back like an overcoat. It took Guan Yu and his attendant three giant steps to reach the riverbank where he shed Zhou Yu on the ground. As he stepped onto the lead sampan with his attendant, the two of them instantly ducked behind the shields held up by the sailors.

THE THREE KINGDOMS   255

All the actions happened in a flash. Before Sun Quan and Zhou Yu regained their composure, Guan Yu's squadron of speedy boats had already reached the opposite bank. As Guan Yu mounted his horse on his side of the river, he bowed in the direction of Sun Quan and Zhou Yu to thank them for lunch before galloping away.

Sun Quan, still sitting at the table in his tent, was seething with anger. He was so shocked and agitated that he could hardly move. Zhou Yu, standing by the shore of the river, felt like a dog, having inadvertently snatched defeat from the jaws of victory.

The repeated failure of his schemes against the Peach Garden Brothers exacted a heavy toll on Zhou Yu's psychological and physical health. Depression plagued him; bouts of palpitation diminished him. He became irascible, and his subordinates often bore the brunt of his temperamental outbursts. But he remained undaunted in his fight on behalf of his master, Sun Quan. His defeat and humiliation at the hands of the Peach Garden Brothers drove him to an obsession for revenge. Even in his dreams, he plotted to have Zhuge Liang and Liu Bei assassinated. All he needed was an ingenious scheme that could catch Zhuge Liang unawares. But duty and logic dictated that regaining western Jing had to be his priority. He would have to bide his time.

Shortly after failing to capture Guan Yu, Sun Quan told Zhou Yu that it was time for war. They amassed their forces on the frontier of Guan Yu's western Jing and prepared for action. In the meantime, Zhuge Liang had sent a large reinforcement from Shu basin to back up Guan Yu. A full-scale war between the two sides seemed inevitable. As Guan Yu shored up defenses along his frontier, a new revelation came to Zhou Yu.

When he reexamined the political landscape of the entire Han nation, it dawned on him that retaking western Jing by force might be tactically feasible at the time, but strategically foolish in the long run. After some calculation, he concluded that Cao Cao remained the dominant power among the three rival groups. Cao Cao commanded the most powerful military force, controlled the choicest territory including the Yellow River basin, and ruled the largest population from which he could draw recruits and collect taxes in support of his military ventures. If Sun Quan and the Peach Garden Brothers were locked in a protracted war, according to Zhou Yu's assessment, both would end up weakened and exhausted, further enhancing and bolstering Cao Cao's dominance. Such a scenario could be disastrous to both Sun Quan and the Peach Garden Brothers. With a clever metaphor, he conveyed his analysis to his lord, Sun Quan, who, at the time, was seething with anger to wage war against the Peach Garden Brothers: "Imagine a jungle in which a leopard, a wolf, and a bear are vying for dominance." Zhou Yu told his lord, Sun Quan, "The bear has size and power; the leopard has speed and stealth; the wolf has endurance and resilience. If the wolf and the leopard are weakened from fighting each other constantly, the bear will be able to pick them off and take the entire jungle. But if the wolf and the leopard form a united front, they may very well be able to expel the bear."

Zhou Yu concluded, "Common sense dictates that the wolf and the leopard should form an alliance, at least until the defeat of the bear."

After a moment of reflection, Sun Quan sighed and said, "I see the merit of your reasoning. But we have already commenced hostile actions against the Peach Garden Brothers. Our attempt to capture Guan Yu was not exactly a friendly gesture. What makes you think that they would care to form an alliance with us now?"

"Yes, we are changing course midstream in view of my reexamination of the three-way contest. Overanxious to reclaim western Jing province, I have rushed into recommending a hostile confrontation with the Peach Garden Brothers. Our cause is just.

Jing province has always been our territory. The Peach Garden Brothers ought to have voluntarily returned the western portion to us. Their greed and intransigence provoked my hostility. But waging a war against them at this time will be strategically foolish in view of the threat from Cao Cao." Zhou Yu explained, "To induce the Peach Garden Brothers into an alliance with us, we will have to compensate for our transgression against them. One possibility is to cede to them a slender corridor in the north of our territory that is the best approach for invading Cao Cao's domain. The ceded territory will not offer much military or monetary advantage to the Peach Garden Brothers because, in a war, that narrow corridor will suffer destruction. Besides, that corridor is hilly and sparsely populated. It doesn't have much economic significance. Depending on the outcome of a war against Cao Cao, the ownership of that corridor will inevitably be determined through negotiations. In a nutshell, offering that slender corridor to them may appear as a momentary concession but is far from a costly concession, whereas an all-out war with the Peach Garden Brothers would be calamitous."

Sun Quan nodded in approval of Zhou Yu's strategic analysis while Zhou Yu continued to elaborate his strategy: "The best way to initiate our peace offer is to contact Zhuge Liang directly. A farsighted, intelligent man, Zhuge Liang wouldn't let our transgression deter him from adopting a winning strategy in this tripartite contest. He understands that, at this point, Cao Cao is a much more dangerous threat to them than we are."

"But Guan Yu is already here in Jing province." Sun Quan responded, "Wouldn't it be easier to approach him first?"

"No, Guan Yu, an intrepid warrior, is not a strategist." Zhou Yu said, "We need to send an emissary to Zhuge Liang with a handwritten letter from you, laying out our proposition and the rationale behind it."

When Zhuge Liang received Sun Quan's letter, he decided to go to Jing province and negotiate with Sun Quan in person. Liu Bei did not disagree with Zhuge Liang's decision but was concerned with Zhuge Liang's safety in Jing province.

"There is nothing to worry about." Zhuge Liang assured Liu Bei, "I will be protected by Guan Yu, the supreme warrior in our world."

In Jing province, Zhuge Liang met Sun Quan and Zhou Yu at a neutral zone to negotiate a peace treaty. By prior agreement, Guan Yu took fifty of his best cavalry as bodyguards to the spot where a tent was set up for the negotiation between the two sides. Zhou Yu and Sun Quan arrived with the same number of troops. The two sides sat down to negotiate at a table with a map of Jing province and Cao Cao's territory immediately to the north.

After two days of haggle and bargain, they reached an agreement. All hostile actions between Sun Quan's army and the force of the Peach Garden Brothers would cease immediately. They agreed to form an alliance on the condition that both sides would recognize and accept the current division of Jing province. They also agreed that, in time, the new alliance would mount a northern expedition against Cao Cao.

At the conclusion of the negotiation, both sides were delighted. They had forged a win-win contract for both parties. In a festive mood, Zhou Yu broached the news that his lord, Sun Quan, had been enthroned as the ruler of a new kingdom called Wu. Zhuge Liang, in his congratulation to Sun Quan, said, "My lord, Liu Bei, is a loyal Han subject. We have made our home in the Shu valley. If you wish, you may refer to us as the Shu kingdom. But our mission remains the restoration of the Han dynasty."

"Well," Sun Quan, in self-defense, declared, "my enthronement is a response to Cao Cao's proclamation of the founding of the Wei kingdom in the Central Plains. The young man, Liu Xie,

THE THREE KINGDOMS

259

or Cao Cao's puppet, who still holds on to the title Emperor Xian of the Han dynasty, it is rumored will abdicate soon. His abdication will formally mark the termination of the Han dynasty. You and I are well aware that, informally, the Han dynasty ended when Dong Zhuo poisoned Emperor Shao and his queen. Since that time, Dong Zhuo and subsequently Cao Cao used Emperor Shao's teenage brother, Liu Xie, as a puppet. Lü Bu murdered Dong Zhuo when the alliance of the nation's commanders expelled him to Chang'an. Today, Emperor Xian of the Han dynasty does not even qualify as a puppet. Cao Cao no longer bothers to pretend that he rules the Central Plain with Emperor Xian's mandate. Confined to the palace in Chang'an, Xian no longer serves any purpose in Cao Cao's design. It is to Cao Cao's credit that he has not killed Xian."

Sun Quan's analysis of the state of the country caught Zhuge Liang by surprise. Zhuge Liang didn't like what he heard, nor could he refute what Sun Quan said.

Being a rational person who never let emotions get in the way of his reasoning, Zhuge Liang conceded, "You are right! The death of Emperor Shao and his queen marked the informal end of the Han dynasty. One could even argue that the death of Shao's father, Emperor Ling, signaled the demise of Han. Shao was on the throne less than four months before Dong Zhuo poisoned him. I have been blinded by my loyalty to the Han dynasty, even though the truth is that a Han sovereign no longer exists. Thank you for opening my eyes! But I have not heard that Emperor Xian is on the verge of abdication. He remains a callow youngster, a tragic figure destined to bear witness to the bitter end of a great dynasty founded by his ancestors. My only disagreement with you is that you credit Cao Cao with refraining from killing Emperor Xian. Cao Cao's every action is dictated by expediency in his pursuit of power. He murdered Emperor Xian's wife not so long ago, didn't he? In fact, he had her entire natal family, young and old, male and female, beheaded in public.

He has no qualms about killing Emperor Xian at a time he deems advantageous to his own ambition. At this point, he still uses Emperor Xian as a figurehead. Death will come to Xian when Cao Cao no longer has any use for him. Cao Cao is every bit as evil and ruthless as Dong Zhuo, only more intelligent, less capricious, and therefore, more dangerous!"

Saddened by the demise of the Han dynasty, which was suddenly and unexpectedly laid bare before him, Zhuge Liang let out a deep sigh. "This is the end of an epoch! The Han dynasty, which endured more than four hundred years, is now history!"

Within a few days after negotiating with Sun Quan and Zhou Yu, Zhuge Liang returned to Chengdu, the capital of Shu basin, and presented the peace agreement to Liu Bei, Zhang Fei, and the senior officers of their army. He pointed out:

First, a war against Sun Quan would be unwise and victory, even by Guan Yu's assessment, was not guaranteed.

Second, a concurrent war against Cao Cao and Sun Quan was not only beyond the military and financial capacity of the Peach Garden Brothers, but also could induce an alliance between Cao Cao and Sun Quan, which would be ruinous for the Peach Garden Brothers.

Third, the proposed peace agreement stood as an assurance of Sun Quan's recognition of the Peach Garden Brothers' sovereignty over western Jing.

Zhuge Liang's rationale for the peace treaty made sense to everyone. They gave their support. Guan Yu, because of his duties in western Jing, could not attend Zhuge Liang's presentation. But he knew of the proposed alliance because Zhuge Liang had already arrived at his analysis of the state of the nation when the two of them were negotiating with Zhou Yu and Sun Quan.

When the Peach Garden Brothers' acceptance of the peace agreement reached Zhou Yu, he was delighted. He could now

THE THREE KINGDOMS

261

focus his attention on the preparation for an invasion northward into the Wei kingdom, Cao Cao's domain.

As Zhou Yu and Guan Yu were coordinating their effort in preparation for war against Cao Cao, a senior deputy commander of the Peach Garden Brothers' army broached a proposal in a private meeting with Guan Yu. This senior commander claimed to speak for many of his colleagues.

"Lord Guan, we, your loyal subordinates, have followed you for many years. Under your leadership, we have won the hearts of the people of Jing province, built a formidable naval force, fought victoriously in the Vermilion Gorge, and held Sun Quan's aggression in check. Our troops adore you; the people of Jing province revere you; if Sun Quan and Cao Cao could enthrone themselves as kings, we would like to declare you the king of a new kingdom, the kingdom of Jing. In our opinion, you are far superior to Sun Quan and Cao Cao."

Upon hearing the deputy's proposal, Guan Yu became angry. He stood up, slammed his fist on the conference table, and growled, "How dare you suggest sedition! I am your commanding officer, *not* your lord. My senior brother, Liu Bei, is your lord. He has been my lord since we formed our brotherhood in a peach garden years ago. If it were not because of your past dedication to our cause, I would have your head chopped off. Now, cast your ridiculous suggestion out of your minds and don't ever think about it again. The meeting is over."

Shaken and chastened, Guan Yu's deputy withdrew in disgrace. He and his colleagues didn't intend to be seditious. Their suggestion arose out of their heartfelt adoration for Guan Yu. But they underestimated Guan Yu's fierce loyalty and total devotion to his sworn brother Liu Bei. That day, they learned a lesson from Guan Yu on the Confucian canon of loyalty.

While Guan Yu quashed his subordinates' idea of establishing a separate kingdom, Zhou Yu, Sun Quan's chief strategist, continued to have serious health issues. He lost appetite, felt faint, and was plagued by chest pain repeatedly. Too weak to bear the heavy burden of the state, Zhou Yu relinquished the role of the chief strategist to his deputy, who happened to be the architect of the alliance with the Peach Garden Brothers. This deputy of Zhou Yu, however, contracted a severe bout of malaria and died abruptly at a young age. His replacement, Lu Su, who espoused an opposite military and political strategy, gained the confidence of Sun Quan. This new strategist had always been leery of Guan Yu. In his view, Guan Yu was an ambitious and dangerous warrior. He warned Sun Quan, "Guan Yu is expanding his army. He built a navy that defeated Cao Cao at the Vermilion Gorge. Since then, he has successfully recruited thousands of soldiers in our backyard. Fighters from the minority ethnic groups love him. Han people of the Jing province admire him. Sooner or later, he will have an army bigger than ours. When that day dawns, I am sure he will not hesitate to attack our territory. While Cao Cao may hold the Central Plain, he is not an immediate threat to us after his debacle in the Vermilion Gorge. He needs time to recover. When he does, we will be strong enough to hold him in check. Currently, we must focus on contending with Guan Yu. Our best approach is to eliminate him before he becomes more powerful than we are. It is my opinion that we should take advantage of our superior strength at this time to regain all of Jing province."

In his sickbed, Zhou Yu was informed of his replacement's proposal. He recognized that the strategy of attacking Guan Yu had some merit, reckoning that Guan Yu, battling Cao Cao in the north, would not anticipate an attack on his back from his putative ally, the Wu kingdom. Such a surprise attack might easily defeat Guan Yu and perhaps result in his capture. But Zhou Yu didn't like to be cast in a duplicitous role, negatively affecting his reputation and standing in history. Furthermore, he recognized that other warlords would be leery to trust him or form alliances with him in the future.

Zhou Yu's sovereign, Sun Quan, however, was more eager to regain all of Jing province and vanquish a powerful competitor, Guan Yu. He was inclined to adopt Lu Su's new strategy even if it implied duplicity. In the end, Zhou Yu, feeling too feeble to mount an effective argument against the proposed plot, acquiesced.

Thus, Sun Quan began moving his army into position behind Guan Yu's northern expedition column, ostensibly as Guan Yu's reinforcement. He also transported troops stealthily up the rivers along the eastern and the western flanks of Guan Yu's column by hiding soldiers in the bowels of junks.

When Sun Quan's forces came onshore from their hiding in the junks to attack Guan Yu's flank on the east and on the west, they surprised Guan Yu as much as their comrades did by attacking Guan Yu from the south. Guan Yu was not only unprepared, he was also dumbfounded.

Where did all these attackers come from? Guan Yu wondered. Wearing Wu uniforms, they are supposed to be our ally.

The ensuing battle was short and decisive.

Chaos, fear, and bewilderment reigned among Guan Yu's troops. They didn't know what to do or whom to fight and couldn't understand what was happening to them. Many of Guan Yu's troops were killed, and many more surrendered. In the confusion, Guan Yu barely escaped with a small coterie of cavalry in the direction of the Shu valley. It was a humiliating defeat for Guan Yu.

Having routed Guan Yu's army and regained a good chunk of western Jing province, Sun Quan mounted a search for Zhuge Liang. He knew that Zhuge Liang had not yet returned to the Shu valley after their mutual negotiation to form an alliance. His spies discovered that Zhuge Liang was visiting an old friend in a small mountain town in western Jing. Sun Quan led a contingent of two hundred cavalry, galloping at top speed to reach that small town.

Luckily for Zhuge Liang, he anticipated Sun Quan's move after Guan Yu's defeat. As a rule, Zhuge Liang always maintained daily communication with his generals in the battlefield through teams of expert horsemen relaying messages between him and his field commanders. Having learned of Guan Yu's debacle because of Sun Quan's treacherous attack, Zhuge Liang suspected that he himself would be a potential target. It was an age-old strategy of pursuit and annihilation in war when your enemy was unexpectedly defeated. But there wasn't enough time to escape from the mountain town where he was visiting his old, reclusive friend. He reckoned that if Sun Quan had come after him with cavalry, the cavalry could arrive at the small city any moment. The situation called for a risky response if he were to escape capture.

Zhuge Liang quickly issued a series of orders to members of his entourage.

A table and a chair were set up on the city wall above the gate in full view of the city's outskirts. On the table lay a zheng, a plucked zither, Zhuge Liang's favorite musical instrument, and a pot of hot tea with a cup. The city gates stayed wide open. Residents in the city carried on with their normal activities. None of his bodyguards could be seen. Zhuge Liang, wearing a flowing robe and a scholar's hat, went up to the city wall, took a seat at the table, and began sipping tea while playing the zither.

By midafternoon, Sun Quan and his cavalry arrived at the city gate. They saw a relaxed Zhuge Liang on top of the rampart and heard a sweet melody flowing from his zither. The city gate was wide-open, citizens were going about doing business as usual, not a single soldier was in sight. Expecting a closed city gate, archers on the city wall, and armed guards by the city gate, Sun Quan and his cavalry were perplexed. When one of his officers sought permission to lead a charge into the city, Sun Quan refused, warning the officer, "This putatively unguarded city is clearly a trap. The shrewd and devious Zhuge Liang has set it up to lure us in. His soldiers are hiding behind the city wall with lance and defensive obstacles to ambush us. Don't charge. Be prudent and wait for reinforcements of archers and infantry tomorrow before launching an attack!"

That evening, under the cover of darkness, Zhuge Liang rolled out of the town from a side exit in a chariot with a few bodyguards and vanished without a trace into the mountains on a long journey to the safety of the Shu valley.

As Zhuge Liang and Guan Yu returned to Chengdu, their home base in the Shu valley, nearly half of western Jing, which appeared firmly in their grasp just a few days ago, had been taken by Sun Quan. It was a devastating experience for Guan Yu, who was unaccustomed to defeat.

At home in Chengdu, Xian-Hui spent days counseling and consoling Guan Yu, trying to lift him out of depression and rebuild his confidence. She told him that setbacks were part and parcel of anyone's pursuit of greatness, that the path to success was never a smooth ride, that obstacles had to be overcome with fortitude and perseverance. Those difficult days, unexpectedly, served Guan Yu well in other ways.

Immersed in his role as the leading warrior for Liu Bei, Guan Yu had not spent time with his family. After the birth of his son, he had been galloping from one battlefield to another, from building a navy to governing western Jing. His son, Guan Ping, now ten years of age, had hardly laid eyes on his father. The name of their son, Ping meaning "peace," betrayed Xian-Hui's fervent yearning for peace in the country so that she could have her husband by her side. The current interlude from Guan Yu's military tours was an unexpected blessing, uniting the family for several months during which Guan Yu experienced for the first time the pleasure of being a husband and a father. He spent time with his young son every day, training Guan Ping in martial arts, exploring the legendary Emei Mountain with Xian-Hui and Guan Ping, venturing into the wilderness to observe wild pandas, exotic monkeys, and vermilion birds, enjoying home-cooked meals with his wife and son, and expanding his knowledge of the classics together with his son, Guan Ping, under Xian-Hui's guidance.

Until this time in his life, Guan Yu had never known or experienced domestic bliss. There was no lack of love in his own natal family when he was a child. But the family was under constant and unrelenting stress, struggling to feed and clothe themselves. Cheerful moments were rare and ephemeral. Now, material provisions being no longer a concern, the family enjoyed delicious food in their own spacious dining room. They wore nice clothing, warm in the cold but airy in the heat. Unlike food, however, clothing was never an important family concern. Xian-Hui, Guan Yu, and Guan Ping were practical but never extravagant in their choice of clothing.

Compared with his own youth, when lunch typically consisted of a jug of plain water plus a couple of wo wo tou (millet balls) and clothing was purchased once a year as the lunar new year approached, Guan Yu, on the one hand, could hardly make sense of his son's life of abundance, and on the other hand, wanted to give Xian-Hui and Guan Ping everything. He was amused by his own oxymoronic sentiments, even though both he and Xian-Hui did not care for luxury.

The greatest reward of family life was Guan Yu's pride deriving from his son's physical prowess and intellectual acumen. It made him happy that his son was superior to himself in every way. He also felt deeply grateful to Xian-Hui for naming his son Ping, "peace," and nurturing him intellectually. That gratitude led to a new recognition of Xian-Hui's sacrifice. He had always admired her intelligence and erudition, loved her with all his heart, and remained faithful to her all these years. Until the occasion of this family reunion, it had never occurred to Guan Yu that he had been neglecting Xian-Hui, as if their matrimonial union were merely a perfunctory milestone and his true devotion was reserved for his military and political endeavors. He could hardly believe how she had stoically endured, all these years, his absence and insensitivity without a single word of complaint. He felt incredibly guilty and swore to make amends. How? he wondered.

Middle-aged now, Guan Yu took stock of his life. He had led an upright life in accordance with the teachings of his parents, his martial arts mentor, and the sages of the past. He felt sheepish about the inadvertent killing of a rapist shortly after leaving the grand master's martial arts camp. But the rescue of a rape victim eased his conscience. He had been an incomparable warrior devoted to the mission adopted by the Peach Garden Brothers. Over the years, he had also become learned and wise in warfare and military strategy. But he had not been a good husband and a dutiful parent. Almost fifty years of age, he was approaching the end of his career as a warrior. Indeed, he reckoned that, with his diminished strength, he could easily die on the battlefield any day. The older he became, the greater the probability of him being killed in action. Death didn't cow him. Neither did it frighten him no matter how he loathed leaving Xian-Hui a widow and Guan Ping an orphan. What befuddled him, at this juncture, was the question, "What is life all about?"

When he was a young boy, he was preoccupied with survival: getting enough food to eat each day, keeping warm in winter, warding off diseases, and staying clear from bandits or unsavory characters. In the grand master's martial arts camp, he was obsessed with training to become a warrior. As a member of the Peach Garden Brothers, he dedicated himself to restoring the Han dynasty.

He had no intention to abandon his patriotic undertaking with Liu Bei and Zhang Fei. Yet he was realistic and keenly aware of the situation confronting him. The prospect of the success of his mission had morphed, at best, into a protracted struggle against Cao Cao and Sun Quan. Was there a chance for victory? Guan Yu didn't have the slightest clue.

Haunted by an uncertain future, Guan Yu felt lost. What he had discovered unexpectedly, as a consequence of his defeat in western Jing, was the glory of domestic bliss in the company of Xian-Hui and Guan Ping. They made him feel strong and wholesome as if he had stepped into a new world hitherto unknown to him, a world that was more fulfilling, comforting, and serene than the pursuit of military victory and conventional success. He wanted more of this newfound fulfillment and tranquility.

Back in Wu kingdom, Zhou Yu, still weak from his illness, was heartened by Sun Quan's victory against Guan Yu. They had not regained all of western Jing, but winning a portion of it was, nevertheless, a significant achievement. He wanted to ride on the crest of that victory by designing a new plot to eliminate Zhuge Liang and the Peach Garden Brothers from the contention for national power.

Conceding that Zhuge Liang might be peerless, Zhou Yu sought to drive Zhuge Liang back to a hermetic life.

Killing Zhuge Liang is too difficult, Zhou Yu thought. He may be as invincible as a dragon, but a dragon who had never harbored an iota of worldly ambition until Liu Bei drew him out of hermitage. Left alone, Zhuge Liang would have preferred to live a secluded life on a remote mountain.

According to Zhou Yu's analysis, the driving force behind Zhuge Liang was Liu Bei, the head of the Peach Garden Brothers. He reasoned, If I can kill Liu Bei, Zhuge Liang will most likely

THE THREE KINGDOMS   269

return to his mountain retreat, and I will have a good chance to prevail against Cao Cao on behalf of my lord.

Following his line of reasoning, Zhou Yu conceived of a plot aimed at killing Liu Bei. It involved deceit and treachery. He justified his ignoble plot to himself with the rationalization that he had already acquiesced to a duplicitous scheme in attacking Guan Yu after forming an alliance with the Peach Garden Brothers. It no longer made sense for him to worry about his reputation in history. If history were to consign him into the category of unsavory, double-crossing politicians, he was resigned to it. Desperate for victory after a string of defeats, he was prepared to resort to any tactic, even if it entailed mendacity, hoax, conspiracy, or other shams and trickeries. He was bereaved and needed to reassemble his shattered ego.

Zhou Yu's new plot was also driven by his fear of Zhuge Liang. In his mind, Zhuge Liang was not only clairvoyant but also endowed with magical powers. The Battle of the Vermilion Gorge proved it.

That man can summon an out-of-season squall! Zhou Yu thought to himself, If I do not checkmate him now, he will bring down the Wu kingdom. My lifelong effort to guide my lord, Sun Quan, to dominance will end in vain.

That evening, Zhou Yu composed a letter to Zhuge Liang, apologizing for the duplicitous attack on Guan Yu's garrison in Jing province and blaming that treachery on his deputy who gained access to Sun Quan during Zhou Yu's illness. He would have never betrayed his ally, had he been in charge, he claimed in the letter.

"You know I am an honest man who has never engaged in duplicity." He wrote, "Now, in convalescence, I am again in charge of the office of chief strategist in the Wu kingdom, and I have righted the ship."

The letter went on to say that having learned of the unexpected loss of Liu Bei's wife to illness, he and Sun Quan sent their condolences. Furthermore, he proposed that at the end of the six-month grieving period, Liu Bei should marry Sun Quan's sister, Sun May.

The letter ended with a warm invitation to Liu Bei to wed Sun Quan's sister at a scenic coastal resort in the easternmost section of Jing province and the promise that the wedding would be staged with fanfare and celebrated with festivities throughout the Wu kingdom.

A special emissary hand delivered the letter to Zhuge Liang.

After reading the letter, Zhuge Liang laughed contemptuously.

"Another humdrum scheme from a dying plotter." Zhuge Liang told the Peach Garden Brothers, "The real purpose of Zhou Yu's proposal and invitation is to lure Liu Bei into Jing province for either imprisonment or execution. Let's gather some information about Sun Quan's mother and sister. Then, we will decide how to respond."

"Why wait to respond," both Guan Yu and Zhang Fei raised their voices in alarm, "if it is a ruse for capturing Liu Bei?"

"Patience, patience, my friends!" Zhuge Liang said. "If the conditions are right, we might turn Zhou Yu's little scheme to our advantage. I just hope he lives long enough to witness what could happen to his dirty trick."

Zhuge Liang then sent several undercover agents to collect information about Sun Quan's mother and sister in Wu kingdom. Weeks later, the agents returned with an unexpected report on the two women.

According to the report, Sun Quan's mother, a powerful and authoritative character, exerted great influence on all members of her extended family, especially her sons and daughter. Perspicacious and intelligent, she was highly respected for her judgments and opinions. In addition, the report noted that she was known for her candor, bluntly speaking her mind to her

THE THREE KINGDOMS

271

elder son, Sun Ce, who, after founding the Wu kingdom, died prematurely, and her younger son, the reigning king, Sun Quan.

The daughter, Sun May, an exceptional personality in her own right, was an aficionado of martial arts. In fact, she was a celebrated expert in swordsmanship, wielding a precious sword forged by the most distinguished blacksmith in the nation. She had been seen, in practice, breaking her opponent's sword into pieces by parrying its blow with her priceless weapon.

Not only was Sun May an accomplished swordsperson, her female attendants and maidservants were all schooled in martial arts. Over the years, she had recruited a staff of women warriors. Some had risen to the grand master level of expertise. Adjacent to her bedchamber, according to the report of the spies, was a large dojo, equipped with straw mats, bronze shields, wooden mannequins, high hurdles for leaping, narrow beams on which to develop balancing drills, elevated stumps on which to perch and move in combat, and a variety of weapons, as well as ersatz ones made of wood. An outdoor archery field was within a stone's throw from her living quarters. When Sun May and her attendants were not strengthening their bodies or improving their combat skills, they competed in archery for entertainment.

Every afternoon, Sun May and her attendants practiced martial arts in her garden. Those practice sessions normally attracted a crowd of spectators outside of the Sun family compound. The women warriors and their martial prowess often elicited awe and applause from the spectators. It was rumored that if Sun Quan had not been an accomplished military man, Sun May would have been the perfect candidate to succeed Sun Ce on the throne of Wu kingdom.

When the report about the two women reached Zhuge Liang's desk, he read it with relish. Afterward, he told Liu Bei, "Lord Liu, you have been favored by the deities with a prospective bride who is ideally suited to you. She complements you perfectly as Xian-Hui complements Guan Yu, but in opposite ways. As accomplished as Xian-Hui is in scholarship, your prospective bride, Sun May, excels in martial arts. Both Xian-Hui and Sun May are superwomen, two incomparable jewels. One is a scholar and an intellectual, the other a martial artist and a master swordswoman. I have no doubt that you will benefit from a wife like Sun May just as Guan Yu has been benefiting from Xian-Hui. In some ways, you are even luckier than Guan Yu, because your prospective mother-in-law happens to be a sagacious and remarkable person. When you go to the Wu kingdom to claim your wife, you will have to win Sun May's heart and charm her mother's soul. Given your charisma and personality, not to mention your good looks and regal bearing, I am confident that you will bring them to your corner in this contest with Sun Quan and Zhou Yu. With your permission, I will compose a letter to Zhou Yu accepting the offer of marriage as well as your consent to go to Jing province for the wedding."

Liu Bei was befuddled.

"But you had explained a few days ago that Zhou Yu's offer of his king's sister was a ruse to capture me. Now you want me to walk into Zhou Yu's trap?"

"Yes, Zhou Yu did use his sister to set a trap to capture you." Zhuge Liang explained, "But we, I mean you, will neutralize it. In fact, his trap will backfire. I will give you instructions before you leave for Jing province. Of course, you will be accompanied by Guan Yu and a platoon of the best bodyguards who will not hesitate to give their lives to protect you."

"Good! With Guan Yu by my side, I always feel safe. He can halt and demoralize an army with one roar." Liu Bei responded, "But walking into our enemy's lair remains a nerve-racking undertaking."

"Yes, there is a tiny risk. Every action we take entails some risk," Zhuge Liang said thoughtfully. "But this one is too minuscule to warrant your anxiety. I have done due diligence in preparation for your mission. According to my calculation, you will

THE THREE KINGDOMS   273

emerge from your visit to Wu kingdom triumphant with a wonderful wife who will love and protect you. But I want to reiterate that, in the end, my recommendation is just that, a recommendation. The ultimate decision rests with you."

"Well, you have always been wise, prophetic, and clairvoyant. I trust your assessment and accept your recommendation."

Having secured Liu Bei's consent to enter the Wu kingdom, Zhuge Liang whispered into Liu Bei's ear detailed instructions on how to prevail in Sun Quan's camp. Liu Bei listened carefully and nodded his head repeatedly.

Before Liu Bei and Guan Yu embarked on their journey, Zhuge Liang also gave explicit instructions to Guan Yu on what Guan Yu should do at different junctures of their visit to eastern Jing. Like Liu Bei, Guan Yu felt somewhat perturbed at the thought of entering the bowels of their enemy's territory without the protection of a full army, but Zhuge Liang bolstered his confidence.

Zhuge Liang's letter took Zhou Yu by surprise.

Expecting his marriage proposal to be rejected as a ruse, he couldn't believe that Zhuge Liang fell for his plot. Ecstatic, and rubbing his hands with glee, he felt he had finally come up with a scheme to triumph over his nemesis, Zhuge Liang. His scheme would result in the capture of Liu Bei without a war, not even suffering a single casualty. With Liu Bei in captivity, the Wu kingdom would be able to take over the Shu basin and emerge dominant in the nation. He knew that even if he captured Liu Bei, Zhuge Liang would remain a formidable foe. But without Liu Bei, Zhuge Liang might lose his zeal and consider resuming his hermetic life in the mountains.

Upon the arrival of Liu Bei and Guan Yu in Jing province, Zhou Yu and Sun Quan welcomed them with an elaborate ceremony, staged an extravagant banquet presided over by Sun Quan's mother the evening of their arrival, and treated Liu Bei and Guan Yu, with all the fanfare and pomp befitting a visiting sovereign. Liu Bei, in return, pulled out his charm, smiled graciously, spoke eloquently, behaved humbly, and thanked his hosts for all that they had done. Totally taken with Liu Bei, Sun Quan's mother couldn't be more pleased after meeting her prospective son-in-law.

My daughter is lucky to have such a remarkable man as her husband. I can now rest in peace, she thought to herself.

During the banquet, Sun Quan's sister, Sun May, sitting at the head table, discreetly glanced in Liu Bei's direction and listened to every word he said. Buoyed by what she saw and impressed by what she heard, she said to herself, Here is a born leader, noble, manly, and attractive! I am blessed to have him as my husband!

The banquet was a festive affair. Sun Quan, Zhou Yu, and all the senior officials in Sun Quan's court toasted the prospective couple so many times that Liu Bei began to feel a little woozy from the drinking. Toward the end of the banquet, Guan Yu walked over to Liu Bei and, with a hand covering his mouth, muttered something softly into Liu Bei's ear. Liu Bei immediately turned to Sun Quan's mother sitting on his left at the head of the banquet table and said in a trembling voice, "My dear mother-in-law, I am afraid your son harbors evil intentions against me."

"No," the elderly lady retorted. "My son will be your brother-in-law. He cannot possibly try to harm you."

"If you are right," Liu Bei asked gently, "why is our banquet hall surrounded by fully armed soldiers?"

"Really?" the lady dowager was taken aback. "How do you know that?"

"My brother Guan Yu detected the soldiers hiding all around us. They are heavily armed. He came over to tell me about it a moment ago," Liu Bei answered.

The lady dowager took in the information, thought for a while, and deduced Sun Quan's scheme. When she did, fury engulfed her. She wasn't just livid, but she also felt humiliated. It became clear to her that her son was using her as a pawn and her daughter as bait to set up a murderous trap of a remarkable man. Her immediate instinct was to spank her son right then and there, as if he were a little boy who had committed serious mischief, publicly embarrassing his mother and family.

"Come over here, son!" she exploded. "Stand next to me."

Flabbergasted, Sun Quan and Zhou Yu were in shock. But filial loyalty dictated Sun Quan's submission.

"How dare you make a fool of me and use my daughter, Sun May, as a lure to harm this wonderful, honorable man?" she roared as she pointed at Liu Bei. "You ought to be ashamed of yourself!"

Confronted with such an unexpected turn of events, Sun Quan was tongue-tied. In desperation, he looked to Zhou Yu for help.

"No, no! Honorable dowager," Zhou Yu muttered sheepishly, "we have no intention of harming Liu Bei, and we certainly did not deceive you. Our proposal for marrying Princess May to Liu Bei is sincere and genuine. We hope the marriage will cement an alliance between Wu and Shu. We have every intention to see our proposal fulfilled tomorrow morning."

"Phew! Liar, why have you surrounded us with armed soldiers?"

"Oh, that!" Embarrassed, Zhou Yu swallowed hard before regaining his composure and coming up with a lame excuse: "They are for your protection. One never knows if Cao Cao's spies might mount a desperate, suicidal attempt to attack us when we are in celebration. Cao Cao is a cunning rival. We must always be on guard against him, especially because the marriage between Liu Bei and Sun May will have a strong impact on him."

Silence followed Zhou Yu's fake excuse as if the banquet hall were suddenly buried in ice. Then, unexpectedly, the dowager's daughter, Sun May, stood up and broke the embarrassing silence: "Don't worry, Mother! My attendants and I will protect our honorable guests. After this banquet, Liu Bei and Guan Yu will retire to the antechamber of my bedroom pavilion instead of the guest quarters that have been assigned to them. All of us will march out of the banquet hall together with Liu Bei and Guan Yu in the middle. Tonight, they will lodge in my quarters until our wedding tomorrow morning."

As Liu Bei bowed and thanked the dowager and Sun May, Zhou Yu, crestfallen and dejected, felt a sharp pain in his chest radiating down his left arm. He collapsed in his chair. Attendants had to carry him out of the banquet room.

At the wedding the next morning, Sun Quan, in a somber mood, congratulated the newlywed with a toast: "This is a glorious day for my sister, Sun May, and a happy day for everyone in Wu kingdom. On behalf of the Sun family, I wish my sister and Liu Bei a blissful marriage and many beautiful sons and daughters. Thank you all for celebrating this matrimonial union with us."

Although the sudden death of his bosom friend and chief strategist, Zhou Yu, after the banquet the previous evening, was weighing heavily on him, Sun Quan withheld the bad news conveyed by his personal physician who, after attending to Zhou Yu on his deathbed, stated: "Zhou Yu died of a broken heart. He had been repeatedly outwitted and humiliated by Zhuge Liang. The humiliation was too much for him to bear."

Sun Quan admonished his physician not to divulge to anyone the cause of Zhou Yu's death. Several days later, hours before Zhou Yu's state funeral, Sun Quan announced that his chief strategist had died from exhaustion brought on by his dedicated service to the Wu kingdom.

After the wedding and two days of exuberant celebration in eastern Jing, Liu Bei returned with Sun May and Guan Yu to Chengdu in the Shu valley. The newlywed couple appeared in perfect harmony, happy and upbeat. They were seen holding hands on a stroll in the garden of the Peach Garden Brothers' headquarters. Zhuge Liang said in welcoming them back home, "In spite of the hazard and trepidation along the path, you've found each other. Your marriage is made in heaven! We welcome our queen to the Shu nation. Long live the queen!"

"Since when has my wife become a queen?" surprised by Zhuge Liang's choice of words, Liu Bei inquired.

"I know it affronts you to consider the demise of the Han dynasty," Zhuge Liang responded. "Steering clear from sentimentality and nostalgia, I wish to present to you, my lord, an unbiased and candid portrayal of our country today. No matter how loyal you and I feel toward the Han dynasty, its demise is undeniable, even though we are loath to accept the truth. Cao Cao is now the king of Wei kingdom; Sun Quan has declared himself the king of Wu kingdom; you, whether you like it or not, are, by default and without pomp or coronation, the king of Shu kingdom. History will remember our time as the era of Three Kingdoms. I hope Shu will emerge triumphant and our country will be unified under your leadership. As your chief strategist, I consider that hope the guiding principle of my service."

As much as Liu Bei didn't want to accept Zhuge Liang's proclamation, he couldn't find a bona fide rationale to counter it. Since organizing a militia against the Yellow Turbans in his home county in the Central Plain, he had been dedicating himself to the restoration of the Han dynasty. Now, he was obliged to recognize that he had failed, and the Peach Garden Brothers had failed. The reality that Zhuge Liang had forcibly presented to him brought tears to his eyes.

For days after Liu Bei accepted the harsh political reality, he wallowed in depression, confining himself in his study, barely taking in any food, and shunning everyone. Liu Bei's indulgence in his grief infuriated his bride, Sun May, and his Peach Garden Brothers. Guan Yu finally had had enough. One morning, he barged into Liu Bei's study, placed a sword on his desk, and screamed at Liu Bei, who looked like a wreck in his armchair.

"Alright, if you want to kill yourself, go right ahead! Cut your own throat with this sword. But I want to remind you of the oath you swore with Zhang Fei and me in the peach garden. We agreed to support each other until our deaths and promised that we would die at the same time. Your suicide will imply our death, the death of your loving wife, and the death of my Xian-Hui. Are you ready to condemn all of us to our graves? If you do, I want to know what we have done to make you think that we deserve such a fate."

Guan Yu's unsparing admonition hit Liu Bei like a roll of thunder.

"No, no!" Liu Bei pleaded, "You, Zhang Fei, Xian-Hui, and Sun May have not done anything to deserve any punishment. On the contrary, you deserve all the accolades and rewards in the world. I respect and adore you all. Lost in my grief, I didn't mean harm to any of you. Please forgive me, my brother."

Liu Bei wanted to say more but lost his voice as he broke down sobbing.

Tears welled in Guan Yu's eyes. He lifted Liu Bei onto his feet, staring at him in his eyes, and said gently, "Look, my dear brother, it's a lovely, balmy day. In the garden, the azalea is blooming, the weeping willows are full of life-yearning buds, the sky is dotted with honking geese as they migrate northward, and the cuckoo birds are singing in celebration of the dawn of a new spring. Let's take a hint from nature's renewal and strengthen our resolve to embark on a new mission to expand the Shu kingdom. Wait for me here while I bring over Sun May,

Xian-Hui, Zhang Fei, and Zhuge Liang and ask the servant to bring some rose liquor. Together we will drink to the future of Shu kingdom!"

The man who succeeded Zhou Yu as the chief strategist for Sun Quan was Lu Su, a plodding but cautious military general and politician. He counseled Sun Quan to lay off the Peach Garden Brothers for a while. After all, Lu Su pointed out, "Liu Bei has just become your brother-in-law. This is not the time to engage in hostility against your new kin."

The news of Liu Bei's marriage to Sun May stunned Cao Cao. Fearful that the matrimonial link would be a harbinger of military alliance, he sent a conciliatory message to Sun Quan, declaring that he had adopted a policy of peaceful coexistence with the Wu kingdom. To demonstrate his goodwill, he reduced the number of troops stationed along their shared border by half and moved them westward toward the Han Zhong region, which remained under the control of a minor warlord, Zhang Lu. Suing for peace with the Wu kingdom, Cao Cao penned a conciliatory letter in which he revealed his new military strategy: "As you know, the Han Zhong region was the birthplace of the Han dynasty. Gaozu, the founding emperor of the Han dynasty, started his conquest of the country from Han Zhong, where he was known as the king of Han. Han Zhong was the reason Gaozu named his dynasty the Han dynasty! It would mean a lot to Emperor Xian if I could recapture Han Zhong for His Majesty. In addition, Han Zhong is the only staging point for an army to enter the Shu basin by land. I am seeking the collaboration of the local commander in chief, Zhang Lu. We hope to invade the Shu basin from there."

Cao Cao's letter made a strong impression on Sun Quan.

When Sun Quan consulted with his new chief of staff, Lu Su, the two of them agreed that if Cao Cao invaded Shu basin from the northeast via the Han Zhong region, the action would not only relieve the pressure on Wu kingdom's northern frontier, Sun Quan could also divert some of his navy and infantry to invade Shu basin up the Yangtzi River via the Vermilion Gorge. Lu Su and Sun Quan estimated that the Peach Garden Brothers would have great difficulty fighting invading forces on two separate fronts simultaneously.

Cao Cao's plan, however, did not pan out smoothly. As his army reached the border city of Han Zhong region, Han Zhong's most capable general, Pang De, a square-jawed hulk of a man, wielding a heavy broadsword, with ten thousand troops under his command, blocked Cao Cao's army on the only road to the heart of Han Zhong. An intrepid warrior and an astute military strategist, Pang De avoided an all-out confrontation with Cao Cao's numerically superior army, but did not shy from individual duels against Cao Cao's generals. Since the road approaching Pang De's military base was a narrow canyon, Cao Cao could not deploy his entire army for a frontal assault against Pang De's citadel. When one of Cao Cao's generals led a light cavalry into the canyon to probe the defense, Pang De emerged from safety behind the tall stone wall with a contingent of elite soldiers and fought courageously. None of Cao Cao's generals was able to defeat Pang De. When Cao Cao sent reinforcements, hoping to overwhelm Pang De's small contingent of troops, Pang De simply ordered his troops to retreat behind a reinforced gate in the middle of a ten-foot-deep barricade consisting of a tall stone wall spanning the width of the narrow canyon. Positioned on top of the stone wall were hundreds of archers ready to rain arrows on attackers.

After one week, Cao Cao switched to a new tactic. Hoping to wear out Pang De, he sent a tandem of warriors forward to challenge him. If Cao Cao's warriors came forward together,

Pang De, hiding behind his stone wall, did not come out to fight. If they came one at a time, Pang De fought them brilliantly. Over several days of such a stalemate, Pang De remained indefatigable even though he was middle-aged. After ten days of bivouacking in front of Pang De's fortified gate, Cao Cao was near the end of his wits. He started sulking and began to think that he should give up his attempt to conquer Han Zhong. Then, one of his officers suggested an innovative approach to solve the Pang De problem.

The officer happened to know of a notoriously avaricious senior officer in Han Zhong named Yang Song. He advised Cao Cao to offer Yang Song a hefty bribe to undermine or destroy Pang De's credibility in Han Zhong. The advice appealed to Cao Cao. To implement it, however, required some ingenuity. Somebody from Cao Cao's camp had to gain access to Yang Song. But Cao Cao was nothing if not an expert at designing crafty schemes.

That night he moved his camp closer to Pang De's fortified gate in the canyon and concealed some of his troops in the hills on both sides of the canyon behind his camp. The next day, he personally led a small coterie of cavalry to probe Pang De's defense along the thick wall of stones. Taking note of Cao Cao's presence on the battlefield, Pang De saw an opportunity to capture Cao Cao. He opened the gate and went after Cao Cao with a platoon of cavalry and several hundred foot soldiers. A warrior wielding a heavy cudgel trotted out of Cao Cao's contingent to engage Pang De in a duel. After a few rounds of combat between Pang De and the cudgel-wielding warrior, Cao Cao signaled his troops to retreat. Pang De and his soldiers immediately gave chase. The chase led all the way into Cao Cao's encampment. Upon entering Cao Cao's camp, Pang De heard a loud explosion and saw hordes of enemy soldiers roaring down the hills along both sides of the canyon. Recognizing that he had been lured into an ambush, Pang De immediately ordered his troops to turn back toward his fortress. In the ensuing chaos, a spy from Cao Cao's army, disguised in Han Zhong military uniform, entered Pang De's camp amid the retreating soldiers. From there, the spy traveled to the capital of Han Zhong and contacted the avaricious Yang Song.

In a private meeting, the spy presented Yang Song with a letter from Cao Cao and a pouch of gold ingots. In the letter, Cao Cao praised Yang Song for his past service to the Han imperial court, and then explained that he intended to pass through Han Zhong on his way to vanquish the Peach Garden Brothers in the Shu valley, not to wage war against Zhang Lu, the chief of the Han Zhong garrison. Cao Cao wrote, "Unlike the treasonous Peach Garden Brothers, your commandant, Zhang Lu, has been a loyal servant of the Han imperial court. By the order of Emperor Xian, my army wishes to pass through Han Zhong to capture the Peach Garden Brothers in Shu basin. Ideally, I would appreciate the collaboration of the Han Zhong garrison. I understand that your commandant has other obligations in maintaining the security of the Han Zhong region. But I am dismayed that General Pang De, in his ignorance and obstinacy, has barred our entry along a narrow path on Han Zhong's eastern border. If you could remove that obstacle to my imperial mission, I would be eternally grateful."

Delighted with the gift of gold ingots and flattered by Cao Cao's complimentary letter, Yang Song told the messenger, "Please let the honorable Cao Cao know that I will take care of the matter."

What Yang Song had in mind was to accuse Pang De of the same transgression and crime he himself was committing, a tactic employed by depraved knaves since antiquity.

The next day, Yang Song reported to Han Zhong's commandant, Zhang Lu, that Pang De, having accepted a large bribe from Cao Cao, not only refused to engage Cao Cao's army but was secretly preparing to surrender. Shocked, Zhang Lu launched an inquiry into the accusation while ordering Pang De to engage Cao Cao's army the very next day, warning Pang De that he could face execution if he refused to engage Cao Cao's army for a decisive battle.

Upon receiving Zhang Lu's order and warning, Pang De was deeply hurt and angry. He felt that Zhang Lu's order constituted not only a grim strategic blunder, but also a major insult to him. A loyal subordinate, he felt, justifiably, that he had been wronged and gravely mistreated.

The next day, he arrived at the battlefield with a bruised ego and a wounded heart. But the sight of Cao Cao sitting on a horse not far from the battlefield gave him hope of a victory and lifted him out of his depression.

Here is an opportunity for me to capture Cao Cao single-handedly, he thought to himself. If I can pull it off, I will be a great hero.

Charging toward Cao Cao at full speed, Pang De thought he would have his quarry in hand momentarily. As he and his horse drew near Cao Cao, the earth beneath them yawned open like a giant maw. Both horse and rider fell into a camouflaged trench. A bevy of Cao Cao's soldiers then overwhelmed him, tied him up, and brought him to Cao Cao.

Stunned and horrified, Pang De expected imminent death. Much to Pang De's astonishment, Cao Cao, instead of demanding Pang De's head, dismissed the soldiers, untied Pang De, helped him to a seat, and politely invited him to switch allegiance.

"You are a great warrior." Cao Cao said with a smile, "I need your service."

Impressed by Cao Cao's magnanimity and courtesy, Pang De felt he was justified to leave Zhang Lu's service and join Cao Cao's camp. After all, Zhang Lu gratuitously threatened him with execution despite his many years of loyal and faithful service, whereas Cao Cao treated him with respect and kindness after capturing him. He graciously accepted Cao Cao's invitation.

After Cao Cao conquered Han Zhong, he appointed Pang De its governor. Zhang Lu was demoted to a subordinate position under Pang De. The only man Cao Cao executed in Han Zhong was Yang Song, the avaricious man, who betrayed his former commander for a pouch of gold nuggets, even though Cao Cao was the one who enticed Yang Song to commit betrayal.

Alarmed by Cao Cao's dramatic acquisition of Han Zhong, Zhuge Liang polled his senior generals for volunteers to confront Cao Cao at the border of northeast Shu basin and Han Zhong. Two elderly warriors, Huang Zhong and Yan Yan, jumped at the opportunity. Late in their careers, they were eager to make a notable contribution to the newly established Shu kingdom and earn some credit before retirement. Since both were middle-aged, Zhuge Liang was, on the one hand, hesitant to entrust them with such an onerous assignment and, on the other hand, loath to dampen their enthusiasm. After he authorized the two elderly generals to lead ten thousand troops to meet Cao Cao's army at the frontier, he discreetly ordered General Zhao Yun to lead another five thousand troops to back up Huang Zhong and Yan Yan at a distance behind the two senior warriors.

A grand master of the spear, Zhao Yun had joined the Peach Garden Brothers after the death of his former chief, Gongsun Zan, the warlord who briefly accommodated the Peach Garden Brothers in Youzhou province of China's northern frontiers along the borders of Mongolia and Korea when the Peach Garden Brothers' county militia expanded into an army. An equal of Zhang Fei and Guan Yu in bravery and martial skills, Zhao Yun was more cerebral and even-tempered than both Zhang Fei and Guan Yu. Poised and unflappable, he preferred problem-solving to violent confrontation on the battlefield. Zhang Fei admired him. Other than Zhuge Liang, Liu Bei, and Guan Yu, Zhao Yun

THE THREE KINGDOMS   285

was the only person whose counsel and opinion commanded Zhang Fei's attention and respect.

At the frontier, Zhuge Liang's elderly general Huang Zhong wasted no time killing Cao Cao's close confidant, an up-and-coming young general, in a duel. The young warrior, suffering from hubris, assumed that his youth and power would easily prevail over an old warrior pushing fifty. But Huang Zhong's experience and skill proved to be beyond the ken of the young man. With a masterful stroke, Huang Zhong feigned a thrust with his sword at the head of his young opponent, only to shift the sword toward the victim's heart at the last moment. Injured, the young general tumbled off his horse. With a collective roar, Huang Zhong's troops charged forward and obliterated the foot soldiers behind the victim.

After his initial victory, Huang Zhong's spies discovered the location of Cao Cao's supply depot near a ravine not far from the battlefield. Huang Zhong figured that if he could take away Cao Cao's supply of food and weapons, Cao Cao would have no choice but to retreat. But clever Cao Cao anticipated that Huang Zhong might follow up his initial swift victory with an attack on the supply depot of the Wei army. Overnight, Cao Cao deployed several infantry platoons on the hills surrounding the depot and personally led the main force of his army hiding in a nearby forest.

Early next dawn, Huang Zhong approached the depot at the head of his force, encountering little resistance. As Huang Zhong's soldiers were piling firewood and incendiary material around the depot to burn Cao Cao's supplies, thousands of Cao Cao's soldiers emerged from the surrounding hills. Huang Zhong tried to turn back, only to find himself blocked by Cao Cao's main column of troops emerging from their hiding places in the forest. Huang Zhong fought bravely, fending off twenty lance-wielding enemy soldiers who encircled him. Then, he heard the rumble of horses pounding the earth of the ravine, heralding the imminent arrival of a cavalry brigade.

Assuming the approaching cavalry belonged to Cao Cao, Huang Zhong thought to himself as he swung his sword to fend off the thrusting lances, This is my death knell.

Yet he remained calm and fearless, bravely fighting Cao Cao's soldiers surrounding him.

When the galloping cavalry arrived on the scene, much to Huang Zhong's surprise and relief, his comrade Zhao Yun was riding at its head, spearing and knocking over Cao Cao's infantry in his path. With lightning speed, Zhao Yun split the lancers, charged toward the encircled Huang Zhong, and lifted him onto his saddle, racing to safety.

Before Zhao Yun departed the Shu basin to back up Huang Zhong, Zhuge Liang had given Zhao Yun an important instruction: "You want Huang Zhong to feel youthful and invincible despite his age. On the one hand, give him a wide berth for his initiatives so that he would not feel that you are there to watch after him." Zhuge Liang told Zhao Yun, "On the other hand, if Huang Zhong enters a battle and fails to emerge quickly in victory, don't hesitate to help him."

Mindful of Zhuge Liang's instruction, Zhao Yun set out to find Huang Zhong sometime after Huang Zhong left camp to raid Cao Cao's supply depot. Luckily, Zhao Yun arrived at the depot in the nick of time when Huang Zhong, surrounded by enemies, began to fade from fatigue.

The report that crafty Cao Cao nearly captured the aging warrior Huang Zhong prompted Zhuge Liang to take charge of the war in Han Zhong personally. With Liu Bei, he led the Shu army to the battle, leaving Zhang Fei to oversee and defend the Shu basin while Guan Yu was in charge of what remained of the western Jing province. Upon reaching the Han River, a major waterway that flowed through the Han Zhong region in the southeast direction, the Shu military column crossed it on wooden

THE THREE KINGDOMS 287

pontoons. On the east bank, they bivouacked at a short distance from Cao Cao's billet.

The location of Zhuge Liang's bivouac surprised Cao Cao. It was against common sense to set camp between one's enemy and a river as deep and wide as the Han River without the backing of a naval fleet. Cao Cao was alarmed. Suspicion and paranoia churned in his mind. He knew that Zhuge Liang, a brilliant strategist and a prudent tactician, would never make such an elementary mistake as bivouacking his army by the bank of a river while facing a formidable enemy. Offhand, he rejected his generals' recommendation to launch a full-scale attack. He believed that the only reason that Zhuge Liang would endanger his troops in such a manner was to lure an enemy into a trap. He didn't want to be ensnared, yet he couldn't fathom Zhuge Liang's scheme.

What scheme has that cunning Zhuge Liang concocted? Cao Cao asked himself, spending several sleepless nights mulling over the question without coming up with a reasonable answer.

Caught between his ever-suspicious nature and his obsession to attack the Peach Garden Brothers, Cao Cao became irritable and petulant. His subordinates, from high-ranking officers to foot soldiers, loathed interacting with him in his agitated state. He was abusive, hollering invectives at his attendants without any provocation. The morale of his army sank, and a general malaise prevailed in his camp. More significantly, he suspected that being overcautious, he might have missed a golden opportunity to vanquish Zhuge Liang's army when they remained on the waterfront.

Two days after crossing the Han River, Zhuge Liang's troops were fully rested from the travail of their journey. They were primed for battle. He devised a three-pronged attack. Liu Bei and Huang Zhong at the head of the bulk of their army constituted the middle column, the main attacking force. Guan Yu with five hundred cavalry vanished into the rolling hills to the left, and Zhao Yun with another five hundred cavalry hid themselves in a wooded area to the right. Both Zhao Yun and Guan Yu were given the instruction from Zhuge Liang: "As soon as you hear drumming from the middle column, order your soldiers to beat the gongs and cymbals in unison as loudly as possible."

When Cao Cao led his generals and soldiers out of their billet to confront Liu Bei and Huang Zhong, Liu Bei's soldiers in the rear started drumming. Immediately, the gongs and cymbals in Zhao Yun's and Guan Yu's columns responded. The east bank of the Han River was suddenly awash in a cacophony of percussion recitals. Startled and alarmed, Cao Cao and his soldiers tried to find out what was happening. They turned left; they turned right; they looked in front and behind. No enemy was in sight. Yet the gongs and cymbals suggested that they were everywhere. As the symphony of percussion raged, Zhuge Liang's troops set off deafening explosions of gunpowder devices all around Cao Cao's troops. The ruckus so intimidated Cao Cao's army that they ran from the battlefield in wide dispersion. In the ensuing chaos and confusion, numerous soldiers in Cao Cao's army were trampled to death. Zhuge Liang then told Huang Zhong, "Now is the time to take Cao Cao's supply depot while Zhao Yun and Guan Yu pursue and annihilate Cao Cao's disoriented soldiers."

Following Zhuge Liang's order, Huang Zhong took a contingent of infantry and marched posthaste toward Cao Cao's supply depot. They met a squadron of defenders at the site. Eager to make up for the failure of his previous raid, Huang Zhong rushed the leader of the defense like a pouncing tiger. In a flash, he cut the leader of the defending force in half with his sword. The gruesome death of their commander sent shock waves through the rank of defenders. Frightened, they turned tail and ran for their lives. Huang Zhong and his soldiers took away as many loads of weapons, clothing, armor, and food as they could carry. Before departure, they set fire to the depot, burning the supplies that were left behind.

In the meantime, Zhao Yun and Guan Yu chased and harassed Cao Cao's retreating army for a full day, raining arrows and heaving spears on them. Cao Cao's forces suffered a tremendous toll. Many deserted or surrendered. By nightfall, less than half of Cao Cao's army remained. Thoroughly traumatized, the survivors dragged themselves, tattered and wasted, toward the east.

The debacle terminated Cao Cao's grand design of controlling the Han Zhong region and spelled the end of his expedition against the Peach Garden Brothers. His only remaining option was to return to the Yellow River basin, his original base.

With the defeat of Cao Cao and the acquisition of Han Zhong region, the Peach Garden Brothers reached a new height in their struggle for power against Cao Cao and Sun Quan. Proud of the Peach Garden Brothers' success, the people of Shu basin celebrated.

Back in his home territory, Cao Cao raged. The Peach Garden Brothers had inflicted two catastrophic losses on him, once in the Vermilion Gorge, and now in Han Zhong. He was humiliated. Desperate for revenge, he began to prepare a multipronged war against the Peach Garden Brothers. As he brainstormed with his generals on how and where they should attack the Shu kingdom, a young member of Cao Cao's court made a proposal: "My lord! Let's not forget that we are in a three-way struggle for supremacy. Waging war and winning battles are not the only means by which one can prevail in such a struggle. Diplomacy also plays an important role. Lately, there has been tension in the relationship between Wu and Shu kingdoms. A few years ago, Sun Quan gave his own sister, Sun May, to Liu Bei as a wife. Last month, Sun Quan's agents kidnapped Sun May in Chengdu and brought her back to Wu kingdom. The incident was a retaliation against Liu Bei's refusal to yield back to Sun Quan the westernmost section of Jing province. Sun Quan had always felt, justifiably in my opinion, that the Peach Garden Brothers should have returned western Jing to Wu kingdom. Sun Quan's inflexible revanchism and his territorial quarrel with the Peach Garden Brothers had already caused a war between Wu and Shu. Currently, the two kingdoms are at the nadir of their relationship. We should take advantage of the situation."

Impressed by the young official's suggestion, Cao Cao looked at him and realized that he was the wunderkind named Sima Yi, who had made a reputation for himself with his quick wit and sharp tongue in Cao Cao's court.

"How do you propose to take advantage of the deteriorating relationship between Wu and Shu?" Cao Cao asked.

"Let's begin with a friendly gesture to Sun Quan, reminding him that we are not his sworn enemy. We can send him a gift in the name of Emperor Xian, thanking him for pacifying the minority ethnic groups in Jing province and the south," Sima Yi said. "The gift is an exploration to find out how he might respond to our overture."

Cao Cao laughed. "Ha! Sun Quan pacifying the minorities! It is, at best, a truth-distorting euphemism. He has driven the Hmong and Mien people into the mountains, sent the Polynesians fleeing into the sea, forced the Tai and Yi into the southern jungles. But if that is how you propose to flatter him, I have no objection. I just hope that the flattery will elicit a favorable response from him."

It turned out that Sima Yi's charm offensive worked beautifully. Lu Su, who became Sun Quan's chief strategist after the death of Zhou Yu, felt that a good relationship with Cao Cao's Wei kingdom at that juncture would be advantageous because the Peach Garden Brothers remained stubbornly uncompromising. Accepting Lu Su's advice, Sun Quan responded to Cao Cao's

THE THREE KINGDOMS   291

friendly initiative with gifts and a letter filled with compliments. In response, Sima Yi sent a missive to Sun Quan in the name of Cao Cao, proposing that the Wei kingdom would assist the Wu kingdom to retake all of western Jing by force. The proposal fell short of suggesting a blanket alliance between the two blocs. He wanted to avoid invoking the concept of alliance, which had implications beyond his current objective. In addition, a full alliance between Wei kingdom and Wu kingdom would be a strong provocation against the Peach Garden Brothers.

Sun Quan was delighted with Sima Yi's proposal. Driven by his revanchism and emboldened by Cao Cao's support, he began to prepare for an invasion of the portion of western Jing under Guan Yu's jurisdiction.

When Zhuge Liang learned from his informants that Cao Cao would support Sun Quan's attempt to regain western Jing, he chose to counter the newly coordinated effort by attacking both immediately.

"Why wait for their invasion? We will destroy them before they mobilize against us," Zhuge Liang reasoned.

He then ordered Guan Yu's army to invade Cao Cao's territory from Han Zhong and Zhang Fei to march against Sun Quan's force in Jing province.

Zhuge Liang's audacious move took Cao Cao and Sun Quan by surprise. Realizing that, once again, the wily Zhuge Liang had seized the initiative, Cao Cao and Sun Quan, once again, found themselves in a defensive position.

At Cao Cao's court, the newly appointed general, Pang De, who had surrendered to Cao Cao in Han Zhong two years earlier, volunteered to lead an army to confront Guan Yu. Ever since his surrender, he had been waiting for an opportunity to show his gratitude to Cao Cao and his newly sworn loyalty to the Wei kingdom. The current military situation provided him with a golden opportunity to demonstrate his sentiments with action. Han Zhong was his home turf. He would love to reconquer it. Sensing Pang De's earnest desire, Cao Cao gladly assigned thirty thousand troops for Pang De's mission. The next morning, Pang De took off with a coffin at the head of his army in front of Cao Cao and his court. Puzzled by the coffin, Cao Cao asked, "Why do you take a coffin with you? Isn't it a harbinger of death?"

"Exactly." Pang De responded, "My lord, I will fight to death on this mission. This coffin will return with either the corpse of Guan Yu or my dead body."

Deeply touched by Peng De's devotion and loyalty, Cao Cao walked down from his throne, took off his golden silk robe, and draped it over Pang De's shoulders. Members of the court spontaneously broke into a thunderous applause as Pang De and his army marched away.

One week later, Pang De and his troop arrived at the city of Fan at the delta of a main tributary of the Han River. From Han Zhong, the city of Fan was the main gateway to Cao Cao's home base, the Central Plain around the Yellow River. The mayor of Fan was relieved at the sight of Pang De and his army. But the city was too small to accommodate Pang De's thirty thousand troops. They had to bivouac on the outskirts of the city. But it was the monsoon season. Incessant rain caused all kinds of problems for the soldiers. The rain made it difficult for Pang De's troop to maneuver in mud, and the tents in which they slept did not fully protect them from the torrential downpour. They were wet, shivering from cold, tired from sleep deprivation, and utterly demoralized. Even the horses of Pang De's cavalry complained against the incessant rain and the humidity, neighing and shaking their bodies constantly.

THE THREE KINGDOMS 293

Guan Yu, in the meantime, arrived by junks on the Han River. Zhuge Liang had insisted that Guan Yu take the river route to the city of Fan despite Guan Yu's objection.

"Why do I have to go to the front line by boat?" Guan Yu protested, "Boats are like prisons. I prefer land to water."

"You will know the reason upon your arrival!" Zhuge Liang answered.

Rain pestered Guan Yu and his troops during their voyage. The level of precipitation that year was exceptional. Water poured down from the clouds everywhere, raising the water level of the river above the surrounding agricultural land. The farmers of this region, aware of the unpredictable nature of the Han River, had built dikes along it to ward off flooding. Guan Yu noticed that the dikes were straining to hold back the raging current. As Guan Yu's flotilla drew near the city of Fan, he saw Pang De's waterlogged camp at a distance outside of the city wall and the reason for Zhuge Liang's insistence on them traveling by boat became clear. The key to victory in this war was the use of floodwater.

At approximately two thousand paces from Pang De's billet, Guan Yu moored the boats and ordered his troops to break the dike. Pang De was in the process of putting on his armor in his tent when he heard the roar of rushing water. Startled, he stepped out and saw a wall of water coming toward him. Fortunately, he was able to grab onto an old willow tree nearby and barely escaped from being swept away. Perched on a high branch of the tree, he was in tears as most of his soldiers vanished into the swirling, turgid flood water. Dazed and despondent, he perched on the lifesaving willow tree like a cowering bird. When a small boat came to fetch him, he didn't even notice that the soldiers in the boat were from Guan Yu's army.

Pang De finally came to his senses when he was brought in front of Guan Yu, who pleaded with him to switch his allegiance to the Peach Garden Brothers.

"Never!" thundered Pang De. "I serve my lord, Cao Cao, Emperor Xian's chancellor. You are a mere brigand. How dare you entertain the thought of my surrender! I am a soldier, and I will die as a soldier."

Guan Yu was moved by Pang De's courage and loyalty to Cao Cao. It was with deep regret that he granted Pang De's wish to be executed. Afterward, Guan Yu buried Pang De with full military honor. On his grave, Guan Yu erected a tombstone and had the following words carved on it: "General Pang De, brave warrior, loyal soldier."

THIRTEEN

AN INJURY

When the rain stopped and the flood began to recede, the city wall of Fan remained intact. From the height of the city wall, the mayor of Fan realized that Pang De and his garrison had perished. He tried to send a message to Cao Cao seeking reinforcement. The messenger managed to escape the city from the other side of the Han River while Guan Yu was searching for a way to breach the city wall. He led a small coterie of cavalry to reconnoiter, galloping around the city. At one point during the reconnaissance, Guan Yu carelessly ventured too close to the city wall. A sharp-shooting archer hiding behind a parapet on top of the wall aimed an arrow at Guan Yu. The arrow hit Guan Yu's left shoulder but didn't knock him off his saddle. Guan Yu pulled out the arrow with his right hand and rushed back to his flagship, a large junk moored by the riverbank. Doctors dressed his wound and commanded him to rest. He was in pain. Several days after the shot, Guan Yu's wound, instead of healing, deteriorated and turned ominously dark while the swelling had spread toward his chest. His physician told him that the arrow that hit him was poisonous and the only person capable of saving his life would be Hua Tuo, who had gained fame several years ago for curing Cao Cao from an ailment with symptoms including an incapacitating headache and a blurred vision.

At the time Hua Tuo was summoned to examine Cao Cao, Cao Cao was totally incapacitated by a pounding headache and impaired vision. Despite the best herbal medicines prescribed by the court physician, Cao Cao's condition deteriorated. After Hua Tuo examined Cao Cao, he said, "My lord, you will not like what I am going to say. But it is my duty as a doctor to tell the truth. Your headache and vision impairment are caused by a malignant growth inside your skull. Herbal medicine is useless against it. The only remedy is to remove that tumor."

"How do you propose to do that?" startled, Cao Cao asked.

"I will have to open up your skull with saws and knives before I can remove it," Hua Tuo answered matter-of-factly.

"Open up my skull?!" Cao Cao was aghast as his paranoia overtook him. "You must be a spy from the Peach Garden Brothers using medicine as a ruse to kill me. Guards, arrest this assassin."

Cao Cao's guards immediately took Hua Tuo to jail and began an investigation of Hua Tuo's background. In the meantime, Cao Cao's headache and blurred vision worsened day by day. Other court officials, swearing that Hua Tuo was the greatest physician in the nation, not a spy in anyone's service, urged Cao Cao to allow Hua Tuo to treat him. Cao Cao, rendered helpless by the intensifying headache and deteriorating vision, finally cast aside his paranoia and agreed to be treated by Hua Tuo.

As Hua Tuo got ready for the surgery, he explained to Cao Cao that there would be pain at the beginning, and therefore, several assistants would have to hold Cao Cao down to prevent him from moving. Cao Cao, after selecting two of his most loyal servants and his two sons for the job of holding him still, submitted to the surgery, which lasted several hours. Contrary to everyone's expectation, the surgery wasn't a gory procedure

AN INJURY 297

with massive bleeding. When he finished the operation, Hua Tuo showed everyone a tumor the size of a plum he had removed from Cao Cao's brain. A few days after the procedure, Cao Cao's symptoms disappeared.

Ever since that operation, Hua Tuo's reputation spread far and wide in China. He was worshipped almost as a demigod capable of dispensing magical remedies. When Guan Yu's condition worsened from the poison arrow, Hua Tuo was brought to treat him.

After examining Guan Yu's wound, Hua Tuo announced that he would have to cut deep into the wound, remove the poisoned tissue, and clean out the wounded area. He made clear that four strong men were needed to hold down Guan Yu during the surgery.

"No need for anyone to hold me down," Guan Yu told the famous physician.

"The cutting will be deep, bloody, and painful," Hua Tuo warned.

"Fine." Guan Yu responded, "Just bring me a big jug of rose liquor. I will sit in my chair when you do the incision. My wife, Xian-Hui, will hold my hand, and ply me with rose liquor."

The surgery went smoothly and successfully. At the end, Hua Tuo sewed up the incision with venison sinew and covered it with a yellowish fuzzy plant material that stopped the bleeding and hastened the healing. Guan Yu's lieutenants, who witnessed the operation, were awestruck by Guan Yu's courage during the surgery.

Two weeks after the procedure, Guan Yu was fully recovered. To show his gratitude, he offered Hua Tuo a pouch of gold. Hua Tuo politely turned down the gift, saying, "I am glad to be of service to a great warrior."

Hua Tuo, already celebrated for curing Cao Cao's headache, became a legend in the annals of Chinese medicine after treating Guan Yu.

FOURTEEN

THE LOSS OF
A BELOVED BROTHER

While Guan Yu was in action against Cao Cao in the north, Zhang Fei, with ten thousand troops in tow, crossed into Sun Quan's territory in Jing province. Obsessed with the thought that he had become a laggard in view of Guan Yu's decisive victory in Han Zhong, he wanted a swift victory over the Wu kingdom. He ordered his troops on a forced march for days, aiming to take Changsha, one of the major cities in Sun Quan's Jing province. But Changsha was a long way to the east from where Zhang Fei began his march. Along the journey, he took shortcuts, away from the main road, whenever he could. But the shortcuts were full of hazards. There were swamps to trudge through, rivers to cross, lakes to skirt, hills to scale, forests to traverse. It was an arduous and difficult journey, made worse by Zhang Fei's impetuosity. As soldiers died from fever and accidents, resentment against Zhang Fei began to brood among the rank and file.

One day, several soldiers walked into a bog and started sinking. Other soldiers behind the trapped victims tried to extract them by reaching for them with lances. But the rescuers couldn't

THE LOSS OF A BELOVED BROTHER

pull the victims out of the sticky muck. The more the victims struggled in the bog, the deeper they sank. Their chilling shrieks before vanishing into the brackish water shook Zhang Fei's troops to the core. Everyone was unnerved.

But the loss of lives in the bog was hardly the only disaster. Two days later, two soldiers died from venomous snakebites. Their bodies turned black and blue from internal bleeding as they writhed in agony before death. Worse than bogs and poisonous snakes, hordes of gnats, mosquitoes, wasps, not to mention critters such as ants, leeches, and poisonous centipedes pestered, bit, and stung the troops every day, especially in the early-morning and evening hours, causing rashes, boils, and hives, gaping wounds that hurt and itched. The march became a catastrophe.

Several days into the march, murmurs of complaints began to circulate openly among the soldiers. Some deserted.

The desertion drove Zhang Fei over the edge. He personally executed two deserters who got caught. The execution made Zhang Fei, already unpopular among the soldiers, into a ruthless tyrant to the rank and file of his army. Some soldiers began to conspire against him.

One night, three conspirators, with the connivance of two of Zhang Fei's personal guards, entered his tent before dawn to attempt an assassination. At that moment, Zhang Fei was snoring in his bed. Assuming that Zhang Fei was sound asleep, the assassins approached him with drawn swords. When they drew close, they saw that Zhang Fei's eyes were wide-open, staring at them ferociously. Frightened out of their minds, they ran out of the tent, expecting to be killed by Zhang Fei, who would come after them with his spear. Much to their surprise, there was no commotion and Zhang Fei didn't come out of the tent. Halting in their tracks, they tiptoed back cautiously and found Zhang Fei in the same sleeping pose with his eyes wide-open, snoring loudly just as he had a few seconds earlier. The assassins realized that Zhang Fei was someone with the strange habit of sleeping with his eyes open. Without any further ado, they slit his throat, chopped off his head, put it in a sack, and fled to Sun Quan's garrison.

A few hours later when Zhang Fei's deputy commanders discovered his headless corpse, they decided to abandon the march to eastern Jing and returned with the remaining army to Shu basin.

In Chengdu, Zhang Fei's death broke Liu Bei's heart. It took all Zhuge Liang's power and his repeated invocation of Liu Bei's responsibility to the people of Shu basin to dissuade Liu Bei from suicide.

The news of Zhang Fei's death hit Guan Yu hard. When a messenger from Chengdu delivered the news, Guan Yu sank to the ground and wept. He withdrew from social interaction and refused food even though he was known for his huge appetite. Xian-Hui tried to alleviate his grief and sorrow, attempting to comfort him with scintillating historical anecdotes, enthralling stories of epic battles of the past, and tantalizing news about Cao Cao and Sun Quan. She kept him in her sight day and night. She wouldn't allow him to consume liquor but fed him different soups that were nourishing and delicious.

Despite Xian-Hui's tender care and devoted effort, Guan Yu visibly shrank from an imposing physical specimen like a sumo wrestler to a regular-sized person in three weeks. No longer barrel-chested, he began to stoop slightly; his hair turned gray; his beard, peppered with white patches, looked as if it had grown bigger, almost concealing his face and neck; his shoulders, having lost much of their muscle mass, looked thinner and narrower; his eyes, awash in tears periodically, looked vacant. No longer an intimidating giant, Guan Yu, middle-aged, bore the wear and tear of decades of waging wars. He seemed to have lost

THE LOSS OF A BELOVED BROTHER

301

his desire to overpower his adversaries. Xian-Hui was beleaguered with anxiety.

One day, unexpectedly, Liu Bei and Zhuge Liang showed up in Guan Yu's billet. Knowing that Guan Yu would be overwhelmed by the loss of Zhang Fei, they came to Han Zhong, unannounced, to give him support. The sudden presence of Liu Bei brought back to Guan Yu memories of his serendipitous encounter with Liu Bei and Zhang Fei on his way to the Han capital, Luoyang, more than three decades ago. Images of the official bulletin board at the gate of a small city and the peach garden of Zhang Fei's family estate floated through Guan Yu's mind. With tears flooding down his magnificent beard, Guan Yu wailed and collapsed in Liu Bei's arms.

Much to Xian-Hui's relief, the presence of Liu Bei and Zhuge Liang, though emotionally jarring at the beginning, jolted Guan Yu out of his bereavement. The friendship and support from Liu Bei and Zhuge Liang gave him a lift. Gradually he resumed his normal life, gained weight, bolstered his resolve, and improved his morale.

During the period of Guan Yu's recovery, Xian-Hui, Liu Bei, Zhuge Liang, and Guan Yu spent many mornings and afternoons promenading along the bank of the Han River. It was as if the four of them were taking a long overdue leave from military battles and political struggles to enjoy each other's company. They loved their time together and drew strength from their friendships.

During one of those morning promenades, the four friends encountered a gaggle of geese on the river, engaged in mutual preening and head bobbing while honking softly to each other. Xian-Hui, in a contemplative mood, asked her companions, "How are humans different from geese? They establish social bonds, eat, reproduce, age, and die just as we do."

"Not much!" Zhuge Liang mused, "Except humans are consumed by the pursuit of power."

"Let's not overlook the fact that humans seek power for a cause. Don't you agree?" Liu Bei quipped.

"Yes, there is always a cause, when one needs a justification," Zhuge Liang riposted.

"But the pursuit of power has led to stupendous human achievements, hasn't it? The founding of the Han dynasty by Liu Bang, for example, is a case in point," Liu Bei replied.

"Yes, the pursuit of power also leads to war, mayhem, savagery, deprivation, and most, if not all, human tragedies!" Zhuge Liang retorted.

"Look," Xian-Hui chimed in. "Geese also seek dominance among themselves. They just don't go to such extremes as humans do in their attempts to dominate others."

"I cannot speak for geese or any other animal." Zhuge Liang laughed. "According to your speculation, animals are better than humans at practicing Confucius's principle of the golden mean. They understand the importance of moderation. Obviously, we are an inferior species."

Everyone broke out in laughter.

Guan Yu appreciated the brief exchange on human nature. He had always loved animals, and he thought to himself, Well, animals might very well be instinctively less brutal than humans. That may be too sweeping a hypothesis that is difficult to prove. But I have never seen animals as evil and mean-spirited as some humans are.

FIFTEEN

THE LAST BATTLE

When Guan Yu overcame his grief from the loss of Zhang Fei, he proposed to Zhuge Liang and Liu Bei that he should head an expeditionary force to attack the Wu kingdom to avenge Zhang Fei's death. Since he had governed western Jing in the past, he argued, it would be natural for him to try to gain it back.

Liu Bei and Zhuge Liang were not sanguine about Guan Yu's proposal. Blessed with a large area of rich agricultural land in Wu kingdom, Sun Quan had amassed a formidable army. His new strategist, Lu Su, who succeeded Zhou Yu, was wily and crafty. Liu Bei and Zhuge Liang did not feel confident that Guan Yu could prevail in a war against the Wu kingdom. They tried to dissuade Guan Yu from taking a reckless action driven by his desire for vengeance. They urged him to assess the situation rationally and exercise patience. But the death of Zhang Fei bedeviled Guan Yu. He was consumed by vengeance against the murderers of his brother. Stubborn as a bull, he refused to heed the advice of Liu Bei and Zhuge Liang. Citing the oath he took in the peach garden of Zhang Fei's estate—"We regret that we were not born together, but we swear on the souls of our ancestors that our allegiance to each other will never alter until we die together"—Guan Yu argued that going after Zhang Fei's killers was his obligation.

During a period of many days, Liu Bei and Zhuge Liang pleaded with Xian-Hui to dissuade Guan Yu from attacking the Wu kingdom. In the end, Xian-Hui told them, "I have tried my best in vain. Guan Yu would not budge. If I bring up the subject again, he will just walk away. On this issue, he is oblivious to my advice."

In the end, Liu Bei and Zhuge Liang relented. Both had a sense of foreboding that Guan Yu's expedition might not end well. In truth, they felt Guan Yu, being middle-aged, was no longer the invincible warrior he had been. Yet, they couldn't speak that truth to Guan Yu for fear of hurting his pride. In addition, they were concerned that if Guan Yu invaded the Wu kingdom, he would be facing a much larger enemy who had the advantage of fighting on their home turf, with better knowledge of the topology of the battleground.

When Guan Yu, at the head of an army of ten thousand infantry and cavalry, marched away from Han Zhong toward Wu kingdom in the southeast, Liu Bei was overcome with sadness. He didn't want Guan Yu to go and blamed himself for failing to dissuade Guan Yu from his mission of vengeance.

Several days after Guan Yu took off with his army from Han Zhong, Cao Cao learned from his spies that Guan Yu was marching against the Wu kingdom. He saw a golden opportunity.

Sending a messenger to inform Sun Quan of Guan Yu's invading army, Cao Cao proposed that when Guan Yu arrived at the city of Fan on the edge of Wu kingdom, Sun Quan should ask the city garrison to refrain from confronting Guan Yu's force and wait for the arrival of Cao Cao's column from the north. In two

THE LAST BATTLE   305

weeks, Cao Cao would adjust the pace of his cavalry column to
arrive at the outskirts of Fan in the middle of the night.

Sun Quan felt Cao Cao's proposal was strategically sensible.
He immediately agreed to coordinate all actions with Cao Cao's
cavalry column.

The night Cao Cao's cavalry column arrived at Fan, the commander of the column, Jiang, wrapped a handwritten message
on the shaft of an arrow and shot it into the city to notify the
defenders to mount a frontal assault on Guan Yu's bivouac next
dawn while his cavalry column would charge into the rear of
Guan Yu's camp. Drumming would be the signal.

When the sun rose the next day, before Guan Yu could detect
Cao Cao's cavalry from the northeast, the defending forces of
the city of Fan, beating one hundred cattle drums, swarmed out
of its western gate to attack Guan Yu's camp. Then, Cao Cao's
cavalry charged toward the rear of the camp.

The two-pronged attack at that early hour surprised and
demoralized Guan Yu's force. The combined force of Sun Quan's
infantry and Cao Cao's cavalry killed Guan Yu's troops at will.
Guan Yu barely managed to escape the massacre on horseback.
He escaped via a narrow mountain path.

Sun Quan's strategist, Lu Su, familiar with the local terrain,
had anticipated that the mountain path could be a potential
escape route for Guan Yu. He had instructed his commanders
to station one hundred lancers over a short stretch of the path
one day in advance of the battle.

As Guan Yu galloped his horse up the path, suddenly he
found himself confronted by a platoon of kneeling lancers,
blocking his way.

Guan Yu turned around.

Within two hundred paces, another formation of Wu lancers
had emerged from a culvert, blocking his retreat.

Guan Yu roared and charged. Instead of defending himself
against Guan Yu's charge, the leader of the lancers backpedaled

into his platoon, forcing Guan Yu to face several rows of lances pointing at him. Furious as a cornered lion, Guan Yu gyrated his halberd and continued his charge with his Breaking the Wave move. But before he could hack away at his enemies, two lances pierced the chest of Guan Yu's mount. The horse collapsed and Guan Yu was surrounded.

When Lu Su and Sun Quan received the news that their troops had captured Guan Yu, they knew they would not be able to persuade Guan Yu to switch his allegiance to the Wu kingdom, no matter how much they desired Guan Yu's service. He was practically the embodiment of loyalty and courage. They also knew that they could not intimidate Guan Yu into submission. Nothing frightened him, not adversity, not imprisonment, not torture, not death. Finally, they understood that the charm strategy of treating him with magnanimity and conferring lofty titles on him would have no impact on him. They were well aware that, years ago, Cao Cao's charm approach to Guan Yu failed miserably. Finally, they were certain that if they freed Guan Yu, he would return as a formidable adversary, fighting for the Shu kingdom, and they might not be lucky enough to capture him again. It was clear that their only logical choice was to behead him. They carried out the execution almost immediately after his capture.

Guan Yu faced execution with equanimity. He only regretted that fate had not granted him the time to expiate his guilt over neglecting his wife, Xian-Hui, and their children.

EPILOGUE

1. The formal end of the Han dynasty occurred in late AD 220 shortly after the death of Cao Cao. That year, Cao Cao's son, Cao Pi, became the sovereign of the Wei kingdom. After succeeding his father, he forced the last emperor of the Han dynasty, Xian, to abdicate and declared himself the emperor of a new dynasty, Wei.

2. After Guan Yu's death, Liu Bei was soundly defeated by the Wu kingdom in AD 222. Bereaved and broken, he died one year later.

3. Following the death of Liu Bei, Zhuge Liang tried in vain to prop up the Shu kingdom with Liu Bei's son on the throne. Failing to prevail over the Wei kingdom and the Wu kingdom, Zhuge Liang died in AD 234, at fifty-three years of age.

4. The Shu kingdom survived Zhuge Liang's death until AD 263 when Liu Bei's son surrendered to an invading army of Wei.

5. The Sima clan replaced Cao Cao's heirs in the Wei kingdom and renamed their domain Jin in AD 265. After conquering the Wu kingdom in AD 280, the Sima clan ended the era of the Three Kingdoms.

ACKNOWLEDGMENTS

I wish to thank my wife, Katherine Saltzman-Li, and my friend Judith Regan for encouraging me to write this historical novel. Without their support, I could not have completed my task. I am grateful to my friend Kate Metropolis for reading a preliminary draft of this book and offering valuable comments and suggestions. Finally, I am indebted to my children, Rachel A. Li and Gabriel E. Li, who are flourishing in their own careers, for inspiring and sustaining my endeavors.

ABOUT THE AUTHOR

CHARLES LI is emeritus professor of linguistics and former dean of the Graduate Division (1989–2006) at the University of California, Santa Barbara. An author and editor of numerous linguistics books and articles, Li's memoir of the first twenty years of his life, *The Bitter Sea: Coming of Age in a China Before Mao*, received wide critical acclaim. The book was chosen by Baruch College of the City University of New York as required reading for the 2010 freshman class and was adapted for the stage at the Baruch Performing Arts Center. In 2017, an NPR podcast featured the book. He is married to Katherine Saltzman-Li, a UC professor of Japanese literature.